"Ready every [...]
team channel.

"I was born re[...]

"Locked and lo[...]u, boss."

"Ready to rumble!"

Lynn's mouth quirked. She simply said, "Roger," and bent her knees, keeping on the balls of her feet, ready for anything the moment they dropped into combat mode. Adrenaline coursed through her limbs, warming her with its familiar, sweet fire.

Time to do what she loved best.

"Going into combat mode in three, two, one. Go!"

Lynn's display flashed to life and her ear instantly filled with a cacophony of sounds. Even as her hands felt the warmth of her morphing batons forming into the familiar shapes of Wrath and Abomination, she was already spinning, slashing out. The two Phasmas she'd dropped nearly on top of exploded into showers of sparks. Abomination barked once, twice, three times and the three demons parked within ten feet of her exploded as well before they could so much as turn and charge.

"There's a freaking lot of them," Mack said, tone somewhere between this-is-really-annoying and I'm-screwed!

"It's called a target-rich environment, Mackie boy," Lynn said between blasting away at the solid wall of Orculls and Spithra headed her way. It took them barely three minutes to deal with the initial wave of lower-level aggressive types surrounding the outskirts of the TDM crowd at the substation.

But the battle was only just getting started.

BAEN BOOKS by JOHN RINGO

TRANSDIMENSIONAL HUNTER (with Lydia Sherrer):
Into the Real • *Through the Storm*

Beyond the Ranges (with James Aidee)

BLACK TIDE RISING: *Under a Graveyard Sky* • *To Sail a Darkling Sea* • *Islands of Rage and Hope* • *Strands of Sorrow* • *The Valley of Shadows* (with Mike Massa) • *Black Tide Rising* (ed. with Gary Poole) • *Voices of the Fall* (ed. with Gary Poole) • *River of Night* (with Mike Massa) • *We Shall Rise* (ed. with Gary Poole) • *United We Stand* (ed. with Gary Poole)

TROY RISING: *Live Free or Die* • *Citadel* • *The Hot Gate*

LEGACY OF THE ALDENATA: *A Hymn Before Battle* • *Gust Front* • *When the Devil Dances* • *Hell's Faire* • *The Hero* (with Michael Z. Williamson) • *Cally's War* (with Julie Cochrane) • *Watch on the Rhine* (with Tom Kratman) • *Sister Time* (with Julie Cochrane) • *Yellow Eyes* (with Tom Kratman) • *Honor of the Clan* (with Julie Cochrane) • *Eye of the Storm*

COUNCIL WARS: *There Will Be Dragons* • *Emerald Sea* • *Against the Tide* • *East of the Sun, West of the Moon*

INTO THE LOOKING GLASS: *Into the Looking Glass* • *Vorpal Blade* (with Travis S. Taylor) • *Manxome Foe* (with Travis S. Taylor) • *Claws that Catch* (with Travis S. Taylor)

EMPIRE OF MAN (with David Weber): *March Upcountry* • *March to the Sea* • *March to the Stars* • *We Few*

SPECIAL CIRCUMSTANCES: *Princess of Wands* • *Queen of Wands*

PALADIN OF SHADOWS: *Ghost* • *Kildar* • *Choosers of the Slain* • *Unto the Breach* • *A Deeper Blue* • *Tiger by the Tail* (with Ryan Sear)

To purchase any of these titles in e-book form, please go to www.baen.com.

THROUGH THE STORM

JOHN RINGO & LYDIA SHERRER

THROUGH THE STORM

This is a work of fiction. All the characters and events portrayed in this book are fictional, and any resemblance to real people or incidents is purely coincidental.

Copyright © 2023 by John Ringo and Lydia Sherrer

All rights reserved, including the right to reproduce this book or portions thereof in any form.

A Baen Books Original

Baen Publishing Enterprises
P.O. Box 1403
Riverdale, NY 10471
www.baen.com

ISBN: 978-1-9821-9384-3

Cover art by Kurt Miller

First printing, November 2023
First mass market printing, December 2024

Distributed by Simon & Schuster
1230 Avenue of the Americas
New York, NY 10020

Library of Congress Control Number: 2023029024

Printed in the United States of America

10 9 8 7 6 5 4 3 2 1

As always
For Captain Tamara Long, USAF
Born: May 12, 1979
Died: March 23, 2003, Afghanistan
You fly with the angels now.
—J.R.

~

To my dear readers:
If you've ever felt overlooked because of who you are,
take heart: you are worth so much more
than you could possibly imagine.
—L.S.

Chapter 1

VANCIL THOMAS WAS NOT ONE TO COMPLAIN. REALLY,
he wasn't.

Sure, being a janitor wasn't the most exciting pro-
fession out there. But being a janitor in a highly
acclaimed, cutting-edge research laboratory wasn't too
bad. The pay was pretty good—thanks Uncle Sam—
and the scientists who worked there were surprisingly
polite, for scientists, anyway.

Not that he had a thing against scientists. Technically he was one himself. PhD in computational
geoscience. But he could never get the funding he
needed for his grants, so, here he was. And he knew
exactly how smug scientists could get when they *did*
get grants for their research.

Especially theoretical research.

But the scientists at DUSEL trying to detect dark
matter were pretty decent. Even said hello to him in
the hall. Didn't treat him like an ignorant interloper

1

who was one mop away from breaking their extremely sensitive equipment and ruining their research.

Not that he used a mop very often. Most of the cleaning gadgets needed to maintain the lab's high-tech equipment and sterile environments were pretty sophisticated. You almost needed a degree just to use them.

It wasn't computational geoscience, but it was important work, and he could live with that.

What he couldn't live with, though, was a subpar electrical system.

"Blast it," Vancil muttered as the bathroom lights where he was cleaning started flickering wildly again for the third time that night. He set down his mop—okay, he *was* using one that night—and stomped over to flip the light switch off and on a few times. Sometimes that worked, sometimes it didn't.

He'd reported the malfunction to the lab maintenance manager several times already. The manager had tersely informed him each time that they'd checked the electrical system and everything worked properly when they ran their diagnostics.

Vancil blamed the giant, experimental machine housed next door—the one they'd developed for the Large Underground Xenon experiment attempting to detect and interact with dark matter particles. Ever since they'd turned it on with the lab's recent inauguration, the electrical systems had been glitchy on this side of the mine. For some reason it never happened during the day when the scientists, lab assistants, and government officials were about and could witness it. Only at night when the place was deserted but for the security team and him.

It was *so* much fun being dismissed for "imagining"

things. As if he didn't have two eyes and a brain between them. He had a freaking PhD for God's sake. He didn't need to be an electrical engineer to know something was up.

Probably government contractors cutting corners on the wiring installation. It would be just like them.

Messing with the light switch did not produce the desired result, so Vancil heaved a sigh and pulled his radio off his belt.

"Hey, John," he said into his crackling handset. "The lights in the bathroom off the LUX-350 chamber are going crazy. Are any other lights in this area doing weird stuff? Flickering? Going off on their own?"

Vancil's question was met with silence, and he scowled at his radio.

"You better not be napping again, you old geezer. The last time—"

The radio crackled to life.

"Who you calling old, Vancil? Can't a man have a few minutes to enjoy his potato chips in peace?"

John Huff on the security team night shift was good people. Their friendly banter during the long, slow nights kept Vancil sane.

"Enjoy your chips after you answer my question. Do you see this?"

"Yeah, yeah, I see it. I was just about to ask what's going on. The lights down your way are going all strobe-light crazy."

"I *knew* it. Promise you'll back me up this time when I talk to that maintenance harpy with a stick up her a—"

The light in the bathroom abruptly went out, plunging Vancil into complete darkness.

"Aw, come on," Vancil yelled at the room, then started muttering curses as he fumbled for the flashlight on his belt.

"What happened?" squawked John's voice.

"I swear, if she doesn't get an independent team in to recertify the electrical system this time, I'm going to—"

A sudden, violent seizure jerked through Vancil's body. The flashlight and radio he'd been holding slipped from his spasming finger and clattered to the floor. His eyes rolled up and he collapsed, head striking the smooth cement hard enough to cause a nasty split in the scalp. Blood began to ooze onto the floor, pooling around his head. He lay there, still as death, cheek squished against the floor and limbs tangled in lifeless disarray.

"Vancil?" the radio squawked again from where it lay nearby. "Vancil, are you okay? Your entire sector has gone dark. I'm sending a team over to check it out. Vancil? Dadgummit, Vancil, say something. Vancil!"

Chapter 2

FIVE MONTHS AGO WHEN LYNN HAD FINALLY DECIDED to be brave and "step into the real," to play the augmented-reality game TransDimensional Hunter, she had *not* signed up to fight snakes.

Spiders she could do. Yeah, they were creepy, but the Charlie Class-2 Spithra she'd been fighting since the summer were big enough that you saw them coming a mile off. Besides, keeping track of their eight spike-tipped legs and poison-spit attack was a fun challenge, one she thrived on.

Creepers were a whole other ball game.

The first time one of the nasty buggers had popped its head out of the tall grass where she and her team had been hunting, she'd almost had a heart attack. Its weird, translucent skin reflected the colors around it so it was almost invisible, and its low, sibilant hiss was easy to miss among the cacophony of TransDimensional Monsters around her. And the slimy bastard was fast.

Really fast.

Before she'd known what'd hit her, it had already

struck her thigh twice, its football-sized head darting in almost too fast to see. While the strikes hadn't significantly lowered her health, it had poison fangs which caused damage over time just like the Spithra's poison-spit attack.

Had she mentioned yet that it was impossibly, creepily *fast*?

As if that wasn't bad enough, the snakelike TDMs came in broods, much like the Rocs gathered in flocks. You'd have five to ten of the fuglies coming at you all at once. If they surrounded you, it was over. You just had to cut and run to avoid a blitz of lightning-fast strikes, machine-gun style. If they didn't get you with their fangs, they got you with their stinger-tipped tails. The only way to avoid damage was to spot them coming and pick them off before they got to you—a challenging feat in and of itself.

Lynn hated them with every fiber of her being.

It was bad enough fighting them on an open field of mown grass. Fighting them in the dim woodland with plenty of underbrush was insane.

But that's exactly what she was doing.

"There are no words to describe," Lynn said, grunting with effort as she whipped Skadi's Wrath around to strike a creeper's head, "how much I hate these *freaking snakes*!!"

"If you spent more time concentrating and less time complaining, I am certain you would have an easier time of it," offered Hugo, the game's AI and sometimes-helpful-but-always-sarcastic guide. His "helpful" commentary in her earbud did not improve her mood in the slightest.

"If you spent—more time—warning me—and less

time—yapping—it'd *definitely* be easier," Lynn panted as she spun around in a circle to make sure she'd gotten all the buggers. Her overhead showed more red dots coming her way, probably a group of Namahags or possibly Managals—the upgrade of the Penagal. She wouldn't know until they got closer because of the woodland vegetation that was only just starting to turn brown and drop now that it was the beginning of October.

At least the weather was cooling off and the crisp fall air filling her lungs was helpfully invigorating. The smell of leaf loam kicked up by her shuffling feet combined with the occasional sound of birdsong through the trees made for an almost peaceful atmosphere.

Almost.

"Remind me why we're fighting in these gawdawful woods?" Lynn grumbled as she backed up, leading the approaching dots back toward her teammates in a less thick section of trees behind her.

"I believe your exact words were 'If one more *bleep*ing paparazzi drone gets in my way while I'm hunting, I will stab somebody.'"

"*Bleep*ing?"

"My content filter prevents me from repeating your words verbatim, Miss Lynn, but I am sure you can fill in the blank."

Lynn grumbled under her breath, knowing exactly why their team was in these woods, and hating it.

When they'd qualified as a TD Hunter Strike Team a month ago and entered the running for the first international championship, none of them had anticipated the fame and scrutiny that would descend upon them overnight.

Mr. Krator had said he was going to make TD

Hunter a global sensation. And now Skadi's Wolves were at the top of the leaderboard for a game that was being obsessively followed by billions worldwide.

Billions.

Most cities had laws against paparazzi drones. The problem was, unlike official media drones that were required to have distinctive markings and broadcast their official credentials, the drones paparazzi used were often indistinguishable from the many working drones that flew all over the city on routine business. The intrusive buggers were incredibly hard to pin down, not to mention track back to their operator and hold them responsible for infringing on city ordinances. They were often tiny and could hide almost anywhere, waiting for their target to appear. AI programmers could make big bucks under the table designing flight algorithms that enabled the little bloodsucking—figuratively, anyway—leeches to move almost as independently as if their remote pilots were right there in tiny little cockpits.

They were a nuisance to absolutely everyone, except of course the rabid celebrity-gossip market that made billions and billions in stream revenue every year. If you were willing to break a few rules and risk hefty fines should your drone be traced back to you, then any Joe Schmoe could become filthy rich with the right footage.

The problem had spawned a whole market in anti-drone technology—some of which was highly illegal itself. If Lynn hadn't needed to focus whole-heartedly on her hunting instead of taking potshots at annoying drones buzzing above her, she might have invested in one of those focus-beam EMP guns. But the permit process for one took six months, minimum. She'd do better with a BB gun or even a slingshot if her aim was good enough.

"A dozen bogies inbound," Lynn said into her team channel. "This should be the last lot, then we can move in on the target."

"What took you so long?" Ronnie demanded over the same channel.

Lynn clenched her jaw against several choice remarks, in the end deciding to ignore the question for the stupid, unnecessary waste of breath that it was.

"Heya, Lynn, you find many broods?"

"Three," she told Edgar. His calm, unhurried question soothed her frazzled nerves. "The first two I was able to take out the buggers one by one, but the last one got the jump on me and surrounded me before I could get them all. Stupid Creepers."

Having chosen to fight in a strip of woodland that day, they were taking turns scouting the clusters of TDMs they found along the line of power nodes they were following. The idea was to draw the aggressive types out to where the brush was thin and the whole team could attack them together. The only problem was the Creeper broods. They were hard to detect until you were on them, much like ghosts, Ghasts, and Phasmas. The six- to seven-foot-long monsters liked to curl up in tight coils and ambush you, like giant cobra-shaped landmines hopped up on speed.

"Okay, guys, I want a semicircle formation, shooters on the wings, heavy in the middle, ready to charge. Let's take this group out nice and clean."

Lynn gave one last glance at her overhead before turning her back completely on the pursuing TDMs and sprinting to her place in the attack formation, between Edgar in the middle and Mack on the left wing. They lined up tighter than usual, so they could maintain visual contact and support each other through the light underbrush.

Fighting in woodland *sucked*.

Ronnie had argued vociferously against it, claiming that it wrecked their accuracy and therefore their team and individual ranking. He wasn't entirely wrong, and Dan agreed with him. But Edgar and Mack had backed her up when Lynn argued that in the city, paparazzi drones and the seemingly ever-present gaggle of lens junkies—fans obsessed with witnessing AR battles live through the TD Hunter Lens app—was just as damaging to their performance. Plus, the medium and upper Bravo Class TDMs tended to avoid buildings and people and stuck to lonelier areas around the outskirts of Cedar Rapids where Lynn and her teammates lived. And the bigger and badder the monster, the higher the reward in experience and loot.

Lynn was more than half convinced that Ronnie *liked* the paparazzi and groupies. He was always extra annoying when they were around, yelling at the team to "tighten up" and "act professional" because they had an "image" to protect.

Image being synonymous with Ronnie's ego.

Dan hated the limited visibility of the woodlands more than the annoyance of an audience or buzzing drones, but then he was their sniper and the most handicapped by the close quarters.

Mack didn't seem to mind one way or the other, and while Edgar didn't *say* much about the spectators, he was always quieter and more tense when they were around.

Lynn loathed them, especially the drones, more

than anything she'd ever hated in life. That included the bullies who'd picked on her mercilessly in middle school about her curvy shape and early-blooming body.

Bullies she could run away from. Bullies were only at school. Bullies she'd learned to tune out.

These stupid drones followed her *everywhere*, and the constant knowledge that the entire world was watching her every move was so oppressive it gave her anxiety attacks.

She didn't dare watch streams anymore, lest she come across some fan reel of herself and inadvertently see the comment section. Sure, there were plenty of positive comments. And then there were the creeps, the trolls, and the CRC groupies who made it their mission to tear her down. Lynn knew Elena put them up to it, or at least didn't say a word against it, since it worked in the favor of the Cedar Rapids Champions, the only other team in their regional area to have qualified last month for the national championship.

Between the constant barrage of fan mail, hate mail, paparazzi, and sponsorship offers, virtual life had become almost as unpleasant as life in the real. Her only escape was WarMonger, where nobody knew she was Lynn Raven, overnight gaming celebrity. On WarMonger she was Larry Coughlin, a grizzled old mercenary who would sooner shoot you as look at you—at least if there was any money to be made out of it.

Or if you annoyed him. Of if he decided you needed to be shot.

The problem was, with school in full swing she barely had time to sleep each night, much less game for pleasure. Every other waking moment was spent hunting TDMs with her teammates or training in the safety of her apartment.

Her life sucked right now, and it was all because of the stupid paparazzi drones. Without them, things might have been bearable. With them, her stress levels were through the roof, and she'd been short with everyone lately, even her mom. She knew she needed to figure out how to adjust, how to cope with this new reality, but any moment she wasn't hunting she felt like she could barely breathe.

How was she supposed to cope with that?

"Give them a few more feet . . . that's it . . . *engage!*" Ronnie's shout spurred her to action while her brain was still trying to shake free of the ever-present worry. Her left hand rose and her finger began rhythmically squeezing as she poured fire from Abomination, the counterpoint to Skadi's Wrath, into the line of Namahags rushing them through the trees. The TDMs moved in a straight line, ignoring the underbrush as if it wasn't even there. They never reacted to organic barriers, only man-made ones. Lynn guessed it was because the game AI had blueprints and aerial footage of man-made structures while it had limited ability to map out every patch of woods, especially considering how much more difficult it was for drones to fly under foliage than out in the open.

Whatever the reason, the TDMs were not hindered by the trees, bushes, and clusters of thorns between them and their prey, while Lynn's team had to be hyper aware of their surroundings, lest they stumble over saplings or get their foot caught in a root and injure themselves.

It was fortunate that part of the prize package

for qualifying as a Hunter Strike Team had included competition-quality uniforms in the generic TD Counterforce colors. Those things were mercifully impervious to thorns and had saved all of them from many cuts and even minor bruises with their built-in impact-distributive panels.

The Namahag in front of Lynn exploded in a shower of sparks and she shifted her fire to the next one in line, then raised Skadi's Wrath and started forward, slightly behind Edgar's roaring charge. The shuffling sound of leaves and brush under their feet combined with the clicks, screams, and growls of the oncoming TDMs, finally enabling Lynn's brain to focus. She sank into that glorious state of relaxed hyperawareness that gave her such an edge as a gamer—and a Hunter. Trajectories and attacks whizzed through her brain as she plotted out each monster's move, knowing exactly what it would do before it got to her. The TDMs all had predictable attacks, at least whenever the game's AI wasn't trying to throw her for a loop, which it did on a disturbingly frequent basis. Her conversations with the game's Tactics Department made her think it acted that way because of how much she pushed its boundaries. The game's AI had been designed to give its players a challenge, and a challenge was exactly what Lynn wanted.

Duck, slash, roll, spin. She was behind the first two Namahags in a flash and gave them both strikes on their vulnerable backs before lunging to the side and rolling again to dodge their inevitable spin and swipe with their foot-long claws. She danced, spun, and struck like a ballerina—a ballerina with a dragon-head-shaped gun belching fire and a wickedly lethal sword carving her enemies into mincemeat.

Not that the TDMs did anything so satisfying as bleed. They just flashed purple with each successful strike and then burst into a shower of sparks once their hit points ran out.

Sometimes Lynn wished they would bleed.

The Namahags weren't quite dead when Lynn was forced to spin and duck under a Spithra's spit attack. The oncoming Spithra took a mere shot apiece from Abomination to end their sorry existence, but by the time she turned back to her other prey, Edgar had already blasted the remaining Namahags to sparks. Quiet descended on their little clearing.

"All right, come on you lot, let's go get this mini boss and get out of here," Ronnie called. "It's getting dark already."

"Good job, everyone. Nicely done," Lynn added on the team channel, mentally smacking Ronnie over the head for forgetting to say it. She'd *told* him enough times over their private link that she thought he'd remember by now. But the leadership tactic of using encouragement and praise to raise morale and solidify camaraderie seemed to go over his head. Or, more likely, he was just too obsessive of a gamer. He got totally focused on the goal and forgot about the "extra" stuff. That was fine for a group of kids gaming for fun in their spare time. But for a team of professional gamers aiming to win the biggest gaming competition in the history of the world, it was a critical mistake.

One they couldn't afford to make.

With an effort, Lynn shoved such thoughts aside and focused on staying in line as they strode through the trees toward their target. By the time they were thirty yards out, they started picking off the straggler

Delta Class TDMs that hadn't been lured away by their scouting tactic. These were so weak compared to the Hunters that Lynn and her fellows could kill any of them with a single shot or a lazy swipe of a Plasma Blade. Edgar barely bothered to aim with this two-handed disruptor cannon, he just blasted in the general direction of the groups rushing them.

Twenty yards out, they spotted the last circle of Namahags that had stayed behind, too stubborn to be drawn away from the "mini boss" TDM that all the other monsters had been grouped around. Lynn had no idea if they were bodyguards or minions used as cannon fodder by the mini boss. What she did know is that the particular monstrosity in the center of the circle wasn't going anywhere, even when all its guards had been reduced to sparks. Maybe it was guarding something. Maybe it was just programmed to stay put.

Their team poured fire into the last Namahags, dodging the tall demon-like creatures' attacks while carefully staying out of reach of the mini boss.

Finally, they turned their attention to the Bravo Class-3 Bunyip crouched like a malevolent hen over the spot it had staked out in the woods close to one of the ubiquitous power-node towers. It was the size of a fifteen-passenger van and looked like a cross between an alligator and a crab, with four long pincer-tipped arms that could snap out in a flash if you got too close. Those pincers packed a punch. Lynn's team had learned the hard way that one solid snap could reduce their health level to bleeding-out. The only way to defeat them was to take out all their guards, then rain down damage on them before more TDMs showed up.

The first time they'd fought one, Lynn had circled

around to attack its rear while it was distracted by her teammates. That's when she'd found out its arms were double-jointed and its huge tail packed a solid punch. After that she'd backed up and opted for the weaker, albeit safer, ranged attack with Abomination.

When the Bunyip finally exploded in an impressive fireworks display, they were able to relax and start collecting loot. Well, mostly relax. TDMs could show up on their radar any time, attracted to the spot by the fighting, as if the deaths of their fellows were some sort of beacon. There were noticeably more TDMs spawning these days than there'd been over the summer—probably because there were so many more people playing the game.

Best to collect the loot and exit combat mode as quickly as possible.

"Aw, *sah-weeet*!" Edgar shouted. "Ammo augment!"

Lynn trotted over from where she'd been sweeping for ichor, globes, and plates and looked on as Edgar shared his inventory view with her.

"They're *incendiary rounds*," he said in a reverent voice.

"I bet you're gonna *love* using those," she laughed, then checked the power-usage levels. "You'll have to use them sparingly, though. They'll dry you up in seconds at your current level."

"Don't worry, I'll save 'em for the big baddies," he said with a grin. "Like the Manticars."

That made Lynn grin with vindictive anticipation. They all hated Manticars. The giant lionlike creatures had three scorpion tails that could strike you anywhere unless you were directly behind them. Thankfully, the creatures were one of the rarer guard types and usually only found around bosses. They were a pain in the *butt* to kill, but the higher Skadi's Wolves got in experience, the less of a threat Manticars were.

"Nah," Mack said as he sidled up to take a peek at the augment, "save them for the Managals. I *hate* those things." He read the stats and gave his chin an absent-minded stroke, plucking at the tiny patch of hair there he'd managed to grow out since the last time his mom had made him shave his fledgling goatee. "Those bullets have pretty good range. I'd definitely save them for Managals. I need all the help I can get killing those stupid things. They split and multiply like giant rabid walking sticks."

"Just wait till we make it to Chimeras," Dan called out, struggling through a tangle of thorns to get the last few pieces of loot. "They breathe *fire*, like a dragon! Isn't that *awesome*!"

"Leave it to Dan to think 'more lethal' is awesome," Edgar grumbled, and Lynn grinned.

"You know you can't wait," she joked, nudging him in the ribs.

He gave her a sidelong grin in return and Lynn was suddenly—and a bit uncomfortably—aware of how close they were. She took a step to the side and swept her eyes across the woods, looking for any loot they'd missed.

"I mean, the faster we go up against the big boys, the faster we level, right?" she said to cover the awkward silence. Was her face hot? Well, duh it was, she'd just finished an hour-long workout. Hunting was physically exhausting, and they'd all been through hell and back that summer acclimating to it as quickly as possible to pass the qualifiers.

"Or the faster we die," Mack pointed out, his tone decidedly less enthusiastic than Dan's had been.

"Okay, okay, enough chatting," Ronnie snapped. "We're here to hunt, not socialize." He pushed past one last bush to stand in front of them, hands on hips.

"Let's see what we got. Team, report!"

"I got a special ammo augment—incendiary bullets," Edgar said. "Looks like it does more damage than the poison DOT ammo augment."

"Good, give the poison ones to Mack," Ronnie said. "Anything else?"

"I found another disruptor cannon," Dan piped up.

"Transfer that to Mack in case he needs it in a tight spot," Ronnie ordered.

Lynn scanned through the items she'd picked up, then sniggered. "Anybody want the 'Loincloth of Lordly Might'? It gives you an *insane* attack bonus." She projected her display and held the item up.

Most of the guys made horrified faces, though Edgar laughed. He took a peek at the stats himself and whistled.

"Ronnie, man, you gotta wear this. Our fearless leader needs all the best augments, right? These damage stats are *sick*."

"I'm not wearing that," Ronnie said, giving the skimpy groin covering the stink eye.

"Why not?" asked Lynn. She worked to keep her face straight but failed. "You could totally rock the Roman gladiator look. Mack, Dan? Back me up here."

"It *does* have really good stats," Dan said absently, as if he were considering wearing it himself.

"I'm not prancing around half naked," Ronnie growled.

"Aw, come on, man. You can modify your avatar to give it a skin suit, you wouldn't be naked, just, you know—" At that point Edgar devolved into sniggers, and Ronnie crossed his arms.

"Put it with the equipment to auction off," he told Lynn, still glowering.

Edgar waved a hand at her, trying to get his breath back. "Nah—nah, give it to me. It'll go great over my plate armor."

Ronnie rolled his eyes as Lynn transferred the item.

"Right, did we get everything?" he asked, not bothering to look around to check himself.

"Pretty sure," Dan said.

"Best we can tell in thick woods like this," Edgar added, still grinning as he unwrapped a new piece of gum and popped it into his mouth. It had taken Hugo a bit of finagling to filter the subvocalization software on Edgar's mic so that the rest of the team wasn't driven insane by the sound of his chewing.

Ronnie's eyes narrowed and Lynn knew he was about to start yelling about how "pretty sure" and "best we can tell" wasn't good enough. Miraculously, though, he kept his mouth shut. Which was fortunate. Lynn was already exhausted and cranky. All she wanted to do was get home, take a shower, and get her homework done so she could collapse into blissful sleep. She would have loved to skip the homework part, but her mother had made it clear in no uncertain terms that if Lynn neglected school in favor of TD Hunter, she would be off the team.

"Fine. We're done for the day, I guess. Let's get out of here."

One by one they dropped out of combat mode. Their weapons, impressive and deadly-looking through the augmented reality glasses they all wore, morphed and reformed into simple batons. These omnipolymer controllers for the game were electric blue, no doubt to make it obvious they were just toys even when they took the shape of whatever in-game weapon they represented.

It was a ten-minute trek back to the closest airbus platform, and Lynn dreaded it, knowing what would happen soon after they left the cover of the woods northeast of Cedar Rapids. She hung back as Ronnie took the lead, Dan trotting beside him as they discussed their latest augments. Then she heaved a sigh and got her tired legs moving. Edgar hung back with her, a silent shadow as usual, while Mack walked slightly ahead of them, chatting contentedly as if he'd never heard of crazy things like "stress" and "anxiety."

"I've got a vidcall with Riko later this evening. I can't wait to tell her about your incendiary bullets, Edgar!"

"Yeah, sure you do," Edgar said as he and Lynn shared a look.

"What?" Mack half turned to glance back at them, nearly running into a thorn bush in the process. "You guys still don't believe me? Come on! Stop being so cynical. Riko is *awesome*, I'm sure you'd like her."

"Mack, the likelihood of you having a girlfriend from Japan is about as high as Ronnie winning a Nobel Peace Prize," Edgar said, his voice slow and bland but his eyes twinkling.

"I'm telling you, she's real!" Mack insisted.

"She's a bot, Mack," Lynn said. "Just accept that and move on."

"You're wrong."

"Just wait, one of these days she's going to come to you crying about how her *ojiisan* is sick and she needs money to pay for his medical bills. Whatever you do, don't give her anything."

Mack reached up to tug anxiously on his baby goatee.

"It's not like that, I swear. She's actually super rich, she doesn't need any money from me."

"Uh-huh," Lynn said, barely suppressing a snort.

"You'll see, one of these days. She says her dad will probably let her fly over for the national competition. Then you can meet her yourself."

"Whatever you say, Mack," Edgar replied. He was much better at keeping a straight face, and his lips didn't even twitch upward as he spoke.

"You talking about your stupid fake girlfriend again?" Ronnie yelled from up ahead.

"She's not fake!" Mack insisted, then broke into a trot to catch up and start arguing with Ronnie and Dan about the tells of scam bots.

"Sometimes I almost feel sorry for him," Lynn said, though she was unable to keep the grin off her face now that Mack had left.

"Don't be." Edgar shrugged. "He'll figure it out eventually."

Silence descended, and Lynn's mind wandered over the idea of a boyfriend halfway across the world. How depressing. What would be the point if you could never see each other face to face or spend real time together? Virtual meetup rooms were all well and good, but they would never be the same as a friend's solid body next to yours, watching your back.

Edgar cleared his throat and Lynn jumped.

"How's your mom holding up?"

"Oh, pretty good," Lynn responded hurriedly. "The hospital is a strict no-go for drones of any kind. Too much risk they'd mess with all the medical equipment and data stations. All the doors and stuff have sensors that keep them out."

"Good," Edgar grunted. After a long silence, he said, "How 'bout you?"

"Oh, me? I'm, uh, fine."

She wasn't, but that wasn't Edgar's problem, so no point bothering him with it.

He fell silent again, and so there was nothing to keep Lynn's mind from obsessing once again over the inevitable attention that would follow her around, watching her, judging her every move—

She could feel her heart rate pick up and her lungs start to feel tight. The sight of the thinning woods ahead of them and the sound of passing air taxis didn't help.

"Hey, Hugo," she subvocalized.

"Yes, Miss Lynn?"

"Pull up the TDH tactical suggestion forum, I wanna see if there's any new posts on Creepers."

"At once, Miss Lynn."

She spent the rest of the trip back absorbed in tactical plans and monster stat lists, studiously ignoring the incessant buzzing around their heads.

"Moooom! I'm home!"

"Hi, honey!" Matilda's voice said from the direction of the kitchen. "I just ordered pizza. The delivery drone should be here in twenty minutes."

"Okay, I'll be quick in the shower," Lynn called back, her tired face breaking out into a smile for the first time in hours. Sunday evening meant pizza and mother-daughter hangout time. They'd used to spend more of the day together, but with school taking up so many hours during the week, Lynn had been forced to compromise.

Lynn slipped her Counterforce backpack off her shoulders and headed for her room. She'd just pushed through the bedroom door when her mother's voice reached her again.

"Uh, sweetie, you're trailing leaves."

Lynn spun around and stuck her head out the door. "Aw, crap. I can't believe the guys let me get all the way home without telling me there were leaves on my back!"

Her mom laughed. "They were probably lodged under your backpack, though there's a few stuck in your hair too. Come here, let me get them out."

Lynn muttered darkly as she obeyed. Boys. They were such heathens.

"Uh, could you check for ticks too while you're at it?"

"Sure, honey."

"I'm *so* glad tick season is almost over," Lynn groaned. She flexed her shoulders, wincing at a sore spot on one shoulder blade. She must have rolled over a particularly pointy root and not even noticed it in the heat of battle.

"You're good, sweetie," Matilda said after a brief examination of Lynn's scalp under her tightly braided hair. "Now go get washed up."

Lynn obeyed, wholly focused on attaining the relief of hot water beating down on her bare skin—and making sure there were no ticks anywhere *else* on her.

Twenty minutes later she emerged, dressed in comfy, baggy t-shirt and sweats, still toweling dry her long, raven-black hair.

There was a soft beep that indicated the pizza delivery drone had arrived at their dock. Lynn yelled "I'll get it," then headed in that direction. She punched in the code at the waist-high portal in their wall by the exterior window, then pulled open the dock door. The delicious smell of melted cheese and tomato sauce greeted her, and she reached for the pizza box sitting in the dock at the same time her brain registered a weird buzzing noise.

What the—

She caught movement out of the corner of her eye and her hand shot out toward it just as the lightning bolt of furious understanding reached her brain.

"What do you think you're doing *sneaking into my house you*—" Lynn's enraged yell devolved into Larry-level profanity. She barely noticed her mother's alarmed question behind her, she was too busy smashing the fist-sized paparazzi drone she'd snatched out of the air. She pounded it against the metal edge of the delivery dock, crushing and snapping it into pieces with each blow.

"Lynn? Lynn! What happened, what is that?"

Her mother's firm grip on her shoulder spun her around and Matilda grabbed her wrist, preventing her from smashing the drone further.

"What in the world...is that a drone?"

"Yes," Lynn panted, fury still simmering. How dare they. Those scumbags, those freaking low-life—

"Let go, honey. Give it to me."

Matilda's firm command cut through Lynn's murderous litany, and she realized she still had a death grip on the now-splintered drone. She relaxed enough to let her mother pry it from her fingers, though she still glared at it suspiciously.

"Throw it out the delivery dock, it might still be recording."

"No, honey! This is evidence of trespassing, we need to turn it in so the owner can be fined and prosecuted. I won't let unscrupulous vultures torment my family without suffering the consequences."

Lynn snorted. "Yeah, like that'll ever happen. It's probably untraceable. Even if it's not, cops aren't gonna waste their time on paparazzi complaints."

"Lynn Raven! That is no way to talk about our men in blue," Matilda scolded, heading for the kitchen to find a bag for the crumbling drone. "I'm sure they'll do whatever they can with the resources they have."

With an effort, Lynn resisted pointing out the number of times long ago when her father had complained about the exact same problem in the Baltimore PD. Their evening had already been ruined enough without bringing up her dead dad.

Once her mom had double bagged the drone and put it back out in the delivery dock—just in case it *was* still recording—they had a subdued meal of deliciously greasy and unhealthy pizza, plus a few bags of steamed broccoli. Matilda was a nurse, after all, and even if "eat your veggies" hadn't already been her constant mantra, over the summer Lynn had developed an obsession with steamed broccoli covered in melted cheese. The sudden increase in physical activity after she'd started playing TD Hunter had triggered a protein and iron craving, and those early days of steamed broccoli had been like nectar from the gods.

She'd been eating significantly more protein than before as well. Lynn had been reluctant to add the expense, but after her mom had seen the way she devoured three steaks in a row during one of their rare mother-daughter dinners out, Matilda had insisted they add more red meat to her diet.

It was glorious, and once Lynn had gotten over the self-imposed guilt, she figured what better way to spend her hard-earned Larry Coughlin mercenary profits than to fuel her new goal as a champion monster hunter.

"Honey?"

"Hmm?" Lynn looked up from where she'd been staring at her pizza crusts.

"Are you doing okay? You've been really...tense lately." Matilda reached out and put a hand on Lynn's arm, giving it a gentle squeeze.

Lynn swallowed. How could she describe the simultaneous awful mental pressure and the constant sick feeling in her stomach she had at all the scrutiny their team had come under since qualifying for the TD Hunter championship?

"Ummmm, well, it's a lot to handle. School, hunting, all the attention...you know."

"Yeah. I'm sorry, sweetie. I know you never asked for this, but...well it's not *all* bad. One of the other nurses, Sandra, sent me a stream of you fighting a few weeks ago with your team, and it looked really impressive—"

"What! Mom, I can't believe you're watching me in the streams!" Lynn flushed and wondered if her mother ever read the comments.

"Why not? Can't I be proud of my own daughter? You know if you made your own stream channel I wouldn't be reduced to scouring the celebrity stream for vids of you."

Lynn's face twisted in disgust.

"And become like Elena? Not in a million years.

You know I hate attention. And besides, I barely have time to get my schoolwork done as it is. There's *no* way I'd have time to manage a stream on top of all that."

"I completely understand if that's the way you feel, honey. I was just surprised, that's all. Ronnie and the others have their own streams."

"You've been watching *Ronnie* on the stream?" Lynn asked, aghast.

"Well, not exactly. More just checked up on him and the other boys. I know they've all had some . . . issues with their families and I can't help worrying about them. They're *your* team. Don't *you* watch their streams?"

"Heck no! I stay as far away from the streams as possible." Just the thought of watching a vid of herself, knowing other people were watching her too, made her skin crawl.

"Well, you're missing out, honey, really." Matilda smiled, obviously trying to be cheerful. "The one Sandra sent me was made using that Hunter Lens app thingie, the one that lets viewers see all the monsters you're fighting? And it was, well, *really* impressive. And kind of scary too," Matilda chuckled. "I certainly wouldn't want to be fighting all those monsters. But you looked amazing, honey. You really did. I am so, *so* proud of how hard you've been working and how far you've come."

The unexpected praise eased the weight on Lynn's chest, and she swallowed.

"You know who else would be proud, sweetie? Your father." Matilda caught her gaze and Lynn could feel a prickle in her eyes even as she could see her mother's eyes shimmering too. "You know, he would have been out there fighting those monsters right alongside you. He would have thought TD Hunter was the most awesome thing in the world."

Lynn gave a wet chuckle that might or might not have had a sob hidden somewhere underneath it.

"Dad was such a dork. I bet he would have preregistered for it the moment it was announced."

"Probably," Matilda agreed, her own voice sounding wobbly. "And with that armor you wear in the game, he would have made sure everybody knew you were his own special Viking princess."

"Mom! Don't be embarrassing."

"You know he would have!"

"Yeah . . . probably."

They lapsed into silence. Lynn appreciated her mother's words, but now the pressure on her chest had been replaced by an old, familiar ache, and she felt even more depressed than before.

"Well, dear, I know it's hard. But you can't let the attention get to you. Nobody's opinion matters but your own, okay? You know in your heart how strong and talented you are, and that's all that matters."

Lynn shrugged weakly, hoping that would satisfy her mother.

Matilda snorted. "Honey, you look *amazing* out there. You're beautiful, fierce, and athletic. I'm not surprised everybody wants to watch you."

"Mom!"

"I'm just being honest, honey. I know that might not make it any more pleasant to be the center of so much attention, but I think it's important you keep some perspective. You are bringing people *joy*. You're fun and entertaining to watch. The way you fight and how hard you work is inspiring. I've read some of the comments"—Lynn sank lower in her seat, face heating—"and I can see how much your fans love you. You really mean something to them, and that's a blessing. It's a blessing to be able to inspire people ... just like your father did."

Lynn swallowed and forced herself to nod. She knew her mom meant well, but Matilda's words only reminded her of all the comments she tried daily to forget. They were relentless, though, wriggling and creeping through any crack in her defenses.

What a joke.

OMG Look at that cow!

I can't believe people actually like watching this train wreck.

Which of those loser boys do you think she's banging? The fatso or the freckly one?

I bet she's doing all of them, why else would they be a team? They're obviously terrible.

"Honey? Lynn!"

"Uh, yeah?"

Her mom gave her a searching look. "I'll do the dishes tonight. Why don't you go pick out a game for us to play before you head to bed?"

"Okay," Lynn agreed woodenly. Anything was better than sitting and thinking.

At least school tomorrow would be completely drone free. The local government and the school board were very strict about such privacy protection when their own necks were on the line. Not that the lack of drones *inside* the school—there were plenty hovering around just outside the school grounds—meant school was stress free. There were her ever-more-difficult senior year classes, including talk of college-prep courses. There was the scrutiny of her classmates, the biting and arguing between her teammates, and the worst of all those put together: the bullying from their rival team, the Cedar Rapids Champions, led by the harpy queen herself, Elena. The icing on the cake was Elena's army of groupies and jocks she sent against them in endless waves of abuse.

No wonder her anxiety was through the roof. Her life felt like a war zone.

If only she could get rid of her problems in the real as easily as she mowed through monsters in TD Hunter.

Chapter 3

"THANKS FOR COMING TO SEE ME, STEVE."

"Of course, Mr. Krator," Steve said, going to military parade rest in front of the CEO of Tsunami Entertainment.

"Oh, cut it out, Steve. I know old habits and all that, but seriously. I'm in a t-shirt and jeans, eating sushi and contemplating how to design a relationship-building AR RPG for nursing homes to help old folks stay connected to their families. I don't have patience for military formality at the moment."

"Got it, sir." Steve grinned and crossed his arms, leaning to rest his hip on the edge of the CEO's massive glass desk. The design genius, CEO, and multibillionaire was sitting in a new-age-looking easy chair to the side of his desk as he ate. "So, what can I do for you?"

"Well, in addition to this old folks RPG I was thinking about, I've also been contemplating our star player."

Steve's eyebrows rose.

"Which one would that be, sir? We have dozens of top-tier TD Hunter players all over the world."

Mr. Krator scowled at him.

"The one who gave us all heart attacks by jumping

inside a TDM boss to game the system and achieve the mission we'd given her at all costs."

"Ah. That one."

"Yes," Mr. Krator said with a sigh. "That one."

"What about her, sir?"

"I'm worried about her."

Steve opened his mouth, thought about it, closed it again, thought some more, then finally spoke.

"Sir, you designed a game to integrate experimental military technology into a globally popular game meant to secretly recruit billions of people of all ages around the world to help fight an invisible invading force of transdimensional entities that could end civilization as we know it within a matter of years—if not sooner. I feel like, at this point, it's a tad late to worry."

"Oh don't be dramatic, Steve. The military was right to turn to the gaming industry. It was the *only* way to deal with a threat this diffuse and multiplicitous. The scientific community nearly had an aneurysm trying to merely *explain* the situation in terms our military could understand and respond to. You'd be surprised how many high-profile examples there are of gaming being used to solve medical, scientific, and even societal problems that were thought unsolvable. One of my favorites was back in 2011 when it took gamers a few weeks to determine the molecular structure of a protein connected to AIDS after scientists had been trying to figure it out for ten *years*. Gaming has been used in almost every scientific field for decades. Back when AI technology was first becoming viable, we quickly discovered that AIs lacked a certain intuition that only humans possessed. Many of our quantum processors were designed by a fusion of AI technology and human interaction within a gaming structure to solve complex problems that even quantum computers couldn't solve on their own."

"Oh, I get it, Mr. Krator," Steve said, holding up both hands. "I wasn't trying to imply that you've put a billion gamers in harm's way without a really, *really* good reason. What I meant was, we're facing civilization collapse. There's a lot to worry about. I guess it feels like worrying about one kid amid millions is... well... selfish. But, if it makes you feel any better..." Steve hesitated, then shrugged. "You're not the only one worrying about her."

Mr. Krator looked up at him sharply.

"You too, huh?"

Steve smiled and shrugged.

"She's got a spunky streak. It's easy to root for her. Besides, it's hard not to have immense respect for someone who has soundly beaten almost every ranked player in the *entirety* of WarMonger over the last four years."

"Too true." Mr. Krator fell silent, seemingly lost in thought.

"So... what, exactly, are you worried about for her?"

Mr. Krator shook himself.

"Yes. Sorry. I'm worried about the pressure she's under right now. The TD Hunter is her natural environment. She'll do fine there—as long as she doesn't pull any more suicidal stunts like the last one. It's a miracle she didn't drop dead. In any case, this is the first time she's gamed without the privacy of a masking account. I know how the gaming industry is—"

"And you think she doesn't? She's not some naive little girl, sir."

Mr. Krator waved a hand.

"That's not what I meant, Steve. It's that I know how the gaming industry and celebrity culture intersect, and what notoriety can do to a person. Especially someone like her."

"And like you?" Steve guessed.

Mr. Krator's wry expression confirmed his suspicions.

"Look, I'm not trying to project," the CEO said. "I just know what it feels like to grow up bullied, and to cope with it by hiding. I'm sure she'll learn how to manage—in fact I *know* she will. She's far stronger than she thinks. But between the fame and the, hm, questionable dynamic between her and Ronnie Payne, well . . . I just want to make sure someone is ready to be in her corner. It can't be me, as I'm sure you understand."

"I do, sir," Steve said, suddenly grinning.

There were many reasons why he loved his job. Not the least of which was because he was no longer getting shot at or having to dodge IEDs. Playing games more or less for a living was a nice perk too. But really, it was getting to mentor players through TD Hunters' tactical department that really made his day. So what Mr. Krator was subtly asking for was right up his alley.

No reason to mention to Mr. Krator that he'd already been doing it since the summer. Heck, Mr. Krator probably already knew. This was just his official—if unspoken—stamp of approval.

"Don't worry, Mr. Krator. I highly suspect Lynn Raven doesn't need our help. But if she does, I'll be damned if I don't give her every ounce of support we can muster."

"Thank you, Steve. I have a feeling she's going to be more instrumental to the success of this program than anyone could have guessed."

"*You* guessed it, sir. Don't think I haven't heard the rumors that you invited her personally. You even had to wheedle her a bit to get her on board." Steve grinned again, and Mr. Krator matched the look.

"I might have been taken by a Delphic fit or two, over the years. It's hard to get to where I am without some sort of intuition. I try not to let it go to my head."

"You do a good job, sir."

Mr. Krator shrugged.

"Thanks for coming all the way up, Steve. This was a conversation I wanted to have in person, off the record, so to speak."

"You got it, Mr. Krator."

"Want some sushi?" the CEO offered, pointing his chopsticks at the still half-full platter on the glass table beside his chair.

"I'll pass, thanks, sir. Never was a fan of raw fish."

"Oh, it's not all raw. In fact—" Mr. Krator must have caught sight of Steve's expression, because the man stopped himself and chuckled. "Once a nerd, always a nerd, I suppose. I'll restrain myself from boring you with the fascinating culinary qualities of this delectable food. I suppose you're a steak and potatoes kind of guy?"

"The bloodier, the better," Steve said.

"My doctor is of the opinion that red meat is poisoning the world."

"What isn't, these days?" Steve asked.

"That is a point. Well, I won't keep you any longer, Steve. Keep me apprised, if you would."

"Will do, sir."

Two weeks after Lynn and her mom had turned in the trespassing drone and filed a police report, they still hadn't heard from the local Cedar Rapids police department. No surprises there, as far as Lynn was concerned. She mostly forgot about it, in fact, because there was a much more pressing threat to keep her occupied: Queen Harpy the Ruthless Attention Whore, otherwise known as Elena.

Every week that the Cedar Rapids Champions failed to pass Skadi's Wolves on the leaderboards seemed to enrage Elena further. Before the qualifiers in September, the leaderboards had only contained individual scores. While Lynn had consistently jockeyed for one of the top ten positions on it as "RavenStriker," that seemed to have mostly escaped Elena's notice. But now there was a leaderboard dedicated solely to the Hunter Strike championship teams, and Elena seemed to take Skadi's Wolves' position on it above CRC as a grave and personal insult.

"So," Dan asked with a little skip in his step, "how many pinecones do you think are shoved up Elena's butt at this point? I bet at least four or five."

Their team was headed down the hall for second-period classes. They always moved in a group, nowadays, or at least in twos and threes. After the multiple assaults Elena's team had made on them over the summer—the last one during the qualifiers which had almost knocked them out of the competition—the guys had been more than happy to follow Lynn's insistence that they never get caught alone at school. They had most of their classes together anyway, so it worked out.

"Maybe her body is a portal to an interdimensional chasm of bitterness and hate," Mack said, grinning. "For all we know she could have *infinite* pinecones shoved up her butt!"

"But to what purpose?" Dan mused. Then he snapped his fingers several times, face lighting up. "I know! She feeds off the anger as her internal power source, so she has to stay perpetually butt-hurt to remain operational. I mean, come on, have any of you ever seen her actually *eat* in the cafeteria? I haven't."

Ronnie snorted, and Mack said, "Nope."

As usual, Lynn felt too grumpy and anxious to participate in the guys' chatter, though Dan's last comment *had* brought a brief smile to her face.

"I've seen her eating salads," she said, and shrugged. "But that doesn't mean she isn't still powered by petty rivalries and childish petulance."

"Speaking of petty rivalries," Edgar rumbled, and put a hand on Lynn's shoulder, stopping her. The others stopped a step or two ahead once they spotted the solid mass of students coming their way down the hall.

"Yikes," Mack muttered, eyes flicking over his shoulder to the empty hall behind them. "Should we turn around?"

"Never turn your back on your enemy," Lynn said. She could tell her tone had changed, lowered, gone almost Larry-esque. But she didn't care. If Elena wanted to pick a fight, she was all for it. She would never hit first, but she would sure as heck hit back.

"Chill out, everyone," Ronnie said. "I just checked Elena's stream. It's live. I bet she wants to insult us to bolster her pathetic ego, maybe provoke us into a fight and get us in trouble. Everyone put on your AR glasses and go live on your own streams. That way she'll know she's being watched from every angle and can't get away with any cheap shots."

Lynn ground her teeth together. It was good advice, which was surprising coming from Ronnie. But they were going to be late for class, and she had zero desire to stand around and be used as a verbal punching bag. She'd endured that for years already and was *done*. Just done.

Without a word, Lynn shouldered her way through her teammates and strode toward the crowd Elena had around her. It looked like the pop-girl had summoned most of the ARS team, including her personal three stooges. The ARS guys stood at the back and the wings, a group of tall, well-muscled guys whose smug, eager expressions told her they'd come ready to enjoy the proverbial cock fight. In the center of the group were Elena's usual gaggle of female flunkies—mostly girls from the cheerleading team but she spotted a few other regulars, including Kayla. The ebony-skinned girl was in the center of the pack, and their eyes met briefly over Elena's shoulder.

Kayla looked away, expression clearly distressed.

"Hugo, tint my glasses, will you," Lynn subvocalized.

"Of course, Miss Lynn."

She always kept the TD Hunter app on these days. It was the only thing that kept her sane, and there was no harm in it as long as she stayed out of combat mode.

Some people counted to ten. Some people visualized sandy beaches. She preferred to bury herself in monster stats and tactical game forums.

Well, and Hugo's dry witticisms helped.

Lynn stopped ten paces away from the approaching group and crossed her arms. She heard her teammates come up behind her and halt on either side. Edgar was a reassuringly solid presence at her left, while

Ronnie mirrored her stance on her right. Dan and Mack shifted nervously on the wings.

Elena stopped a mere five paces away, and her posse shuffled to a halt amid whispers and giggles.

Lynn didn't say a word, just waited for Elena to dig her own grave.

"You're in my way, fatso," Elena said, her artificially refined voice dripping with scorn.

"In case it is a relative point of interest, Miss Lynn, my omnisensors estimate your current measurements and body-fat percentage are equal to or less than twenty-five percent of the females surrounding Miss Seville."

"You shouldn't insult your friends, Elena. It's not nice."

"W-what? You're not my friend!" Elena spluttered.

"Thank God for that," Edgar muttered over Lynn's shoulder.

"I'm talking about your flunkies, genius," Lynn said, suppressing a snort at Edgar's comment. "I'm the same size as some of them, so the whole 'fatso' insult just doesn't work. I'd recommend you come up with something more creative, at least if your tiny brain is capable of that much intelligent thought. We've wondered about it from time to time."

Elena's face reddened and her eyes narrowed.

"You're an ugly, fat cow," she hissed. "Just because you squeeze yourself into some sort of fat-compression suit so you'll fit those lame clown uniforms you hunt in doesn't mean you're anything like my girls. I can't watch a single stream with you in it, you're so disgusting to look at."

"Pity," Lynn said calmly. So calmly. "If you watched a few you might learn something useful about, oh, I don't know, the game you're trying to compete in?

Did you know you're not even in the top one hundred on the individual leaderboard?" Lynn didn't know Elena's exact ranking because anyone not in the top one hundred wasn't worth her time to track down.

"Ahem, Miss Lynn, apologies for the correction, but she is not even *on* the individual leaderboard. It cuts off at one thousand."

"Oh, sorry," Lynn said, a mile-wide grin spreading over her face. "My AI just informed me you're not even *on* the individual leaderboard. For the captain of a Hunter Strike Team, that's pretty pathetic. Have you even killed a single TDM yet?"

Elena's mouth worked silently for a moment, then she spluttered.

"I've killed plenty! And my team—"

"Isn't aaaanywhere close to mine on the team leaderboard, Elena. Why don't you take your little flock of sycophants and go practice your combat moves. That'll get you closer to a championship win than throwing around pathetically lame insults and begging people to pay attention to you like a sorry little loser."

Elena gasped theatrically and put a hand to her chest, her voice wobbling unconvincingly as she said, "Connor, you're not going to just sit there and let her insult us, are you?"

There was a beat of silence as everyone in Elena's group looked around.

"What?" Lynn asked, apparently puzzled. "Missing your pet dog? I'm actually more impressed that he's not here. At least *he* has the sense to focus on getting work done while you prance around like a pigeon who thinks she's a peacock."

Elena flushed a deeper shade of red and dropped

the "close to tears" act, shifting her focus to Ronnie.

"You're a pathetic coward, letting a *girl* do all the talking for you."

Ronnie's pale, freckled face flushed pink, and Elena's eyes lit up with savage glee.

"What, are you too afraid of opening your mouth in front of your betters to stand up for yourself, you little baby? Who's the team captain, anyway? Because it's certainly not *you*."

"Shut your mouth, you b—"

"Ronnie!" Lynn's hand shot out and grabbed Ronnie's shirt sleeve as he surged forward. He spun on her furiously, breaking her grip.

"I didn't ask you! Now shut up and stay out of my way."

"Whoa, Ronnie, chill, man," Edgar said, shifting his stance.

Elena crossed her arms again and cocked a hip, all smugness once more.

"I see. So, you let a *girl* and a *dumb gorilla* talk for you? You really are a pathetic sop."

Ronnie started forward again, but this time Edgar snagged the back of his shirt, and that wasn't a grip Ronnie—or anyone else—could break.

"Calm down, man," Edgar said quietly. "We're streaming live, remember? She's just pushing your buttons because Lynn wouldn't get mad. Don't let her get to you."

Ronnie stopped trying to advance, though he was still breathing hard, furious eyes locked on Elena.

"You can call me pathetic all you want, *Elena*, but I'm not the one who can't hunt to save my life. You're the one who's a pathetic leech, feeding off everyone else's hard work. You're nothing without your dad's money, and I've done *research* on him. He's not even a real businessman, just a stock trader who got lucky a few times. I even found an open investigation on his firm, so I bet your dad is a cheating criminal too—"

"*You liar!*" Elena nearly screamed, and now it was her who was trying to advance while her flunkies anxiously grabbed her arms. The guys of the ARS team shuffled aggressively, popping knuckles and looming closer as if waiting for an excuse to attack.

"You filthy, creepy *liar*! If you ever talk about my daddy like that again, I'll—"

"Hey. *Hey*! What's going on here?"

Connor's loud, commanding voice—the voice of a true leader used to controlling his team on the field— cut across Elena's ranting. The tall, blond former ARS captain shouldered through the crowd.

"ARS boys, get out of here, this is none of your business," Connor snapped, sending a glare around at the guys in the group.

They shrugged collectively, some of them looking amused, others disgruntled. Even so, they began drifting back down the hallway, throwing surreptitious looks over their shoulders as they went.

"Elena, what the *hell* do you think you're doing?" Connor said through barely moving lips. He shot a wide, charming smile in the direction of Skadi's Wolves, obviously for the benefit of their livestreaming glasses, not them.

"None of your business," Elena huffed, crossing her arms again. "Though I notice you were conveniently *absent* when these losers started insulting me for no reason."

"That's because I was in *class*, Elena, where *you* are supposed to be as well. Now *come on*."

He smiled again at Lynn's group, then took a firm grip on Elena's hand and began dragging her down the hall after his ARS team. Elena's flunkies hurried after them like a clutch of ducklings, though Kayla, who lagged at the rear, looked back at them several times as she slowly followed. It looked as if she wanted to say something, but then decided against it and trotted to catch up with the other girls.

Lynn was staring after her former friend, wondering at the odd behavior, when Ronnie turned on her.

"*Never* do that again!" he hissed, fists clenched.

"Wait, what? What'd I do?"

"Usurp my authority and show me up in front of everyone!"

"Uh, Ronnie, we're still—"

"Then turn it *off* you moron!"

Lynn's glasses hadn't been streaming in the first place, just recording, since she didn't have a stream channel anyway. But all the other boys paused and blinked as if they were busy shutting their streams down.

"Look," Lynn said, trying to stay calm, "I'm the one Elena always picks on. I'm the one she sees as a threat. So, I figured I might as well confront her and get it over with."

Fatso. Cow. Disgusting.

Lynn gritted her teeth and focused on Ronnie's furious face. Honestly it wasn't much better than the demoralizing barbs that whispered in her head in Elena's taunting voice.

"Well, you were wrong," Ronnie snapped. "*I'm* the captain of this team, and from now on I'll be the one speaking for us in any situation, with other teams or with the public."

Lynn threw up her hands, sick and tired of the whole situation.

"Then why didn't you say something before? Like, when I marched up to her and you lined up silently beside me? Don't pretend you weren't fine with me taking all the punishment from that harpy until she questioned your *manhood*. Good grief, Ronnie, you're almost as bad as her!"

"I'm *nothing* like her!"

"Well you could've fooled me!" Lynn yelled back. She snapped her mouth shut on more words that pushed against her tongue, clamoring to get out. They were Larry's words, not Lynn's words—all the truth of Ronnie's incompetence and idiocy she'd endured for *months*. But she bit her lip and turned away from Ronnie's puce-colored face as his mouth worked up a reply.

"Just forget it, Ronnie. Sure, you can be the spokesperson, whatever. I don't care. And I won't bother trying to stand up for us in the future, since you want that job so badly."

"W-wait a minute, I'm not done!"

Lynn didn't bother responding, lest she say something she'd regret.

"Come on, Ronnie," Mack said, ever the peacemaker. "We're late for class as it is. Everyone was just trying to help, okay? No biggie."

Lynn could hear the guys' low voices behind her as they belatedly followed her down the hall.

Crap.

She'd thought Ronnie was getting better. He *had* been getting better. But then they'd become an official

Hunter Strike team, had launched to the top of the team leaderboard, and the world's attention had descended on them like an army of vultures—and it had been slowly picking them apart ever since.

Lynn wondered how professional gamers coped with it. It was maddening. *She* was going mad. And she didn't know how much longer she could hold up under the stress before something gave way.

Just hold on, Lynn, she told herself grimly. *Hold on.*

After school was hunting time. If they rushed, they could get changed and meet up with a precious few hours in which to hunt before dinner and parent-imposed curfews.

Dan's seven p.m. curfew was the worst. In the aftermath of their qualifier win, their team had been featured on the local news and Dan's cover had been blown. While Mr. And Mrs. Nguyen's reactions were filtered through Dan's glum description, it seemed to Lynn they'd been more furious that Dan hadn't actually gotten into robotics camp than that he'd lied about what he *had* been doing all summer. They'd promptly forbidden him from ever playing TD Hunter again, to which Dan had calmly—according to him—pointed out that he'd already become a local celebrity, and it would be a big embarrassment for him to suddenly quit for no reason. He might have also mentioned the cash prize, college acceptance, and assured gaming career waiting for him when he won—which, of course, was inevitable.

Lynn assumed it must have been a gut-wrenching choice for Mr. and Mrs. Nguyen: Have their son publicly fail at something or have him become a *professional gamer.* The choice had probably been a near one, too, but in the end, they'd allowed him to keep playing on the condition of perfect grades—thus the seven p.m. curfew.

Mack hadn't fared much better in the parental-wrath department, at least from his mom. But, for the first time in his life, perhaps, Mack had stood up to her and told her he was going to keep playing whether she liked it or not. They were all proud of him for it, though Lynn suspected there had been a lot more diplomatic wheedling and a lot less heroic defying than Mack had implied in his retelling. The mention of prize money and guaranteed future prospects hadn't hurt in Mrs. Rios's case either. The end result—an eight p.m. curfew—wasn't much better than Dan's situation, though at least both of them were blessedly free on the weekend.

Edgar, of course, was over eighteen, and from his comments Lynn gathered his mom had always been distantly supportive of whatever he did that kept him close to his friends and out of trouble. Mrs. Johnston worked multiple jobs to support her five children and considering how mature and independent Edgar had always been, Lynn figured he'd earned enough trust that his mother wasn't worried about his ability to balance responsibilities. He *had* been forced to promise a significant portion of his winnings to his younger sister, a year his junior, to take over the bulk of his duties taking care of their siblings. But Lynn had met his sister at the qualifiers, and she seemed to love and look up to him just as much as the rest of his siblings, so her mercenary demands were probably more due to Edgar's good-naturedness than her reluctance to help.

Ronnie never said a word about his father or any sort

of curfew, so Lynn could only assume he had free rein over his schedule. Heck, she didn't even know what his dad did. Perhaps he traveled extensively for work or didn't get home until late in the evening. Or maybe he simply didn't care what Ronnie did. Ronnie had always been a closed book when it came to his personal life.

As for Lynn, she'd already come to an understanding with her mom over the summer. As long as her grades stayed up and she stuck close to her teammates out on the street, Matilda trusted her to manage her own schedule. That didn't mean her mom didn't worry. But then, what mother *didn't* worry about their child?

Considering Lynn barely had time for any solo hunting, there wasn't much to worry about. She was always with the guys, and even if she hadn't been, she was constantly followed by a buzzing swarm of drones. Creeps harassing her on the street were a distant worry of the past—her biggest danger now was a stress-induced aneurism.

She'd half-heartedly tried to wear a disguise for a while. But considering the body-scanning and facial-recognition programs easily available to any paparazzi hobbyist, she'd quickly found it was wasted effort. Plus, there were four other people she could be predictably found around, and they all had streams, not to mention were considerably more open to the public's attention. So if the drones didn't find her, they inevitably found Ronnie, despite her protests that the buggers were a distraction to training. Ronnie, predictably, was too busy strutting and angling for sponsorships to do more than pretend to listen.

Thus, when school let out that day, Lynn turned her Skillet playlist up to full volume and shaded her AR glasses to the max before following Mack and Edgar out a lesser-used side entrance to avoid the crowds of kids streaming toward the school airbus platform. They headed to the nearest commercial airbus stop, where they would meet Dan and Ronnie, who were coming from a different class. The drums, guitar, and melodic screaming in Lynn's ears drowned out any overhead buzzing nicely, and the guys knew better than to try and talk to her out in the open. Too many listening ears. If they wanted to converse, they always pinged each other in the TD Hunter app anyway. Not all the guys were as good at subvocalizing as her, but they were good enough that they could carry on private conversations if they needed to. Not that they *remembered* to, half the time—but at least they had the option.

They'd reached the airbus platform and were waiting for Dan and Ronnie when Lynn got a ping from Edgar. She looked up to see him watching her with a seemingly serene look on his face. But she'd known him long enough to notice the little wrinkle between his brows. She opened up a voice channel and gave him a small nod of acknowledgment.

"You okay, Lynn?"

Not really. I want to punch everything in sight and wish I could eat paparazzi drones for breakfast.

"Yup," she subvocalized.

One dark eyebrow quirked, just enough for her to know he didn't believe her. She rolled her eyes.

"I'll be fine. I just want to get hunting. What's keeping Ronnie and Dan, anyway?"

Before he could reply, Lynn spotted the two hurrying toward them from the direction of the school, and a group message from Dan popped up in her vision.

RAN INTO ELENA AND FLUNKIES ON WAY OUT.
DON'T ASK RONNIE ABOUT IT.

Lynn checked and confirmed that Ronnie was not
one of the recipients of the message. Then she replied-
all and promised SURE THING.

The two joined their group and they all stood around
waiting for the next airbus to appear. Dan and Mack
started arguing, obviously continuing a conversation
they'd been having earlier. They were debating the
proper ranking weight of various TD Hunter scores,
such as kill-to-damage ratio, which Dan was better
at, versus overall kills, where Mack excelled. Those
two were always ragging on each other about scores,
sometimes pulling Ronnie and Edgar into their debates.
Lynn never talked about her scores, though she kept
a careful eye on them.

Their hunting schedule had already been decided for
the evening: they were going to visit one of their old
stomping grounds near the original electric substation
where Lynn had first fought the TDMs en masse. It
was about a fifteen-minute airbus ride northwest, not
quite on the outskirts of town, but close to it. The
substation itself was surrounded by an open field with
woods north of it, the St. Andrew's golf course to the
west, a quiet subdivision to the east, and the backs
of several businesses bordering the field to the south.

It wasn't the most secluded spot to hunt, especially
not since word had spread on the TD Hunter tactical
forums that substations were a TDM magnet. But so
far, they hadn't had any clashes with other Hunters.
Players were usually more interested in watching Skadi's Wolves work than competing for hunting grounds.
After all, if you could watch through the TD Hunter

Lens app, it was a pretty spectacular sight. Almost as good as watching ARS games.

Or, at least, that's what Lynn had heard in virtual. She was too busy keeping focused on her performance and avoiding the streams to check it out herself.

At their stop, they left the airbus in silence and trooped along the quiet road that led to the substation. When they rounded the last corner, though, and the substation field came into view, Lynn stopped dead in her tracks.

"Uh, guys, do you see that?" she subvocalized on their team channel.

"Whoa, what are all these people doing here?" Mack asked, slowing.

"Ignore the spectators," Ronnie barked, not breaking stride toward the field that already had a healthy crowd of people milling around its southern edge. Lynn noticed Ronnie raise his head more and throw back his shoulders, as if preparing to give a speech before a crowd of adoring fans.

Lynn put two and two together.

"Ronnie, you *told* them we were going to be here!" she subvocalized, unable to add the appropriate amount of rage and indignation into her words without shouting.

When her team captain didn't reply, she broke into a run and caught up to him.

"What the freaking *hell* do you think you're doing, Ronnie?" she subvocalized on their private channel, a compromise they'd come to over the summer with the idea that as long as Lynn gave Ronnie advice privately, he would pay attention to it. "Our last recon showed a significant uptick in TDM activity at this substation. We can't take on that many TDMs with this crowd of lens junkies in .the way! And look at all the drones! What about other teams copying our tactics? I thought we'd agreed to *keep our heads down*."

"We're public figures," he shot back. "You can't expect we wouldn't attract attention in a competition like this. We need to learn how to adapt and over-come, no matter the battle conditions."

"That's a load of crap, and you know it. We've never attracted even a quarter of this many spectators, even when we hunted in the middle of the city. You *invited* these people here to watch as some kind of ego trip, didn't you?"

Ronnie refused to look at her.

"Shut up and get back in formation, soldier. We've got a job to do."

Lynn almost slapped him then and there. Soldier? What were they, twelve years old and playing Call of Honor? She had a name! Only the swarm of drones circling overhead stopped her from strangling Ronnie on the spot.

Well, the swarm and the several dozen fans running toward them.

Lynn took a deep breath and let her Larry brain take over, enabling her to put aside all her anger, frustration, and other distracting emotions. Larry mode was cool, focused, and blessedly free of her hang-ups. It was the only way she could hunt sometimes—the only way to forget all the anxieties that held her back.

Or, in this case, her simmering stress that was about to explode and take Ronnie with it.

Only one thing mattered in Larry mode: winning. It was something Lynn forgot, at times, and she was grateful to be reminded of it.

"Tighten up, team," Lynn subvocalized, falling in right behind Ronnie. His shoulders twitched, as if annoyed she'd beat him to the command. But in Larry mode, Lynn didn't care what Ronnie thought. If their glorious leader was going to be an idiot, then it was up to her to take up the slack. He should have already briefed them on everything that was going to happen, not blindsided them with this ridiculous circus. Even if, in some deranged recess of his mind, this audience was necessary for "publicity" and not just to stroke his own ego, then he should have taken command of his team's attention and confidence from the moment they realized the situation.

For all of Ronnie's gaming experience and positive potential, his ego turned him into a childish moron. And "Larry the Snake" knew exactly what happened to childish morons: they got themselves and all their men killed in battle.

Well, not on her watch.

"Ignore the spectators," Ronnie subvocalized into their team channel—*finally*. "Just don't respond and keep going to our usual rally point in the field. From there we'll spread out and go into combat mode."

"Roger that, boss," Edgar said, pulling a stick of gum from one of the tight pockets on his TD Counterforce uniform, unwrapping it, and popping it into his mouth.

Ronnie marched straight toward the gaggle of amateur paparazzi, lens junkies, and fans clutching TD Hunter swag and waving Ever Bright signing markers in their direction. Fortunately, the crowd was smart enough to part like the Red Sea when Ronnie loudly declared, "Stand aside. We have a mission to complete," like some sort of four-star general.

Lynn rolled her eyes behind her tinted glasses. She supposed she should be grateful Ronnie didn't try to stop for a photo op or to sign some fangirl's t-shirt.

*Un*fortunately, however, the crowd didn't *stay* where they'd stopped, but reformed behind Skadi's Wolves and followed, chattering excitedly to each other—or to themselves in the case of those livestreaming their "exclusive experience." The gaggle of people followed them all the way out into the field, staying ten paces or so behind. Their presence made the back of Lynn's neck itch, and she resisted the urge to keep looking back.

About a fourth of the way across the field, Ronnie stopped and their team gathered round, some ignoring the spectators better than others. Mack—the little dunce—kept looking over at them and grinning. At one point he even waved at the drones overhead and mouthed, "Hey, Riko!"

It would have been cute if it hadn't been so annoying.

"Okay, team, listen up," Ronnie said, drawing every-body's focus. Lynn noted that not only did he fail to subvocalize, but he didn't even bother trying to keep his voice down. Her ire ticked up a few more notches, but she concentrated on staying in Larry mode and not letting it get to her. "Based on what we've seen at this substation before, we can expect a larger-than-normal aggressive and guard-type presence around a series of stationary gatherers—probably Bunyips. Our mission is to completely clear the field. That means we'll have to resupply on the move and we'll be attacking in a series of waves and feints. Consider this a training exercise to take on bosses."

A thrill tingled up Lynn's arms and she flexed her fingers, anticipating the feel of her game batons in them.

"We'll start in a quad wedge without stealth. Dan, you're on takedown to get rid of any fliers we draw in. After that we'll advance far enough to get a good idea of the opposition and trigger their attacks, then fully stealth and retreat back toward the rally point, picking off as many as we can. Finally, we'll switch to a strafing line and start whittling down the guard circles. Refill levels as needed and call out if you need a supply transfer—don't leave it to the last second. Got it?"

The team responded with a chorus of assents.

"What about them?" Lynn asked, jerking a thumb over her shoulder.

"I already told you, ignore them," Ronnie said, not meeting her eye.

"They're going to get in the way."

"They're TD Hunter fans, not idiots. You think they don't know how to stand on the sidelines and watch?"

Lynn gritted her teeth.

"Some of them, sure. But what about the paparazzi trying to get the best stream angle? Those crazies will do anything for a good shot. And I wouldn't put it past some fans to jump in the middle of a battle with a championship team for a selfie. Would you?"

Ronnie gave a dismissive snort.

"Just focus on hunting and ignore them."

"You know," Dan piped up, "I saw this crazy lady in Germany throw herself at a Hunter Strike Team during battle to ask one of them out on a date. You should probably say something official sounding, just to warn people to stay back. You're the captain, after all."

That gave Ronnie pause, and finally he sighed and shook his head.

"Fine. Wait here."

As he marched back toward the crowd, Lynn met Dan's eye and gave a little nod of thanks. She doubted anything Ronnie could say would dissuade obsessed fans or jerk paparazzi, but hopefully the bulk of the spectators would stay the heck away from their battlefield.

Their "glorious leader" said his piece—it sounded a lot more like a welcome than a warning, but it would have to do—then rejoined them and finally switched to subvocalization to give the "Form up!" command.

They got out their batons and moved into their first formation, spreading out enough to give each other plenty of room for melee maneuvers. The quad wedge called for Edgar and Ronnie abreast at the front as the heavy hitters with Lynn and Mack behind and to the side to provide fire support and guard their flanks. Dan stood in the middle behind Edgar and Ronnie where he would be protected from melee attacks and could concentrate on taking out any Tengu or Rocs hanging around, or just picking off ground targets to thin out the crowd.

Lynn fell easily into position on Edgar's right and shook out her limbs, getting the blood flowing and preparing to *finally* get some action.

"Hugo, get ready to drop me in combat mode on Ronnie's mark. No stealth. I want those bastard Tengu rushing in like starved vultures."

"Very good, Miss Lynn. Would you like me to put on one of your playlists for background music?"

"Not today. Put TDM sounds on my left bud, coms on my right, and leave both open to ambient noise. I don't trust this crowd. Oh, and could you warn me if any of them gets dumb and decides to get close?"

"Unfortunately, I am unable to report on the movements of civilians in real time, only Hunters in combat mode. However, if I do notice any disturbances within your field of vision, I will certainly bring them to your attention."

"Good enough," Lynn grunted.

"Ready everyone?" came Ronnie's voice over their team channel.

"I was *born* ready!"

"Locked and loaded, boss."

"Ready to rumble!"

Lynn's mouth quirked. She simply said, "Roger," and bent her knees, keeping on the balls of her feet, ready for anything the moment they dropped into combat mode. Adrenaline coursed through her limbs, warming her with its familiar, sweet fire.

Time to do what she loved best.

"Going into combat mode in three, two, one. Go!"

Lynn's display flashed to life and her ear instantly filled with a cacophony of sounds. Even as her hands felt the warmth of her morphing batons forming into the familiar shapes of Wrath and Abomination, she was already spinning, slashing out. The two Phasmas she'd dropped nearly on top of exploded into showers of sparks. Abomination barked once, twice, three times and the three demons parked within ten feet of her exploded as well before they could so much as turn and charge. In another ten seconds she'd cleaned up a handful of Grumblins and a clutch of death worms, finishing her sweep of the immediate area around her as her teammates did the same. Dan remained fully stealthed so he could focus on his sniping, and from the sound of it he'd already spotted some airborne targets, likely Rocs since Lynn didn't yet hear the distinctive "missile" screech of an incoming Tengu.

Despite how easily they took out the scattered Delta and Charlie Class targets, there was no time to relax. Their sudden appearance, especially with no stealth, drew in every TDM within thirty yards like enraged water buffalo.

And there were *a lot* of TDMs within thirty yards.

"Shit," Mack said, tone somewhere between *this-is-really-annoying* and *I'm-screwed*. "There's a freaking *lot* of them."

"It's called a target-rich environment, Mackie boy," Lynn said between blasting away at the solid wall of Orculls and Spithra headed her way. "Consider it a gift to your kill-to-damage ratio." She lunged to the side, avoiding a stream of Spithra poison and grinned at Mack's disgruntled grumbles barely audible over the grunts and yells of Ronnie and Edgar wading into the oncoming TDMs.

It took them barely three minutes to deal with the initial wave of lower-level aggressive types surrounding the outskirts of the TDM crowd at the substation.

But the battle was only just getting started.

"Everybody grab supplies while you can," Ronnie shouted as a solid mass of Namahags and Penagals marched toward them from the direction of the substation. Those TDMs were joined by more Spithra and Orculls streaming in from the sides and waves of obviously suicidal, but still determined, demons and Grumblins from the rear.

And that wasn't counting the Phasmas and Ghasts popping up and sneak attacking at every opportunity.

"That's a *looot* of monsters," Dan muttered, echoing Mack. "Ronnie, I already took out the local Tengu, and most of the Rocs are too busy at the substation to notice us yet, so I'm switching to dual pistols to clean up this mess behind us so you guys can focus forward."

"Roger," Ronnie replied.

Lynn glanced over at the tight sound in Ronnie's voice. At least thirty towering Namahags followed by an equally dense line of Penagals were ten yards from Ronnie and Edgar. Dozens of other TDMs were closing in on her and Mack from the sides. All four of them were pouring fire into the monsters and doing significant damage. But for every TDM that exploded, there were more behind them, as evidenced by the thick clusters of dots on Lynn's overhead.

So much for the "significant uptick" in TDM activity around the substation. This wasn't an uptick, it was a flood. What had happened to change the algorithm's spawn rates so drastically? Had a boss moved into the area that they didn't know about?

Lynn gave a very Larry-worthy curse and refocused on her slaughter of Orculls and demons trying to rush her from the side. She had to get her area clear, or she would be too tied up to support Edgar, who was about to get swarmed, big time.

What a freaking Charlie Foxtrot. They should have scouted the area further out instead of assuming they knew what force levels they were up against.

Ronnie and his sloppy impatience, for the win! her Lynn brain said.

You let him. You should have been looking out for the team better, her Larry brain replied.

"Whooooa, man, this is *so cool!*"

Lynn nearly jumped out of her skin at the voice right behind her. She spun on instinct, Skadi's Wrath whipping out toward the target. She barely managed to pull back in time to avoid walloping some random middle-schooler right across the face. True, the kid's full-face AR helmet would have protected him from any serious damage, but it sure wouldn't have looked good on the kid's no-doubt-active livestream.

"WHAT THE HELL ARE YOU DOING ON MY BATTLEFIELD! GET LOST!" Larry-Lynn bellowed at the top of her lungs, right in the kid's face. Then she spun back, sweeping Wrath in a figure eight to cut down the three Spithra that were right on top of her, stabbing with claw-tipped legs at her face. They'd already gotten her solidly with their poison spit while her back had been turned.

"Please tell me the kid ran off," Lynn subvocalized to Hugo.

"I believe he retreated a dozen yards but is still watching. And he is not alone," Hugo informed her as she rolled forward, avoiding the swings of two Orculls that were trying to pincer her between them. She came up and stabbed one in the back and shot the other, then took a precious second to scoop up some ichor and an Oneg before dodging a charging demon. She wouldn't need the Oneg herself—probably. But Edgar was nearly invisible beneath the Namahags mobbing him and would be guzzling the stuff.

Lynn didn't have time to worry about idiots who got too close. She had to get rid of this mob on her, *stat*. Edgar's whoops of battle lust had already turned to grunts of concentration as he jumped and dodged as best he could while blasting away. Mack and Dan had drawn closer together to cover each other and were similarly subdued as they focused on aiming, shooting, and dodging as fast as possible. Ronnie was also silent as he joined his twin pistols together into a Plasma Sword and tore through his crowd of monsters in a complicated dance of swinging, fiery death.

But silent was bad. Silent meant they were too pressed to keep tabs on one another, too pressed to even call for help when they needed it. They would get separated and defeated in detail.

She gave herself thirty seconds of one hundred percent focus on her area of responsibility.

Thirty shots of Abomination. All instant kills.

Thirty stabs and swipes of Wrath, every lunge and spin sending up more showers of sparks.

Thirty seconds and dozens of dead TDMs, then Ronnie's time to take charge was up.

Larry was in charge now.

"Ronnie," Lynn subvocalized on their private channel, "there's heavier forces than we predicted. We need to blink out and regroup."

"No," came her captain's reply between grunts of effort.

Lynn's eyes scanned the ground, and she snatched up as many piles of ichor, armor globes, and Oneg capsules as she could while shooting Ghasts with her other hand, aiming mostly by sound.

"What do you mean, no? We're going to get killed and there's no point taking the ranking hit."

"Can't blink in competition. Shouldn't do it here."

Lynn cursed under her breath and glanced at Dan and Mack, her Larry brain calmly sorting options, putting together pieces. They were still plugging away, and didn't look like they were about to die. But only Ronnie, their captain, had the team's health and other levels available on his display, so she had to guess.

She sprinted toward the mass of TDMs around Edgar as her Larry side finished the puzzle.

"You didn't care about blinking out two days ago when we were jumped by Yaguar," she subvocalized, one hundred percent cold, ruthless Larry. "You just don't want to look bad in front of an audience. Well newsflash, you incompetent prick, you're going to look awful idiotic when we all get picked off, one by one, like some amateur bunch of noobs."

Then she was on the Namahags and the time for words was over. Wrath scythed and flashed as she stabbed up under armor plates and took out three brutes in seconds, giving her an opening to get at Edgar. She didn't dive into the circle, just held the gap, widening it so Edgar would have a path of retreat.

That's when she saw the pair of guys in t-shirts and cargo pants, back-to-back, AR-visored heads uplifted in awe as TD monsters swarmed around them and poor Edgar blasted away, his AR-augmented body armor flashing with red damage again and again as he soaked in the damage that even his cannon couldn't keep back. A dozen drones buzzed overhead, dipping down low, almost to head level, trying to get close-up shots of Edgar in action.

What the actual—

No. No time for anger. These idiotic paparazzi were just terrain. Rocks in her path. Their drones were tree branches blowing in the wind.

Her Larry mode logged the terrain features and kept fighting, focused with every fiber of her being.

But deep down somewhere inside, Lynn was screaming in rage and pulling her hair out.

"Wow! Look, RavenStriker is here!"

"Quick, get the drones on her!"

"This is stream gold, we're gonna get so many followers from this."

Buzzing around her head, drowning out the all-important TDM sounds. Shapes flashing in the corners of her eyes, making her glance away from her target.

"Miss Lynn, you're taking thirty percent more damage per second than usual, might I suggest we retreat and—"

"Block out ambient noise, now!"

The buzzing and paparazzi chatter cut off.

"Were you also aware that you are still fully unstealthed, Miss Lynn? That likely accounts for at least twenty percent of the increase in hostile attention."

Foxtrot, foxtrot, foxtrot.

"Skadi's Wolves, stealth fully now if you haven't already!" Lynn yelled, mentally kicking herself for the oversight. Ronnie should have reminded them to fill their globe slots the moment he realized how badly they'd underestimated the TDM numbers.

Skadi's Wrath hit something solid as she swung it up in an arch to cut down another Namahag. The force wasn't much, but it was enough to make her electric blue sword bend and completely distract her. In that split second, three Namahags pounced and started pummeling her, and she had to roll blindly to get away.

"Down to fifty percent health, Miss Lynn, and I doubt Edgar is doing any better."

Lynn kept rolling, pausing just long enough to order Hugo to refill all her slots for health, armor, and globes before gasping out on the team channel.

"Edgar, do you need Oneg?"

"Yes!"

Lynn wasted precious seconds transferring her extra Oneg to Edgar, then dodged further away. She was turned around, had lost track of Edgar and the rest of her team, and was still beset on all sides by TDMs. A quick glance at her overhead reoriented her—and made her Larry curse again.

They were all over the place.

"Ronnie, we need to blink and regroup," she panted, her focus fractured and not even bothering to use their private channel.

"No! Just—focus—we'll be—fine," came his disjointed reply.

"We're taking too much damage, we're in a terrible position, this is a waste of ranking!"

It wasn't pride talking. Their ranking determined their experience bonuses, not to mention her ability to keep earning the incredibly valuable pieces of the Skadi armor and weapon set. They were gambling their championship odds on a pointless battle, all because of Ronnie's ego.

"I'm low on Oneg again!" Edgar shouted. "And I think I hear a Manticar coming!"

"Edgar, blink out *now*!" Lynn commanded.

"No! Don't you dare, Edgar—"

There was an ear-splitting roar in Lynn's left ear and she winced.

"Oh shit—"

Edgar's blue icon disappeared from the overhead.

"Dan, Mack, blink now!"

"Uh, but Ronnie said—"

"Do it now, Hunters!" Lynn roared, busy herself dodging the long reach of some Penagals that stood between her and where she'd been trying to rescue

Edgar. But now he was gone, and she saw the golden-maned head of a Manticar lift in another roar over the sea of TDMs. She *could* take on one herself, as long as she had the space and time to dodge its tails and whittle it down.

In the current mass of enemies, it would kill her in seconds.

"Ronnie, you too, get out of here!" she yelled, just as the Penagals in front of her parted, drawing back from the Manticar loping toward her. "I'm out," she yelled, and Hugo blinked her out just as the Manticar pounced.

The abrupt quiet and emptiness around her made her momentarily dizzy, and she locked her knees, trying to orient herself.

"RavenStriker! Over here! That was amazing!"

"Tell us about your battle. What made you exit the game?"

"Can you share your training regime? I have millions of followers dying to know."

"Will you sign my backpack?"

Voices washed over Lynn and her vision was blocked by a crowd of people all pressing in. Drones buzzed low overhead, filling her ears with that uniquely annoying sound that was as grating as fingernails on chalkboard.

"I—I—" She blinked, tried to back up, ran into someone, and flailed. People were touching her, grabbing her arms. She had her batons, she had to fight back—

"MOVE!"

The bellow came from in front of her, and there above the heads of the crowd, Edgar's scowling face loomed.

The press of people scattered and within seconds Lynn could breathe again. Edgar came to stand beside her, looming with deadly menace as the last few paparazzi types backed up and the ring of hopeful fans clutching swag eyed him warily.

"Lynn! Lynn! You okay?" Dan's panting voice came from behind her and then Dan and Mack came shouldering through the crowd.

Lynn scowled and didn't respond. Her body vibrated with anger and unspent adrenaline even as her stomach twisted in fear. She could still feel the hands grabbing her, pulling her, hungry for pieces of her.

"Listen up you lot!" she called out in her best Larry battle voice. "You're interfering with the training of a Hunter Strike Team, and every second of this is on livestream. TD Hunter security is watching you as we speak. Anyone who doesn't clear out right this second will regret it!"

Her threat echoed across the field, and to her relief, most of the onlookers started backing up. Some hurried away as they glanced nervously up at the many hovering drones. Others went slowly, clearly still riveted by the drama.

As long as they gave her space, she didn't care.

The swiftly departing crowd finally revealed Ronnie, standing on the outskirts with his arms crossed, virtually ignored by the spectators. He marched toward their team, face as red as Lynn had ever seen it.

"What the—" He devolved into a stream of Lithuanian curses that even Lynn hadn't heard before. But she could guess what they meant.

"Keep your voice down, Ronnie," Lynn hissed. Her skin prickled uncomfortably, all too aware of how many people were staring at them.

"You usurped my authority and disobeyed a direct

order!" Ronnie yelled, completely ignoring her words and getting right up in her face.

That raised Lynn's hackles.

"If you hadn't set us up like some sort of performing circus to bolster your own pathetic ego, none of this would have happened!" she snapped, trying but probably failing to keep her voice down herself. "We should have scouted the area first and been more careful going in, or at least pulled out a lot sooner and came up with a different plan as soon as we saw we were outgunned."

"*I'm* the team captain, and *I* make the plans! If you had followed orders, we would have been fine! But *no*, you're an emotional *girl* who couldn't keep it together. You got scared and pulled out! You have no idea how to be on a team or to trust your—"

"I *what*?" Lynn interrupted, completely losing it. "I got *scared because I'm a girl*?? Do you hear yourself, Ronnie? You're so incompetent and fragile you can't even take responsibility for your team—who *you* are in charge of—much less for your own actions! *You're* the one who led us in blind. *You're* the one who got so bogged down you forgot to tell us to stealth up. *You're* the one who let us get separated and defeated in detail. All *I* did was salvage our situation so the whole team didn't suffer 'cold chill of death' penalties!"

"I had a plan—"

"It was a stupid plan! And I could have told you that if you'd have taken five minutes to run me through it beforehand! But *no*, I'm a *girl* so obviously I know *nothing*! You're so freaking stupid, Ronnie, I can't believe I ever thought you could lead Skadi's Wolves."

"This is *my* team! I've been leading these guys

for years and you're just a noob wannabe we let tag along because we needed another player! You're not even a real gamer!"

Lynn saw red. She actually saw red, like in the cartoons.

"Ronnie, shut up," Edgar said, "You're being a douchenozzle." He laid a hand on Lynn's shoulder, as if he could sense that she was seconds away from ripping Ronnie's head off his shoulders.

"Shut up yourself, Edgar! She's a liability and I won't play with someone we can't trust. I want her off the team!"

A ringing silence followed, broken only by the incessant buzzing overhead.

"Wait a sec, Ronnie, you can't do that," Dan said, brow furrowed as he looked back and forth between Lynn and his captain. "She's our best player. How are we going to find a replacement who can even begin to match her stats and combat experience?"

Ronnie hesitated a fraction of a second, but then crossed his arms. "We're a Hunter Strike Team. Everybody wants to be us. It'll be easy to find a fill-in."

"Maybe we should talk about this somewhere else," Mack said, looking around at the thinner but obviously riveted crowd. "I know we have some bumps to smooth out as a team, but let's not make any hasty decisions. We can figure this out."

"If she won't follow orders, she's out," Ronnie declared, shooting a glare at Dan and Mack instead of meeting Lynn's furious gaze.

"Hey, chill out, Ronnie," Dan said. "For real, we should talk about this, and we shouldn't do that here."

"No."

Everybody turned to Lynn. She only barely recognized her own voice as she continued in tones of icy steel.

"This team is a waste of everybody's time. Ronnie has made it abundantly clear that he's an incompetent captain, and there's no way in a thousand lifetimes we'd ever win the championship like this. I'm here to win, not to be constantly ignored, belittled, and insulted. And I won't stand by and let our team lose to spare Ronnie's fragile ego. I'm out."

With that, she turned and walked away.

Tears blurred her vision. Not tears of hurt, but tears of anger and frustration—at wasted dreams and the futility of everything she'd fought so hard for.

Vaguely she heard voices behind her.

"Hey! Edgar! Where are you going?"

"I'm with her. If she's out, I'm out."

Ronnie's protests faded behind her as she walked as fast as she could toward the road, desperately ignoring the stares and whispers of the random strangers who had witnessed their team's untimely end. Buzzing followed along overhead, but for her own sanity she tried to block it out.

A warm presence caught up to her and began pacing silently alongside. A soothing warmth filled her chest, but she didn't look over at Edgar. She couldn't even bring herself to say anything—not yet at least, with a crowd still watching.

But she was grateful. So, so grateful.

They were silent the whole way back to the airbus platform. Lynn didn't ask where Edgar was going, and Edgar didn't say, but he didn't get off on his stop. He stayed beside her all the way to the platform by her apartment complex. He stayed with her up to her building, and through the front doors, leaving their tail of buzzing drones behind. They didn't say anything in the elevator, and when Lynn finally stopped in front of her door, they just stood there for a moment, silent.

"So, what's the plan, boss?"

A fleeting smile lifted Lynn's lips, but then the enormity of the situation crashed down on her.

"I have no idea."

"Hey, don't sweat it, Lynn. We'll figure something out. I believe in you."

She didn't know what to say to that. There weren't any words to describe the warm pressure in her chest, pushing up into her throat. It was a comforting pressure, and she clung to it. But she couldn't speak past it.

"Get some rest," Edgar said, filling the silence and giving her an encouraging squeeze on her shoulder. "See you tomorrow at school."

Lynn forced herself to look up at him and meet his warm eyes as she nodded in thanks. His face crinkled in a good-natured smile, and he gave her a two-fingered salute before turning and ambling down the hall, digging in his pocket for another piece of gum as he went.

Chapter 4

KAYLA SWAIN HAD IT ALL: GOOD GRADES, GOOD looks, a rich stepdad, and a prized position in the most exclusive clique at school.

She was also deeply, deeply unhappy.

"This is *wonderful*!"

Elena's squeal of joy made Kayla wince.

"I knew they were all losers. How could you *not* be with a stupid name like Skadi's Wolves? I'm just glad they did my work for me and gave up on their own."

Connor didn't respond from where he sat on one side of the perfect cream-colored sectional couch, perpendicular to Elena. Kayla noticed he had the faraway look of someone watching a stream on their retinal implant.

"I mean, how dumb could they be?" Elena went on, ceasing her excited bouncing to lean back and cross her long, shapely legs. She was either oblivious to or just ignoring Connor's lack of enthusiastic agreement. Probably the latter. Elena ignored a lot of things because in Elena's mind, if she ignored it, it didn't exist. Kayla would know, considering *she* didn't exist half the time.

Like now.

They were at Elena's house off Blairs Ferry Road,

a huge six-bedroom estate house, even though the only people living in it were Elena and her mother—Elena's father was almost always away on business. They were supposed to be prerecording some "slice of life" videos of Elena and Connor, the "perfect" gaming couple, relaxing and being...whatever. Cool, rich, sexy, and everything else enviable among stream celebrities. It was Kayla's job to take the videos and craft the posts, which Elena would then approve. If she liked what Kayla wrote, Kayla was invisible. Just an obedient little cog in Elena's machine.

If Elena *didn't* like what Kayla wrote...well, then things got unpleasant.

Kayla's stepdad owned a big PR firm based out of Des Moines, and Kayla had always had a knack for social media. When she'd first volunteered to help Elena manage her public image, she'd been desperate to please, not to mention a lot younger and more naive.

Now, though, she understood.

She was just a fly on the wall to Elena. Not even enough of a person to bother worrying about overhearing what Elena said.

"I bet they planned the whole thing ahead of time, just to get attention." Elena examined her perfectly manicured nails as she spoke. "If they're just going to lose anyway, they might as well get as many followers as possible while they're trending. It's what I would have done—if I was losing, *obviously.*"

Connor still didn't respond.

Kayla glanced at the muted livestream minimized in the corner of her AR contacts—no implants for her, her father wouldn't hear of it. *I work in the industry, honey. I know what those things are capable of,* he always told her whenever she'd begged him for implants like all the other rich kids. He didn't seem to understand the stigma that came with something so gauche as AR glasses. At least he'd allowed contacts, even though they irritated her eyes.

Lynn and the rest of Skadi's Wolves had long since escaped the camera drones of *HotGamingCelebs'* livestream, but Kayla guessed Connor was watching the replay of the argument.

As soon as it had started some fifteen minutes ago, one of Elena's clique had pinged them all.

OMG LK AT HGC STREAM!!! LMAO, LOSERS TOTES LOSING THR SHIT!!!!

Elena had immediately dropped everything—even though Kayla had been trying for a solid thirty minutes to get the perfect shot to satisfy her—and had been glued to her stream ever since. Kayla had caught most of it herself, and she winced in sympathy at the memory. Poor Lynn. Kayla didn't know Ronnie Payne herself, but from what little she'd observed, he really did seem like a world-class jerk.

"Connor? Connor! Are you even listening to me?"

Connor's ice blue eyes focused on Elena, his expression aloof.

"No."

Elena uncrossed her legs and stomped her heeled foot. She actually stomped it, like a three-year-old child. Sometimes, Kayla could barely believe Elena was for real.

"Stop obsessing over Skadi's Wolves and listen to me! They're history! We don't have to worry about them anymore. This is our big opportunity to cement our position. We need to go live now and say something impressive. Something about how, unlike *some* people, *we* won't let the city of Cedar Rapids down, yada yada yada. Okay?"

"I don't think so," Connor said softly, back to focusing on his implant screen.

"What? Why not? You think we should be more aggressive? I'd love to, I just thought—"

"No, idiot. I don't think Skadi's Wolves are done for."

Elena reared back, staring at Connor as if she couldn't believe her ears.

"W-what did you just call me? How dare you!"

"You underestimate Lynn Raven," Connor said, tone casual, almost thoughtful. "You always have. She's not going to give up so easily."

"I don't care about Lynn Raven! She's done for. She's been humiliated on livestream. Everybody is going to drop her like the trash she is. No more '#teamraven-striker,'" Elena said in a mocking voice, then made a face like she'd just gotten a whiff of rancid milk.

Connor stared at her, his perfect face unreadable. Finally, he shook his head.

"Like I said, Elena: you're an idiot."

Elena's eyes narrowed.

"Watch your mouth, pretty boy. You are *nothing* without me. *I* paid for all your equipment, *I* got you sponsorships, and *my* stream is making you famous. You were just a dumb jock before I picked you to be on my team and made you into something!"

"Maybe," Connor said after a pause, then shrugged. "But I'm the one who knows how to lead a team and win this championship. Stream celebrities are a dime a dozen, and if Lynn started her own channel, she'd have double—probably triple—your followers *overnight*."

He paused and gave Elena a long, evaluating look.

Kayla held her breath, for once praying *not* to be noticed. She wanted to melt into the background, but she stayed where she was by one of the patio windows looking over the Sevilles' expansive lawn.

"You're dead weight, Elena," Connor finally said. "Especially after that stunt you pulled at school, confronting Skadi's Wolves. Drama might up your viewing stats but looking like a complete fool on your own stream is a great way to lose any credibility our team has built."

"*You* looked like a fool because *you* weren't there to back me up!"

"I didn't look like a fool, Elena. You did. You know calling people 'fatso' and 'cow' is fat shaming, right? It's not cool anymore. You need to get with the times."

"B-but she *is* fat!"

Connor shrugged.

"Doesn't matter. What works in high-school cliques isn't what works in professional gaming. That's what you don't understand. If I'd realized how inept you were at adapting, I wouldn't have made our deal."

"I—I—" Elena's mouth opened and closed like a fish trying to breathe.

"Maybe it's time I reconsider it."

"Y-you can't do that!"

Connor's gaze sharpened.

"Oh? And why is that?"

"You're nobody," Elena huffed. "You're nothing without me and my influence. I'll call my daddy and have him tell the college board to rescind that scholarship offer they made you. You only got it because of Daddy. You *have to* abide by my terms, or you'll lose everything." She crossed her arms and smirked at Connor, but Kayla could tell she was nervous. She kept shifting her head and shoulders like she always did when trying to make sure her hair was falling just right.

"A threat like that might work with one of the others, Elena. But I know what I'm capable of. Just because our deal expedited some things doesn't mean I can't do it on my own. *My* ARS team is first in the state. Or did you forget that part?"

Elena's nostrils flared, and for a moment Kayla thought she was going to start yelling again. But then a seductive smile spread over her face and she scooted along the couch until her and Connor's knees were touching. She laid a hand on Connor's leg.

"Don't be like that, Connor. We make the perfect couple. Everybody loves us! There are a lot of . . . benefits to being on my team, as you well know." Her smile broadened and she shifted, conveniently tugging the hem of her blouse down a little further to show the lacy edge of her bra. Kayla nearly threw up in her own mouth, watching the display.

"We have the perfect opportunity to show a strong front. We could even play it up a bit for the livestream. You know how much stream fans love romance, right?" Elena scooted a little closer and her hand drifted up Connor's thigh.

Kayla looked down, face heating. Being a fly on the wall was sooo awkward.

Next thing she knew, she heard someone stand, and her eyes shot up again. Connor was looking down at Elena, his expression as unreadable as ever while Elena had a pout on her face.

"As much as I've enjoyed our little arrangement, I think I'll be leaving now."

Elena's eyebrows scrunched.

"What do you mean?"

"Always a pleasure, Kayla," Connor said without looking over at the patio window.

Kayla jumped and blushed harder.

"Wait a minute, why are you talking to Kayla? I'm right here, Connor. Right here, hellooo. What do you mean, you're leaving? We're not done with our stream shoot yet."

Connor ignored Elena completely and strode toward the door without a word. Elena jumped up from the couch.

"Wait! Where are you going? You didn't mean—you can't leave the team, if that's what you mean. We have a deal! Is that what you mean?"

Still, Connor said nothing as he disappeared through the living room door, headed for the front of the house.

"Stop! Connor!" Elena hurried after him, and Kayla heard her continued yelling as it moved through the echoing house.

"I said stop! You can't leave, you have *nothing* without me! If you even think about it, I'll—I'll ruin your name! I'll dox you! I'll say you raped me! You'll never get any scholarships ever again! Your sports career will be ruined! Connor, stop!!"

There was the sound of the front door opening, then Elena's voice faded further, as if she'd followed Connor outside to the front patio. Fortunately—or unfortunately, depending on how you saw it—her voice rose in pitch to a scream and Kayla could still hear her words as clear as a bell.

"*Fine*! You disgusting pig! I never needed you anyway! I've got dozens of pretty boys just like you lining up to take your place! What the heck, I don't even need them to be pretty! Anybody could take your place, you filthy traitor! Even that stupid boy from Skadi's Wolves, Donnie or whatever, I bet even *he* could do your job! Do you hear me? *You'll regret this!!*"

There was the sound of a revving engine, then the squeal of tires and the engine sounds faded.

Kayla remained frozen by the patio window, mind racing. What should she do? Elena was about to come storming back into the house and, as the only other person there, Kayla knew full well who would bear the brunt of Elena's wrath. Could she get away with disappearing and sneaking out the back? How badly would she pay for it later?

This was a nightmare.

The unhappy, sick feeling in Kayla's stomach intensified as she heard the front door slam and the furious *click-clack click-clack* of Elena's heels marching across the marble floor of the foyer.

Before Kayla could make a decision, Elena stormed back into the room. The cream rug muted the lethal-sounding staccato of her heels, but the quiet didn't last for long.

"What are you staring at, you useless idiot!"

Kayla flinched.

"Um, nothing! I was just figuring out a better angle for the, uh, shot when, well..." she trailed off helplessly.

"When what? What, exactly, do you think just happened?" Elena's sharp voice cracked across the room and her eyes narrowed dangerously.

"O-oh, n-nothing!" Kayla said hurriedly.

"That's right, nothing, you little creep. Why were you standing there the whole time like some kind of paparazzi sneak, eavesdropping on our *private* conversation? If you breathe a *word* of anything that happened here—if I see a *single* mention of it show up on any stream, I will hold *you* personally responsible, Kayla! Do you understand?"

"Y-yes, of course. I won't breathe a word!"

"You better not, you worthless lump. What are you even good for?" Elena yelled, switching tracks and picking up steam for a really good rant, just like Mrs. Seville did whenever they got in her way. The woman wasn't often in the house—her many social activities and beauty appointments kept her out and about. But when she was there, they knew to make themselves scarce if they didn't want to be lectured on their inadequacies or hear endless rants about Mr. Seville. "You've spent hours trying to get one measly shot and wasted all our time! I bet *you're* why Connor walked out, because you're such a massive waste of air and space. Can't you do anything right?"

"I-I was just doing what you told me to, Elena. You didn't like the first shot—"

"Because it was a worthless piece of garbage, just like you!"

Tears pricked the corners of Kayla's eyes, but she blinked them away. You couldn't show weakness in front of Elena, you only made it worse on yourself.

"Look, Elena," Kayla tried, keeping her voice as calm and pleasant as she could.

"Shut up and get out of my house, you little shit! I'll do my own posts for today, no thanks to *you*! You're worthless. You're *all* worthless! I have to do everything myself, just like always. Why am I the only competent person in this entire city?"

Relief flooded through Kayla. She grabbed her bag and was out of there like a shot, leaving Elena's voice echoing behind her as the girl continued to rant at the empty room. Kayla's own heels click-clacked across the marble foyer and she felt a sudden surge of loathing for them. She would kick them off the second she got home. They were uncomfortable and completely clashed with her personal style. She wore them because *Elena* told her to. In fact, every stitch she had on had been prescribed by Elena. Most of the clothes and shoes in her closet too. To be a part of Elena's clique, you had to dress the part, or you weren't allowed.

Usually, Elena called her an air taxi to take her home, but now Kayla would have to do it herself and linger awkwardly on Elena's front porch until it arrived.

She couldn't take that—she would wait at the front gate.

Kayla clacked her way down the stone steps of the Seville's front porch and started off along the twisting driveway toward the road, hating her shoes, Elena, and herself every step of the way.

How had her life come to this? When was the last time she'd been happy? She could barely even remember a day when she didn't have this queasy lump in her stomach, always making her anxious, worried what everyone—i.e., Elena—would think or say.

The last time she'd really been happy had been in sixth grade, when her mom had finally left her dad and they'd relocated to Cedar Rapids for a fresh start. They'd moved into that apartment complex and she'd met Lynn and they'd had so much fun together. Sure, it had been awkward starting out, but what twelve-year-old wasn't awkward? Lynn had been a good friend: quiet, but full of fun and interesting ideas once you got her out of her shell. They did silly, fun things together, even taught each other how to braid the other's hair and traded favorite braid patterns.

But then Kayla's mom had remarried, and they moved up in the world. Kayla's stepdad was one of the "country club" crowd and had a big house not far away in Linn Junction. Moving there had been like a dream come true. Her stepdad was actually pretty cool, and she and her mom suddenly had all the money they could want to go shopping, buy better clothes, and get all the toys Kayla had ever wanted. She missed playing with Lynn every day, but she'd been sure there was plenty of room in her new life for her friend too.

At least, until Elena Seville—the most beautiful and popular girl in middle school—marched up to Kayla, looked her critically up and down, then shrugged and said her daddy had told her to be nice to Mr. Swain's new stepdaughter. Kayla was one of *their* crowd now.

From that moment on, Elena's will dictated what she wore, what she said, and most importantly, who she was seen with.

And Lynn was *not* on that list.

Kayla remembered Elena's words so vividly, as if she'd spoken them yesterday.

You can't be around people like that *anymore, Kayla.*

But why not? Lynn is nice.

Who cares? She's so fat, and have you seen the clothes she wears? My daddy says fat people shouldn't be allowed out in public where everybody has to look at their ugly bodies. He says his tax dollars pay for their healthcare, so they should be shut away until they learn how to eat right and look decent. It's their own fault, you know? How ugly they look? If they weren't so disgusting and greedy they could all be thin and beautiful like us.

It had sounded ludicrous to Kayla, even then. But she was out of her depth, surrounded by a whole crowd of girls she was desperate to fit in with, and they all agreed with Elena. They couldn't *all* be wrong, could they? Maybe Elena really did know what she was talking about. After all, she *was* the most beautiful girl at school, so she must know something about how staying thin worked, right?

At least, that's what Kayla had convinced herself at the time.

Thinking about it, Kayla felt her face flush hot with shame. She knew better now—it'd taken years, but she'd finally gotten sick of Elena's preaching and started doing her own research on health and fitness, only to find that humans came in a dizzying array of natural body and metabolism types. She knew all about the body-image sickness in the celebrity industry.

The information was there for anyone who had the guts to be confronted with it.

And yet, despite what she knew to be the truth, she stayed a part of Elena's clique. Rejecting Elena was paramount to suicide. She'd seen a few girls try it, and Elena had *destroyed* them. The bullying had been so bad that the girls had eventually transferred schools.

Kayla tried to kick a stray stone on the driveway in front of her, tears of frustration and shame welling in her eyes. She missed and nearly overbalanced, then cursed herself seven ways to Sunday.

This was stupid. *She* was stupid. Why was she *letting* Elena abuse her?

Suddenly, Lynn's words from the livestream echoed in her head.

I'm here to win, not to be constantly ignored, belittled, and insulted... I'm out.

Kayla felt emotion well up in her throat. Her friend—no, her *former* friend—was so brave. Lynn had everything Kayla wished she had and was too afraid to reach for. Lynn knew her worth, held her head high, and refused to take the abuse.

Why couldn't she be more like Lynn?

Feet throbbing, Kayla finally reached the front gate. She checked her LINC and saw she still had at least a five-minute wait for the air taxi she'd ordered. She wrapped her arms around herself, sniffed, and shivered. The early October sun was out and the air wasn't too chilly, but Kayla still felt cold and miserable.

She wished she could talk to Lynn and ask her how she was so brave and confident. But Lynn would never talk to her again, not when Kayla had stood by for *years* and let Elena insult and torment her without raising a finger to stop it. There was no apology that could make up for how terrible a friend she had been.

On a morbid whim, Kayla pulled up the *HotGamingCelebs* stream again and skipped backward until she could rewatch Lynn standing up for herself to that jerk captain of hers. She watched it again, and again, zooming in on Lynn's face and trying to puzzle out how the girl was staying so strong.

It was a shame Lynn didn't have her own stream. If she gave the fans exclusive, first-person content there wouldn't be such a demand for hot takes from paparazzi vultures. The poor thing was probably going crazy with all those drones following her around.

An idea struck Kayla with such force that she rocked back on her heels and almost lost her balance.

It was brilliant.

But would it work? More importantly, could she do it?

For the first time in years, hope filled Kayla's chest, and she was actually smiling by the time the air taxi pulled up.

Lynn had just gotten out of the shower, dressed in her most comfortable baggy clothes, and was braiding her damp hair when her LINC beeped, indicating a call was coming through. She hesitated. Did she *want* to talk to anyone right now? But years of being drilled in responsibility and responsiveness by her mom propelled her toward her desk where her LINC ring lay. She slid it on and popped in her earbuds, from which she heard:

"Call from: TransDimensional Hunter technical support line. Accept call?"

Lynn was so shocked she didn't respond right away, and her LINC's answering service repeated the request.

"Y-yeah, sure," Lynn said, though nervousness filled her gut.

What did they want? Did they know she'd been kicked off her own team? What would she say?

"Hey Lynn! It's James over at TD Hunter technical support. How you doing today?"

"Um, great! Just, uh, great."

"Glad to hear it! I won't keep you long, I was just following up on some unusual activity your LINC had sent us. You recall that after the beta testing period, you agreed to let your LINC continue sending us data the TDH app collected to help us continue to improve our users' experience?"

"Uh, yeah, I guess?"

"Well, the system noticed you were recently in a very high level of activity engaged with a large number of TDMs when you left combat mode quite abruptly. It looked enough like the black-out glitches we ran into during beta that we just wanted to follow up and make sure there hadn't been some malfunction in your equipment or the game app."

"No, no. That was on purpose. It's, uh, all fine."

"Okay! Great. How're the new team items and special rules working out? Any user-related questions I can help you with?"

"Um, nope," Lynn said as casually as she could manage. "We're good, thanks."

"Excellent. We want to make sure we provide the best support possible for our Hunter Strike Teams to make sure your experience is smooth, considering our shorter-than-usual beta testing period. Remember, any questions or issues you have, please don't hesitate to give us a call. We're here to help."

Lynn swallowed.

"Thanks, James. I appreciate that."

"Great! Well, if there's nothing else I can help you with . . ." James paused, and Lynn shifted uneasily in the pregnant silence.

"Can I talk to Steve?" she blurted out before she could change her mind.

"Sure! Let me ping the tactical department and check that he's not already on a call. Give me a sec, okay?"

"Okay . . ." Lynn was already regretting her request, but there was no backing out now. Within seconds, Steve Riker's gravelly, clipped voice came online.

"Hey kid. You rang?"

For some reason, the sound of Steve's voice made Lynn relax, not tense up further like she'd expected. Her dad had always called her "kid," and the familiar epithet just seemed to hit the right spot in the tangled ball of frustration and emotion jammed up in her chest.

"Um, well, yeah. About that . . ."

Steve chuckled.

"No worries, kid. I saw it all."

"You did?" Lynn gasped. Her cheeks heated.

"Yeah, our tactical team likes to, uh, keep an eye, shall we say, on certain streams known for harassing gamers. It's so our legal department has a head start if there's ever any cause for lawsuits. They flagged that stream—hey, what was it called?" Steve half yelled as if calling over his shoulder to someone else in the room. "Yeah, *HotGamingCelebs*. Jeez. What a dumpster fire. Anyway, they flagged it as soon as they saw some of the audience getting in the way of players, and I watched the rest live, so . . . yeah."

"Yeah," Lynn echoed, shoulders drooping. She suddenly felt exhausted beyond belief and stepped over to flop down on her bed and stare listlessly at the ceiling. The familiar smell of her comforter surrounded her but didn't make her feel any better. "Maybe I should just give up and go back to being Larry Coughlin and making bank in WarMonger. At least then I had complete control over my life and I could make reliable money."

Steve chuckled.

"I know quite a few players who would be quaking in their boots at the idea of Larry showing up again."

Lynn snorted.

"And," he continued, "I know quite a few players

who would *love* to have Larry back. I won't lie, teaming up with Larry Coughlin to kick some Tier One a—I mean butt was seriously good times."

Rather than make her feel better, Steve's praise made her groan.

"I really miss it, you know. I just don't have time anymore! And it annoys me to think of all those 'young upstarts' getting overconfident and running their mouths because the Boss Snake isn't around to put them in their place."

"I know, kid. Believe me, I know. It sucks to give up things you worked hard for. Look, though, you sound pretty down about the whole TD Hunter situation, but you shouldn't be."

"What do you mean?" Lynn moaned, now covering her face. "I got kicked off my own team! I'm basically out of the championship running. What am I supposed to do now?"

"You've got a couple options, actually. First option: join another team. You are in the top ten TD Hunter players *in the world*. There's dozens of teams that would simply kick out their weakest player to give you room to join, if you put out that you were looking."

Lynn removed her hands and made a face.

"That . . . doesn't seem right."

"Maybe, but it's the truth. Of course, there's the problem of location. Not many top-tier teams in Iowa—just yours, actually. But if it was important enough to you to relocate, you'd be welcomed pretty much anywhere in the world."

The idea was slow to sink in, but when it finally did, Lynn was speechless. People all around the world knew who she was, *and* they wanted her on their team? The surrealness of it was overwhelming, but it did take the edge off the crushing disappointment and panic that had been sawing at her insides.

"I—that's great news, but...yeah, I don't think we can relocate. This championship thing isn't a sure bet, and my mom would have to give up her job."

"Don't shortchange yourself, Lynn. You could make more in sponsorships than your mom's annual salary *easy* if you put the word out you were looking."

Lynn shook her head in disbelief.

"Maybe, but that would only last until after the international championship—if I even make it that far. And what if I lost?"

"Then the publicity would cement you as a top-tier professional gamer and you could go on to some other gig. Believe me, ad companies are *always* looking for top players to promote their brands. Virtual ads can only get a company so far, and large swaths of the population pay to block them. How better to get eyes on their products than to have uber-popular stream celebrities wearing them and talking about them? What I'm trying to tell you, kid, is you've got options. You just gotta think big."

But Lynn still shook her head.

"Mom loves her job. It's her calling. I couldn't ask her to give up nursing."

"Understood," Steve said. "Which brings us to your second option: reform your team."

"But it's not *my* team. Ronnie is the captain."

Steve snorted.

"Come on, Lynn. I know you don't like the idea of being in the spotlight but be honest with yourself. It's *Skadi's Wolves*, not *Ronnie's Wolves*. Heck, at least one of your teammates"—there was a pause—"Edgar

Johnston, right? He quit with you. And the other two, ah, Mr. Rios and Mr. Nguyen, both seemed opposed to the breakup. There's nothing stopping you from reforming the team and replacing Mr. Payne."

Lynn's mouth dropped open. She hadn't even considered the possibility.

"B-but it's Ronnie's team. He registered it and everything."

"I doubt he read the fine print. Did you?"

"Er . . . some of it. It's all kinda vague in my head though, I'd have to go back and check."

"I'll save you the trouble. You all paid your registration fee, you all registered as members of Skadi's Wolves under your own names. The designation of Team Captain is simply for organizational purposes and for in-game mechanics. It's not legal. Up until the week or so before the national championship, the team captain and team members can change. Generally pro teams who do this for a living have a pool of alternates they tap into if any team member gets sick or an emergency comes up. For the TD Hunter championship, you have to have your team set and your alternates designated by . . ." There was a silence while Steve looked for the information. "June 1st, it looks like. The championship will be held on June 15th, one year from game launch. Until then, everything is up for grabs except the team name—though you could even change that if you were willing to jump through the hoops."

"But, what's to stop the team from splitting up and creating multiple new teams?"

"Can't register new teams after qualifications," Steve said. "Teams are a democracy, not a dictatorship. Whatever the majority of the team decides, goes. We step in and arbitrate if there's a dispute that can't be worked out internally, but that's a last resort."

Lynn's brows scrunched together. She vaguely recalled reading those details before the qualifiers, but ever since her blowup with Ronnie she'd been so upset she hadn't remembered them.

"So...if I got Mack and Dan, or even just Mack, to side with me..."

"Yup."

Lynn considered that, then remembered who would likely have to become team captain in such a scenario. She groaned.

"I don't want to deal with all this drama. I just want to kill monsters!"

Steve chuckled darkly.

"I get it, kid, I really do. You have *no* idea. But every opportunity has its challenges. And I suspect you'll find help to overcome them in the most unexpected places."

"What does that mean?"

"It means you're not in this alone, so don't go all fatalistic on me. At least, not unless you want to go with your third option."

"What's that?"

"Quitting. But if you tried that, I'd be over there to kick your a—I mean posterior back into the game so fast you wouldn't know what hit you." The grin in Steve's voice was obvious, and Lynn grinned back.

"Golly, Steve, if I didn't know any better, I'd say you cared."

"Nah, kid, don't let it go to your head. We've just got some friendly bets going on in the Tac, and my money's all on you. I'm too poor to lose, so don't you go quitting," he teased.

"Yessir."

"That's what I like to hear. Oh, and a word of advice?"

"Yeah?"

"Don't make things personal, okay? I know what that jerk said, I saw the whole thing. But two wrongs don't make a right. If you really want this championship, you have to stay focused on what's important: winning. Not getting even, not humiliating the people who've wronged you. Just forget that kid. Forget what he said. You've got nothing to prove—you've already proven it. Focus on the mission. Got it?"

"Yeah . . . I'll try. Thanks, Steve."

"Anytime, kid. And good luck."

Lynn smiled.

"Thanks. RavenStriker, out."

A while later, Matilda and Lynn had just finished their "breakfast" together and Lynn was cleaning up while her mom got ready to go to work when there was a knock on the door.

"Mom, are you expecting anyone?"

"No, honey," Matilda called from her bedroom.

"Okay, I'll get it."

Newer apartment complexes had fancy smart doors that announced who had arrived based on their public LINC broadcast. But their complex had been built before Lynn was born and only the most basic and necessary conversions made. Things like the drone delivery docks, which were required by law for each habitable apartment once a bunch of accidents in the early days of drones had led to a blanket ban on airborne devices indoors.

They did, at least, have a peephole. But when Lynn

looked through it and saw Kayla Swain, of all people, she was so shocked she didn't move for a good ten seconds.

There was another knock, soft and unsure.

Lynn shook her head. Why was Kayla here? Had Elena sent her? Was this some sort of setup? Was she going to throw eggs in Lynn's face and record it to further humiliate her after the public breakup of Skadi's Wolves?

She considered not opening the door, but her curiosity got the better of her. With a twist of the knob, she opened it just a crack.

"What are you doing here?"

Kayla jumped.

"O-oh! Hi Lynn! Um...could I please come in?"

"Why?"

"Oh, well, to talk, if that's okay?" Kayla smiled nervously, and Lynn noticed her fingers pinching and twisting the hem of her shirt. The old familiarity of that tic hit Lynn right in the chest. She frowned, though she did open the door enough to look fully into her former friend's face. Kayla's frizzy hair was unbound and windswept, like she'd pulled it carelessly from the updo she normally tamed it with at school.

"Kayla, you haven't spoken a word to me in five years. Why should I even give you the time of day? For all I know, you're a spy for Elena and here to do something awful."

To Lynn's astonishment, tears filled Kayla's eyes and the girl bit her lip, obviously trying to keep her composure.

"I-I know, Lynn. You're right. You don't owe me anything and I—I can never make up for how horribly I've treated you all this time. B-but I *swear*, Elena didn't send me. I'm here because I w-want to talk, that's all. And . . . and I hope you can see it in your heart to hear me out. Please?" she finished in a whisper.

Lynn's mouth twisted to the side and she raised an eyebrow. Was Kayla faking it? It didn't look like it, but her old friend had changed a lot since they were twelve, and Lynn had no idea what she was capable of.

She did, however, know what Elena was capable of.

"I want to believe you, but I don't trust Elena further than I can throw her—less, actually, since I could throw her skinny butt at least across the room."

The comment prompted a wet chuckle from Kayla, but she immediately looked guilty for it and dropped her eyes. Lynn stared at her for a moment, then went on.

"Anyway, you could be recording this conversation and feeding it back to Elena. Maybe you're here to talk *and* Elena manipulated you into livestreaming the whole thing, or whatever. I'm pretty sure she'd do anything she thinks she can get away with."

"O-okay. This isn't that, I promise. Let me prove it to you." Kayla dug into her purse and pulled out a little round contact case. "Here, I'll take out my lenses."

"You wear lenses? I thought you had implants like all the other girls."

Kayla made a face.

"Yeah, so does Elena. But my stepdad won't let me get them. So, I wear really discreet lenses at school and glasses at home. The stupid lenses kill my eyes."

"Yeah, mine too, that's why I don't wear them," Lynn said without thinking. Kayla looked startled, then smiled tentatively.

As Lynn waited, the girl took out both AR lenses, put them away in their case, and replaced it in her purse.

"There, see? No recording."

Lynn squinted.

"You could still be recording with your LINC omnisensors."

"Oh, uh, I guess. Well, here." Kayla reached up and unclasped the silver chain that held her stylish LINC medallion around her neck. She slipped that into her purse too. "See?"

Lynn made a face again, brows drawn down. But her former friend looked so miserable and hopeful at the same time that she finally sighed and opened the door wide.

"Fine. But leave your purse on the kitchen counter. We'll go talk in my room."

"Thank you, thank you!"

To Lynn's relief, her mother was still in her bedroom, thus avoiding another awkward conversation.

"Mom! A, uh, friend from school came by to talk, we'll be in my room!"

"Okay, honey!"

Lynn knew her mother would find out about the argument with Ronnie eventually. She was hoping she could figure things out and break the news herself before the bombshell landed. It would be bad for Ronnie's health if Matilda saw firsthand what he'd said. Lynn wouldn't put it past her mom to call Ronnie's dad and chew him out *and* chew Ronnie out too. It would be so much easier to wait until she had a resolution and could calm her mother with assurances that no real harm had been done.

Kayla made straight for Lynn's bedroom and Lynn followed. It felt . . . wrong that Kayla knew exactly where to go, as if there weren't a gaping five-year chasm of hurt between them and their twelve-year-old selves. Lynn shut the door behind them, crossed her arms, and propped a hip on her desk. Kayla looked around the room, twisting her hem nervously again, before finally sitting gingerly on the bed.

"Okay. Talk," Lynn said.

For a long moment, Kayla just stared at the ground, hands folded tightly in her lap.

Lynn sighed.

"Come on, Kayla. Out with it. What's this about."

"I'm sorry!" the girl blurted, finally looking up. Wet trails were visible on her dark cheeks, and she sniffed.

"Okaaay..." Lynn didn't know where this was going.

"I'm s-sorry for everything. For ghosting you when we were kids. For ignoring you all this time. For staying quiet while Elena was horrible. I'm sorry for hurting you and not being the friend you d-deserved." Kayla hiccuped on her last word, then swallowed. Her eyes were so big and round and pleading. Just seeing her back in this bedroom dredged up old hurts that Lynn had long since accepted and moved past. It made her want to lash out, to make Kayla understand how much her actions had hurt.

But Lynn wasn't twelve anymore. She took a deep breath.

"Okay. I hear you. But I don't get why you're here now."

"I-I wanted to apologize, and say how sorry I am, and that it's all my fault and you didn't do anything wrong. I know there's no excuse for my choices, b-but I hoped you might be able to understand"—Kayla's voice descended to a miserable whisper—"well, understand how hard it is to do the right thing around Elena."

Lynn sighed bigger this time and reached up to rub her temples. She hated drama. It was exhausting and confusing. But she *did* know what Elena was like, and since Kayla had arrived, she'd done nothing but show how sincere she was. As much as Lynn wanted to say, "Thanks, bye now," and kick Kayla to the curb, that was what Elena would do, not her.

"Okay. I get it. Elena is a manipulative harpy, and if you get on her bad side, she makes you wish you'd never been born. I just don't get why you ghosted me in the first place. Did our friendship really mean so little that you threw it away just to chase after Elena and her clique?"

"No! And...and yes," Kayla said, looking down at her hands again.

Lynn finally pulled out her body-mold chair and slouched into it.

"When my mom remarried," Kayla said to her hands, "it moved us to an entirely new social circle. I didn't realize it then, but I think my stepdad and Elena's dad were in business together, and Elena's dad told her to make friends with me, maybe to get brownie points with my stepdad or something? Anyway, she tracked me down and *told* me I was going to be in her clique. I know I could have said no, but I felt desperate to fit in." Kayla looked up, apology and pleading in her eyes.

"My therapist is always on me about that. She says I don't have to please people all the time and my worth isn't dependent on others but that's...just how I am. And I was twelve, Lynn! I was an idiot. All I wanted was for my new stepdad to like me and to not screw things up for my mom. My biological dad was...terrible, and Mom seemed really happy with my stepdad. Anyway, Elena declared I was hers and that I couldn't hang out with 'losers' anymore. She—" Kayla stopped and squeezed her eyes shut, then opened them and looked out the window.

"She said lots of horrible things about you, and I just accepted them, because it was that or get rejected myself. And after a while...well, Elena and that crowd was all I had. She cut me off from everything else and made it really clear that anyone who betrayed her would regret it for the rest of their lives. I felt stuck."

Lynn shook her head, still angry but also incredulous at the stupidity of teenagers. Okay, so *she* was still a teenager, too, but she'd never been *that* stupid.

"I know...I was stupid," Kayla said miserably, as if echoing Lynn's thoughts. "But I'm not strong like you, Lynn."

The comment startled Lynn, and she looked at Kayla more closely. The girl's shoulders were curved inward, as if to protect herself from unseen blows. It reminded Lynn a lot of herself and all those years she'd been afraid to be seen, knowing the abuse that happened when you brought attention to yourself.

Lynn got up and went to sit beside Kayla on the bed. She hesitated, then gave her former friend an awkward pat on the shoulder.

"Kayla...I'm not strong. I spent *years* being bullied and my only defense was hiding. Being invisible. It's only been recently that I've figured out how to stop hiding. But I'm still a work in progress. And honestly, I couldn't have done it without my mom and some great people who've supported me and given me advice. I guess what I'm trying to say is, I'm nothing special. I didn't *choose* anything heroic, I just tried to survive, like you. And I think I understand how hard it was for you, but that doesn't change the choice you made. Or how much it hurt me."

"I know," Kayla sniffed. "I'm not even asking you to forgive me, I just saw how you stood up to your team captain on livestream and it...it inspired me. I can't take Elena anymore. I don't know what to do or how to get away from her, I've just been so miserable for so long. I want to be different. I...I want to be more like you."

Lynn had no idea what to say. She couldn't help being suspicious of Kayla's motives, no matter how sincere she sounded. It was almost as if she couldn't allow herself to hope Kayla was really sorry, because if it was all a trick, she couldn't take being betrayed *again*. And yet...

And yet Kayla obviously needed help. Lynn's mom was a nurse, and her dad had been a cop. Helping other people had been drilled into her since she was a little kid. She couldn't just reject Kayla outright. But she also needed time and space to think.

"Look, Kayla. Thank you for apologizing. It was the right thing to do, and I appreciate it. If you really want to be different, then the first thing you need to do is tell Elena—in public, to her face—to go stuff it. Don't make it about getting even or anything, just make it clear, in front of everybody, that you're not going to let her push you around anymore."

Kayla was already shaking her head, and her hands were back to twisting in her lap.

"I can't do that! She'll skin me alive! I'd never be able to show my face again at school, Elena would make sure of that."

"Bullshit."

"What?"

"I said bullshit. That is complete and utter crap, and you know it. Elena doesn't own you. She doesn't control your life. She is nothing to you if you choose. The only power she has over you is the power you give her. You have to make the choice to stand up on your own two feet and not care what she says or thinks. Yeah, it sucks, *a lot*. But I've survived it since sixth grade, and you can too."

"B-but my stepdad—"

"Would probably tell you the same thing, Kayla. Seriously? If he loves you at all, he would never want you to be in an abusive friendship. Does your stepdad love you?"

"Yes! Of course he does."

"Have you ever told him, or your mom, for that matter, what Elena is really like?"

"No," Kayla said in a small voice.

"Yeah, not the smartest move."

"I know!" she wailed. "I'm sorry. I'm such an idiot."

Silently, Lynn agreed, but didn't let the words escape her lips. Instead, she tried to think what her mom would say.

"Maybe you've made some stupid decisions, but you're not an idiot. You're doing the right thing now, and that's what counts. It's going to be hard, but you can't back down. Not ever again. Got it?"

"O-okay."

Lynn shook her head ruefully and stood. Look at her, doling out advice like Steve.

Crazy.

She was glad Kayla seemed to be coming round, but she still didn't trust her. It was too soon for that. "Thanks for coming over and all, but I've still got school to do tonight. So, uh..." She gestured at the door.

"Oh! Sure, of course. But, um, there's one more thing I wanted to tell you—or, I guess, ask you? It's really important, and I had to apologize first and everything. If you don't mind...?"

Lynn sighed.

"Sure, what is it?"

"Well, I, um, saw the stream of...you know." Kayla made a sympathetic face, and Lynn's stomach twisted.

"Yeah, so what?"

"I was at Elena's house, and obviously she was totally disgusting about it, but she and Connor got into an argument and Connor stormed out! I think he may be quitting the team, I don't know—"

"What!"

"I know, right? But anyway, that's not even what I wanted to tell you," Kayla rushed on, her words tumbling over themselves in their hurry to get out. "I've been managing Elena's stream for *years* because, well, I volunteered at first so she would like me and then, you know, free labor and everything. But I'm pretty good at it, and my dad owns a big PR company, and he's asked about you a few times, and now that I'm done with Elena, and things would be *so* much easier for you if you had your own stream so paparazzi would stop bothering you so much, and so I thought maybe I...maybe I and my dad...well, maybe we could help? Maybe represent you or something?"

Kayla finally finished and seemed to hold her breath, as if expecting a slap. Lynn, though, was still digesting the flood of words and could only stare blankly at the girl on her bed.

"I-I haven't mentioned it to my stepdad yet, of course, because I wasn't sure you'd be interested, so I don't know all the details of how it would work. But I know from working with Elena that there's probably lots of people trying to message you and get your attention and ask for interviews and exclusive shots and everything. It's probably really overwhelming, and since you've maybe ignored it all up to now, but there's still demand, that could be why you're being harassed by stream vultures—"

"By what?"

"Oh, that's what we call paparazzi in the biz." Kayla shrugged, and it was such a nonchalant, authoritative statement that Lynn laughed.

"So, your stepdad..."

"Yeah! He owns Global Image Consulting—or, at least, he owns part of it. It's got a board and everything, but he's on it, even though he still handles some clients personally, and—"

"Whoa, whoa. Back up, Kayla."

The girl snapped her mouth shut and looked hopeful.

"Let's just say *if* I wanted your help and *if* I worked with your Global Imaging or whatever, how much would it cost? I'm not Elena. We're normal people, I don't have a rich dad who can throw money at whatever I want."

"That's the best part!" Kayla chirped, bouncing on the bed in her excitement. "You're already such a big name that it wouldn't cost you anything! You'd agree for Global Image Consulting to be your representative— your agent, you might say—to work on your behalf negotiating sponsorships and stuff, and they'd get a small percentage of whatever deals they made. So, basically, it wouldn't cost you a thing!"

Lynn's expression turned skeptical. It sounded too good to be true.

"Look, let me talk to my mom about it and I'll... I'll be in touch, okay?"

"Honey! I'm leaving for work! Is your friend still here?"

Matilda's voice came from the living room, making Lynn jump. She'd forgotten she wasn't alone in the apartment. She shot a nervous look at Kayla, but there was no help for it.

"Come on," she said, jerking her head at the door. She went out into the living room and smiled at her mom. "She was just leaving."

"Oh! Kayla? I, um, haven't seen you in a long time. How have you been?" Matilda's eyes flicked to Lynn and her eyebrows rose, but Lynn just shrugged.

"I'm good, thank you Mrs. Raven. I'd better be going, though." Kayla turned hesitantly to Lynn and caught her eye. "Um... I'll see you at school?"

Lynn nodded.

"Yeah, I guess so. Good luck tomorrow. You can come have lunch with me if you want, after... you know." She gave Kayla a significant look, and the girl's dark complexion seemed to pale.

"Yeah. Thanks. I'll see you then." Kayla hurried off, grabbing her purse from the kitchen counter on her way out the door.

Matilda looked from the door to her daughter and back.

"What was that all about?"

Lynn let out a breath. She was even more exhausted than before, and she still had school work to do.

"I'll explain later, you're going to be late for work."

"Oops! You're right. Love you, sweetie. I'll see you

in the morning." She leaned over to press a kiss on Lynn's damp hair, and Lynn smiled.

"Love you too, Mom. Have a good shift."

Soon, the echo of the closing door and her mom's footsteps down the hall faded, and Lynn was finally alone in the apartment.

Good freaking grief.

She had a lot—*a lot*—to think about.

But first, she had math homework.

Chapter 5

"HEY, LYNN!"

The call down the school corridor made Lynn jump. People had been staring and pointing at her and talking in not-so-quiet voices all morning. She'd simply kept her head up, ignored it, and tried to get to class as quickly as possible. Thankfully, Edgar had stuck by her side like a particularly large and persistent bur, so no one had bothered her. But still.

She knew what they were all talking about.

By the time she'd spun to look for the voice, her brain had kicked in and told her the voice sounded suspiciously like Connor. Sure enough, the blond-headed poster boy for good-looking jocks everywhere was trotting down the locker-lined corridor to catch up to her and Edgar, who were on their way to the cafeteria.

Lynn looked suspiciously up and down the hall, but there was no sign of Elena, her posse, or the rest of Connor's ARS team.

"Thanks for waiting up," Connor said when he reached them, not at all out of breath.

"What do you want," Lynn said flatly and crossed her arms. Edgar came to stand beside her, arms hanging loosely at his sides. Connor gave him a once over, but it seemed to be an evaluating glance, not a hostile one.

"I need to ask you something, if that's all right."

Lynn raised an eyebrow.

"Do you plan to insult me before or after your question? And where are your thugs? If they're going to jump me, I'd rather just go ahead and get it over with."

Connor sighed and shook his head.

"It's nothing like that, and I'm sorry Elena has been so unprofessional. She's got most of the ARS team wrapped around her little finger. I keep telling the boys to ignore her, but..." He trailed off and shrugged.

"Regardless, you're the captain of a rival team. What is there to talk about?"

Connor chuckled and lifted a hand to rub the back of his neck.

"Well, considering I left the Cedar Rapids Champions yesterday, quite a bit."

Lynn's mouth dropped open, then she realized she was staring and snapped it shut.

"That's crazy. What is this, some kind of ploy to make us less suspicious of you so you can sabotage our team?"

"What team?" Connor asked, raising his own brow.

The comment sent heat to Lynn's cheeks and she scowled. Connor raised his hands defensively.

"I'm sorry, that came out wrong. I was at Elena's house yesterday when she started watching the livestream of your team's... argument. I couldn't help but see what happened. As an athlete and a captain myself, I can say I was completely embarrassed by Ronnie Payne's behavior. It was obviously petty and unprofessional, and nobody should be subjected to that kind of treatment, much less a stellar player like you."

Connor's words sent a shock of surprise through Lynn. Annoyingly, her cheeks heated even more.

"Thanks," she muttered, though she was still suspicious. First Kayla, now Connor. What the heck was going on? "But what's any of that got to do with you? And why are you saying you're not part of CRC anymore?"

"Like I said, I was at Elena's house yesterday. I guess her reaction to the livestream was the final straw for me." He sighed and shook his head. "I've been reconsidering my place on the team for a while, but more so after Elena's idiotic bullying stunt the other day. This whole competition has clearly gone to her head and impaired her judgment. I can't be a part of it anymore, so I told her yesterday I was out."

"Okay," Lynn said after a moment.

She was impressed, despite herself. She'd wondered if Connor would ever have the balls to do more than tell Elena to shut up. Apparently, he did. But that didn't mean she trusted him.

"No offense or anything, but we all know perfectly well you and Elena are in the same...crowd. She's been a cheerleader as long as you've been on the ARS team. You *know* what she's like. Why did you team up with her in the first place?"

Connor cleared his throat, showing the first signs of discomfort Lynn had seen.

"To tell you the truth, I shouldn't have. I was always skeptical about whether or not she'd be able to cut it. I was willing to try because...she promised she could get me a full-ride sports scholarship to my top college pick. Her dad has plenty of connections, and she said he could put in a good word on the selections board. Augmented sports is all I ever want to do, so I took a calculated risk." He shrugged. "Unfortunately, Elena proved to be even more erratic and untrustworthy than I'd realized."

"Erratic and untrustworthy? More like cheating and backstabbing. You were *there* when she and your teammates tried to beat me up. You just stood there!"

Connor raised his hands again, palms out.

"I was as shocked as you when it happened. The only reason I didn't intervene was that by the time my brain caught up with things you'd already maced everyone and run off." He grinned at her, and the smile made his perfect face even more annoyingly handsome. "Believe me, I chewed them all out after you'd left, much to Elena's displeasure, as you can imagine."

"Then what about at the qualifiers when you all broke Mack's equipment in the bathroom?"

"I had no idea she was even planning that. I only know it happened because Elena was complaining about it afterwards, mad that it hadn't gotten you disqualified. How could I have stopped something I didn't even know was going to happen?"

Lynn's mouth twisted and she chewed on her lip. Part of her wanted to believe Connor. He hadn't gone to the same middle school as her, and so hadn't been around during the worst of the bullying she'd endured. Would he have participated in it if he had been? Since starting high school, most of the bullying had come from Elena and her crowd, with only a few of the nastier members of the ARS team aware enough of her existence to pick on her. Connor had always seemed much too focused on classes and sports to bother wasting time on the unpopular kids. But neither had he spoken out against

Elena or his teammates' behavior, at least not in public. So, what did that make him? Was he trustworthy?

Somehow, Lynn felt like he was up to something. The question was, what?

"So, you told Elena to stuff it. Congratulations. Why do you want to talk to me?"

"Well," Connor said, and gestured toward Lynn and Edgar, "it seems to me like we're in the same boat. Just because I can't stay a part of CRC doesn't mean I'm throwing in the towel on TD Hunter. I gave up my place on the ARS team to do this. I took a calculated risk to achieve something greater, and there's no way I'm giving up. Neither are you; I would guess. That's what I wanted to talk to you about."

Lynn gave him a skeptical look.

"Go on."

"It's simple," Connor said. "We join forces. We're both top-tier players who are dedicated to winning. Think of what we could achieve together?"

"Us and what team?"

"Skadi's Wolves, of course."

"But that's Ronnie's team now," Lynn said, keeping her tone neutral, despite the way her throat tightened at the thought.

"Not if you all agree to remove him as captain. TD Hunter isn't like school sports. I read up on it last night to be sure, but from what I can find in the TD Hunter competition regulations, if teams have any sort of internal dispute, then they're supposed to work it out among themselves. So, all you have to do is get the rest of the team on your side and contact the competition registration people to let them know who the new team captain is."

Lynn pursed her lips. She'd been mulling over Steve's advice all night and all morning, and now here Connor was, suggesting the same thing. She looked at Edgar, who only shrugged.

"Okay, so what if we do? What's in it for you?"

"A chance to win, of course. That's why we're all competing, isn't it? And it's not like I can just create my own team from scratch any more than you can. Only teams that qualified can go on to the championship."

"And how do we know we can trust you?" Edgar rumbled.

Lynn nodded. It's exactly what she'd been thinking too.

"What you can trust is my track record," Connor said evenly. "I'm a winner, a team player, and a good captain. Our two teams were well matched before, with some weaker and some stronger players. But if we combine our teams by making me your captain, we'll be invincible. The question is, do you want to win, or not?"

"Whoa, hold on there, buster. Who said anything about making *you* captain," Lynn said, eyes narrowing.

Connor looked surprised. "I have the most experience and based on what I've observed of you so far, I assumed you didn't want to be captain. Was I wrong?"

The question hit Lynn right in the chest, and for a moment all she could do was stare at Connor.

Of course she didn't want to be captain. She *hated* being in the limelight.

And yet...what a relief it would be if people finally took her as seriously in the real as they took Larry Coughlin in virtual. In WarMonger, her authority was based on her very real track record and leaderboard ranking.

But was that worth dealing with all the attention and responsibility?

"I want to win this competition," she finally said, sure of that, at least. "To do that, we need a *good* captain. Are you going to be a good captain?"

Connor smiled, showing his perfect white teeth, and Lynn's stomach swooped alarmingly.

"I'll be a fantastic captain. Guaranteed. What do you say?"

While Lynn was trying to restart her brain, Edgar beat her to a reply, drawing Connor's attention to his stoic face.

"I'd say we talk it over with the team and decide together."

The brilliance in Connor's smile dimmed slightly, but he still nodded.

"Perfectly reasonable. I'd do it quickly, though. Every day of missed training takes us further from the championship."

"We'll be in touch," Edgar said noncommittally.

Lynn nodded in agreement.

"Okay, well, thanks for hearing me out. I guess I'll talk to you again soon." Connor put a finger to his forehead and gave a mock salute, then strode off down the hall, looking just as confident and relaxed as always.

"I don't like him," Edgar said quietly once Connor was out of earshot.

"Mm," Lynn said. She shouldn't like the guy either, but he *was* probably the best shot Skadi's Wolves had at winning, now that Ronnie had officially lodged his head so far up his back end that it would never be found again. "Whether we like him or not, he's a

hella more competent than . . . well our other options.
I think we need to take his offer seriously."

Edgar didn't reply, just gave a jerk of his head
and started down the hall toward the cafeteria. Lynn
followed, but her mind wasn't on lunch, it was rolling
over Connor's words in her head.

Could they trust him? Had he really broken with
Elena? Or was this an elaborate plot?

After they'd collected their lunch, Edgar led the
way to a table, and it wasn't until he'd pulled back a
chair with a scrape and plopped his big frame down
into it that Lynn realized where she was. Dan, Mack,
and Ronnie stared back at her from around the table,
each one frozen in various states of putting food into
their mouth.

Ronnie was the first to recover.

"What do you think you're doing?" he hissed at
Lynn, though his eyes flicked briefly to Edgar too.
"You're off the team. Go find somewhere else to sit."

"She's not off the team," Edgar said evenly, then took
a large bite of the apple in his hand. The slow, crackling
crunch of the crisp apple seemed overloud in the little
pool of tense silence at their table, even though the
chatter of hundreds of students swirled around them.

Ronnie's brow darkened and he sat up straighter.
"Yes she is."

"Not until we all agree on it, she isn't," Edgar said
around his mouthful of apple. "Team's a democracy,
not a dictatorship. Game rules say so."

While Ronnie spluttered, Lynn took a deep breath
and forced herself to speak, even though it was the
last thing she wanted to do.

"I'm on the side of Skadi's Wolves. I'm here to win

this championship, and anyone who isn't on board with that needs to get out of the way so we can do what we formed this team to do."

"*I* formed this team," Ronnie spluttered. "*I'll* make sure we win, but not with subpar players who won't listen to orders!"

"*We* formed this team, and *we'll* decide who plays on it based on what's best for the team," Lynn said, slamming down her lunch tray with more force than she'd intended. Her food bounced, some of it scattering across the table, and she glared at it before yanking her chair back and sitting. While she retrieved her lunch, Edgar calmly addressed Ronnie.

"You're my man, Ronnie. We've been tight for years. But you've got some serious issues, and I think you know it, deep down. I blame your old man, but it don't matter in the end. You've been making dumb calls, and we all know it. We were just too loyal or whatever to say anything. Lynn's got bigger balls than all of us put together, and she calls it like it is. Either you get that through your thick head and start treating her like one of us, or *you're* the one who's not a team player and needs to go. *Malamalama*?"

Despite the seriousness of the situation, Lynn had to resist a smile. When it came down to it, Edgar sure did have a way with words. But when she looked up from her tray and saw Ronnie's pale face and clenched, trembling hands, it was clear the words had been wasted breath.

"You've got no idea what you're talking about. You've always been soft on her, and you're not even that good of a gamer yourself! If you want a *girl* to lead you around by the nose, be my guest. We'll find real gamers to replace you, won't we Dan?"

Dan looked back and forth from Ronnie to Edgar to Lynn, his face drawn in distress.

"Look, Ronnie, we've been friends since, like, elementary school. But you've been acting pretty weird lately and—"

"Not you too!"

A few heads turned their way, and Ronnie lowered his voice.

"I can't believe you'd take her side. What are you, a pussy?"

"Come on, dude, don't be like that. This is *Lynn*, she's cool—"

"She's a *girl*—"

"You know, I think I finally get it."

Lynn's comment was quiet, but its hardness cut through the conversation like a diamond blade. Ronnie blanched and looked at her, then dropped his eyes. She didn't blame him. Though she couldn't see herself, she could tell by the coldness in her chest that murder was in her eyes.

"I finally understand what you mean when you say 'girls got no game.' It has nothing to do with me, or even girls. You're really just saying 'I'm a sniveling coward with an ego so fragile you could break it with a feather.'"

"Lynn, don't—" Edgar muttered as Ronnie flinched, but Lynn was past listening.

"You're so weak and cowardly, the only way you can cope is by tearing everybody else down. You're probably just like your dad, aren't you? Is that what he does, too? Tear you down to make you feel small and worthless so he can feel better about himself?"

"Lynn!"

She felt Edgar's big, calloused hand grip her wrist

tightly in a warning gesture, but she didn't look at him. She just kept staring at Ronnie, daring him to meet her eyes.

But he wouldn't.

"I don't have to stay here and listen to this crap," he spat, then shoved his chair violently back and grabbed his tray. "You're all a bunch of filthy traitors!" And with that, he stormed off. A few curious sets of eyes at nearby tables watched him go, but for the most part the noisy room was oblivious to the drama.

Edgar gave a heavy sigh and let go of Lynn's wrist, going back to his food.

"Well ... that was ... awkward," Mack said, poking at his own tray gloomily.

Dan was still staring after where Ronnie had disappeared, looking torn. If Lynn had been feeling more generous, she would have been sorry for Dan. He and Ronnie were best friends.

But she was all out of craps to give.

Dan finally turned back to their table, expression troubled as he chewed on his lip. When he glanced up at Lynn, she met his furrowed gaze unflinchingly.

"That was ... did you really need to be so harsh?" he asked quietly.

"It was the truth."

Dan's shoulders drooped.

"Yeah ... maybe ... that's what worries me."

"Are you going to join him?"

"What? No, of course not. But ... he's still my friend."

The concerned look in Dan's eyes sucked all the fight out of her and she let out a weary breath. Part of her regretted her words, or at least regretted how they'd hurt Ronnie. But they were still true.

"I know, and you shouldn't stop being friends. He probably needs you now more than ever. But . . . I don't think he should be on the team anymore." She glanced at Mack, who was still staring morosely at his tray. "If we all agree on that, we can contact TD Hunter after school and make it official."

"Why the rush?" Dan asked. "He might come around, you never know. Why don't you let me talk to him?"

"Dan, I'm sorry, but we've already done this before. Many times before. I thought things had gotten better when we passed the qualifiers, but then we got all this stupid media attention and it went straight to Ronnie's head. This is the biggest competition of our lives and all of us have futures at stake here. I'm sorry about Ronnie, but every day we let this distract us from training and leveling, our chances of winning drop. We're going to be killing ourselves as it is to keep up our grades *and* hunt enough to reach level 40 by next June."

"But we still have to find a replacement. That could take a while, right? So why don't you focus on recruiting a replacement and I'll try and talk Ronnie around, just in case?"

Lynn exchanged a glance with Edgar, who shrugged.

"Well, the thing is, we already have a possible replacement."

"What?" Mack said, finally looking up.

"Yeah, uh, Connor got fed up with Elena and quit the CRC. He wants to join Skadi's Wolves."

The exclamations from Mack and Dan turned more heads, and they quickly quieted and leaned in.

"What the heck, Lynn?" Mack whispered furiously. "Those goons assaulted me in the bathroom. We can't trust them!"

"The other CRC members did that, not Connor. And he claims he didn't know about it until after the fact."

At Mack's unconvinced glare, she went on.

"Look, I'm not saying I trust him. I'm still half convinced this is an elaborate ploy by Elena. But at the same time, he's CRC's *best* player, and he's not like Elena at all. He's a pro and focused on actually *winning*, not getting attention. I can't see him playing along with one of Elena's petty tricks when he knows it will only hurt his own team's chances just as much as ours. I'm convinced enough that I think we should hunt with him a few times and give it a try, to see what we think of him. We can always change our minds later and kick him off the team, right?"

Mack didn't look happy, but at least he seemed to be giving it some thought. Dan had slid on his AR glasses and was obviously checking something.

"His ranking and kill stats are pretty impressive. Not in your league, of course," he said to Lynn, glancing at her with a grin. "But they're above mine and Ronnie's. He's no slouch, that's for sure. Still..."

"I just want to give him a try," Lynn insisted, "see how he fits in with the team. We already know making him team captain doesn't give him power over us, we can still—"

"Whoa, whoa, hold up, team captain?" Dan protested. "You never said anything about team captain. I thought you'd take over that role?"

A little glow warmed Lynn's chest and threatened to spread to her cheeks, but she did her best to play it cool. "Connor has years of experience leading a team in augmented reality sports, which are very close in function to TD Hunter, even if the strategy is different. His ARS team has been top in the state the past two years, so we shouldn't doubt Connor's leadership skills."

"We can doubt his judgment, though," Mack muttered, still not looking happy with the arrangement.

"Yeah...I know," Lynn admitted. "But if we give him a try now, we can keep training and moving forward while we look for alternatives. We'll need a few alternates anyway, come June, in case one of us gets injured, so our team won't be disqualified at the last minute. So...what do you say?"

Dan shrugged.

"I'm willing to give it a try. He seemed professional enough when we teamed up in the qualifiers."

Lynn turned to Mack, who groaned.

"Don't give me that look! I can't say no when you look at me like that."

"What??"

"Like you actually trust my judgment and are expecting me to make a good decision. It makes me scared to let you down."

Lynn felt like a deer in the headlights.

"R-really?"

"Yeah! You're always so encouraging and helpful, and you're our best player. I don't want Connor on our team, but if you think it's a good idea, well..." He gave a helpless shrug. "I can't say no."

"Um, okay, thanks," Lynn said, escaping Mack's soulful gaze to look at Edgar. The corners of his mouth twitched downward and his brow furrowed.

"I don't trust him."

"I know. But will you give him a chance? For the team's sake?"

Edgar held her gaze long enough that she had to resist the urge to fidget. Finally, he snorted.

"Sure, I guess. If you think we should. You're the *Toa Tama'ita'i*, after all," he said with a half grin.

"Errr, right." Lynn shot a nervous glance at the other two, who were looking back and forth between her and Edgar. "So, I'll ping him to meet us after school. That cool?"

They all nodded, then got back to their various lunches. Lynn picked unenthusiastically at hers as she looked to the far end of the room, trying to spot Elena's crowd. They usually sat at the front of the cafeteria, nearest the lunch dispenser machines and the big windows that looked out on the sports fields. Sure enough, there they were, and she could just see the top of Elena's head, her brilliant blond hair caught up in a high ponytail. Lynn searched, but didn't see the dark, frizzy hair of Kayla in the group, and that made her chew on her lip in worry. Was Kayla all right? Had she already confronted Elena? Had Elena done something to her?

Though she couldn't find Kayla in the sea of heads around her, she did spot Connor sitting with his former ARS team. They were usually to be found in Elena's general vicinity, but today they sat on the other side of the room. Suddenly, Connor looked her way, spotted her staring, and gave a little nod, a half smile on his face. Lynn ducked her head hurriedly and tried to make herself enjoy her lunch. It seemed bland and lumpy in her mouth.

She was just contemplating pushing her tray over to Mack, who had his usual disheartening salad, when all the lights in the cafeteria went out.

A few people screamed in surprise, and one particularly loud male voice rang out, "Somebody grabbed my butt!" The large windows on one side of the cafeteria let in plenty of light, though, so there was more of a general shuffle and mutter of confusion than any kind of mass panic. There was a brief lull in the noise, as if everyone was waiting with bated breath for the power to kick back on. But as the moments passed and it became obvious this was more than a temporary glitch, the noise level grew again and students started yelling out to each other, trading theories and wondering what to do. The handful of adults at the tables in the teacher's corner were huddled together and looked as bewildered as everyone else.

For a second, Lynn wondered why someone hadn't already gotten on the intercom system to announce the issue and tell everybody to calm down. But then she remembered—duh—the power was out. She was just putting on her AR glasses to check the school app's announcement boards when the cafeteria doors burst open and in came the vice principal, huffing and puffing like she'd run all the way from her office.

"Calm down, everyone. Calm down!" she called out. Her voice didn't carry well, but one of the teachers shouted to get everyone's attention and the room quieted. "Thank you, Mr. Rosenburg. Now, everybody please remain seated and calm. There has been an issue with the school's power grid, but our maintenance team is looking into it now and I'm sure it will be resolved shortly. You may go ahead and finish your meals, but please remain in the cafeteria until we have the power back on. Thank you."

The vice principal then bustled over to the teacher's

table and all the grownups started a whispered conference.

Lynn shot a look around her table. Mack seemed worried, but Dan was all curiosity and excitement. Edgar looked as calm as usual. He shrugged at her and went back to his fries.

"What do you think happened?" Dan asked, leaning in and speaking in a low voice as similar hushed conversations started up again all around the cafeteria.

"Just a glitch?" Edgar said. "Like the man said?"

"Never happened before, though," Lynn countered, looking around the room with furrowed brow.

"I saw in the news that city power systems have been glitching all over the country," Dan said. "My mom says it's all GForce Utilities' fault. She says they've been skimping on infrastructure for decades and pocketing the profits, and now it's coming back to bite them in the butt."

"I don't know," Mack said. "Riko mentioned they'd been having power-grid issues in Japan too. It's been on their news. Japan doesn't use the same power company as the US, does it?"

Dan rolled his eyes.

"Of course not, dummy. And I don't know why you'd believe anything that bot tells you."

"Riko isn't a bot!"

"Yes, she is, Mack. The odds of *any* of us having a girlfriend, much less a super-hot one from Japan, are about as good as getting a perfect kill score in WarMonger."

Lynn hid a grin. She'd gotten a perfect kill score plenty of times as Larry Coughlin. So where was her hot Japanese boyfriend? She shook her head at the silliness of that thought.

"I'm telling you, she's not a bot. She's really into AR games and spends a lot of time chatting in virtual with American and British players to practice her English. After we aced the qualifiers, she saw us on the Hunter Strike Team list and was intrigued by our team name because Skadi is a character in one of their really popular classic video game series that her dad always liked."

"Yeah, yeah," Dan chuckled. "A likely story. The problem is, if she *was* real, she would have definitely contacted *me*, not you. I'm way more handsome."

Mack reddened, but jutted his chin stubbornly.

"Yeah right. Compared to a twelve-year-old kid, maybe. You barely even reach my chin. She said she was attracted to my manly facial hair," he finished loftily, giving his scraggly goatee a stroke.

Lynn barely managed to hold in a fit of giggles at the sight. She looked at Edgar to save herself and saw his eyes twinkling merrily.

"Definitely a bot," they said in unison, and then they both burst out laughing.

While Mack and Dan continued to argue, Lynn got control of herself and checked the school app like she'd meant to do earlier. It had a general announcement for all students to remain where they were while the school performed emergency maintenance, but other than that there was no more information.

Huh.

It was a good thing nobody at their school depended on power to keep them alive, just continue their education. The similarity between what was happening now and the fiasco at her mom's hospital over the summer, not to mention that power outage at the Lindale Mall, was suspicious.

Remembering what she'd found outside of Lindale Mall around its power generators, she brought up the TD Hunter app.

"Hey Hugo, how's it hangin'?"

"As I have neither a physical manifestation, nor any sort of quantifiable health prognosis, I am not certain how you wish me to answer that."

"You could just say 'I'm great, you?'"

"Very well. I am doing admirably, and yourself?"

Lynn snorted.

"Good try. But never mind that. I want to go into combat mode and see what kind of TDM activity is around this school."

"Certainly, Miss Lynn. But first I would advise you to remove your batons from your backpack."

"Er, why?"

"Because in their current weapon configuration they will morph into items longer than your backpack and might become damaged as a result."

"Oh, yeah." Duh. She should have thought of that.

Moving as surreptitiously as possible, she reached down with a hand to unzip her backpack and dipped into it to pull out her batons, which she laid flat in her lap under the table.

"There should be enough room under the table, right?" she subvocalized.

"As best as I can determine from your LINC's current position, yes."

"Okay, let's fire this thing up, then."

Lynn's combat screen came to life and the sight of her overhead map made her blood run cold.

"Oh *shit.*"

"What?" Edgar whispered, leaning over.

"Check your TD Hunter map," she breathed. "But take your batons out of your bag first."

A few moments later, Edgar echoed her curse.

"Why the heck is the school surrounded by monsters?" he whispered to her. "I mean, we're not exactly in the middle of downtown or anything, but still. We've never hunted around the school before because the pickings were too slim to be worth it. What's changed?"

"The school isn't exactly surrounded," Lynn pointed out, her pattern-wired brain kicking in as the strange flash of panic she'd felt faded. "Remember the layout of our campus. Most of the red dots are grouped on the north side, around the generators and sports fields, and leading up into that patch of woods behind the school. It's a lot less thick on the other three sides around the roads and airbus platform. I'll bet those dots are mostly Delta Class. Also, remember we don't normally go into combat mode around the school. We've leveled a few times since we last checked, so we can see more TDMs now. Maybe that's why..."

She fell into thoughtful silence, and they looked at each other.

"I dunno," Edgar muttered. "That's a *freaking lot* of monsters."

"Well, we can't do anything about it now. Once school's over, though...I think we should get Connor to join us and try hunting out behind the school today. I'm curious to see what's out there, maybe we'll discover an unknown or something."

Edgar nodded, and they both exited combat mode, stowing their batons back in their bags. By the time they returned their attention to their lunch trays, Dan and Mack were still bickering good-naturedly, none the wiser.

Lynn had been all prepared for an agonizing afternoon of trying to concentrate on class while her mind was distracted by what she'd seen on her TD Hunter map. Fortunately for her sanity, "class" never happened.

They waited in the cafeteria for what felt like forever. Thirty minutes after class was supposed to start, the vice principal came back and informed everyone that the maintenance workers were still trying to fix the error, and for everyone to sit tight. What had been a relaxing break from class turned into a boring wait. Some people submerged themselves in virtual, ignoring school policy of mesh-web use during class hours in favor of keeping themselves entertained. Others got rowdy, and the teachers that had stayed in the cafeteria had their hands full breaking up arguments and telling kids to get off the tables. One food fight even broke out. But with most of the food already eaten, there wasn't enough ammunition for it to last long—especially not after Elena started screeching in a panicked rage about food getting on her clothes.

By the time the first afternoon period had passed and the second was starting, the school administration realized a major incident was going to happen if they tried to keep so many teenagers cooped up. The principal appeared this time, announcing that they were sending everybody home for the day.

"Saaa-weeet," Dan said, getting up with a bounce in his step. "No English period today! I totally forgot about that essay we were supposed to hand in. I've been sweating bullets about it all morning."

Lynn snorted, knowing perfectly well Dan had been doing no such thing. He probably wouldn't have batted an eyelid at getting a zero for his missed essay. Having parents unhealthily obsessed with grades seemed to have given Dan a perpetually sunny attitude when it came to school performance. If he did well, his parents spent less time trying to restrict his gaming hours. If he did poorly, he got to enjoy the futility with which they tried to restrict his gaming hours.

It was a win-win, in his book.

Of course, with TD Hunter being augmented reality instead of in virtual, he'd been forced to put more effort into his grades to keep his parents from locking him in the house or taking away his batons.

As everyone flowed toward the doors at the front of the building, Lynn hurriedly looked up Connor in the school roster and sent him a ping. She'd been so busy contemplating the strange influx of TDMs around the school she'd forgotten to do it earlier. With no class to distract her, she'd had Hugo take her back into combat mode so she could study their positioning. She'd run a dozen theories past Hugo, hoping he'd give away some tidbit of information about the game algorithm that she didn't already know. Predictably, he'd been as opaque and evasive as ever. Lynn understood it would spoil the game if he just told her whatever she wanted to know, but it was still annoying.

After that, she'd turned to the tactical forums, on as well as off TD Hunter, looking for recent mentions of increased TDM spawning, especially after Level 20. She found quite a few posts, but everyone seemed to think the phenomenon was a natural result of being higher level.

That *did* make sense. But something about it still bugged her.

She and the guys weren't even halfway to the front doors when Connor messaged back that he'd meet them behind the school by the ARS training building. Lynn in turn pinged the rest of the team, relaying the plan. Soon after, they emerged into the mid-October sunshine. Lynn tensed automatically and glanced at the sky, but they were still close enough to the school building that the airspace above it was clear. Over by the airbus platform, though...

Lynn nudged Edgar and jerked a thumb toward the bushes beside the front of the school. Edgar, in turn, gave Mack and Dan's sleeves a tug and they all slipped out of the stream of students headed for the airbuses. None of the other students gave them a second glance, and Lynn led the way around the school, trying to keep under trees or behind bushes as much as possible. For all she knew, word had already gotten out about the school's early closing, and reporter drones might be circling the area soon.

Nervous tension crackled through Lynn's limbs as she wondered about Connor. Would he be waiting with Elena and the ARS team to ambush them?

Her fears were unjustified—this time, at least. They found Connor alone, leaning casually against the ARS training building. When he spotted them approaching, he pushed off the brick wall with a smile.

"Great. Now that we're all here, we can get started."

Lynn raised her eyebrows and glanced at her team-mates. Their expressions ranged from suspicious to disgruntled, but nobody said anything, so she shrugged and looked back at Connor. She was willing to wait and see what he did as their new "captain."

"I assume everyone has their hunting gear with them?" Connor asked, looking around.

Everyone nodded. They usually changed after school let out.

"Okay. Since the power is out and they've shut down the main building, we can't use the bathrooms there. I have the access code to this building, though, from when I was ARS captain. It'll be dark in there, but there are windows to let in light, so I think we'll manage. Sound good?"

More nodding.

"Right, let's get going."

Connor waved his LINC—a ring like Lynn's—across the access panel, and the door's lock clicked. Fortunately, the locks had their own internal power, one of the few things besides the emergency exit signs that did. Once the door closed behind them, it took their eyes a moment to adjust to the gloom. Connor moved forward confidently across the main training floor, obviously familiar with his surroundings. He led the guys to the men's changing room and pointed Lynn toward the women's. They changed and were back out in the fresh air with a minimum of stumbling about.

"Listen up everybody," Connor said once they'd gathered around him in the shade of the building. "For me to do my job as team captain, I need to get a handle on your usual team tactics, weapon capabilities, augments, et cetera. I know you all have quite a bit of experience in virtual gaming, and I'm happy to hear any suggestions you have for strategies in TD

Hunter. I've studied everything the game's tactical section has to offer, and of course I have plenty of experience leading an ARS team. But not all ARS tactics translate well to this game, so I'm depending on you all to get me up to speed."

Lynn's eyebrows climbed higher and higher as Connor spoke. Despite herself, she was impressed. Not only had he complimented them, but he'd actually asked for their *advice*. The last time Ronnie had done that was, well . . . never.

Not everybody was so impressed, though.

"You're right, we *do* know more about gaming than you do," Dan said, crossing his arms and glaring at Connor. "So how do we know you're not just here to spy on us and learn all our secrets? You could easily hang around for a few weeks, then run back to CRC and steal all our best moves for your own team."

Connor nodded at the accusation, seeming unfazed.

"I'd have the same worry if I was in your position. On one level, it just comes down to trust. I've expressed my honest intentions to you all, and there's nothing more I can do to prove them. At the same time, think of it this way: if all I thought CRC lacked was some tactical finesse, then anything I might learn from you all wouldn't make up for the training time lost while I was here 'learning your secrets.' Besides, TD Hunter's tactical forum is one of the most robust I've ever seen. I doubt there's much you all are doing that I couldn't glean from there with enough time and patience."

That sounded reasonable to Lynn, though Dan snorted and maintained his glower as Connor continued.

"Look, how about I start by explaining CRC's usual formations and how we would go about tackling various

TDM placement scenarios. Then it will be a fair trade of information and we can decide which tactics to use for Skadi's Wolves based on what sounds best overall."

They agreed—albeit begrudgingly—and Connor started in on a summary of how CRC worked. As she listened, Lynn began to feel sorry for the former ARS captain. He'd had to bend his team completely out of shape to accommodate Elena's ridiculous antics. Dealing with Ronnie had been a cinch by comparison. At least *he* was a skilled player and willing to take some advice, as long as it was given privately.

It turned out the CRC's tactics and formations were not that different from what Skadi's Wolves had developed. When Connor finished his overview and none of the guys seemed overly eager to share in kind, Lynn rolled her eyes and started explaining how Skadi's Wolves fought. Connor paid close attention, asked clarification questions, and seemed genuinely delighted with what he learned. At one point he smiled and said: "Wow. It's going to be so refreshing to lead an actual team instead of Elena's popularity circus."

When she was done, Connor clapped his hands together and looked around.

"Great. We have plenty of work to do to become a cohesive unit, so let's get started. First things first: I created a hunting group for everybody to join so we have a shared channel to use until you get me added as team captain."

They fired up their apps and accepted the group invite Connor had sent, though Lynn felt a flare of annoyance at the name of it.

Connor's Team.

She wasn't sure why it rankled her. He *was* going

to be team captain. Maybe she was simply still on edge from all the drama of the past few days.

Once she'd joined, she saw Connor's blue icon pop up on her overhead—her other teammates were already there as part of Skadi's Wolves.

"It's standard in AR sports to call everyone by their last name, so that's what we'll be doing on this team."

"Why?" Dan said. "We just use first names."

"Because it's not only standard, it's more professional, and prevents confusion over similar first names."

"But we don't have any similar first names."

"Not now, perhaps, but what if one of you gets sick or hurt and we have to play with an alternate? It's better to use last names, so that's what we'll do."

Dan frowned but didn't protest further.

"Now, as far as role assignments, Johnston, Raven, and Nguyen, you'll stay the same. Rios, I'm moving you to assault with Raven and I'll take over tactical."

"Uhhh, you sure?" Mack asked, looking nervous. "I'm not all that great at melee, I've been specializing in ranged."

"You'll adapt fine, I'm sure. The team captain should always be in the tactical role so they can keep a clear head and maintain oversight on the playing field. I'm certain one of the reasons Payne was such a terrible captain was because he insisted on charging into the thick of things and was always too distracted to lead properly."

Mack glanced at Lynn, but all she could do was shrug. She didn't like Mack's reassignment any more than he did, since it really wasn't the role he was best suited for. But Connor did have a point about Ronnie.

Of course, *she'd* led teams in WarMonger just fine

while assaulting the enemy. But then, she'd rarely been up against more than a couple dozen combatants at a time. Not hundreds, like the swarming monsters of TD Hunter. Maybe it *would* be better to have the captain in a supporting role, though with only five Hunters against hundreds of TDMs, Connor would be just as busy as the rest of them no matter his position.

Hopefully, with time and practice, Mack could adjust to his new role. There was still the problem of what weapons Mack would use, though. The two-handed Plasma Sword Ronnie preferred took significant practice to wield competently, and Plasma Blades weren't strong enough to go up against Level 24 monsters. Fortunately, Connor had a solution.

"Use these for now, Mack," Connor said, his eyes flicking back and forth as he manipulated his TD Hunter app with just his gaze. "You should get one of them automatically as soon as you level to 25, and I'm sure someone will find another as loot soon after, so you can give these back to me then."

Eyes alight, Mack used gestures to equip whatever Connor had given him and projected it for them all to see.

"Cool!" Lynn exclaimed. "An ArcLight Pistol and a Splinter Blade? Those don't show up till Level 25, and you're the same level as us. So where'd you get them? The TD Hunter marketplace?"

"Yes, and they weren't cheap."

Lynn nodded in understanding. It was exactly how she'd intended to monetize TD Hunter before she agreed to fight in the championships: hunt as much as possible and zoom through the levels, then sell your loot to impatient players willing to shell out large amounts of money for any advantage to climb the leaderboards. The weapons in TD Hunter had a minimum use level five levels below the level at which they dropped as loot. That meant that even though they wouldn't achieve a free ArcLight Pistol or Splinter Blade themselves until they reached Level 25, if they got ahold of the weapons some other way, they could use them as early as Level 20.

"Let me guess," Lynn said. "Elena uses her daddy's money to buy all the weapons and augments available as early as possible?"

Connor shrugged.

"What she does with her money is no business of mine, but I certainly wasn't going to turn down the advantage."

"It's perfectly legal," Dan pointed out.

"I know," sighed Lynn. Every cent she owned she'd earned through blood, sweat, and tears, and it was painful to part with it, even for a good cause. She wondered what it would be like to have as much money as you wanted without ever lifting a finger to get it.

Probably horrible.

She was proud of her hard work, and it didn't take a genius to look at history and society and recognize the dangers of being spoiled by wealth and power you never had to strive for.

"We could all have that kind of money if we landed the right sponsorships," Mack piped up, eyes still wide and a grin on his face as he examined his new weapons.

Connor chuckled.

"It doesn't quite work like that, Rios. But yes, sponsorships can help. I'm surprised you all aren't covered in company logos already." Though his words were addressed to the group, it was Lynn he looked at, giving her an inquisitive arch of his brow. She ignored the implied question.

If only he knew.

The thought made her remember Kayla's offer. She wondered if she really would get some peace and quiet if she had a PR person. That would be amazing. But could she trust Kayla? And where had Kayla gotten to? Was she all right?

On a whim, Lynn pulled up the school directory again and sent a ping to Kayla while the others talked about sponsorships.

Didn't see you at lunch. You okay?

"Ronnie had some small-time offers he took up," Dan was saying, "but that's cuz he was team captain. I'm sure we'll get plenty of offers ourselves the more we play."

"That's certainly possible," Connor said diplomatically. "Now, we only have so much daylight, so let's get to work. I took a peek at the area map when I was inside, but does anybody else have thoughts on a good place to start our sweep around the school?"

Lynn didn't immediately reply, not wanting to be the first to say something. But when the other guys just looked at each other and shrugged, she finally spoke.

"I think we should start on the east side near the generators. There's a thick group in that area, but I've found TDMs near high-traffic buildings are usually lower-class monsters. So it should give us a chance to get used to working together without much risk."

She didn't voice her real reason for starting there: she wanted to see if the school's power grid came back on once they'd cleared the electrovore-type monsters away from the generators, as had happened at Lindale

Mall. It was a stupid, crazy theory—this was just a game, after all, and couldn't affect reality—but she was still curious. Her patternist brain had to know if there was a correlation, or if the mall had just been a coincidence.

"Sounds like a solid plan. Once we clear that area we can make our way northwest around the athletic buildings and up toward the woods behind the school where the largest clusters of monsters are," Connor finished, looking around at everybody. "Right, let's get into position!"

They followed Connor toward the east corner of the school, tightening straps and adjusting equipment as they went. They all used their compact, high-performance backpacks they'd won at the qualifiers as their school bags now, so they had everything they needed close at hand. Lynn gripped her two batons in hands damp with sweat despite the cool October air.

She wanted this to work out so badly.

If Connor was sincere and their team learned how to work well together, maybe the championships could become the wonderful dream come true she'd hoped for instead of the hell it had been the past six weeks. Well, the stupid media attention would still be there. But at least she wouldn't be isolated and hung out to dry by her own team.

The mini substation behind the school that fed and regulated its section of the power grid was tucked up next to the brick school building and surrounded by a wooden privacy fence. Outside the fence there was a strip of grass, then a sidewalk, then another strip of grass with some ornamental trees. Beyond that were the sports fields and activity buildings, built on what had long ago been the parking lot for school games and activities. Teachers and parents used the airbus or rideshare carpools these days, though. The few students—like Elena—whose wealthy parents had bought them little electric cars kept them parked in the small remaining lot out front.

Connor had them gather on the sidewalk. There was still one wing of the school jutting out from the east side that sat between them and the street to the south, so unless any drones got nosey and decided to fly illegally over school airspace, they were assured some measure of privacy. If the school was always so empty in the afternoons and evenings, Skadi's Wolves would have spent much more time hunting around it. The grounds were usually populated with students participating in various sports, clubs, and other activities, but the power grid issue had canceled all activities on campus that day.

Hopefully none of the maintenance guys working inside came out to fiddle with the substation while Skadi's Wolves were hunting, or they'd get run off.

"Johnston," Connor said, pointing to Edgar, the tallest of their group, "I want you closest to the school wall. You're our anchor. Advance as slowly as you need to toward the corner, clearing everything in your path. Raven and Rios, you're next. You'll support Johnston and keep the swarms down. I'll be next in line monitoring everything and providing support. Nguyen, you're the winger on the end, it'll be your job to pick off stragglers and deal with attacks from above or behind. We'll likely catch the attention of patrolling aggressives who will swarm in once we start wiping out the feeders. Got it?"

They gave a chorus of agreement, and Connor nodded.

"Excellent. Spread out, take your positions, and prepare to enter combat mode on my signal."

Lynn took up her spot to Edgar's side, about seven feet away from him and fourteen from the brick wall of the school building. The corner of the building and the fenced in generators were about twenty feet ahead. While everybody else lined up, Lynn looked around and a shiver ran down her spine. It was eerily quiet without the constant hum of generators that should have been coming from behind that fence. Lynn had never seen her school campus this empty or desolate.

She shook her head and tried to refocus.

"Hugo, how close are we to leveling?"

"This batch of enemies is likely to do the trick, if it is thick enough, Miss Lynn. You are all about five percent away from your next goal."

Lynn frowned. She'd hoped to have more wiggle room than that. She'd checked the individual leaderboard after that Charlie Foxtrot Ronnie had led them into the other day. To her dismay she'd found that her main rival for top kill-to-damage ratio, a Canadian with the handle DeathShot13, had pulled ahead of her. Normally that wouldn't be much of a problem. They were always jockeying for the top spot. But this close to Level 25 it was critical that she was number one, or she might not earn the next item in the Skadi named set.

"Stupid, idiotic, arrogant jerk face," Lynn muttered.

"I beg your pardon?"

"Not you, Hugo. Ronnie."

"Ah. Mr. Payne. What entirely avoidable mistake has he succumbed to this time?"

"Never mind. I just hope this swarm is pretty easy

because I need to be untouchable for the next fifteen minutes."

"We can always hope," Hugo replied in his usual dry voice.

"Hey Mack," Lynn said on the team channel, "be sure to let me know as early as possible if you're feeling overwhelmed or if you spot anything big coming at us. We're about to level and I've got to make sure I get this next Skadi piece, so I'll be pretty focused."

"Got it, Lynn."

"Last names, everybody. Last names," Connor's voice broke in.

Lynn sighed internally. At least they didn't have to worry about leveling unevenly anymore. Once they'd become an official team, all kill experience was evenly distributed between them. They could still hunt on their own and gain extra experience but hunting alone meant they didn't get their team experience bonus or damage modifier, similar to the area bonus her Skadi's Horde item granted. Anyone over Level 20 could form a team with three to six members to gain those basic advantages, as well as to find and use team weapons such as cannons. But being a Hunter Strike Team gave them functional perks as well, like glowing auras on their TD Hunter skins. They could choose between various colors and effects like lightning or shadow tendrils that made sure everyone who saw them in-game knew they were a championship team.

Of course, the extra attention was the last thing Lynn wanted, but the effects *were* really cool.

There was also a rumor that Hunter Strike Teams got a loot-drop bonus that gave them better weapons and augments. But maybe it only seemed that way because of the superior fighting abilities of the Hunter Strike Teams.

"Everybody ready?" Connor's question came over the team channel.

"Affirmative," Lynn said, and tightened her grip on her batons as the rest of the team sounded off.

"Good. Enter combat mode in three, two, one, go!"

"Hit it, Hugo!"

Lynn was moving before Wrath and Abomination were even finished forming. They'd entered combat mode right in a sea of imps interspersed with demons and death worms. Lynn danced back, getting out of the closest demon's swipe range. Then she charged, Abomination thundering and Wrath slicing through the air. The demon exploded into sparks along with the imps around it, and Lynn was already turning, taking out all the aggressive types within her circle of responsibility so they didn't rush her from behind as she advanced.

Within fifteen seconds she'd cleared her area and was advancing in line with Edgar, who was blasting away huge swaths of imps with every fiery belch of his cannon. Since they were so much higher level than these TDMs, their weapon range reached further than the monster's ability to detect them. It made for an anticlimactic, if satisfying, bloodbath for the first minute, until they rounded the corner of the school and the mini substation came into sight.

"Shit! That's a lot of Rocs!!" The sharp *crack* of Dan's sniper rifle increased in tempo as they beheld the literal cloud of Rocs hovering low over the substation. At Dan's attack, the closest half peeled away and came diving toward the team.

"Retreat five paces and hold," Connor commanded crisply. "Raven and Rios, support Nguyen. Johnston, provide perimeter support while we take care of these Rocs."

With only a slight delay, they shifted their attention and executed the order. Their line was a bit ragged, but the tactic worked beautifully. Lynn dodged as she shot, avoiding the diving Rocs and occasionally spinning to take out a ghost or Ghast that tried to sneak up behind her. She did take a few hits—there were so many Rocs, it was impossible to dodge them all. But she was able to thin them out enough that she wasn't completely overwhelmed when the line of Spithra got within spitting range. The gaggles of Orculls would be close behind, but they didn't have a ranged attack so Lynn didn't worry about them yet.

She was about to ask Hugo to open a private channel to Connor and suggest they retreat when their captain's voice barked out again.

"Retreat ten paces, slowly. Keep drawing them out and picking them off as we go, but don't let them overwhelm us. Nguyen, take out the Spithra before they get too close, Raven and Rios can finish up the Rocs."

Relief swept through Lynn. It was almost laughable how thankful she felt over something as small and routine as a measured retreat order. It just went to show how much Ronnie's spotty leadership record had scarred her.

With the superior range on his sniper rifle, Dan made quick work of the scuttling Spithra, marching exploding sparks down their line before they could get close enough to rain down poison spit. Lynn dodged a few stray attacks while taking out the rest of the Rocs with Mack.

"Hold here and let the Orculls come to us," Connor said once the last of the Spithra exploded.

Lynn bounced on the balls of her feet, itching to charge. But she understood why it was better to hold. They didn't want to attract any more enemies, for now.

They were able to take out half the Orculls with aimed fire before the beasts even reached them. Once they were close to melee range, Lynn finally charged. She dove between the two in front of her, their swinging attacks passing over her head before she came up and twisted to slash in an arc, catching both Orculls in their lightly armored kidney areas. The monsters exploded and she lunged through the glittering sparks to stab a third that was going for Mack.

It was clear Mack was struggling with his new role and weapons. He kept his Splinter Blade moving, but the attacks were sloppy and slow, an obvious afterthought as he poured fire into each monster's center mass with his ArcLight Pistol. Thankfully, the Orculls were low-enough level that the weapons' high damage made up for Mack's inexpert tactics.

That wouldn't keep working, though.

"Doing great, Mack," Lynn said in a brief lull after the last Orcull exploded. "Just make sure you stay light on your feet. I know you're not as used to melee, but you have to keep moving. Never stay in one place."

"Got it," Mack said, face flushed and expression sheepish.

"Get ready to advance again," Connor called out. "Looks like we'll need to draw away a few more waves before we have a clear shot at whatever is in the middle."

They repeated their advance-retreat routine, catching the attention of another wave of Orculls, Spithras, and some Penagals. They resupplied as needed from the plethora of loot scattered around them—the only evidence left of their grand slaughter. Dan kept the skies clear, though there was a bit of a panic when a Tengu showed up during the fiercest fighting of the third wave. It dove straight for Lynn and only Hugo's proximity warning got her rolling to the side in time. She took a raking strike from an Orcull—her fault for rolling directly into its path—but it wasn't as bad as a Tengu dive-bomb would have been. Dan took the toothed-vulture monster out as it screamed in fury and flapped its ugly wings to gain altitude again.

By the time they reached the last cluster of TDMs around the generators, Lynn was suspicious. She'd expected to spot a Bunyip between the ranks of monsters, hunkered down by the security fence, waiting to attack anyone who got close enough. But the space seemed empty except for a strange distortion that Lynn didn't get a chance to examine right away. An entire new flock of Rocs showed up just as Skadi's Wolves engaged the last wave of guards. They were more of a nuisance than anything else, but they forced Lynn to pour every ounce of concentration into her immediate surroundings to keep from taking hit after hit from the opportunistic buggers.

She was down to two Namahags and an extremely skittish Penagal when her display started flashing a rhythmic red for no reason at all.

Something was trying to kill her.

Chapter 6

"WHAT THE FRICK, HUGO! WHAT IS THAT?" LYNN
yelled, disengaging from the two Namahags.

"You appear to be taking damage, Miss Lynn."

"No duh, genius! Did you figure that one out all
by yourself?"

"As a matter of fact, I did. Are you proud of me?"

"Stop being sarcastic and figure out *what the heck
is killing me!*"

How close was she to leveling? Had she taken too
much damage?

She dove forward and stabbed upward at the
closest Namahag, exploding it into a thousand sparks
before surging to her feet and charging the second
Namahag, taking it out too. But her display kept
flashing red.

"Hugo, refill all my armor and globe slots! What
the freaking hell is killing me and where is it?"

She spun around in a circle, searching for some
stray Spithra or a Roc above her, but there was
nothing in sight.

"Raven, what's going on?" Connor called from down
the line. He still had a few Penagals he was cleaning
up but he'd clearly heard her yelling.

"Something's shooting me but I can't find it! It's got to be an unknown or something new with crazy high stealth!"

Edgar had his cannon raised in readiness and was spinning too, eyes searching everywhere.

"I don't see a thing, Lynn! We've killed everything within range."

"Is anyone else taking damage?" Connor asked.

A chorus of noes answered him.

Lynn ground her teeth. Stupid, freaking algorithm, picking on her at the worst possible moment. She cursed at it with her choicest Larry maledictions as she tried rolling and dodging randomly, hoping it would throw off her invisible attacker's aim.

"Everyone, retreat as a group back the way we came," Connor said. "Let's see if we can get out of range or if it moves with us."

The command almost sent Lynn sprinting away— she was desperate to stop taking damage. But just as she was turning, her eyes flitted over the spot by the fence where she'd seen a distortion before. The sun had been shining down brightly at the time, banishing any trace of shadow. But now a cloud had moved in, dimming the direct light, and Lynn suddenly realized what she was looking at.

She charged.

"Raven! What are you doing?" Connor yelled.

"It's an unknown and I think I know what it is," she yelled back.

Actually, she didn't think. She knew *exactly* what this stupid, sneaky, good-for-nothing glob of plasma was.

She attacked the faint sparkles of the sneaky unknown with everything she had, ignoring the steady flash of damage as she slashed, stabbed, and shot round after round into it.

"What's Lynn fighting?"

"I don't know, I can't see anything to target!"

"There's nothing there on my overhead."

"Are we not high-enough level to see it?"

Lynn ignored the confused chatter of her team as she focused on destroying her attacker with extreme prejudice. Wrath and Abomination did their work well, and soon the sparkling mist exploded in spectacular fashion, making Lynn suspect the unknown had been quite large.

"Congratulations, Miss Lynn! You have discovered a new unknown and you have also leveled. As per your previous instructions, all your leveling information has been minimized to your option menu, you can review it at any time. Please stand by while my unknown-entity analysis completes its review."

Lynn turned so the wooden fence was at her back and she had a clear view of her surroundings. She stood there, chest heaving, weapons held loosely at her side, as a riot of anticipation and dread stormed through her.

She'd leveled to twenty-five. There was no going back now.

Had she achieved her next Skadi item? Or had she missed it?

Why was Hugo taking so long?

Her teammates came up and stood in a loose semi-circle around her, still alert for TDM attacks as they traded silent glances.

"Everything okay, Lynn?" Edgar asked.

"Yeah. Waiting on Hugo's analysis of the unknown. Did you all level?"

"Yup," Dan said, and the other two nodded.

"And nothing jumped us?" Lynn asked with a frown.

"The day is still young," Edgar muttered, his eyes scanning their surroundings.

"Maybe it's because we're right next to a building?" Mack said. He sounded as nervous as Lynn felt.

"Let's stay focused, team," Connor broke in. "Everybody refill your slots, top off your health, and keep an eye on your overhead map. Johnston and Nguyen, you provide overwatch while me and Rios go pick up loot, then we'll take a look at it and distribute as needed."

Lynn listened with half an ear but was distracted when an image of the new monster popped up on her display. As she suspected, its bulging, tentacled form looked like a bigger, meaner version of the Lecta and Lector.

"The unknown entity has been designated as a Lectragon, a new Bravo Class-1."

"Called it," she muttered.

Hugo didn't stop to congratulate her on her powers of prediction, simply continued his spiel.

"It appears to be another electrovore with similar feeding habits to the Lector and Lecta. This entity has a plasma-beam ranged attack, significant stealth capabilities, and a defensive particle shield. Defeat of a Lectragon should yield ten globes and roughly eighty ichor points. Excellent job, Miss Lynn. Credit for the detection, defeat, and analysis of this unknown has been added to your Hunter profile and the official list of TDMs."

"Sneaky bastard," grumbled Lynn as she scanned the entity's details. They were accompanied by her experience bonus and reward loot, including a significant haul of Oneg. Helpful, but not worth the dip in her kill-to-damage ratio.

Dread twisted in her gut, and she hesitated before finally selecting her menu to pull up her leveling announcement.

All the usual stuff was there: experience bonus, extra loot, and a new weapon selection—she chose the ArcLight Pistol to give to Mack in case he wanted two of them. None of the standard, single-handed weapons would ever come close to Wrath or Abomination, which leveled with her and maintained their damage advantage.

But that's all there was. No announcements and no special bonuses achieved.

Lynn's throat constricted and her heart sank like a ten-ton boulder. She had to swallow before she could subvocalize a question to Hugo.

"Um, Hugo, I, uh, don't see anything about a new Skadi item. I guess I didn't make the cut?"

"Pardon? Do you mean a new rare item in the Skadi's Avatar named set?"

"Um, yeah." Her eyes felt hot and prickly. She would *not* cry. Really, she wouldn't. It was just a game. She was never emotional about games. Never.

"Ah! There is no notification because there is no item, Miss Lynn."

Lynn froze.

"What?"

"There are six items total in the Skadi's Avatar set, which can be achieved at Levels 5, 10, 15, 20, 30, and 40. The next item in the set is available—"

But the rest of Hugo's info dump didn't even register in Lynn's brain. She was too overwhelmed by a flood of intense relief to do anything but stand there and breathe deeply, trying to slow her galloping heart.

She had no idea why, without realizing it, she'd gotten so attached to this item set. Somehow it had become a part of her identity as a Hunter, and she would have felt miserable missing even one piece of it. There wasn't a wiki on it yet, probably because she was one of the first to achieve it, so she'd simply assumed the pieces came every five levels.

Lynn relaxed, letting her head droop as she recovered from the emotional roller coaster. That was when she spotted something shining in the grass half under her foot. She stepped to the side and reached down to tap the glowing item. It disappeared from the grass and popped up on her display, rotating slowly. It looked like a standard Army-green ammo can. On its side was painted the TD Counterforce logo.

Hmm? Was this some new special ammo?

Then Lynn spotted the augment's name and she snorted in laughter.

"What is it?" Edgar asked, glancing over at her.

Lynn pressed her lips together and took a deep breath to suppress more giggles.

"I, uh, just found an item called the 'Ammo Can of Holding.'"

Dan guffawed.

"For real? What does it do? Give you an infinite supply of Oneg?"

"That'd make Edgar happy, for sure," Lynn said, selecting the new augment to read its description. "Whoa... even better than infinite health..."

"What could be better than infinite health?" Edgar said.

Lynn grinned at him.

"It doubles my personal augment capacity."

"*Whoa-ho-ho-ho! No way!!*"

"Yes way."

"What did you find, Raven?" Connor asked, coming over with Mack now that they were done sweeping the area for loot.

Lynn showed him, and he whistled in appreciation.

"That will come in handy."

"You're telling me. We *all* need one of these."

Connor scratched his head.

"I've kept a pretty close eye on the auction listings since the summer and I've never seen one listed."

"I bet people are only just now finding them," Lynn pointed out. "The description says it's a Level 25 augment with Level 20 minimum requirement. If it's relatively uncommon, that probably means not many are being found and those that do find it are keeping it for themselves."

"Possibly," Connor agreed. "Whatever the case, I'll keep an eye out for it in the marketplace. They're bound to go for a lot, but we'll see."

Lynn wasted no time equipping her new augment while Connor went over their haul.

"It's not much, just a few offensive and defensive augments. I'll post their stats in the group chat and you all let me know if they're better than anything else you have. Also, everybody put their current supply numbers in the chat so I can see who's low and Rios and I will distribute what we found—"

A sudden buzzing hum behind Lynn made her jump and everybody turned to stare at the wooden security fence.

"The regulators. They restarted," Mack said. "Does that mean the school power is back on?"

The others looked at each other and shrugged, while Lynn just stared at the fence. The power station at Lindale Mall had come on almost as soon as she'd finished clearing away the feeders around it. But this one had taken five minutes or so to restart. Did that mean Lindale Mall truly was a coincidence and the school maintenance techs had simply fixed the glitch just now? Or had the larger mass of feeders done something more lasting to the grid that caused a delay before the power came back on?

Lynn gave her head a shake to rid it of ridiculous thoughts. She was letting the game's realism get to her. It spoke well of Mr. Krator and the other game designers because she was not the kind of gamer who enjoyed role-playing and subversive storylines. She was too analytical. All she wanted was to find the patterns, figure out how to beat it in the most efficient way possible, and make money while doing it.

Yet this game . . . it was wreaking havoc on her instincts. She blamed the ground-breaking algorithm they'd designed to generate the monsters and battle scenarios. Powered by cutting edge AI, it was no wonder the game seemed so real. It was truly making her question the line between game and reality.

Well done, Mr. Krator, she thought ruefully, and refocused on what Connor was saying.

"—still plenty of time before sunset, so I think we'll push north next and clear around the sports field toward the woods. I'm curious what we'll find. Has everybody made their new weapon selections and switched over their augments?"

They all made various noises of agreement, and Lynn happened to glance at Edgar. She did a double take, noticing a change in his armor's appearance.

"Oh no! You had to replace your Loincloth of Lordly Might?"

"Yeah," Edgar said, making a mournful face.

Dan slapped him on the back.

"Time to rejoin the real world with all us lowly, loincloth-less mortals."

"It was a good item," Lynn said, struggling to keep a straight face. "Loyal, brave, and true. We should light a pyre for it and celebrate its passing into Valhalla."

"Wait," Mack said, "isn't that where dead warriors go? Why would a loincloth—"

"Sully not the Loincloth of Lordly Might's memory with your unclean lips!" Lynn cried out dramatically as Edgar wiped away fake tears and Dan held a hand over his mouth to keep his laughter in.

"All right, team," Connor said, giving them a hard look. "We have hunting to do. You can horse around on your own time."

"I *am* going to miss it," Edgar whispered to Lynn as Connor continued his directions.

"Your noble frame just won't be the same without its Lordliness gracing your nether regions," Lynn whispered back, cheeks burning from the effort of suppressing her grin.

"Let's make a long sweep line," Connor said loudly, and shot Lynn a look. "Spread out about thirty feet between us. I'll hold the middle to keep an eye on things. Johnston and Nguyen, take the left, with Nguyen on the wing. Raven and Rios take the right, with Rios on the wing. We'll advance across the fields and clean up anything we find between here and the woods. The dots didn't look too thick when I checked the map earlier but support each other as needed. If we come up against anything big or unexpected, we'll pull in and make a tighter line. We might not all be in visual contact from end to end, so be sure to pay attention to the team channel. Got it?"

Lynn took a deep breath and sounded off with the others. She felt light, almost buoyant, and full of energy. After so many weeks of walking on eggshells and always worrying about having to clean up after Ronnie, it was incredibly relaxing to have someone reliable and level-headed in charge.

Okay, so the day was still young. But Connor *did* seem to have his act together.

As they set off around the school buildings and across the activity fields, it was all Lynn could do not to break into a jog, picking off TDMs as she went. She fairly bounced as she strode forward, keeping in line with Connor to her left and Mack on her right. The sunshine warmed her back and shoulders, helping dispel the chill that had set into her muscles while they'd gathered loot and talked.

They took their time sweeping the school grounds, using the opportunity to find a new equilibrium as a team. Connor remained professional and competent, critiquing and praising in equal measures. He did get on Dan's case for excessive chatter. Lynn didn't mind it and thought it improved team morale, but she could see Connor's point that it was distracting from the mission.

Overall, it was a pleasant hour of vaporizing Delta Class TDMs and practicing accuracy and combat technique against the Charlie Class. They saw a few Bravo Class monsters, but not many. By the time they reached the woods north of the school, they were all ready for a breather. Connor had them exit combat mode and group by the fence that bordered the school grounds. Lynn munched on an energy bar while Connor gave Mack some pointers on melee fighting.

Edgar wandered over and stood beside her, sipping occasionally on the tube of the built-in hydration pack of his TD Counterforce backpack.

"You doin' okay?" he asked quietly, glancing down at her.

"Yeah, actually. Today's been great. No Ronnie, no drones, and no drama. It's almost too good to be true," she said with a smile. The invigorating hunt combined with residual elation that she hadn't missed the next Skadi item had made her much more chipper than usual. It was a weird feeling. "You?" she asked.

Edgar grunted and shot a sidelong look at Connor, which sobered her up.

"Still waiting for the shoe to drop?" she asked, lowering her voice.

He nodded.

"He might be a good hunter, but I still don't trust him."

Lynn shrugged.

"If he's playing some sort of game, it's a long game. Don't worry, we'll keep our eyes open." Her words didn't seem to reassure Edgar, who just grunted again and took another swig of water.

Connor rounded them up soon after, and one by one they jumped the school fence into the unmown grass and brush beyond that swiftly turned into woodland.

Lynn had never explored the area during her time in high school, considering her extreme aversion to the outside. But she vaguely remembered that these woods surrounded a major power-node tower, with a neighborhood to the east and a highway bordering it to the northwest.

Once they had gathered again on the far side of the fence, Connor started laying out his strategy for their advance when the faint sound of buzzing grew overhead. Lynn groaned and glanced up. Sure enough, there was a sleek little drone overhead to the west, circling the perimeter of the school grounds. It would spot them in seconds, if it hadn't already. She was honestly surprised it had taken the resident vultures this long to sniff around the back side of the school, though . . .

She glanced at the corner of her display and saw it was a little after when school normally let out. Maybe they'd figured it was finally safe to encroach on school airspace now that classes were officially over. Whatever the case, it meant the end of the brief respite she'd been enjoying so much.

Connor spotted the intruder, too, and sighed.

"Let's switch to subvocalization only from now on," came his voice over the team channel, "at least until we get under some cover."

Lynn gritted her teeth and resolutely fixed her eyes on the woodland in front of her.

"Hugo, can you put on my 'Burn It Down' playlist, low volume, left ear, but also overlay game sounds, normal volume on both ears?"

"Certainly, Miss Lynn."

"Thanks."

"Okay, team," Connor continued, "let's line up on the fence and continue our sweep, but no more than ten feet between us. The underbrush should thin out once we're under the trees and it'll be easier to keep together. For now, let's get through this border area and make sure we aren't leaving any monsters to sneak up behind us. If we run into any big clusters of TDMs, pull in and reform as an attack-V with Johnston at the point."

They lined up silently, then jumped back into combat mode on Connor's signal. Lynn dropped in almost on top of a Grumblin, but it didn't immediately react. That few-second delay gave her batons time to reform as deadly weapons of mass "murderation," and she dispatched it with a quick slash. By then the rest of the scattered monsters in the area had taken notice, and the whole team switched to ranged weapons to pick them off as they rushed to attack.

Once the immediate area was clear, Connor called an advance and they waded forward through the tall grass. Lynn was *very* glad it was no longer summer— she still checked for ticks every night out of habit, but the cold weather seemed to have killed them off. Soon, Skadi's Wolves were pushing through saplings, brush, and brambles, attempting to stab at the odd monster that glided right through the tangle to attack. Here, their high-performance uniforms made things infinitely easier. Thorns, stickers, and prickly brush slid right across the fabric's tough surface, allowing them to slip smoothly through the thicket.

Inside the woodland the underbrush thinned out, making it much easier to see each other through the tree trunks. Most of the trees were medium sized, a mix of oak, hickory, ash, and maple. Lynn knew, because she'd been studying the woodcraft book Edgar had given her for her birthday. In fact, she had it with her in her backpack. In a way it was silly to be lugging around a *book* made of *paper* when she had the entire mesh web at her fingertips. All she had to do was ask Hugo and he could identify every tree in sight down to their species name. But the book had felt like the sort of gift that ought to be used, like her father's pocketknife, which was tucked securely into one of her uniform's discreet pockets. Plus, the extra weight enhanced her strength training. Win-win.

It didn't take them long to hit the southern edge of the thickly clustered dots they'd seen on their overhead. Right off the bat, groups of Spithra and Orculls peeled off the mass and charged toward them. The assault wouldn't have been much more than an annoyance if it weren't for the pairs of Phasmas that kept popping up at their backs and attacking while they were distracted at the front. Then they stumbled on a Creeper nest and everything went to hell. Connor called a quick retreat and they backed up, killing Phasmas as they went and pulling the TDMs after them. Once they got rid of the first wave they cautiously inched forward again, trying to take out the Creeper nest without attracting another wave of aggressives.

And then they did it again. And again. And again.

It might have become tedious and repetitive, but every engagement was different and there wasn't a moment Lynn could slack off and lose focus. She'd checked her individual ranking when they'd crossed the fence and had seen that she'd slipped to third in kill-to-damage ratio. To regain top position she had to be at her very best for every second of battle, landing every blow, dodging every attack like smoke on the wind. Otherwise, the rest of the Skadi set might slip through her fingers. Connor's professional and timely commands kept the chaos manageable, and Lynn was able to sink into her Larry brain for long stretches, letting her hunter instincts push away the incessant buzzing of life's worries.

Connor did a good job gauging the heat of their engagements and kept them from being overwhelmed by plenty of well-timed retreats. They scooped up loot and resupplied as they went, checking each area for items before moving on to the next. It might be an hour or more before they headed back through the woods to get home, and by then the loot would be long gone. Eventually the waves of Charlie Class TDMs gave way to Bravo Class, which Lynn enjoyed because they were more challenging.

But not everybody was doing as well.

Mack was struggling to keep up, not only in kill rate but also responding to commands and movement changes. Privately Lynn thought Connor should have let him stick to double pistols and simply upgraded his weaponry rather than assign him an entirely new fighting style. But she hadn't wanted to confront Connor right off the bat. Maybe she was being too protective of Mack—maybe the struggle was good for him. At least Connor wasn't berating him for mistakes like Ronnie had. But it was clear through the tone of his voice and his clipped instructions that he was impatient with Mack.

There wasn't time to worry about it, though, and

since Edgar was between her and Mack there was little she could do to help. Instead, she focused on slaughtering monsters like an unstoppable machine so Edgar's load was lighter and he could help cover Mack.

Eventually, even Lynn started getting fatigued from the constant battle. Moisture wicking and odor resistant her uniform might be, but it couldn't entirely erase the smell of hard-earned sweat. They'd never faced this many monsters in successive waves while Ronnie was captain, and still the mass of dots to the north seemed just as thick as before. Where were they all coming from? Had they been camped out here the entire time? Or were they congregating around something?

A part of her suspected there was a boss out there, probably near that node tower. But depending on its level, they might not be able to see it, much less fight it. As long as they had an endless supply of monsters to kill, though, and were able to retreat when needed, she was happy to keep chipping away at the successive rings of TDMs guarding whatever it was.

They were just regrouping for another advance when Lynn heard a telltale roar ahead of them. A shiver ran down her spine, and for once she didn't feel the usual thrill of bloodlust fill her. That was a Manticar, and she was *so* tired. At that point facing one of them would be an annoying obstacle instead of an exciting challenge.

Sure enough, a lone dot that the other dots pulled away from was headed straight toward them from the north, as if it had been sent out to do battle by its commander. In a sudden rush of panic, Lynn realized who would be facing it up close and personal: her and Mack. One glance down the line and she could see

Mack was almost stumbling in weariness. Honestly, they all were.

"Connor," she subvocalized on their team channel, "that's a Manticar about to jump us and it's been a long day. If everybody else will pull back a little to draw it away and distract it with ranged fire, I'll get behind it like I've done before and take it out from the rear."

"It's Bancroft, and that's a job for more than one. You and Rios are on assault, you'll take the Manticar together. Johnston and Nguyen, fall back with me and concentrate all fire on the Manticar."

Lynn gritted her teeth but didn't argue.

"Mack—I mean Rios, just follow my lead. We have to attack it head on and slip behind to get under the stinger where it can't strike us. Then we just slash at its legs and keep moving with it, and it'll be dead in no time."

"O-okay," Mack said, clearly unhappy with the situation.

There was no time to reassure him, so Lynn simply charged forward and hoped he followed. If he held back and tried to dodge the stinger from the front, the Manticar would take him out in a few strikes.

The Manticar loomed up out of the trees, charging straight through trunks and bushes. Lynn's path was less straightforward, but she still headed right for its head. At the last second she dodged to the side and rolled under its first stinger-tipped strike, coming up beside its flank. She gave the huge muscled leg a slash with Wrath, then spun, ready to lunge again and move with the Manticar to stay under its stingers where it was safe.

That's when she spotted Mack, and she groaned. Her teammate had skidded to a stop in front of the Manticar, which had turned to roar in his face and attack with all three stingers. Now Mack was back-pedaling to stay out of reach while shooting the beast in the face. Lynn would be the first to admit that the eight-foot-high augmented-reality monster was as intimidating as heck. But she also knew its weakness and had killed multiple Manticars before with just this technique, so there was nothing to hold her back from diving right at it. Mack was used to sniping Manticars from a distance, and instinct or fear had held him back.

Common sense told her to stay put and take out the Manticar as quickly as possible, capitalizing on the distraction Mack was providing. It was what Larry would have done.

But this wasn't WarMonger2050, and she wasn't a mercenary looking out for her bottom line and ready to cut her losses if need be. Maybe Mack's life wasn't in danger, but the pressing urge in Lynn's chest to dash forward and help him was no less strong.

Lynn saw the Manticar's stingers descend once, twice, three times on Mack, and then she couldn't take it anymore. With a curse she dashed around the creature's legs, so close she could have run her fingers through its fur—if it had been any more than a visual illusion, of course. Rounding its shoulder she lunged to put herself directly under its huge head and then let loose with Abomination's armor-piercing special ammo. She pumped round after round into it as fast as her finger would move, all while stabbing it repeatedly through the throat and up into its head.

Understandably, her attack distracted it from its current prey, and it reared backward with an earsplitting roar. The air and even her own body seemed to vibrate with its ferocity—some kind of weird side effect of her earbuds vibrating against her ear bone, probably.

Far from intimidated, Lynn lunged forward to stay under its head and keep shooting...

And ran face first into a tree trunk as big around as she was. She bounced, quite literally, off the tree and fell backward, landing hard on her butt then flopping onto her back, all the wind knocked out of her. Thankfully her fall was cushioned by flimsy bushes and a thick layer of leaves. She lay motionless where she fell, stunned and head throbbing.

"Lynn! Are you okay?" Mack shouted and ran forward, still shooting. More fire was pouring in from the front and sides, and she felt a vague sense of relief when sparks burst above her head and the roars of the Manticar went abruptly silent.

"Everybody, exit combat mode!" Connor shouted. There was a crashing of brush as the guys gathered round.

Lynn stared up at the four heads leaning over her.

"Oops," she said, suppressing a weird urge to giggle.

Connor frowned.

"Are you injured?"

Edgar shot him a glare.

"She's got a knot the size of a walnut oozing blood on her forehead. Of course she's injured!" He crouched down and held up three fingers in front of her face.

"How many fingers am I holding up?"

"Three, silly. And no, I don't have a concussion again. I'm fine. Just kinda winded."

Edgar's eyes narrowed like he didn't believe her. But instead of fussing, he held out a hand to help her up.

"Whoa, take it slow," he murmured, and Lynn couldn't have agreed more. Her head was spinning.

Ow. That tree had *hurt*.

"That was sooooo cool!" Dan gushed, once it was clear she wasn't in imminent danger. "I can't believe you just got right under its head! You were, like, stabbing it in the brain! Man, Lynn, sometimes you make me wish I wasn't a sniper. You get to have all the fun!"

"Like running headfirst into trees?" she muttered, and Dan laughed.

"You should get checked out," Connor said. "That knot looks pretty bad." He'd backed up and was now standing, arms crossed, watching her with that expressionless face of his. She couldn't read him. Was he concerned? Angry? Annoyed?

"I'm fine," Lynn insisted, letting go of Edgar and stepping away. Her hand felt hot and tingly where it had made contact with Edgar's skin, and she got busy brushing leaves and dirt off herself as a distraction. "Besides, my mom is a nurse. She can look at it when I get home."

Connor's expression didn't change, but he nodded.

"Miss Lynn," Hugo said in her ear, "are you sure I should not summon a medical transport? Head injuries can be quite dangerous and you are hardly in a position to judge your own level of fitness considering you attempted to brush off a Grade 2 concussion mere months ago."

"Lay off, Hugo," she subvocalized, "I'm fine. I didn't black out or anything."

"But—"

"We're done for the day, then," Connor was saying, and Lynn focused on him so she could ignore Hugo's fussing. "Good work, team. We made great headway to Level 26 and team cohesion is ... getting there." He glanced at Mack but didn't say anything. Even so, Mack seemed to shrink in on himself in response.

Lynn frowned. She bet her friend felt responsible for her getting hurt, even though it wasn't his fault at all.

"Hey, Mack, thanks for keeping that Manticar distracted for me," she said, giving him a smile. "It worked out great. Well, except for me being a complete klutz."

That brought a tentative grin to Mack's face.

"No problem. But next time, let's do it in a field or something. We wouldn't want you getting another concussion."

"Well, I can't make any promises. But I will definitely keep a sharper lookout for trees hiding inside TDMs."

"Come on," Edgar said, forestalling any further banter. "It's a long walk back to the airbus platform, and Lynn should go home and get some ice on her head."

Lynn wouldn't admit it, but she was grateful for the suggestion. Her head was throbbing with what she suspected was the beginnings of a massive headache.

They all turned and headed back the way they'd come. Their path of advance through the woods was easily visible by the trampled bushes and kicked up forest loam. Lynn made a mental note to never go hunting in a garden or nature preserve. The environment would not thank her for it.

Speaking of environment ... Lynn took a whiff of her uniform and wrinkled her nose. After her little stunt she now smelled of sweat *and* dirt. Yippee. She couldn't wait to get home and take a shower.

Edgar stuck close by her side as they walked, though he was as silent and placid as ever. Connor walked in front talking battle tactics with Dan, whose hands were dancing with excitement as he exclaimed over various ideas. Clearly, he'd warmed up to their new captain over the course of the afternoon. Mack walked silently between their two groups, tugging on his fledgling goatee as he lost himself in his own thoughts.

Lynn wasn't inclined to talk either, though for her it was because noises were doing painful things to her head. She'd resigned herself to a miserable trip home until she suddenly remembered she had pain reliever stashed in her backpack. It, along with sunscreen, bug spray, and energy bars, made up her "essentials hunting kit." In the past she'd needed it for sore muscles protesting about all the new ways she was pushing them. But her body had adapted and changed, toughening up with the constant training. Without stopping, she swung her TD Counterforce bag off her back and dug for the little bottle, then swallowed a few pills and washed them down with water.

"You okay?" Edgar asked once she'd replaced her backpack.

"I'll be fine. Just a headache, totally expected after running headfirst into a tree." Out of the corner of her eye, she thought she saw a grin lift Edgar's lips. "Hey, you're not laughing at me, are you?"

"Who, me? Laugh at a *Toa Tama'ita'i*? To her face? I'm not *that* dumb."

Lynn narrowed her eyes, but Edgar's expression

remained passive, even if his eyes danced when they glanced over at her.

"Humph," she snorted. "I'm just glad the woods were too thick for drones to follow us. If one of them had caught my flub on camera I'd become the laughingstock of the global gaming community. I might as well kill myself now and avoid the misery."

"Nah, it wouldn't be that bad."

"Don't try to sugarcoat it, Edgar. Heck, *I'd* love to see a vid of what happened. I'd probably laugh myself hoarse. If 'epic fail' footage like that made it to the mesh web, I'd become a meme within seconds."

Edgar didn't reply, but when she looked over at him, she realized it was because he was too busy holding in his laughter.

She rolled her eyes and lengthened her stride so he wouldn't spot her involuntary grin, though she had another motive too. Coming alongside Mack, she glanced over.

"Hey. Penny for your thoughts?"

He gave her a worried look.

"They're probably not worth even that."

"Yeah, you're probably right if they're anywhere along the lines of blaming yourself for me trying to bulldoze a tree with my head. It's *not* your fault. Got it?"

Mack sighed.

"I know you're right, but I still feel bad. I really suck in this new position and I feel like I'm letting the whole team down."

"Good grief, Mack, no. *Connor* made the assignment, so if you want to blame someone, blame him. Anyone would need time to adjust to new weapons, new fighting style, and new position. You just need practice. You can work on it in the evenings with the training simulations. You'll be back to your usual standards in no time."

"If you say so," he muttered, sounding unconvinced.

By then they'd reached the edge of the woods and conversation died down as they pushed through the thick brush and came out near the school fence. Lynn had already known from the growing buzz above what awaited them, and the knowledge made the throbbing in her head worse. She refused to look up and acknowledge their existence, though. Stupid drones. When their team jumped the fence and headed across school grounds, the buzzing sound lessened, but didn't disappear.

As they rounded the school building and the deserted airbus platform came into view, Connor slowed and dropped back to walk on Lynn's other side opposite Edgar.

"How are you feeling?"

"Took some pain reliever, I'll be fine," she said with a shrug.

"Still, just to be safe, I'll be escorting you home."

"I'll take her home," Edgar said, his tone unusually harsh.

Connor's reply was cool.

"I'm the team captain. It's my responsibility to look after my team."

"I'm her *friend*, it's *my* responsibility to make sure she's okay."

Lynn scowled and she wished someone would hurry up and invent teleportation devices—right after they invented invisibility cloaks. What the heck was up with those two?

"Um, okay, so, everybody calm down. One, I'm fine. Two, nobody needs to 'take me home.' My head feels better already, and my mom will check me out when I get home."

"Actually, Lynn, I need to talk to you about a few things for the team anyway. Run some feedback past you. It'd be easier if we chat on the airbus, since I've got some things going on this evening."

"Uhhh, okay." Lynn glanced at Edgar, who was looking at Connor—and not in a friendly way. "Um, Connor, usually Edgar, Mack, and I take the same airbus, we all live in the same direction."

"Ah. Makes it simple, then. We'll all ride together."

He didn't mention where he lived, but Lynn was pretty sure it *wasn't* in the same area of town as her, Edgar, and Mack.

Once on the airbus, their uniforms made a few heads turn, though everybody soon went back to minding their own business. One kid near the front turned in her seat and gave them an open-mouthed stare that morphed into a mile-wide grin. She mouthed "So awesome" and gave them a double thumbs-up over the back of her bench. Lynn surprised herself by grinning in return and giving the tween a wave. She was so obviously starstruck it made Lynn's heart warm.

Lynn sat down next to Edgar and Connor took the empty seat on her other side. Lynn immediately regretted her choice of seats as the warm presence of not one, but two male bodies, both a head taller than her, loomed on either side. It wouldn't have been so bad if they hadn't spent the entire afternoon exercising. Edgar smelled as bad as she did. Almost worse, Connor *didn't* smell bad. He exuded a kind of musky, woody scent that made Lynn want to lean away from Edgar and toward him.

She sat as straight as a board, hands on her back-pack between her knees, hardly daring to move as weird thoughts raced through her head.

Connor had been doing sports for years, so he'd probably invested in some new expensive deodorant that turned his sweat smell into cologne, right? That was a thing, wasn't it?

Which one of them had more muscle? Obviously Edgar was bulkier, built more like a wrestler, but Connor's skintight uniform made it abundantly plain that he was all lean strength with barely an ounce of fat on him.

Not that she'd been looking. Had she? Well, obviously she'd been looking at him off and on all afternoon, but not like *that*.

Lynn felt her face grow warm and she hurriedly fixed her eyes on the floor between her feet. She needed something else to think about, *stat*. What homework did she have to do when she got home?

That was the moment Connor decided to chat about "a few team things." It was all Lynn could do to answer in intelligible English. It was mostly routine stuff, though, not the strategy or performance feedback she'd expected. In fact, the questions were almost sociable, such as how she liked the game and what her favorite monster to fight was. Edgar was silent throughout, as was Mack without Dan there to laugh and banter with. Normally Dan rode with Ronnie since they lived in the same area, but now Dan was riding home by himself.

When they finally reached Lynn's stop, she nearly jumped out of her seat.

"This is me! See you guys tomorrow."

Connor stood as well. "I'll see you to your apartment. I had one more thing I wanted to ask you about."

"Uhhh." Lynn's brain failed to give her a coherent response, and she was distracted by the hard stare Edgar was aiming at Connor.

"Do you want me to come with you, Lynn?" Edgar asked quietly, shifting his gaze to her.

Lynn was pretty sure if she spent any more time sandwiched between two large, smelly men, she might have a mental breakdown, so she hurriedly shook her head.

"I'll be fine. I'll ping you when I get to my apartment, okay?"

"Okay . . . be safe," he said.

"Uh, right, will do," Lynn said, and fled the airbus.

Somehow, she'd hoped that walking as fast as she could might make Connor magically disappear. To her annoyance, he trotted to catch up and easily kept pace with his long legs as they descended the platform and headed to her apartment complex. To make matters a hundred times worse, there was a cloud of drones hovering above the stop—paparazzi drones just waiting to pounce. Their buzzing followed her and Connor along the sidewalk, making her neck and shoulders tense uncomfortably.

"So, um, what did you want to ask about?" Lynn said without looking over, hoping to get whatever it was out of the way so she could go home and hide from everybody and everything.

"Oh, well, mostly I wanted to thank you for giving me a chance with the team. I really enjoyed today. It was certainly an eye-opener. You did a great job.

You're even more impressive up close than on the TD Lens vids I've seen."

"Um...you're welcome? You, uh, weren't too bad yourself."

She actually had no idea how he'd done. She'd been too busy focusing on her kill-to-damage ratio to ogle Connor fighting monsters in his skintight uniform. The thought made her face heat again, and she sped up even more.

"I do have a bit of feedback, though," Connor said, keeping pace.

"Could we, uh, voice chat," Lynn asked, jerking a thumb upward.

Connor glanced up, seeming to notice the drones for the first time. He shrugged and switched to subvocalization.

"I know you were trying to help Rios with that Manticar, but you took a big risk and ended up injuring yourself. In the future I expect you to stick to the assignments I give you and trust in the rest of your team to support you."

"Uhhhh, okay?"

"Everybody was concentrating fire on the Manticar, we would have destroyed it soon enough without you needing to take risks."

That made Lynn look up, brows drawn together.

"But Mack wouldn't have survived that long. I know how much damage those stinger strikes do, and it was going at him with all three!"

"And you think I didn't know that?" Connor said, raising one eyebrow.

"Well..."

"I'm the team captain, Lynn. It's my job to know

those things, and my job to make the calls. How can we fight as a team if I can't trust my subordinates to do their jobs and stay in their lane?"

Lynn's mouth opened and closed a few times as an embarrassed prickle made her skin itch. How could she explain her decision? Mack dying would have been bad for the team—not to mention Mack—and everything would have been fine if that tree hadn't been there. Yes, she'd lost situational awareness, but the same thing might have happened if she'd stayed at the Manticar's rear like she'd meant to.

"I-I wasn't doing anything you didn't tell me to do. You said to assault the Manticar, and that's what I was doing."

Connor shook his head, a little smile on his lips.

"Yes, I suppose so. But it was still a risky move and you know it. Besides, Mack made a mistake and didn't follow orders either. It was good for him to understand the consequences of his actions. If he died, then he died, and that would have been a useful lesson for him. You weren't helping by saving him from that."

Conflicting thoughts swirled in Lynn's head, so she didn't reply. His argument made sense, but it also felt . . . off. Yes, Mack needed to learn how to fill his new position competently. But letting him die just to teach him a lesson? It didn't feel right, but they *were* competing in an international competition with astronomical stakes. Connor had been leading a team in high-stakes competitions longer than her, though her mercenary jobs in WarMonger had probably earned her far more money than Connor had ever made off sponsorships at a high-school level. The thing was that Lynn's in virtual missions had all been one shots.

There was no long-term team development or strategy. The only thing that mattered was whatever worked for *that* battle, nothing more.

"In any case, as brave as your move was, it was the wrong one for that situation. In future, I'd appreciate it if you stuck to your role and let us all work together to support each other, rather than doing anything stupidly heroic, okay?"

They'd arrived at the front doors of her apartment building, so Lynn slowed and forced herself to face Connor. She gave him a serious, professional nod. "Got it."

At that point she expected—and hoped—he would say goodbye and walk away. Instead, he lingered, looking at her with an unreadable expression.

"I'm not Ronnie, you know," he said out of the blue, leaning forward slightly. "You can trust me to take care of you and the team."

What the heck?

"Uhhh, sure. I know."

"Good. Because I know you're used to second-guessing your captain's every order. But you can't do that with me. I know what I'm doing, Lynn."

"Yeah, sure. You're a pro and all that. I get it."

"I'm glad you do," he said, and smiled. It wasn't his usual reserved, polite look, but rather a full-face smile showing off his brilliant white teeth. It lit up his whole face and . . . wow. That blond hair and those blue eyes . . .

There was another awkward pause, then Connor chuckled quietly.

"You know you really are an amazing player, Lynn. It is truly an honor to have you on my team. I don't think I've ever seen anybody move with such fierceness and beauty. You look fantastic out there."

Lynn's brain, which was busy sorting through conflicting emotions, stuttered to a halt.

What?

"I'm not surprised everybody is so obsessed with you. You're beautiful, smart, and a phenomenal gamer. How are sponsorship companies not already breaking down your door?"

"Uhhhh...th-they are," she said, uncomfortably aware of the faint hum above her head.

"Really?" he said, and took a step closer. "Why haven't you accepted any of them?"

"Uhhh..."

Because I hate attention, her brain said, but her mouth didn't seem to get the memo.

"I can help you with that, you know. I've already got quite a bit of experience in negotiating sponsorship contracts. In fact, why don't we get together and talk about it? We could grab dinner sometime."

"Uhhh..."

"Miss Lynn, are you in need of assistance?" Hugo's voice said unexpectedly in her ear. "Your speech center seems to have malfunctioned. Shall I summon your mother to run interference?"

"No!"

"Pardon?" Connor said, brow creasing at her sudden yell.

"Oh, sorry, I was, uh, talking to, um, my personal AI," she said hurriedly, going back to subvocalization. "It, uh, came on because I'm so close to my apartment and it started doing stuff and...sorry. Um, what was your question?"

"I was just asking when you'd like to go out for dinner, to talk about sponsorships?" Connor repeated, a little half smile back on his face.

"Uhhh..." Had she said yes to dinner? When did she say that? "I don't know, everything's really busy with school and hunting and all that."

"But sponsorships are important for the team too. The more you have, the more it will attract offers for everyone else. And we can use the extra funds to outfit our team better. It's really a team matter, so I think it would be entirely appropriate to make time for it. How about this Saturday evening? I can pick you up at seven, does that work?" He gave that brilliant smile again and something swooped in her stomach.

"Uhhh, I'm not sure—I mean, I think—um, I have to ask my mom?"

"Oh?" Both his eyebrows rose. "I didn't realize you still let your mother run your schedule. I guess I assumed with all the hunting you have to do for this competition that she trusted you to take care of your own affairs."

"I mean, she does," Lynn said, waving a hand dismissively and hoping her face wasn't turning red. "I just, you know, want to run it past her. We're pretty close."

"Of course," Connor said, his smile back in place. "I'm sure she'll be fine with it. It's for the competition after all, and what parent doesn't want to support their child?"

"Uh, yeah," Lynn agreed faintly, head still spinning. Had she just agreed to go on a date?

"Well, I'll see you tomorrow after school for another hunt, but I look forward to Saturday." Connor waved and turned away from the complex doors, heading back the way he'd come. Lynn stared after him, not really consciously. She still didn't know what had just happened.

Had he really called her beautiful? Did he mean it? Or was he just being nice?

Nobody had ever called her beautiful before. Well, her mother did sometimes, but that didn't count, obviously.

Wait . . . was this some sort of trick? But no, it couldn't be, not after everything Connor had already invested in becoming a part of their team. Could it? He *had* cut ties with Elena, hadn't he?

But hadn't he and Elena been a thing? Elena certainly seemed to think they were, but Lynn honestly couldn't ever remember a moment when he'd seemed pleased to be around her. She'd never seen them make out at school or anything, and Elena was notorious for PDA with her revolving door boyfriends. That pop-girl was a "marking her territory" kind of predator and wasn't afraid to show it.

Suddenly Lynn realized she was still standing out in the open, watching Connor's well-built form disappear down the street like some kind of lovelorn idiot.

She fled inside, trying not to think about the ubiquitous sound of humming overhead.

Chapter 7

THE NEXT MORNING AT SCHOOL, WHISPERS AND
pings were flying as hard and fast as poison spit
from a mob of Spithra. The school had various news
boards on their virtual wall, but they also had chat
boards for each class and each student year. Lynn
never touched those—she knew the kind of veiled
bullying that went on in them despite the supposed
monitoring of the teachers. But there was a running
count of the number of posts and conversations on
the school's main virtual wall, and it had jumped by
nearly thirty percent overnight.

Lynn had assumed it was chatter about the power-
grid escapade the day before, but her "Larry sense"
went off when Dan and Mack came running down
the hall to greet her outside their first class. Their
faces were pale and their eyes were wide as they
huddled close, backs turned against the curious stares
of passing students.

"What's up?" Lynn asked in a low voice.

"Nothing good," Mack said.

"You won't *believe* this," Dan hissed at the same
time. "We had to come show you. It's just too unbe-
lievable for a ping! Look at this!"

A tiny stream-vid icon popped up in Lynn's message

box in the top right corner of her AR glasses, which she'd already put on to check class topics for the day. Lynn maximized it by focusing on it and blinking twice. An image of Elena and her flunkies standing in front of a local restaurant filled Lynn's vision. But it was the person standing beside Elena that made Lynn's jaw drop open.

"I'm *sooo* excited to announce the newest member of the Cedar Rapids Champions. He's actually the former team captain of Skadi's Wolves. But obviously he could see how superior the CRC is and he was thrilled and honored to be invited to our team. I only allow the best players in my team, of course, and I'm dedicated to making sure we're always on the top. So stay glued to your streams, my lovely fans. You'll be seeing a lot more *amaaazing* battles from us. We're the top team in the region and we'll be training tirelessly to make sure we win the national championship!"

Lynn barely even registered the next few seconds of the stream because she couldn't seem to rehinge her jaw to her face and make it close. She stared past the stream image at Mack and Dan in front of her, her mouth still gaping. Both stared back with similar expressions, though their mouths were pressed into worried lines, not flapping stupidly like hers.

"W-what? Ronnie? In the CRC?? Wha—" She cut off abruptly and refocused on the stream image as a familiar voice interrupted the gush of Elena's drivel in response to one of the onlookers' questions.

"Elena and I are working *together* to make sure this team is second to none. Elena does, well, this part"—he smiled painfully at the camera—"and I'm in charge of training and leading the team, since I have many, many years of gaming experience. The only way *any* team has a chance of winning is *loyalty* and *cooperation* under a strong leader. So watch out, Hunter Strike Teams, because we're coming for the prize and nothing can stop us!" Ronnie gave another painfully awkward smile at the camera and pumped his fist in the air. Elena, standing beside him with her arms crossed, visibly rolled her eyes and then hip checked him out of the way to start talking again with a brilliant smile of white teeth and perfect lipstick.

"So be sure to like and follow our stream, and don't forget to set your notifications to 'always on' so you don't miss a single juicy update!"

The stream clip ended with a spinning, flashing logo of a fearsome hawk, wings spread across the city symbol of Cedar Rapids and the name "Cedar Rapids Champions" wrapped around the upper curve of the image.

A few seconds of stunned silence passed before Lynn rediscovered her vocal cords.

"Whaaat?"

"I know, right?" Dan said, hands twisting and squeezing each other in front of him. "Did you hear him? Loyalty and cooperation? Talk about unsubtle digs." His tone was scoffing, but Lynn could tell Ronnie's words had bothered him. Dan wore every feeling and thought on his sleeve, and his guilt was palpable.

"It seems kinda extreme, even for Ronnie," Mack said quietly. "I mean, joining *Elena's* team? Is he crazy?"

Lynn shook her head, not in negation but because she simply had no words. What was that idiot thinking?

The hostility and disgust between him and Elena was so painfully obvious it had made his awkward speech look even worse. Did he really think Elena was going to follow orders and support him in whipping CRC into shape? Not that Lynn thought Ronnie was capable of whipping anyone into shape, much less a fractious group of self-serving airheads.

She couldn't fathom what Ronnie thought he was going to accomplish by it all. Unless that was exactly it: he *hadn't* been thinking? But he hated Elena, so what could have prompted him to take up such a terrible offer? Was he really *that* desperate to compete? Or was the move made out of revenge and spite? Or maybe Elena was blackmailing him?

"Hey, have you all seen—"

"Yes," all three of them answered in unison as Edgar strode up to their huddled group, his sneakers squeaking overloud in the nearly empty hall.

It was almost time for class.

"Look, everybody," Lynn said. "I don't know *what* has gotten into Ronnie, but he obviously wasn't ready to give up and drop from the competition. We should be grateful he didn't recruit four random people and try to hijack Skadi's Wolves." They hadn't yet called TD Hunter support to make the team member change official. They needed to do that *soon*. "The important thing is that he's got his own team now, and we can leave him to it. Ignore the CRC. Don't watch their stream, don't comment on their wall, don't talk about them at all. We need to *focus*. It's the only way we'll stay on track. We've got a lot of work to do, but we've got good players and I think Connor is going to be a good team captain. So let's keep our heads down, get our schoolwork done to keep our parents off our backs, and keep training and hunting like professionals. Got it?"

Everyone nodded, though her little pep talk hadn't lessened the worry or guilt in their faces.

"Come on, we'll be late for class," Lynn said, and jerked her head toward the door to their room.

It was hard to stay focused at school, but at least there were no more confrontations in the halls between periods. Perhaps Elena had decided ignoring Skadi's Wolves was the best way forward, and Lynn could not have been more pleased.

Lunchtime brought a surprise, though.

"Um, c-can I sit with you all?"

Lynn and the guys looked up in surprise to find Kayla standing there, lunch in hand and expression hesitant. She was wearing unusually casual clothes— at least compared to what she used to wear around Elena—but her face was freshly made up and her hair was perfectly styled. Lynn thought her eyes looked rather puffy, though.

"Sure," Lynn said, thankfully finding her tongue before any of the guys had a chance to say something nasty. She'd completely forgotten to tell them about Kayla's surprise visit and change of heart. At the looks of confusion from around the table, Lynn hurriedly gave them the cliff notes version while Kayla pulled out her seat and settled carefully between her and Mack.

"So," Lynn finished, directing her gaze at Kayla, "how did it go yesterday? With Elena?"

Kayla bit her lip and poked at her food, but then looked up and gave a weak smile.

"About like you'd expect. I went home early afterward."

"Wait," Dan said, "so you weren't here for the power-grid failure?"

"No, though I heard about it. What happened?"

That was all the encouragement Dan needed to embark on a dramatic retelling using a hapless fry to gesture like a conductor's baton.

"Dude, eat that fry before it breaks and goes flying," Edgar said, shaking his head.

Dan didn't miss a beat but stuffed the fry into his mouth and kept right on going. Lynn noticed with interest that the antic made Kayla smile shyly as the girl listened and nibbled at her food.

Once that story had run its course, Dan launched into another about the time a storm had knocked out the power in his house right at the climax of a vital boss battle in one of his MMORPG games. Lynn ducked her head to hide her grin with bites of her sandwich. Dan was always chattering on about one thing or another, but now he was barely even pausing to draw breath. It was as if the presence of a pretty female at their table—Lynn didn't count, obviously—had made him incapable of closing his mouth for even a second. As for Kayla, her eyes hadn't glazed over—yet—and she seemed happy listening. Maybe she was simply relieved to hear something other than mean-spirited gossip.

Either way, it was nice to have another girl at the table. At the very least, it distracted Lynn from the mountain of worry scrabbling for her attention. But more than that, it brought a bit of optimism. Kayla would probably never be the friend she'd once been. But it sure was nice to see Elena's perfect little façade of popularity and control crumble, first with Connor, now Kayla.

HEY.

A ping from Kayla popped up in the corner of Lynn's vision.

I TALKED TO MY DAD. HE WOULD LOVE TO REPRE-SENT YOU. HAVE YOU THOUGHT ANY MORE ABOUT IT?

Lynn scrunched her nose in thought, then subvo-calized an answer.

HAVEN'T HAD A CHANCE TO TALK TO MOM ABOUT IT.

Kayla didn't visibly react to the answer, but her reply popped up soon enough.

WE CAN DO A VIRTUAL MEET WITH MY DAD SO HE CAN ANSWER ALL YOUR QUESTIONS. YOUR MOM TOO.

The idea of doing anything of the sort made Lynn want to throw up—not the meeting part, but the discussing of her bizarre and still-surreal rocket to international fame. But she knew deep down that ignoring her problems never led anywhere good. Better to face it head on, even if it was the last thing in the world she wanted to do.

SURE, she finally replied. I'LL ASK MOM ABOUT IT TONIGHT.

She thought that was the end of it, but a few sec-onds later a last reply from Kayla popped up.

THANKS FOR GIVING ME A CHANCE. I WON'T LET YOU DOWN.

An echo of old hurt twisted in Lynn's gut, but all she did was give a little nod. *No reward without risk*—that was Larry's motto. When the only thing at stake was her mercenary reputation in WarMonger, though, such a life philosophy seemed easy.

In the real it was much harder.

Edgar suddenly reached to the side, wrapped his right arm around Dan's head, picked up a handful of Dan's fries with his left hand, pried Dan's mouth open, and shoved the fries into the teen's mouth.

"Eat," Edgar growled, as Dan choked on the fries. "Eat food and for God's sake *shut up*."

"Buff Ah wub just talging abow..." Dan said, spitting fries everywhere.

"Eat food," Edgar growled again, forcing Dan's mouth shut. "Enough *talkie-talk!*"

Everybody was laughing, though Kayla was holding her hand over her mouth in a ladylike fashion as she did so. She met eyes with Lynn and nodded at her.

"Thank you for letting me sit with you," Kayla said, smiling faintly. "This is fun. Way more fun than Elena's crowd."

"That's 'cause we're dorks," Mack said. "Dorks have all the best fun."

Lynn shook her head with a smile as Edgar and Dan continued to argue and Mack seized the opportunity of Kayla's undivided attention to tell her about his "definitely real" girlfriend from Japan.

Class after lunch dragged by, but finally the end-of-day tone rang out and they were free to rendezvous behind the school with Connor to start hunting. They met at the edge of the sports fields and Connor was all business from the start. His plan was for them to go into combat mode near the woods, far enough away from both the school and the mass of TDMs further north to quickly carve out a foothold and then assess their next move. He didn't mention it, but Lynn wondered if he was as interested as she was to see how much the TDMs had respawned where they'd cleared out yesterday.

Things were rough at first—it was clear Mack was feeling nervous and that affected his performance. But Lynn opened a private channel with him and coached him through the best attack strategies using both a melee and ranged weapon in tandem. She didn't ask Connor's permission to do it. She was afraid he'd tell her to leave Mack to figure things out on his own—better to ask forgiveness and all that. Besides, the first half hour of clearing they did was comparatively easy, so she could afford to split her attention.

Once they'd cleared enough to take a breather, they gathered to inspect the overhead map. Southward looked like it had yesterday, though from experience Lynn knew more of the red dots would be aggressive patrolling types than the numerous gatherers they'd faced yesterday. She had no idea why aggressive types respawned faster and in greater numbers than gather types, but at least it meant there was never any shortage of monsters to kill for experience.

To the north, though, things were different.

"Whoa," Mack said.

"Yeah, really," Dan agreed. "What does the game think we are, terminator bots? It would take us *days* to kill that many monsters, at least if we care about our health and combat scores."

Lynn didn't respond, and neither did Connor. Whether to present its players with a challenge, or because the algorithm was hiding some sort of big prize up that way, the clusters and curving lines of red dots blocking their way north had grown thicker and extended even closer to the edge of the woods than yesterday.

"I wonder..." Lynn began, then realized she'd said it out loud and stopped.

"Go on," Connor said, giving her a nod.

"Well, I wonder if the TDM increase is a higher spawn rate, or if the game is shifting forces in response to our attack yesterday."

"How so?" Connor asked.

"Think about the TD Hunter's storyline," she said. "I know the in-game narrative is a bit lighter than most gamers are used to, but this is a global fight of man versus monster. We're supposed to advance in levels to gain enough power and experience to take out the monsters before they overwhelm everything. But also, our 'forces' don't know much about these monsters in the first place, so part of our job is collecting data and identifying new threats. These bosses the TDMs circle around seem like an important key. I mean, the gather types we kill don't respawn as much as the aggressives do, so maybe that's the TDMs' weakness, you know? And that's why they protect them like they do?

"I like the way the game's algorithm keeps us guessing and the narrative doesn't lay out a linear storyline like a lot of other FPS games. It's kinda open world meets adventure puzzle game meets first-person shooter. Obviously, we can never win the game by killing *all* the TDMs, that'd be impossible. And obviously the game is trying to hint at *something* by massing all these monsters between us and whatever is north. I wonder what we'd find if we made a big circle instead of trying to assault directly through."

Lynn looked around at the guys and noted with

satisfaction that Dan's expression had transformed
into one of intense thought as he stared off over
their heads, while Connor had that unfocused look of
someone studying their AR interface. Mack's brow was
furrowed in worry—probably still hung up on the solid
mass of red on their overhead map, but Edgar looked
oddly amused. When their eyes met, he tapped the
side of his forehead and nodded at her in approval,
as if acknowledging some brilliant leap of deduction
on her part.

She rolled her eyes, but Edgar just winked.

"That's a very interesting observation, Raven," Connor
finally said, his eyes refocusing on their group. "We may
even check it out at some point. But with the national
championship ahead of us, our priorities are clear. We
aren't here to play through the game narrative, we're
here to reach Level 40 and become the most technically
skillful players in the world. That's the only way we'll
win. So, for now, let's stick to the basics and work on
our assault technique while using this helpful mass to
accelerate our leveling. Hunting near the school gives
us more time to practice. Obviously, the terrain isn't
ideal." He glanced toward the woods and frowned.
"But it will be good practice for whatever they set up
at the national competition. We don't know what sort of
terrain they'll use, so we should be ready for anything."

It wasn't what she wanted to hear, but Connor's
point made sense, so she suppressed her curiosity
to focus on the fight ahead. She'd never been one
for game storylines, preferring to stick to what she
was good at: killing things in the most efficient way
possible. There was just something about this game
that irked her, something that made her curiosity itch.

Now was not the time to be curious, though. Instead, she put on her Larry calm and got out her batons while sinking into that ultrafocused mindset she'd used for years to kick butt and earn money.

The next few hours were grueling but satisfying. More than once, Lynn was grateful that it was October and not August. The day was cloudy and their exertions kept them comfortably warm instead of giving them heatstroke. The massive amounts of experience they were racking up got them to Level 26 late in the afternoon after a fight with a crowd of Managals that split and split again each time one of them was killed. The willowy, long-limbed monsters were unusually aggressive, more so than Lynn remembered when they'd first encountered the monster type several levels ago. Did it have anything to do with what they might or might not be guarding?

Lynn put it down to her imagination and focused on keeping Mack's head in the game. He was improving but had a tendency to get overwhelmed when they were in the thick of it. Edgar was as unflaggingly enthusiastic about blasting things to bits as always, and Connor was as quietly efficient as Dan was noisily lethal. Their team captain's reprimands for Dan's constant quips grew less as the battle grew more fierce, and Lynn was silently grateful. As much as she appreciated Connor's experience and professionalism, they weren't his ARS team, and he shouldn't try to make them fit his boring, vanilla athlete mold.

They were gamers and geeks, and proud of it.

By the time they'd made it a hundred yards further into the woods than the previous day, Connor finally called it quits. With the coming evening they'd started getting harried by Yaguar, the scarily fast upgrade of Stalkers. It reminded Lynn of the Vargs' behavior, though the wolflike monsters were so low level they were merely a nuisance now.

Skadi's Wolves were met at the southern edge of the woods by a larger group of drones than yesterday. Lynn wondered with a sinking stomach if the word had spread and drones would now start camping out around this hunting site like they often loitered around her apartment. If this kept up, obsessed fans and lens junkies were sure to follow, eager to watch battles live. That was why Skadi's Wolves had always rotated hunting spots before, so their movements wouldn't be predictable.

Well, Lynn wouldn't say anything. Connor either knew what to expect and had a plan, or would come up with a plan when the time came.

Connor didn't try to "escort" her home this time, a fact which seemed to cheer Edgar up immensely. On the airbus ride he was unusually chipper, at least for Edgar, which meant he was mildly talkative instead of mostly silent. Lynn enjoyed their quiet banter, and Edgar even asked how her "other" gig had been going. His exaggerated eyebrow wiggles made it clear he meant WarMonger, but she just shook her head, since Mack was sitting right next to them.

Besides, thinking about WarMonger made her sad. She missed playing it—missed being Larry with no worries but winning her fights and collecting her bounty, missed the quips, even missed her late-night research on military forums. There simply wasn't time anymore. She had different priorities now, though that didn't soften the ache of knowing all the years she'd spent building her reputation was slowly wasting away.

After she made it home, she took longer in the

shower than normal. Her muscles needed it. Connor had pushed them *hard*, which was good for them, but also incredibly exhausting. She still had homework to do, not to mention catching up with her mom who she'd hardly seen all week. That Friday Matilda had only a half shift, so they were having a late dinner together.

Lynn ate heartily, but quietly. So much had happened in the last few days, and she wondered if she could get away with not mentioning most of it. That, though, ran the risk of Matilda catching the gossip from the streams rather than the real story from her, and that wouldn't be good.

"Honey, the school sent me a notice that they had a power malfunction yesterday that cut the school day short. Did everything go all right today?"

So much for not mentioning it.

"Um, yeah, it was all fine. And yesterday wasn't a big deal. We just sat around in the cafeteria for a while, then they sent us home early. Though, I stayed and went hunting with, um, my team."

"I bet a lot of students wished you could have a few more power malfunctions," Matilda said, smiling.

"Yeah, probably." Lynn grinned back.

"Well, thank God it wasn't the hospital again. They claim they've fixed the glitch that knocked out our backup system when the grid went down. I really wish GForce would get its act together and figure out what bug keeps causing all these blackouts. Did you hear there was another airbus crash in New York? There were no casualties this time, thankfully—the nearby power nodes got it enough juice to slow before it hit the ground. But no one in the news can explain why fully charged batteries would spontaneously just shut off. Like they'd been sucked dry in an instant or something. You wouldn't believe the conspiracy theories I've heard flying around."

"Let me guess," Lynn said, stabbing a chunk of cheese-covered broccoli with her fork, "somehow the Chinese are involved, right?"

Matilda snorted and shook her head.

"Apparently this is just the start of a global takeover by the Commies, either Russia or China, take your pick. Most are betting on China, since they're obviously the ones in charge of the TransAsia alliance, no matter what the PR streams say. I've heard every bit of nonsense you can think of, from remote-activated EMP chips in every battery manufactured in China, to hackers taking over the power grid, to backdoor kill switches in the algorithms running global infrastructure."

"To be fair," Lynn said, gesturing with her fork, "you've been telling me about how the Chinese have been tightening their hold on their global 'partners' for years in, like, South America and Africa. Why else would they have invested billions in building up those developing countries? But the US is different, right? I thought the last president promised a complete ban on Chinese-made parts for all critical infrastructure and military equipment?"

"Just because he promised it doesn't mean it *happened*, dear. That's the beauty of being a politician. Once you've been elected, you don't have to keep your promises unless it's politically expedient. Besides, what about the companies who found creative workarounds through third-party suppliers to cut the cost of such a massive transition?"

Lynn frowned and chewed her food, troubled by the thought.

"But enough about gloomy politics. How is hunting going? Find any new monsters recently?"

Lynn nearly choked on the bite she was swallowing but managed to wash it down with a few gulps of milk without killing herself.

"Uhhh, it's been good..."

"Why does it sound like there's a 'but' in there?" Matilda asked, raising an eyebrow.

"Weeell, the team has, um, switched a few things up."

"Do tell," her mom said, obviously having no intention of letting Lynn off easy.

Lynn took a deep breath, then spoke in a rush.

"Ronnie kicked me off the team because he's an insecure jerkhole, but then we voted *him* off the team instead, and then we recruited Connor Bancroft to fill his spot as team captain, and Connor is *a lot* better and we're doing good now. Oh, and Kayla has dumped Elena's crowd and wants us to be friends again."

In the stunned silence that followed, Matilda blinked a few times, then cleared her throat.

"Goodness. Well, that all sounds like a change for the better, but isn't Connor Bancroft the captain of your rival team?"

"Yeah, he used to be. But he got sick of Elena and quit to come to our team."

"Oh. Are you sure he's...right, for your team?"

"Because people who hang out with Elena tend to be arrogant bullies?"

Matilda nodded, a wry look on her face.

"Yeah, I was worried about that too, but...well, so far he seems okay." She didn't mention his odd behavior the other evening. She was even tempted to "forget" to mention their Saturday plans but couldn't quite bring herself to stoop to that level of dishonesty, despite Connor's veiled barb about Lynn's lack of autonomy. It had been very difficult for Matilda to adjust to Lynn's newly active life after all those years Lynn had spent gaming safely in her room. Lynn knew exactly how hard it was to face your anxiety, whether you were an image-conscious teenager or a trauma-scarred mother. She didn't want to betray her mother's trust after they'd worked so hard to build it.

"Oh, and, um, I'm having a meeting with Connor tomorrow evening to talk about team stuff and how to recruit sponsorships for Skadi's Wolves."

"A meeting?" That really got Matilda's eyebrows up.

"Yeah, a meeting. Nothing weird, he just offered to help strategize since he's negotiated a few sponsorship contracts before—you know because he's captained the ARS team at school and everything."

"I see." Lynn's mother pursed her lips. "And this 'meeting' is in a public place?"

Lynn rolled her eyes.

"Yes, *Mom*. We're going to grab a bite somewhere cheap after we finish hunting for the day."

"Oh? A dinner meeting? Sounds . . . portentous."

"*Moooom*," Lynn groaned. "It's not like that."

"Don't be naive, sweetheart. I know you've . . . struggled with how you see yourself. But even you can't deny you've really changed over the past five months. You looked good before, but now you look fantastic. Don't underestimate the effect that has on boys. They can't help it. It's biological—and a good thing too, or the human race would have died off millennia ago."

"The guys on my team never seem to make a big deal about it," Lynn argued.

"They're your childhood friends, honey. That gives them some familiarity to hide behind. But I wouldn't say *none* of them have noticed."

Lynn's brow creased.

"What are you talking about?"

Her mother pursed her lips again, but this time in an unsuccessful effort to hide a smile.

"Don't mind me. You'll figure it out, if he ever gets up the guts to say something."

"You're crazy, Mom," Lynn said, shaking her head and absolutely *not* thinking about Edgar. Her mother was imagining things, plain and simple.

"Well, just promise me you'll be safe. No going anywhere alone with this Connor. I made an exception for Edgar when you needed to practice your gaming because you all have known each other for so long. But you don't know Connor and it's just good sense to be cautious."

"I get it, Mom. I promise, I'll be careful."

"Good. Now, what is this you mentioned about Kayla? She was visiting the other day and I was really surprised to see her. I thought you two..."

"Yeah," Lynn shrugged. "Well, apparently she's finally 'seen the light.' I kinda feel sorry for her, having to put up with Elena for years. She said Elena has always bullied her and the other girls in their clique. Elena is a poster girl for controlling, spiteful, and mean, so it doesn't surprise me. I'm just glad she finally got up the nerve to tell Elena to get lost. I'm not sure about being friends, but...well she offered to help me."

"Oh? In what way?"

"Do you remember her stepdad? Apparently, he owns some kind of PR company called Global Image Consulting and is interested in representing me, or maybe the team. She made it sound like his company would act as a go-between and manage our public presence so we can focus on competing."

"That sounds wonderful, dear! You don't seem very excited, though. What's the matter?"

"Well..." Lynn paused, not wanting to sound petty or whiney. "I guess I'm still coming to terms with Kayla *not* being one of the mean girls, you know? Not that she was ever really mean personally, she just hid behind Elena. But she stood by for years while... you know." Lynn shrugged, not sure what else to say.

"Oh honey," Matilda said, and reached out to squeeze Lynn's hand. "That must be really hard for you." She was silent for a while, her eyes going distant in thought. Finally she said, "Life is never simple, and I don't have a perfect answer for you. I wish I did. As your mom I wish I could just make everything better. But that would rob you of the important experience of dealing with life yourself and growing into the wonderful, mature woman that you're becoming." She smiled at Lynn and gave her hand another squeeze, then let go and leaned back.

"I will say, though, that people *can* change. Forgiveness isn't about ignoring the hurt done to you, or about allowing someone to *keep* hurting you. It's about willingly accepting the *burden* of that harm, and in doing so taking away its ability to keep hurting you. You can forgive Kayla and overcome how she hurt you in the past without having to be friends with her now. Maybe you'll never be friends again. But *you* have the power to lay to rest whatever is between you. It won't be easy. It never is. But that's your decision, and nothing she can do will change that, because it's your choice to accept. Or not. Friendships are hard, sweetie. So hard. But the reward is worth the risk, even when you get hurt."

Lynn made a face, but nodded, her mind full of things to think about. There was a moment of silence, then her mother spoke again, her words hesitant.

"Do . . . do you want to know how I learned all that about forgiveness?"

Lynn's eyes widened, and she nodded eagerly. Her mother took a deep breath.

"A long time ago, when you were very little, I hurt your father. Badly. I won't go into details because it doesn't matter. It was stupid and impulsive and foolish, and he had every right to hate me for it. There was even a part of me that *wanted* him to hate me for it, because I honestly deserved it."

"But he didn't, did he?" Lynn whispered. Her eyes burned and her heart ached, knowing exactly what her dad had done, because that was the kind of person he'd been.

"No, he didn't," Matilda echoed, then smiled, though it was overshadowed by the lines of sorrow on her face. "Of course, he needed some time to come to terms with it—anyone would have. But instead of holding onto my mistakes and letting them fester between us, he wholeheartedly accepted the hurt and then let it go. He never brought it up again in any argument and never made me feel guilty about it, even though I'm sure the pain of it affected him for years afterward. He bore the burden of it for my sake, and it set the example for our relationship for the rest of our marriage."

"Wow."

Matilda nodded, and after that neither of them spoke for a while. They finished their meal and then went about the cleanup together in a silent dance of familiarity built over their years of loneliness together.

After they finished, as Lynn was heading out of the kitchen to get her homework and evening training done, her mother spoke again.

"For what it's worth, honey, I do think you should give Kayla a second chance, if you can. I've heard good things about her stepdad, and I'd be interested to hear what his company can offer. You need all the help you can get, and I hate watching how much stress you're going through without being able to do a darn thing to help. You know my schedule for the weekend, maybe you could contact Kayla and arrange a conference call or something with her stepdad?"

Lynn took a deep breath, then nodded. She hated the idea of contacting and arranging and conference calling. But hopefully if things with Kayla's stepdad worked out, she wouldn't have to worry about it—or the paparazzi—anymore.

The very last thing Steve Riker wanted to do was talk to a punk like Ronnie Payne. The kid reminded him of some of the nightmare officers he'd had during his career—the kind you couldn't work with, you just had to endure until you could escape them.

But he'd promised Mr. Krator he'd look out for Lynn, and despite Ronnie's most recent asinine choices, Steve had a feeling about the kid's future with Skadi's Wolves. And heck, that kid needed the mentoring *way* more than Lynn did. That girl had her head on straight. She only needed a nudge here and there to remind her of her own worth.

But Ronnie Payne? Steve had shaken his head sadly after refreshing his memory on the kid's file. That boy had really gotten the short end of the stick. Didn't excuse his behavior, but what kid whose mom had abandoned him to run off with another man, and whose dad buried the pain of his wife's betrayal under flaming misogyny, wouldn't be messed up?

There would be no "fixing" Ronnie Payne. But maybe Steve could get the kid to open up a bit and start thinking about his behavior and how it could be better.

Talk about a Hail Mary. But he had to try.

He put the call through, and fortunately—or unfortunately, depending on how you saw it—Ronnie answered.

"Uh, hello?"

"Mr. Payne? This is Steve from TD Hunter customer support. I'm calling to follow up on your recent team assignment changes. We wanted to make sure everything on our end was working and you didn't need any further support." As far as excuses to start a conversation went, it wasn't a bad one. Now all Steve had to do was get Ronnie to open up.

"Uh, no, I'm good, thanks."

"That's great. We at TD Hunter are dedicated to making sure our players have a seamless experience on our platform. Now, I also work in our tactical department, and I know something like a team change can be disruptive to your normal training regime. Can I offer any advice or resources to help you and the CRC continue to advance toward your goals?"

Steve didn't even need a script by this point. He'd

become fluent in "customer supportese" pretty quickly, considering the hundreds of calls he'd made since he was pulled into this whole circus. Plus, it wasn't that different from the diplomatic bureaucratese enlisted guys like him used on their officers. Well, the bad officers anyway. The good ones you could just talk straight to.

Good ones like Lynn.

"Uhhhh, I don't think so," Ronnie replied. The hesitation in his "uhhhh" belied his words. Steve smiled grimly and dug deeper.

"It's perfectly normal to feel out of place when learning to work with a new group of people, Mr. Payne. It's one reason we offer the full spectrum of support that we do, from technical to tactical. Are there any particular concerns on your mind?"

"So, what, you all are giving out relationship advice now? That seems weird."

To you and me both, kid. To you and me both.

"Think of it more as navigating the tactically nuanced minefield that is team dynamics. Since the TD Hunter championship is team based, and the technology of it is so new and cutting edge, we wanted to make sure we offered every possible tool to our Hunter Strike Teams that we have available. Believe me, Mr. Payne, not every player gets personalized calls from TD Hunter support." Steve smiled as he spoke, using a conspiratorial tone to make the kid feel special. Stroking Ronnie's ego was kind of the opposite of what the kid needed, but how else was he supposed to get Ronnie to open up?

"Well, that's cool, I guess. I dunno...my team captain is...not that great."

If only you knew the things Lynn has said about you, kid. Steve shook his head; glad he wasn't on a vid call and having to keep a straight face.

"How so, Mr. Payne? If you give me a little more detail, I could offer some advice."

"Uhhh, well, she's pretty much incompetent, knows nothing about gaming, and only cares about her stream followers. I don't even know why she's playing this game."

"I see." Steve grinned to himself, unable to hold it back at the ridiculousness of the situation this kid had gotten himself into. But he carefully wiped it from his face before he went on. Hearing smiles was a real thing. "It's understandable that some team dynamics don't work out. Have you considered joining a different team?"

"Well, yeah, my *own* team that I built from the ground up," Ronnie said, resentment lacing his words with ugliness. "They mutinied and kicked me out over some petty argument."

Steve took a deep breath and reminded himself that the customer was always right, while simultaneously wanting to smack this kid over the head. How in the world did he say "You done screwed up" without saying "You done screwed up"?

"That sounds . . . terrible. What was their grievance? That might shed some light on the best way to tackle the situation."

There was a pregnant silence and Steve mentally crossed his fingers.

"They, uh, said I wasn't a team player," Ronnie muttered.

Understatement of your life, kid.

"But it wasn't my fault, I swear!" the boy continued. "There's this girl on the team who's always doing her own thing and never listens to anything I say. The guys all *get* gaming, you know? But this girl just doesn't understand. Totally unreliable. I told her to shape up or get out and the rest of the team turned against me."

Steve rolled his eyes. He knew in far greater detail than either Ronnie or Lynn would ever suspect *exactly* what went on in Skadi's Wolves. This kid was blowing smoke up his anus and right out his mouth.

"Ah! I see. So, I suppose this incident occurred *after* you'd already explained the problem to her in detail and worked one-on-one to understand her specific struggles while improving her professional development and team-building skills? You know, all the usual things a team captain is in charge of doing?"

"Uhhh, what?"

Give me one week with this kid in basic training. One week. That'd shape him up.

"Well, generally in team environments," Steve explained with methodical patience, "the members of the team are the captain's responsibility. Not just their welfare but their performance. And it's in the captain's best interest to develop rapport and understanding with his team members so as to best address each one's specific issues and help them overcome their weaknesses. After all, we each have our own foibles and areas we can improve. It's up to the team leader to identify those areas and come alongside their members to grow as individuals and team players."

There was a long silence.

"Uhhh, sure, sure. Yeah. That stuff. I did ... something like that, I guess."

Steve rubbed his temples. If only this kid would stop lying to himself for one second. Maybe if Steve gave him a little push...

"And, of course, a captain is also responsible for his own professional development, so I'm sure you engaged in regular self-reflection, sought feedback from your team members on your leadership effectiveness, and conducted further reading and research to expand your knowledge of sound leadership techniques?"

"What? No. We barely had time to get our homework done and still hunt enough to qualify for the competition. I didn't have time for all that shit."

"Understandable," Steve said, consciously relaxing his jaw to avoid gritting his teeth. "Would you say your current team captain engages in any of these proven behaviors to improve team cohesion and effectiveness?"

Ronnie snorted.

"Absolutely not. She's a total airhead and a jerk. But, I mean, she's a *girl*, so you can't expect much else."

Oooh boy. Here we go. Time to take off the kid gloves.

"Of course. It all makes sense, now. Because having breasts and a vagina obviously make it impossible for girls to become competent in basic human skills like logic, reason, problem solving, hand-eye coordination, and following instruction?"

"W-what? I mean—that's not—they're just—"

"Can you explain to me exactly, in scientific terms, why a girl would be any less competent at games than a boy, Mr. Payne?"

"I-I don't like your tone, man. I thought this was supposed to be customer support or something."

"This *is* customer support, Mr. Payne." *Support to*

all our other customers who have to put up with you. "Knowledge is power, and we want to do everything we can to empower you to succeed. Are you aware, for instance, that here at Tsunami Entertainment, our user base is evenly split, fifty-fifty between male and female?"

"Whaaaat? No way. Girls don't game."

"Our registration servers would beg to differ. Are you also aware that, on average across game genres, women make up approximately thirty-five percent of top-tier players?"

"That—that, sounds weird. I game a whole lot and I don't see girls in the top tiers."

"You game 'a whole lot' *in virtual*, where a person's avatar and account name often have no bearing on their sex. Is it possible you have gamed with many top-tier women, and simply weren't aware of it?"

"I mean . . . I guess it's possible, but I doubt it. I can tell when I'm playing with a girl, they just act different."

You poor, clueless child. I hope I'm there to see your face on the day you find out who Larry Cough-lin really is . . .

"Speaking as someone who works in the industry," Steve said, unable to keep the dryness out of his voice, "I can assure you the statistics from the last decade show that, not only do women game just as much as men, they make up a statistically significant number of professional gamers. There is no evidence whatsoever to back up the idea that women are less capable of gaming or less capable of gaining advanced skills for those who spend comparable amounts of time on it as their male counterparts. Therefore, it would likely be in your best interests as an aspiring professional gamer to base your actions and attitudes on the proven and vital role women play in the gaming industry as a whole. Otherwise, you risk lessening your potential for success."

There was a long silence, and Steve hoped and prayed that something, *anything* he'd just said had made it through Ronnie's thick, clueless skull. When the silence kept stretching on with no response from the kid, Steve cleared his throat.

"Are there any other questions or issues I can help you with today, Mr. Payne?"

"Um...yeah, maybe. Let's say, hypothetically, one of my teammates was a girl."

Hypothetically? Steve thought. *What is Elena, chopped liver?*

"How do I...well, how do I deal with them? Like, how do I know how to talk to them and stuff?"

Steve rubbed his temples again, holding on to the shreds of his patience and reminding himself that Ronnie Payne had grown up without a mother, and likely no female role model in his life beyond various teachers. For a brief moment, he fantasized about putting the kid's *dad* into boot camp for a week—the jerk of a man obviously had no idea how to be a father if his kid was *this* clueless about women at almost eighteen years old. *The odds that this kid is a virgin is one thousand percent,* Steve thought, and took a deep breath.

"I suggest, Mr. Payne, that you treat them like a person."

"Uh, okay?"

"As confusing as women might be at times, they are not a different species. Men and women are all human beings, and a good place to start would be to treat your teammates—*all* your teammates—with civility and respect, regardless of how they look or act, and regardless of your opinions toward them. A little humility goes a long way too," he added because he just couldn't help it.

"Okaaaay, but—"

A slamming sound in the background of Ronnie's voice feed interrupted the kid, and shouting became audible.

"Ronnie? Where the heck is my food? How many times do I have to tan your hide to get it through your thick skull that I expect my food *ready to eat* as soon as I get home from work?"

"Calm down, Dad. It's keeping warm in the oven!" Ronnie yelled.

"You can tell time, can't you, boy? Why isn't it on the table? You better not be playing games in your room again. I told you, no more gaming nonsense if you got another C or below—"

The call abruptly cut off, and in the ensuing silence Steve stared blankly at his display screen in front of him.

"Good luck, kid," he finally muttered to himself and shook his head.

Lynn both welcomed and dreaded Saturdays. No school meant a full day of training and hunting. But training meant she had to complete The Run From Hell. It consisted of slipping out a side door of her building and sneaking behind it and through the greenway to run a few laps around the Heather apartment complex. She was grateful for the later sunrise of the coming winter because it meant she didn't have to get up as early to avoid nosey drones.

Even so, she still hated running with the burning

passion of a thousand suns. Every time she passed someone else jogging on the sidewalk who smiled and waved cheerily, she had to resist the urge to punch the perky look right off their faces.

After exercise, a shower, and going through some simulator exercises, she headed out to meet the team back at their school. She took the roundabout way to the airbus platform and wore a bulky coat with the hood up to avoid detection from the cluster of drones hovering above it. It wouldn't throw off those who would just show up at the school anyway, hoping her team would be there. But there was nothing she could do about that.

Sure enough, a flock of buzzing "stream vultures" were already hovering over their team meeting place behind the school when Lynn got there. She was the last to arrive, so they got right to business. Connor set up a group call to TD Hunter support and they took care of changing the team membership, all of them subvocalizing in their interactions to avoid the eavesdropping drones above. It went smoothly, as if the tech who helped them had been expecting their call—which, maybe he had.

It felt weird when they all had to verbally confirm Connor as their new team captain. A twinge of unease in her gut made her wonder if they were making the right decision, but she shook the feeling away and focused on moving forward and making things work.

The rest of the day was one long, grueling battle. They took a break at noon and retreated to the edge of the woods to order a drone-delivered lunch. But other than that, it was hours of slashing, stabbing, and dodging. Even Lynn, who loved the thrill of the hunt and relished the time and space to keep perfecting her technique, was flagging by the late afternoon. Connor didn't seem too affected, but then he was the only one among them who was a professional athlete and had the body to back it up. Edgar, Dan, and Mack didn't complain—well, not much—but their form and tactics slid further and further the later in the day they fought.

And still, the monsters kept coming.

Lynn began to think that their frontal assault, beyond the benefit of experience gain, was never going to succeed, no matter how hard they fought. The sheer number of monsters that kept coming, rank after rank, reminded her of the qualifier tournament and what it must have felt like for those unfortunate teams who'd tried to run straight into the fray from their original lineup instead of skirting the edges and coming in from the side like Skadi's Wolves and the CRCs had done.

By the time Connor called for a final retreat and they exited combat mode to head back through the woods toward the school, it was after five and starting to get dim under the cover of the trees.

"I'm so tired I think I'm going to die," Dan groaned, dragging his feet dramatically through the leaf litter.

"Buck up, Danny boy," Edgar said, "at least you aren't Ronnie. He has to fight *and* deal with Elena."

Dan shuddered. "I'd rather fight a campaign-level raid boss by myself. I'd have a better chance of survival."

"I wonder how he's doing," Mack said, sounding genuinely worried despite his own drooping shoulders and dragging feet.

"Reaping the rewards of his own decisions," Lynn replied shortly. She wouldn't wish Elena on her worst enemies, but she still refused to feel sorry for Ronnie. He'd made his own bed, now he could sleep in it. "Hey, Mack, you did great today," she went on, hoping to distract her teammates from gloomy thoughts. "Your practice is definitely paying off."

"Really?" Mack asked.

"Yeah, totally. The way you took on that brood of Creepers that popped up while I was being mobbed by Namahags was perfect. You kept your head, stayed moving, and got the job done."

"Thanks, Lynn," Mack said, and grinned.

"You'll still never pass me on the leaderboards," sang Dan, making little shooting motions at Mack.

"Gloat all you want, Dan. You can just never admit they weigh the stats unfairly."

"You're just sore that I'm better than you because of my super-ninja Bruce Lee-level Asian powers."

"Riiight," Mack said, and exchanged a long-suffering look with Lynn.

"Hey, is it just me, or is your goatee a little longer?" Lynn asked, noticing it for the first time.

Mack actually blushed.

"Uh, yeah. Riko likes it, so I told my mom I wasn't going to shave it off anymore just because she thinks I look scruffy. It's had a bit more time to fill in."

"Mack and a scam bot, sittin' in a tree, K-I-S-S-I-N-G—" Dan sang.

"Shut up! You're just jealous that being a famous gamer hasn't gotten *you* a girlfriend."

"Are you kidding me? They're lining up in virtual, begging for my attention. I could have my pick if I wanted."

"In virtual, huh?" Edgar asked, eyes crinkling in amusement. "You know most of them are probably bots, too, right? That makes you exactly the same as Mack."

Dan elbowed Edgar, which was about as effective

as elbowing a mountain. Then the three of them were off bickering good-naturedly again.

Lynn rolled her eyes, trying not to think about the topic of boyfriends and girlfriends and dating. Connor walked on the opposite side of their group from her, quiet as usual. But she still felt unnaturally aware of his presence, as if he were staring at her, even though he wasn't. She was grateful for the distance between them, so she didn't have to feel awkward every time she glanced his way and noticed his form-fitting hunting uniform. It was impossible to look at him and *not* notice it. He was eminently noticeable, and that didn't bode well for her, considering she was meeting with him later that evening.

Somehow, she got home without collapsing and took a very hot shower, hoping it would relax her. When all it did was make her sleepy, she turned the cold water on and finished up hopping from foot to foot and cursing under her breath, alert even if she wasn't very happy.

On a weird whim, she left her hair unbraided and brushed it out over her shoulders. At least with it down, she could hide behind it if need be. She didn't have any "nice" clothes, so she simply wore her most flattering pair of smart clothes she'd bought at the Lindale Mall for school. The autumn yellow she'd picked for the blouse brought out the gold of her wolf eyes in a way she really liked, and she made the skintight jeans black to match her hair. She slid her dad's knife into one of her pockets and patted it through the fabric, reassured by the weight of it there.

"You look nice, honey," Matilda commented from the couch when Lynn exited her room shortly before seven.

"Uh, thanks?"

Her mom smiled.

"Remember to stay in public and be back by nine, all right?"

"Got it." Lynn gave her a thumbs-up. "Have fun mindlessly browsing the streams."

"Oh, I think I'll catch up on the news," Matilda commented, to which Lynn made a face of disgust. "Don't give me that, young lady. Someone has to pay attention to what's going on in the world, otherwise who will keep the politicians accountable?"

"Yeah, yeah, yeah. I know. I just hate the idea of having to wade through it all, trying to figure out what's true and what's lies."

Matilda sighed. "Me too, honey. Me too."

"Good luck." Lynn gave her mom a little wave.

"You too, and be safe."

Her mother's words echoed in her ears as she headed for the front doors of her building. At the entrance she spotted Connor waiting for her on the bench outside, the same bench she'd sat on many times with Edgar. She was distracted from that thought by the inescapable image of Connor's six-foot-plus frame lounging across the bench, his well-fitted t-shirt and jeans proclaiming in no uncertain terms that he had a gorgeous body and absolutely knew it.

The sight stopped Lynn short just inside the doors, and she swallowed.

"Are you quite all right, Miss Lynn? Your heart rate has increased precipitously and your core temperature is rising as well. Are you unwell?"

It took two tries before she successfully subvocalized a reply.

"I'm fine. Ignore your sensors, they're probably malfunctioning."

She'd left the TD Hunter app running mostly as a safety backup, even though there were any number of security apps she could have used, or even the built-in service AI of her LINC. But none of them were Hugo. She knew it was silly to feel a connection with a computer program, but she couldn't help it. So, she chalked it up to user preference and let the app run.

"I beg your pardon! My sensors are most certainly *not* malfunctioning, and if they were, I can assure you that I would know."

"Don't get your panties in a wad," Lynn subvocalized, still trying to will her feet to move. Conner had noticed her and was rising from the bench, a handsome smile on his face. "Just hush up and stop distracting me. Your job is to call the police if Connor tries to ax murder me, not to track my heart rate and body temperature."

"Do you anticipate such an eventuality? Or are you simply indulging in the annoyingly human pastime of exaggeration?"

"You're the genius computer program, you figure it out. Now hush. I have to pretend to be functional and you're not helping."

She exited the doors and attempted a polite smile as Connor approached, though she suspected a glance in a mirror would have shown something more akin to a grimace. He looked her up and down, and his smile turned even brighter.

"Hey Lynn. You look really pretty this evening. Ready to grab some food?"

She nodded, tongue-tied and glad nothing Connor had said required a verbal response. He'd noticed her body, which triggered years of learned anxiety and trauma . . . but the notice had been positive, so that did all sorts of weird and new things that she had no idea how to deal with. Was feeling elated and mortified at the same time a normal thing? Or was her brain malfunctioning?

More importantly, could she pretend to have sudden onset muteness all evening and get away with it?

He led her to the small parking lot of her apartment complex, where finally she became aware enough of her surroundings to notice the flock of drones following them.

Well, duh.

Lynn ground her teeth together and resisted the urge to look up. How could Connor act so at ease with this mob after him? Maybe he was used to it? Or maybe she was just messed up and normal people didn't get anxiety attacks from being followed around by cameras.

It turned out Connor—or perhaps his father— owned a small electric car. Most people just used public transportation or ride sharing, since it was far cheaper and almost as convenient. But some people had the luxury of affording the privacy and autonomy of their own car. Lynn was simultaneously relieved and annoyed by it. It meant no staring strangers, but also no buffer between her and Connor.

Well, except Hugo, for whatever he was worth.

The space inside the car felt ten times smaller than it probably was, though Connor seemed completely unaffected. His entire demeanor was relaxed, and he chatted casually about their recent hunting trips as if this little "meeting" was the most normal thing in the entire world.

It took all of Lynn's self-control to relax her muscles and respond in an equally casual tone. Fortunately, the ride was short. Connor kept things as simple and casual as he'd promised, taking them to a nearby pizza parlor that offered all of Iowa's most delicious and outlandish pizza toppings. Lynn concentrated completely on the food, an easy thing for her to do since she was absolutely starving after all the calories she'd burned that day. Connor took her silent concentration as an invitation to tell her all about his ARS sponsorships, complete with his team's win stats and the records they'd set. It all sounded suspiciously like bragging, except that it was the whole point of their meeting, right? Plus, Connor spoke so matter-of-factly that Lynn couldn't tell if he was incredibly humble, or so massively arrogant he didn't feel the need to hype things up the way Ronnie did all the time.

Whatever the case, the difference between him and Ronnie, not just as team captains but as normally functioning human beings, was stark as day and night.

Good grief, Lynn thought. *Even Connor struggled to deal with Elena. Ronnie is going to get eaten alive.*

"So, what do you think?"

"Huh?" Lynn said, suddenly aware Connor had asked her a question.

A corner of Connor's mouth twitched.

"I said, do you think you'll start taking on sponsorships now?"

"Uhhhhhh, probably?" She'd zoned out of the last few minutes of conversation, so she played it casual and hoped Connor hadn't noticed.

"Good. Just make sure you require that they include the whole team. That way our uniforms will match and we'll get more publicity that way."

"Oh, uh, right. Got it." She didn't, that must have

been part of the conversation she'd missed, but it kinda made sense?

"So, now that we've got that topic out of the way, I'm curious, do you have any big plans after we win the world championship?" He smiled, then took a bite of pizza, making headway into his mostly untouched plate.

"Um, well, probably just go to college and get a degree in game design. That's the prize, after all. I'd love to work for Tsunami Entertainment afterwards, maybe doing play testing or designing mechanics for various games."

"That's cool. So you don't intend to pursue professional gaming as a long-term career?"

Lynn thought about that—*really* thought about it. Nobody had asked her that before, not even her mom, and she wasn't entirely sure of her answer. Finally, she shrugged.

"I really like gaming, but the stress of the competition is pretty intense. Maybe after a while I'll get tired of it, you know? If I have a degree and a job at Tsunami, I can enjoy gaming without all that stress. What about you?"

For some reason that made Connor smile, though it wasn't his usual charming grin. Lynn could see hardness under it, the same hardness she imagined in Larry's eyes whenever she was talking to some cocky newbie who thought Larry was an old geezer who couldn't back up all the hype surrounding his reputation. It was a hardness that demanded respect. And caution.

She kinda liked it.

"Oh, I'm an athlete, through and through," Connor said, mirroring her shrug. "It's what I'm good at, and I enjoy it a lot. Winning is what I do—why fix what isn't broken?"

That was logical enough. It was similar to how she'd felt about WarMonger, at least until TD Hunter had come along.

"So, after TD Hunter, do you think you'll go back to AR sports? Or focus on more traditional gaming? I'm sure there's going to be lots of AR games coming out now that TD Hunter has been such a global hit."

Connor took another bite and thought while he chewed.

"It will likely depend on what opportunities are out there. ARS is what I'm more familiar with, but I'm finding I really enjoy the less ... constrictive aspects of gaming over school sports. Sometimes in ARS, the fun of the game gets lost under a pile of rules and regulations. TD Hunter has been incredibly refreshing. And the company isn't bad either." He winked at her, and Lynn felt her face heat. She ducked her head and took a bite of pizza, hoping Connor hadn't noticed.

This was so, *so* weird. She was having a normal conversation about things she actually cared about with one of the most popular and hot guys at school—a guy that *Elena freaking Seville* had marked as her own. What alternate reality had she been transported to? Was this all some massive joke, and the CRCs were about to jump out from behind the booth on either side and dump ice water on her or something?

"You know, I'm really surprised someone like you has managed to fly under the radar for so long," Connor said, leaning forward and propping both elbows on the table.

Mouth full, Lynn tried to hide her startled look under polite interest, but probably only managed to look constipated.

"You're smart, hardworking, and incredibly skilled

at what you do. It's a good thing you've only gotten into shape recently, or I might've had to fight off all the other boys at school to get to you."

Lynn choked. That led to a coughing fit as she tried to eject pizza from her lungs. She was too busy regaining normal breathing function to object when Connor slid around the table to the bench on her side to give her some helpful slaps on the back.

When she could finally breathe again, she took a long drink of ice water, mostly to cool her flaming cheeks. Not only had she made a fool of herself right after Connor had complimented her, but she was now trapped between a wall and the incredibly well-muscled Connor Bancroft. They were so close she could feel the heat coming off his skin.

"You okay?" he asked.

"Y-yeah," she wheezed. "Just peachy. Thanks."

"Good, I wouldn't want to have to perform CPR, it's not as fun as it looks in the movies." He grinned at her, his eyes on her lips.

CPR? Fun?

"O-okay. Well, now that you mention it, I don't think I can eat anymore, so I should probably be getting back home, you know?"

"Of course. Just let me finish my pizza real quick. It would be a shame to waste such perfection."

Lynn could only nod and sit as still as a statue, afraid if she moved she might accidentally brush up against the statuesque physique beside her demanding her full attention by way of extreme proximity.

"Are you sure you are well, Miss Lynn?" Hugo's voice queried in her ear. "Your heart rate and core temperature have skyrocketed again. According to available medical research, such symptoms indicate the possible onset of heatstroke. Should I summon emergency medical services?"

"I'm inside, you idiot! How could I be getting heatstroke?" Lynn subvocalized, never more grateful for the skill than at that moment.

If an AI could have sniffed in affront, Lynn imagined Hugo would have done so. As it was, Hugo's only means of expression seemed to be with words, which the AI wielded with its usual precision.

"Madam, I am a gaming AI, not a medical diagnostic program. I can only work with what is in front of me, and *you* appear to be on the brink of collapse."

"I'm *fine*. Can you make him eat faster? Because if not, then bug off!"

"That is, I regret to admit, outside my abilities to influence. Therefore, I will, as you say, 'bug off.'"

Lynn might have worried that she'd offended the AI, if she'd had any spare brain cells left to rub together. Unfortunately for her, all of her brain cells were occupied thinking about certain *other* things rubbing together.

Somehow, she survived the excruciating few minutes until Connor finished his food and stood.

"That was some good pizza. Shall we?" he asked, offering his hand.

Lynn froze, staring at the hand like it was a snake about to bite her.

"You know, this is usually the part where you take my hand and I help you out of the booth," Connor said, laughter in his voice. "Did that ice water give you brain freeze or something?"

Or something, Lynn thought and swallowed hard.

Then she summoned all her courage, wiped her sweaty palm on her jeans, and took Connor's hand. It was warm and strong, which made her even more conscious of how clammy her own hand was. Before she could think anything else, he was tugging on her arm and she had to slide out of the seat and stand up to avoid being pulled over face first.

"There we go. That wasn't too hard, now was it?" Connor gave his trademark brilliant smile and Lynn was pretty sure her heart stopped for a second or two for no reason at all.

Yup. No reason.

"Come on, let's get you home."

Instead of letting go, Connor tightened his grip on her hand as he turned toward the door to leave.

"B-but we haven't paid," was all Lynn's panicked brain could come up with as she tried to parse through the possible responses to having her hand held.

Punch him in the face?

Yank her hand away and run like a bat out of hell?

Kiss him?

What the heck?

"Oh, I already paid when we ordered, don't worry about it," he replied, looking at her. He gave an encouraging smile and tugged on her hand. "Come on."

Somehow her leg muscles still functioned, and she found herself walking out of the restaurant, hand in hand with him, a picture-perfect couple for the dozen or so tiny drones hovering outside the entrance. They buzzed about as if in excitement, but Lynn was too busy trying to unfreeze her brain to notice.

Before she'd made any progress, Connor had gotten her into the car and they were headed back toward her apartment. The drive was short and gave her little time to figure out what to do or say when they arrived. She realized too late that her dazed lack of response gave Connor the perfect excuse to come open her door for her and offer his hand again to help her out once he had parked.

"Uh, I'm f-fine, thanks," she said, and heaved herself out of the small car, hoping she didn't end up colliding with Connor's chest in her desperate attempt to escape. He took the hint and stepped aside, but then fell into step very close beside her as she speed walked back to her apartment. His stride was so long he seemed to put forth no effort to keep up, and when she didn't so much as pause at the doors, he nonchalantly followed her in.

When he continued to follow her to the elevator, she stopped and spun around, only to find him so close they were almost touching.

"Oh! Uh, hey, um, I'm j-just going back to my, um, apartment, now. Bye?"

"I had a great time too," he said with a smirk. "And you're welcome." With that, he leaned down and kissed her on the cheek. It was a chaste kiss, but he lingered there for a second before drawing back, the smirk still on his face. "We should do it again sometime. Well, see you Monday!"

Connor turned and left, hands in his pockets, posture relaxed as he swaggered back toward his car. As for Lynn, her brain was making feeble reboot noises in her head as she attempted to regain control over her limbs.

"Miz Raven? Lynn? Is that you?"

An elderly voice called down the hallway, making

Lynn jump and turn, then clutch her chest in relief as she saw who it was.

"Oh, Mr. Thomas. Sorry, I didn't see you there."

"No need to apologize, young lady," the old man said, coming out of his ground floor apartment and closing the door behind him. "I was just heading out to get some fresh air and I thought I heard your voice in the hallway."

"Y-yeah," Lynn laughed, rubbing her damp palms furiously on her thighs, "that was me."

"And who was that handsome young man with you?"

Lynn gulped. "Uhhhh, just some guy?"

"Well, times have certainly changed from when I was your age if young ladies are letting 'just some guy' give them a goodnight kiss." He smiled knowingly as he approached, leaning with every step on his cane.

"Oh, no, no, that wasn't—I mean we're not—I mean he isn't—"

Mr. Thomas held up a weathered hand.

"Do not worry yourself, Lynn. I was merely teasing. Such exploits are far too tiresome to bother with at my age, so I must simply live vicariously through the young and adventurous."

"B-but I'm not living adventurously! I swear!"

By this time her elderly neighbor had reached her, and he raised his hand to give her a gentle squeeze on her shoulder before dropping it again to join his other on the head of his cane. To Lynn's surprise, the kindly gesture made her relax and feel a warm glow in her chest, the exact opposite of what she'd felt mere minutes before when Connor had touched her.

"There is no need to justify yourself either way to

me, my dear. Youth is a time of great uncertainty, change, and exploration. How else are young ones to learn and grow?"

Lynn gave a nervous laugh and rubbed the back of her neck.

"I'm really not looking to learn in, well, *that* department. At least . . . I don't think so? I don't know. It's all pretty confusing."

Mr. Thomas nodded sagely.

"I remember the feeling well. It is perfectly natural. I would advise you to take things slowly, and do not be afraid to ask those you trust for advice. While exploration is healthy, acting in ignorance or on impulse is not, so do not keep your questions and fears to yourself."

"Right. Thanks, Mr.—I mean, Jerald. Thanks." Lynn gave him her first genuine smile of the evening.

"Any time, Lynn."

"Enjoy your walk!"

"I shall endeavor to do so. Have a good evening."

"You too," she said, and gave a wave, then headed off down the hall toward the stairs. As exhausting as the day had been, she needed to burn off some energy. And cool down. Definitely cool down.

Chapter 8

THOUGH CONNOR ARGUED AGAINST IT, THE REST OF them agreed that they still needed to take Sunday off, at least from group hunting. Maybe Connor's parents were used to him being gone every night of the week and all weekend doing training for ARS tournaments, but the rest of their collective parents weren't. Dan's father actually threatened to lock him in his room if he didn't spend at least part of Sunday working on school, and they all agreed they needed a day off if they didn't want to exhaust themselves.

Or flunk out of school.

Lynn slept in—meaning she got up at eight instead of six—and spent the morning doing homework and struggling to stay awake. It wasn't so much that school was boring, but . . . well, most of it was boring. There were exceptions, like her Global Politics and Religion class, whose teacher was rumored among the students to be so controversial that the principal had threatened to fire him multiple times. As far as Lynn could tell, the most controversial thing he'd ever taught them was "trust, but verify," which was pretty much what her mom said anyway.

Near lunchtime she gave up and, desperate for some

way to wake herself up and blow off some steam, logged into WarMonger.

Percy Mustela was not happy. His investment firm had lost a big client, and another one was teetering on the edge. He didn't *know* that it had anything to do with their rival firm's winning streak in their unofficial wargaming. But it sure *felt* like it.

"Bobby, you idiot! Where's my cover fire?"

"One of Grayson's mercs took me out again, that prick. I only just respawned. I don't know if I can get back to your position."

Percy groaned.

"We're never going to hear the end of it if we lose *again*. And I think our senior manager might ban WarMonger completely. Says it's bad for morale."

"It's not our fault! Grayson's team dug up some crazy Tier Two mercs and they're crushing us. I can't even find them half the time. If the team from Investments International hadn't allied with us, we'd already be toast."

"Killing enemy mercs is not your job, moron. That's why we hire our own mercs. Your job is to stay alive!" Percy swore under his breath as streaks of tracer fire missed his head by a breath. He ducked his avatar back behind cover and slammed a health pack. He'd bought the "unlimited first aid" cheat code off some snot-nose teen, so he was popping them like pills. "Just get over here, will you? I'm stuck behind that bombed out hospital. I think they've got a sniper up on the cell tower."

"I'm trying. Ever since Larry Coughlin bought it, none of the other guys we've hired seem to live up to their rep, you know?"

"Larry Coughlin didn't die, you idiot. He probably

just had a medical issue come up or something that keeps him from playing. I heard he's as old as dirt, lives in a wheelchair because of an op gone wrong back when he was a government spook."

"What? No! Larry was spec ops, everybody knows that. He got out and switched to contract work stateside after he caught some shrapnel over in the sand box. Have you *seen* his ranking history? He lives and breathes this stuff. He wouldn't just up and disappear. I'm telling you, he's gotta be dea—"

Bobbyboy123 has been terminated by NewCenturion.

"Bobby, you idiot!" Percy yelled for what felt like the hundredth time. The guy was their firm's best account manager, but his enthusiasm for WarMonger far outstripped his meager talent at virtual gaming. He was the one who hired all the mercs, though, so he was sort of a nerd about them. He was as bad as the lame-os over in HR with their fantasy football teams.

Percy stayed put behind the crumbling hospital wall, trying to decide what to do while explosions and *rat-tat-tat* fire sounded around him. Could he ping one of Investment International's mercs and give them the location of the sniper on the tower?

"Ohmygodohmygod Percy, *he's back*. Larry Coughlin! He just pinged me while I was in cooldown, said he's got some time to kill!"

There was an embarrassing resemblance between Bobby's high-pitched words and the sound Percy's girlfriend made whenever her favorite stream celebrity replied to her comments.

"What are you waiting for? Get him in here! Now!"

Seconds later a notification popped on Percy's display. *Larry Coughlin has joined your team.*

The tension in Percy's chest eased and he felt optimistic for the first time in days. Seconds later, a gravelly voice came over their team channel.

"BenDover69, get off your pimply butt and run for that cell tower."

Percy's optimism disappeared as fast as it had come.

"What? No way, that sniper will frag me before I get even close!"

"You hired me to win, not babysit! Move! Or I'll frag you myself."

That grating, stone-cold voice sent shivers down Percy's spine, and his haptic glove-covered fingers fumbled as they gestured to get his avatar up and running.

"Okay, okay! I'm going, Mr. Coughlin, sir. I'm going."

He didn't even take time to scan for bogies first. He just dashed into the open, juking back and forth in a vain hope that it would keep him alive a little longer.

A loud, echoing crack rang out over the match arena and Percy almost pissed himself. He expected his avatar to drop, but instead a game notification flashed across his vision.

NewCenturion has been terminated by Larry Coughlin.

"Yessss!" Percy said, punching the air and making his avatar do a flailing roll straight into the burned-out husk of an ambulance.

"Stop dancing like a cheap hooker and get under cover!"

Percy swore and followed orders, even as he did an internal dance of glee. *Take that, Grayson.*

The match didn't last long after that. Larry Coughlin rallied the Tier Three mercs Bobby had originally hired to fight for them and they joined up with the mercs from Investments International to sweep the board of the other team. The mercs fought in eerie silence, moving as one as if they shared a hive mind—though probably Larry had just made a private channel to coordinate or something. There were a few more-clever holdouts on Grayson's team, but Larry seemed to know exactly where they would be and took them out like an all-seeing god of WarMonger. Percy laid low and stayed alive, only emerging at the end to meet at the rally point so his avatar could do a victory dance and rub it in Grayson's face.

He saw some of Investments International's mercs at the rally point too, and those sneaky bastards were just standing there, motionless, as if they were going out of their way to keep their avatars from showing any body language or facial expressions via their haptic controllers. They were probably talking in their own private chat, too, like they were too good to mingle with "normal" players.

He made ten times more in the financial industry than any of those creeps could ever dream of, but they thought *he* was the pathetic loser?

He would show—

"Nice doing business with you, BenDover69."

Percy—and his avatar—jumped and he almost squealed like a pig at the ghostly bass voice that caressed his ears. He spun his view and there was the bastard in his legendary Alice the Strange armor.

"*Now* you get to dance," Larry said. "Don't count your money when yer sittin' at the table, don't do a victory dance 'til you're takin' a tally of your slain."

"R-right. Yeah. Thanks, Mr. Coughlin. Bobby'll take care of your payment."

"Already did. He's a decent kid. Good head on his shoulders. You, on the other hand... You're the reason we're called snake eaters, we usually kill and *eat* something like you. 'Cause they're a dime a dozen, there's no season, and they taste like chicken."

Percy was too busy trying to moisten his suddenly dry throat to come up with a retort—which was probably for the best. But he did make a mental note to have Bobby throw something extra nice to the merc to keep his firm on Larry's good side. Last thing he needed was Grayson offering the guy a better price on their next game.

Larry Coughlin's avatar ambled over to the group of other mercs, and one broke off and approached him as if they were having a conversation. Percy shook his head and turned away, putting them from his mind. He had a victory dance to do and he never passed up an opportunity to gloat.

"Hey, kid, fancy meeting you here."

"Hey Steve," Lynn said in Larry's gravelly voice, then remembered to switch off her voice modulator. "Figured you'd be sleeping in on a Sunday. Don't they work you hard enough over at TD Hunter?"

"Ha! Yeah, but between sleep and shooting things, shooting things keeps me more sane."

Lynn grinned. Steve was her kinda guy.

"What about you, kid? I thought you were too busy to play with us mere mortals anymore."

"Oh, I needed a quick pick-me-up. I was falling asleep over the massive pile of homework I gotta finish today."

Steve made a sympathetic noise, but there was humor in his tone when he spoke again.

"The fact that you consider it a pick-me-up to hop into a multiteam battle between a bunch of skill-less Wall Street suits is one reason why you and I get along. Don't think I didn't see you baiting that poor bastard, what's his name, BenDover69?"

Lynn giggled, unable to hold it back when Steve said the idiot's handle out loud.

"Did you see how high he jumped when I came up behind him?"

"Yup. Wouldn't be surprised if the guy pissed his pants in the real."

"I hope he didn't soil his precious suit."

"Come on, kid. That guy isn't in a suit on Sunday morning. He's probably playing in his underwear in some giant New York penthouse apartment."

"Ew. I did *not* need that mental image."

Steve's barking laugh made Lynn grin again. It was *so* nice to be herself around someone who understood both sides, Lynn *and* Larry. She vaguely wondered what it would be like to play WarMonger with Edgar, but Steve's voice distracted her from the thought.

"Hey, I'm glad we bumped into each other. I had an idea about something you said the other day when we were talking—about you not having time to play WarMonger much anymore."

"Oh?"

"Yeah. You were worried Larry was losing his hard-earned rep, and you had a point. Plus, if he disappears entirely just when you're skyrocketing to stardom in TD Hunter, some people might put two and two together."

Lynn hadn't considered that second part, but it made sense.

"So I was thinking: What if you give me and some

of my boys over here at TD Hunter permission to play Larry for you?"

"Uhhh, what?"

"I've already cleared it with Mr. Krator, and it's not like we don't have access to your account."

Lynn's immediate gut reaction was *hell no*. Larry was *hers*. She'd built him from the ground up, put her blood, sweat, and tears into him. Larry wasn't just hers, he was *her*. Sort of. In a weird way.

"Look, kiddo, I know what you're thinking. But you don't have to worry. I know how much Larry means to you, and we over at Tsunami Entertainment respect the, er, heck out of what you've done with him. I promise I won't let anyone within spitting distance of him who I don't personally vet and deem worthy of taking on the mantle of the notorious Larry the Snake. You have my word."

"I . . . well . . . maybe?" she finally said. It wasn't a bad idea, but she felt too emotionally conflicted about the idea to give a straight answer.

"I've got it all worked out," Steve assured her, and Lynn couldn't help but grin at the enthusiasm in his voice. "You'd be surprised how many of the top-tier mercenaries you've already worked with are employees, or at least contractors, here at Tsunami. I know a lot of 'em personally. It's a smaller industry than you'd imagine. Anyway, I'll hand pick a few and swear them to secrecy. I won't even tell them Larry is you, just that Larry's handler is OCONUS for a while and asked for some help keeping the account fresh. Make sure nobody gets cocky and thinks ol' Larry has finally kicked the bucket. We won't do anything crazy. I know you've got some regulars you usually merc for who've taken a pounding in the ranks without you there. I'm sure they'd love to see Larry back. We'll just aim to have him pop up once a week or so, frighten all the newbies, put in his time, and disappear again. It'll keep your name fresh, plus provide the proof you need that Lynn Raven isn't Larry Coughlin, in case anyone starts throwing around theories on the streams or forums. Sound good?"

Lynn had been on the fence, but the more Steve talked, the more comfortable she felt and the wider her grin spread.

"You can't *wait* to swagger around as Larry Coughlin, can you?" she accused him, still smiling. "You sound like a pimply teen about to get his hands on a sweet hotrod."

Steve laughed heartily. "You've caught me. I guess there's no point denying it. I enjoy playing FallujahSevenNiner, but I've just never had enough time to establish a rep like you have. Comes from being a boring adult with responsibilities. You kids spend insane amounts of time in virtual, you know that?"

"Hey, gotta enjoy it while I'm young, right?"

"Ain't that the truth. So what do you say, kid? Will you let me help you out?"

"You mean, will I magnanimously allow you to put your pimply teenage butt in the seat of *my* hotrod?"

"Hey now, I remember a time or two when Fallu put Larry in his place, you can't deny that."

Now it was Lynn's turn to laugh. "Yeah, yeah, I know. But really, if you or anyone else screw up my rep and rankings, I will personally see to it that you are blackballed from WarMonger. *Permanently*," she finished in her best gravelly impression of Larry.

"Says the *actual* pimply teen to the Tsunami employee who has Robert Krator's ear."

"I don't get pimples, thank you very much. And I'm also one of Mr. Krator's star TD Hunter players, so he has every reason to keep me happy. Plus, I'm prettier than you. So suck it."

"Jeez Louise, kid, you ain't Larry Coughlin for nothing, are you?"

"You can bet your britches I'm not. So watch yourself and your buddies like a hawk. If Larry dips below Tier One, even for a second, there's nowhere you can hide in virtual where I won't find you."

"I thought you were too busy winning TD Hunter tournaments to beat people to a pulp in WarMonger?"

"Oh, I don't need to do it personally. I *know* people."

"Riiight. Of course. You've got me quaking in my boots, kid. But seriously, we'll take good care of Larry. I promise."

"You'd better," Lynn said, switching her voice modulator back on so Steve could have the full effect of Larry the Snake in threatening mode. "I think we'd better do a deathmatch just to make sure you're up to snuff. Whippersnappers like you always talk big, but you don't *really* know a man until you've tried to kill him. Besides, I'm pissed at the paparazzi but can't beat their faces into the ground, so your face will have to do."

Steve laughed.

"Whippersnapper huh? You're on, kid. You're on."

Lynn's mini break in WarMonger left her with a spring in her step and a lighter load on her shoulders than she'd had in a while. Which was good, because she needed all the positivity she could get to face the second conversation she was forced to have that day.

"Do I *really* have to do this?" Lynn whined, knowing she sounded pathetic.

"Yes!" her mother said. "You can't back out last minute after Mr. Swain was so gracious as to give up his time on a Sunday to talk with us."

"But it's so embarrassing!" Lynn slid down further on the couch, as if she could somehow sink into its cushions and disappear. They were sitting in their living room together, and Lynn had linked in their wall-screen opposite the couch so it would display their upcoming vidcall and its sensors would broadcast their images in turn.

"Why in the world do you think it's embarrassing? I think it's exciting. Imagine, my daughter? Famous? You'll be wearing sponsorships in no time and everybody will know who you are."

"That's *exactly* the problem," Lynn muttered, arm flung over her face.

"Come on, honey," Matilda said softly, laying a hand on Lynn's shoulder. "I know being in the spotlight has never been comfortable for you. Your father was the same way. But just like him, I know you have the courage to face the unpleasant necessities and turn them to your advantage. You have *every* right to be proud of your accomplishments, and *nothing* to be embarrassed about. Do you hear me? Now sit up straight and act professional. You're still my daughter and I raised you to be polite."

Lynn groaned, but said, "Yes ma'am," and did as she was told.

Soon their meeting time arrived and the wall-screen lit up with GIC's logo. When the logo disappeared it revealed a man in a crisp suit sitting at a large desk in a tastefully decorated office. He looked about in his fifties with warm brown eyes and a touch of gray in the dark hair at his temples. With his apple cheeks and the shape of his handsome face, he could have easily been Kayla's biological father if Lynn hadn't known better.

"Good evening, Mrs. Raven, Lynn," Jamal Swain said, nodding to them. "It's a pleasure to meet you both. I'm glad you reached out. Kayla has been talking my ear off about you, Lynn, and your team."

"She has?" Lynn said, swallowing nervously.

Mr. Swain smiled.

"Don't worry, all good things. I'm sure you both have lots of questions, though, so let me give you the elevator pitch, if I may," Mr. Swain said, nodding again.

"Of course, sir," Lynn replied, formally, as her mother also murmured her assent.

"Global Imaging Consultants is exactly what its name implies," Jamal said calmly. "We manage images for personalities around the world as well as dealing with the myriad fractured laws regarding such images. Since before the internet, there have been issues regarding the balance of the public's need or at least desire to know about the lives of public persons, celebrities, politicians, and so on, and the fact that they are people who have lives and wish to live them.

"GIC is in the business of balancing that for our clients by creating a public image, using information processes to maximize the value of the image potential, personal value, and financial value, while still helping them live their lives. Some wish to constantly be in the public view. I have one client who literally has a camera in her bedroom. Even I find it creepy, but she likes to have people watch while she sleeps."

"That *is* creepy," Lynn blurted. "She likes that?"

"She is narcissistic to the point of severe addiction," Mr. Swain said with a shrug. "But she has an interesting secondary point that if someone breaks into her home, there are several thousand people, minimum, just watching her sleep, and the other cameras in her house, that will contact the police."

"That's . . . a point," Lynn admitted, glancing at her mother. Matilda had an incredulous look on her face, but she kept her opinion of crazy celebrities and their insane ways to herself.

"Then there are those that when a certain door closes, they prefer to have their own lives," Mr. Swain said. "From the sounds of it, you're that type."

"Yes. Absolutely. I'd *really* prefer if nobody even knew who I was," Lynn said. "I'm not a fan of being noticed."

"Well, you've breached that barrier and that is a permanent thing," Mr. Swain said. "Mind if I discuss that for a moment? It could be helpful in making your decision on what you want to do moving forward."

"Not at all, sir," Lynn said.

"Good. Let me start with the question: Do you have any religious objection to evolution?"

"Uhhh . . . no?" Lynn glanced at her mom, who gave her an unhelpful "don't ask me" look.

"Good. Then always keep in mind that the gene is selfish, and we are barely evolved monkeys," Mr. Swain said, grinning. "And we act like them. Especially when it comes to fame and attention."

"How?" Lynn asked.

"Monkeys and early humans existed in small bands, troops. Within those bands, what was critically important for survival, for reproduction, was the Alpha or

Alphas of the troop. Keeping an eye on the Alpha, mimicking the Alpha, trying to become the Alpha, was what promoted the survival of the individual. With me so far?"

"Yes," Lynn said slowly.

"And, again, we are barely evolved. So when people lock onto a celebrity, what they are locking onto is 'this is the troop Alpha.' Some girl halfway across the world, for example, will view some video of you and want to be just like Lynn Raven. They'll want to copy your dress, your hairstyle, talk like you, et cetera.

"Since the mindset is of a small troop of monkeys where everyone knows everyone else, there will be people who will instantly assume that you are friends, because you are the Alpha of the monkey troop. Complete strangers will walk up to you and carry on a conversation about who you should or should not date, what you should or should not wear, how you should or should not act. Because they are part of your monkey troop, at least in their minds."

"Ugh," Lynn said.

"Once you breach the barrier, it's a permanent thing," Jamal said, shrugging. "There could be people you run into when you are in your sixties who still remember Lynn Raven."

"That's nuts," Lynn said, grimacing. She looked at her mom again, but Matilda was staring at Mr. Swain with a grave expression and pursed lips.

"Then there is the fact that the Alpha always gets picked on. It's a test to see if they're still worthy to be the Alpha. So, people will denigrate you, cut you down. Cyberbullying. Fortunately, with some of the laws out there, the extremes of such things are illegal."

"Faketime porn," Lynn said with a shudder.

"What? What is that?" Matilda asked, eyes flashing like someone had just personally threatened her child.

Lynn shook her head.

"Believe me, Mom, you don't want to know."

"But it *is* a reality of the mesh web that we must keep in mind. That as well as aggressive stalking," Mr. Swain continued. "I understand you had a drone come into your home?"

"Through the delivery chute," Lynn said unhappily.

"Which is remote trespass and home invasion which can be charged," Mr. Swain said. "If you're our client, report it to us and we'll see about tracking down the perpetrator, wherever on earth, and trying to get them charged. Which we often do."

"Mom already tried that. The police didn't care," Lynn said.

"When you become a celebrity of even the most minor sort, you create 'your' troop of monkeys," Mr. Swain said, shrugging again. "That troop has a value. Financial, yes, but also in terms of influence. Your home invader might be in Challah, India. But if the Challah police are contacted and fail to take action, one response, fairly automatic, literally handled by an AI, is to contact their PR people and let them know that it was home invasion of an influencer, an Alpha. When the Challah police arrest the malefactor, Lynn Raven says nice things about them and people say nice things about the Challah police and the Challah police increase their points. He or she might only briefly see the inside of a jail cell, but they do. And that reduces the number of people willing to invade your home to find out what you wear when you're eating pizza."

"Sweatpants and a t-shirt," Lynn said. "But keeping up with all of that..." She thought about her schedule and grimaced.

"Who said you keep up with it?" Mr. Swain said, chuckling. "We do that. That's what we're for. And the cease-and-desist orders to all the people swarming you with drones for financial gain. Legal AIs covering statutory laws and precedents in the various jurisdictions and ensuring that people aren't breaking them with your image. We have teams of people, including lawyers and AIs, who do nothing but that all day long. Teams who review copy from AI-generated text, thanking the police as if it were you; responding to comments, keeping very close to the character of Lynn Raven; people and AIs who scour for mentions or videos, looking for anything that's off or wrong. Yes, anything that breaks image but also fakes and frauds, lies and calumny."

"So...what pays for all of that?" Lynn asked.

"That would be the news streams that want to know whose shirts you wear,'" Mr. Swain said, sitting back and steepling his fingers. "Though it's really the monkey troop who wants to know whose shirts you wear. The news streams are just doing advertising. You said sweatpants and a t-shirt. What brand? No particular brand? I have some suggestions for brands who will send us money if you just say you wear them, no need to go out in them and demonstrate. You use high-performance gear while you're hunting, yes? Whose might I ask?"

"Uh, mostly NanoTechLabs," Lynn said.

"Not a brand we work with, but we can either try to get them onboard or, if you're willing, find one we already have contacts with," Jamal continued. "Those are the sort of minor and noncompulsory actions on your part that are important. If you're promoting Brand X, make sure that Brand X is what you want to eat, drink, wear, use. Because if you're videoed eating, drinking, wearing Brand Y instead of Brand X, it's a headache.

"Flip side is, at a certain level of points, depending on certain factors you may or may not yet be at, you can generally get whatever it is for free. If you drink a particular sports drink, the brand will likely be willing to provide the product for free if they see you as a valuable influencer."

"That would be nice, honey," Matilda said, smiling broadly. "And it'd be a good chance to expand your wardrobe."

"*Mom*," Lynn said through gritted teeth, trying not to be grumpy at the thought of miserable chores like *shopping* and *trying on clothes*.

Mr. Swain chuckled.

"So, you get free stuff and get paid to promote it. We get fifteen percent and we'll be pushing for every brand we can find to enhance your income and ours."

"What if I prefer to get my clothes at thrift stores?" Lynn said, crossing her arms.

"That's workable," Swain replied. "There are some great thrift-store brands we could work with. You could even promote a charity, probably without an income stream but goodwill, as a term of art, is a multiplier. Doing interviews is part of the job; talk about it. That promotes the charity and builds goodwill."

"Okay," Lynn said, dubiously.

"You want the drones to mostly go away?" Swain asked.

"Yes, *please*."

"We can get them to mostly go away. *Mostly.* There are a few caveats you need to know that are important and there's a much longer briefing you will have with your PR manager if you decide to sign with us about some of the dos and don'ts but these are the most important."

"Okay," Lynn said.

"I am literally in the job of vanity," Mr. Swain said. "But even I recognize that vanity is incredibly destructive. I'll reference again one of my clients who has people watch her while she sleeps. She obsesses constantly about her looks, her weight, and she's gone through rounds and rounds of plastic surgery. It's her life, I just craft it. But I do worry because it is extremely unhealthy, and I worry about my clients. With me?"

"Yes, sir," Lynn said. "But I don't think that will be a problem with me. I just want to vanish."

"Won't happen, I'm afraid," Mr. Swain said. "Even if you dropped everything, now, and tried to disappear, decades down the road there will still be people who will wonder about Lynn Raven. But what I would also counsel you on is that fame is an addictive and subtle drug. You might want to vanish, now, but that can change in strange ways. Try to keep that humble attitude, it will anchor you to reality and the values that are important to you. Among other things, it's a fantastic public image. In ancient past, triumphant Roman generals riding their chariot through adoring worshippers would have a slave sit out of sight and repeat over and over 'Remember that you, too, are mortal.' Keep that in mind at all times as you enter the world of the monkey troop Alpha. Yes?"

"Got it," Lynn said, sitting up straighter.

"The second is a tricky and evolving legal issue," Mr. Swain said with a sigh. "The 2032 Federal Image Control Act seemed simple on initial passage. If a person has, intentionally or unintentionally, become a public figure they are subject to certain privacy rights when the invasion of privacy is for commercial purposes as well as laws against things like fake porn videos. The push for paparazzi laws, as they're called, go back decades, at least to a princess of England who was killed in a car crash, and they really picked up steam with those fraudulent sex vids of the president's daughter."

"Oh, yeah," Lynn said, grimacing. "Those were sick."

"Wait a second." Matilda turned to Lynn. "How do *you* know about those vids? That was over a decade ago."

Lynn rolled her eyes.

"Come on, Mom. Nothing in the mesh ever goes away. Besides, it was national news. I might have been young but I wasn't blind. Kids can get anything—and I mean *anything*—in the mesh if they go looking. They just need to know the right person to ask. All that age restriction stuff is about as effective as wet toilet paper."

Her mother's mouth opened and closed a few times, but then she glanced at the flex screen and obviously decided now wasn't the time. "Apologies. Please continue, Mr. Swain."

"Yes, well, after that there was a lawsuit that created the politicking carve-out," Mr. Swain continued, politely not commenting on the interplay. "A senator who was a strong environmentalist was caught tossing a piece of trash by a paparazzi drone in a wilderness area. The senator argued the footage should be suppressed—increasing the viewership by the way—since he had a reasonable right to privacy and it was his image. But the owner argued that it was politically consequential free speech and that it was protected by the First Amendment."

"I think I remember that from class," Lynn said, frowning.

"The Supreme Court ruling was that anyone who engages in political speech is not entirely fair game but generally fair game," Swain said. "So, every politician has to live in a fishbowl. Sucks and it probably causes some people to not run for office but it's a reasonable legal argument. If a congressman runs as a vegan and gets caught eating steak, it shows they're a hypocrite which is something people should know.

"Since then, two other suits have extended that to any public figure who engages in 'politicking.' So, if an Alpha of whatever troop wears a t-shirt emblazoned with a political slogan of any sort, they are now in the 'politicking' realm and their privacy protections are essentially nil. Because political speech. Let's say an influencer who was always wearing t-shirts that read 'Meat is murder' got caught by a drone eating a steak. The 'Meat is murder' shirt is considered political so, again, hypocrisy which influences the political response of the Alpha's monkey troop. Engage in political speech and you're less protected. Make sense?"

"Yes, sir," Lynn said.

"If you decide to work with us, our first job is tracking who is sending the paparazzi drones and sending cease-and-desist letters," Mr. Swain said. "The process is pretty automatic, generated by a legal AI. And they'll be responded to by the paparazzi's legal AI as 'politically protected.' Have you made any political statements since the event? Not before you were noticeable but since?"

"Well, no," Lynn said, "but that's because I don't make statements, period. What about casual conversation with my friends while we're walking down the street? Am I allowed to have an opinion about political events and issues?"

"Of course you are, but that is an important and, unfortunately, difficult point you make. Once you're an Alpha of a troop, everything you say in a public space is considered a 'statement,' whether you mean it to be or not. Most of the time casual conversation for a celebrity whose sphere of influence has nothing to do with politics isn't an issue. That is, until a streamer or paparazzi decides they can make money by posting a vid of you discussing a controversial topic. And what qualifies as a 'controversial' topic changes with the times and the culture."

"Good grief," Lynn said. "Guess it's a good thing I don't talk much."

"Yes, that could certainly be seen as a virtue when it comes to being a public figure. For now we'll operate on the assumption that you're not in the 'politicking' realm. So, in the case of the drone operators claiming political speech protection, we would respond with an automatic 'prove it' and when they can't, they'll withdraw the drone. But if you do engage in political speech, it gets harder."

"Okay," Lynn said, shrugging. "Shouldn't be a problem though because I'm not that into politics."

"Good," Mr. Swain said with a sigh. "Stay away from it. It's evolving. The current argument making its way through the courts, because of the 'Meat is murder' case, is that it suppresses political speech. Which is true. What I just said to you is an example.

We'll see how it shakes out. But if the politicking exemption goes away, then it's all 'protected speech' and essentially most of the Act goes out the window and we're back to square one."

"Ugh," Lynn said, shaking her head.

"We're a party in one of the suits," Mr. Swain said. "We're arguing for the current precedent. There used to be a rule in PR, a long time back, 'stay away from politics.' I strongly encourage my clients to follow that rule and I've gone so far as to drop some that just got to be too much trouble because of their politicking. If you pick side A or side B all you'll do is drive off the other side and reduce your marketability. Okay?"

"Yes, sir," Lynn said, and nodded.

Mr. Swain's lips twitched and he shook his head.

"You know, that reminds me, the strangest argument I've heard in the area is that 'all actions and speech are political.'"

"What?" Lynn asked.

"You've said 'sir' multiple times since we started talking, did you notice?" Mr. Swain asked.

"Uhhh, I guess?" Lynn said, then, "Sir."

"That's something that is... unusual for most in the entertainment industry," Swain noted. "Take my client who sleeps while being watched. She sleeps in the nude I'll add."

"Agh!" Lynn said, grimacing. "Didn't need to know that."

"Clearly not a philosophical conservative," Swain pointed out. "While she stays away from direct politicking, thank God, she's very liberal. 'Sir' and 'Ma'am' tend to indicate that while you are not necessarily conservative, some of your personal philosophies may be. She's never called me sir, just 'Jamal' or 'Jammi.' Please don't call me Jammi, by the way. I hate it."

"I never would, sir," Lynn said.

"You also are self-effacing and give others credit. That's been argued to be 'conservative political speech,' believe it or not."

"O . . . kay," Lynn said. She did not consider herself a conservative. "I'm just . . . polite."

"Some on the political left reject politeness as an outdated social construct," Mr. Swain said. "So, your use of 'outdated social constructs' like politeness, humility, being self-effacing, giving credit to others, can be viewed as taking a political stance in favor of conservative philosophies and thus politics and thus everything you are, every action you take, what you wear, how you speak, is political. I've seen the argument. It's been upheld on merit grounds in a case. We'll see where it goes.

"Getting away from that, there's the 'incidental' rulings," Mr. Swain continued. "Say you go to a concert with friends and someone who is filming the concert catches you on camera. All well and good. People can comment on it 'Hey, there's Lynn Raven!' But if the streamer promotes that it's Lynn Raven in the video, if the video 'concentrates' on the figure, then they owe commercial fees and/or can be ordered to take down or cut out that portion of the video.

"We're . . . gentle on that with minor streamers. Minor streamers don't make much money and we don't ask for much. And we'll even help out, depending. Though what we actually send is in more formal language, our message more or less says, 'Hey, we represent Lynn Raven. Know you were just covering the concert, but you focused on her dancing for x minutes and you promoted it with her name and likeness. Know you don't make much money, but you owe some to Lynn, see fee structure. If you agree on that, we'll have Lynn promote the video which will get you more hits and if you don't then you have to cut her out and take down the promotion.' Sound about right?"

"I . . . guess," Lynn said. "I don't want to be plastered everywhere but, yeah, if some streamer happens to . . . Would some streamer actually use me to promote their stream? I mean, covering a concert or something?"

Mr. Swain chuckled, and his eyes unfocused for a moment as he manipulated his LINC display. Their view of Mr. Swain's office cut to a stream vid of Lynn and the guys walking into Happy Joe's Pizza Emporium, the vid obviously taken from a drone hovering nearby. One corner of the stream vid was a cutout view of the streamer's face as he commented on the action.

"So, turns out Lynn Raven's totally into Happy Joe's. Just more proof that she has good taste!"

The streamer looked to be in his early twenties, with lanky hair and a pimply face.

Lynn's mouth set in an uncertain line as the drone footage zoomed in, obviously trying to get a shot of her through the restaurant's windows.

Why did anyone care what pizza she liked?

Their screen view switched back to Mr. Swain's office, and he gestured with a hand.

"SevenFourNine is, despite his looks, a known Augmented Reality Game streamer with sixty-two million followers," Mr. Swain said, "And he is heavy on TD Hunter. He covered the beta with support from the company. My people did a bit of research when we were building a proposal to present to you, and they checked with Happy Joe's. The restaurant saw a twenty percent jump in sales after this streamer's mention."

Lynn's eyebrows shot up, and she glanced at her mom, who looked equally shocked.

"In addition," Mr. Swain added, "since he's someone we correspond with, we were able to reach out and he said he saw a jump in his own view numbers when he started covering Skadi's Wolves, and especially you, Lynn, after the qualifiers. You're popular. And, since no good deed goes unpunished, now he's one of your loyal stalkers. He's actually one we probably won't cease-and-desist unless you insist, since he's one that's generally sane in comparison. If we cease-and-desist all of them, it won't work. There has to be some source of coverage, or people will just stalk. The monkey troop must be fed. Fed pizza apparently."

Lynn resisted the urge to slouch down into the couch and throw an arm over her face again. Her fateful choice last June to compete in TD Hunter had taken away her anonymity, and she wished she could have it back.

But that was not how the world worked.

"Most of the drones *will* go away," Mr. Swain assured her, perhaps guessing her thoughts from her expression. "Not all. But, yes, people are already using your likeness to promote their streams and there is secondary promotion, too, Happy Joe's as an example. But look on the positive side: you helped out your favorite pizza place on a slow night."

"Is eating taco pizza a political statement?" Lynn asked.

"To some of the people making these psycho legal arguments, probably," Mr. Swain. "I could go on for hours on the topic, but let's refocus on the matter at hand: you've found yourself in need of someone to intercede, shall we say, between you and the world. I've clarified your position and gone over some of what you could expect from GIC. We'd be honored to represent you, but I'm sure you have many more questions. I'll have my secretary send an information packet to your LINCs and—"

"Can we start today?"

Lynn's question seemed to catch Mr. Swain off guard, and Matilda shot her a questioning look, too.

"I'm sorry, Lynn, do you mean can I answer more questions today?"

"No. Can I sign up? Right now? Can you make the drones go away today?"

"Honey, don't you want to take some time—"

Lynn shook her head and sat up straighter. She'd been thinking hard while Mr. Swain talked. It had become more and more clear that she was in over her head. Actually, at this point she felt like she was chained to an anchor at the bottom of the sea. She wanted—*needed*—what GIC had to offer. And if doing some streams and promoting some products was what it took, then so be it.

"You've told me everything I need to know, sir."

"Right, well, I'd be glad to connect you with a few of our previous clients if you'd like some references before you sign." He seemed to be looking more at Matilda than Lynn as he said it, but Lynn still shook her head.

"Thank you, sir, but that won't be necessary. You're obviously very competent and knowledgeable, and you're generous with your time when you could have sloughed me off on one of your employees. And you treat Kayla well. It's obvious she loves you. That's a good enough reference for me," she finished with a shrug and looked at her mom. Matilda seemed more hesitant, but after a searching look in Lynn's eyes, she nodded.

Mr. Swain chuckled.

"Well, then, I guess that settles it. Welcome to GIC, Lynn."

It took time to go over all the legal particulars. But true to Mr. Swain's word, he had her own personal stream set up, complete with shared admin, within hours—the first step to cracking down on the drones. He handed off the day-to-day management of the account to their head PR manager, Mrs. Pearson, but he promised to check on the status of things personally for the first couple weeks to make sure everything got off to a good start.

Mrs. Pearson was as no-nonsense and straightforward as anyone Lynn had ever met. She called Lynn that very evening, and by the end of their conversation, Lynn was convinced that nothing on earth would ever dare get in Mrs. Pearson's way, at least if it valued its life. The woman promised to get on the ball immediately, and told Lynn to expect several interviews that week, with more to come. Lynn shuddered at the thought, but she'd committed to this, so there was no backing out now. Plus, Mr. Swain's promise that GIC's efforts would substantially diminish the drone presence fairly quickly gave her the motivation to grit her teeth and tell herself it would be worth it.

Monday morning, Lynn didn't notice much difference in the size of the "flock" that followed her to school.

Tuesday morning, she was pretty sure it was smaller.

By Wednesday, the first day she was scheduled to have an interview, it was starkly obvious there were fewer drones.

And, of course, her teammates noticed it as well. She didn't even have to tell them, since they'd all been sent contract offers from GIC as well. Mack and Dan signed theirs immediately, and talked about it incessantly any time they weren't actively in class or hunting. Edgar took more convincing, but in the end he seemed to resign himself to his fate. Connor didn't say a word about his offer, but Lynn could only assume he'd accepted his as well, since Mrs. Pearson had sent her a few messages about doing a team interview the next week and setting up a Skadi's Wolves stream channel, which meant GIC must have gotten the contracts for all five of them.

Lynn had been worried about the hassle of collecting content for their collective streams, especially considering how Elena pranced around the school doing constant livestreams and being obsessed with perfection every moment of the day. But it turned out to be a lot simpler and stress free than she'd expected. Mrs. Pearson simply had her authorize GIC's proprietary app on her LINC which enabled Lynn to share what she saw through her LINC or AR input any time she wanted. She could share live, with or without sound, or record for later sharing, so she could record clips of their fights to send to Mrs. Pearson for editing, touch-ups, and ad insertion. All Mrs. Pearson required was at least one clip a day of something, *anything*, and at least one sizable clip a week of hunting TDMs with plenty of action in it.

That, Lynn could do.

Her first interview was...not as bad as being strapped to a chair and having her teeth pulled out one by one, which was what she'd expected going in. Parts of it were even a little fun. She'd been leaving her TD Hunter app on almost all the time, mostly because it made hopping in and out of it easier, but also because Hugo's sarcastic quips and observations were quickly becoming a form of moral support Lynn had never known she needed. The interviewer for Lynn's first appearance was mostly interested in hot takes and juicy behind-the-scenes information, though at least he didn't ask any creepy personal questions. Lynn didn't have much in the way of "juicy" details, but she did share about her training routine and what it was like being a normal teen while competing in a game that had become a global phenomenon.

Her second interview at the end of the week was pure awesomeness. The interviewer was a famous female gamer that Lynn had followed for years. They spent over an hour talking about what it was like being a "gamer girl" in an arena still dominated by male players and sensibilities. Lynn didn't name any names—she had *some* honor, after all—but she was pretty sure that if Ronnie ever watched the interview, he would want to punch her face through a wall.

The next few weeks were an exhausting blur of high highs and low lows.

They sped through Levels 27 and 28 and picked up some awesome augments.

Lynn got an F on one of her English assignments and had a very difficult conversation with her mom about it.

Mack's individual ranking on the leaderboard surpassed Dan's for the first time—only for a day, but still, Lynn was certain Mack would never stop crowing about it.

Their team got completely wiped out by a hoard of Rakshar, a new Bravo Class-4 monster that was an upgrade of the Namahags. That led to a stern talking to from Connor, which didn't quite reach a Ronnie level of berating, but edged uncomfortably close. It also set Lynn back in her kill-to-damage ratio after she'd only just begun to claw her way a few percentage points above DeathShot13.

The drones following them around dwindled to almost nothing.

Connor kissed her again—she wasn't sure if that was a high or a low, or maybe just a confused middle. He overheard her admit her abysmal English grade to Edgar, who was having similar woes, and later offered to tutor her since English was his "strong suit." Her mom agreed to it as long as they met in a public place, and his tutoring skills turned out to be surprisingly good. He made sense of some things she'd been struggling to wrap her head around and she did a lot better on her next essay. She relaxed more around him, though she still wasn't sure how to react when he did things like compliment her or hold her hand. He didn't seem to need or expect any kind of reaction, and even her awkwardness appeared to amuse him.

It was all very confusing, but his behavior was miles above the bullying, insults, and abuse she'd received from virtually every other guy throughout her school years. So, she decided to ignore her misgivings and give him a chance.

What did she know about dating anyway? Maybe everything he did was perfectly normal, even the way he would touch her unexpectedly, brushing her arm or laying a hand on her back, as if he were acclimating her to his presence. That was normal, right? And it wasn't as if she *dis*liked it. It was just...weird. But then she'd spent years flinching from every touch, expecting it to be a cruel pinch or an inappropriate grab. So maybe the weirdness was all in her head. She did notice that he never touched her in front of their teammates—when they were hunting, he was all coolness and professionalism. But he didn't seem afraid to compliment her or show affection in public, so he certainly wasn't trying to hide what he was doing.

The whole thing gave her so many conflicting emotions that she opted to simply let it happen, at least for now. After years of being torn down by everyone, she couldn't summon the willpower to tell the one person building her up to stop—no matter how weird it felt. Well, the one person besides her mom, who didn't count, and Edgar, who usually turned his compliments into a joke. Besides, Edgar had gotten weirdly quiet and broody lately, and Lynn couldn't figure out why.

By the first week of November, the weather had turned decidedly chilly, and it was fortunate Lynn had signed on with GIC when she had, because they all needed new sets of cold-weather high-performance gear. The sponsorships pouring in were enough to cover the new equipment, which was *not* cheap. Sometimes Lynn felt like a walking billboard, but at least she had the freedom to refuse any sponsorships that required her to say something on camera or talk about a specific product. She had enough offers that she got by just fine with those she wore as logos on her uniform and displayed as ads or sponsors on her stream—well, that

Mrs. Pearson and her team displayed. The cut GIC was taking of her sponsorships was a pittance compared to Lynn's gratitude at not having to mess with all the hassle herself. And for her uniform, all she had to do was add the programming patch the sponsoring companies messaged her and the smart fabric did the rest itself.

Beyond necessitating a wardrobe change, the cold weather had the benefit of cutting down on the number of random strangers who asked for her autograph and the number of TD Hunter fans who followed her around while she was hunting. Thankfully, Connor handled the fan interruptions like a pro, because any time Lynn spotted one, she wanted to go all Larry the Snake on them and threaten to cut off their ears. Connor had this little spiel about how they appreciated the support but required observers to stay so many feet back for their own safety, blah-blah-blah. The few times people ignored him, the intimidation factor of Connor and Edgar together looming over them convinced them to back off.

By the end of November, Lynn was feeling less enthusiastic about a future craze in AR games. Hunting in the snow was *not* fun and they slipped enough times that Connor had to severely limit their activity during certain weather to keep them from getting injured. Bad weather and approaching finals slowed their leveling process and put a strain on all of them, especially Connor. Lynn knew he was thinking about what sort of pace they could maintain all winter and whether it would be enough to get them to Level 40 by June 15th.

She knew because she worried about the same thing.

"Okay, people. We're doing something different today," Connor said on their team channel after school let out the Thursday after Thanksgiving. "Today we're going to do some recon. Everybody meet up behind the ARS building, and try to avoid notice. I don't want hangers-on for this exercise."

Lynn shot Edgar a quizzical look but he just shrugged and led the way out of the mass of students heading to the front doors. These days they exited the school out the back to minimize their time in the biting wind. Their cold weather gear was great at insulation—so much so that overheating was often a problem during hunts. But winter wind in Iowa sucked no matter what you were wearing.

They didn't have to wonder about Connor's cryptic statement for long. He was waiting for them when they arrived, and Dan and Mack were close behind.

"I've been switching up where we hunt the past few weeks to make sure we didn't become too comfortable in one terrain," he began. "But this TDM mass north of the school still offers the largest amount of potential experience in one place that we've found so far. I know we were getting bogged down assaulting from the south time and time again. Less loot was being dropped and the monsters were fighting in more difficult formations. Maybe the game is designed to respond to such tactics with increased difficulty to encourage players to spread out and vary their hunting habits. Whatever the case, our progress and efficiency were dropping, so it made sense to shake things up.

"But with the increasingly bad weather I've been doing some calculations and come to the conclusion that we have to start attacking higher-value targets. I've also considered changes in tactics for the winter that emphasize ranged weapons so we have less chance of injury hunting in the snow. We've all put enough time, sweat, and tears into this competition that I don't want to rely on one thing or another for success. We're going to try everything we can think of to increase our experience gain, so don't be shy if you have any ideas."

He paused to look around their group, but everybody was nodding in agreement and looking determined, so he went on.

"Today we're going to make a wide circle around the edge of the woods, out of combat mode. At strategic points around the perimeter, we'll hop into combat mode to check the map and see if we can spot the center of this TDM mass. Hopefully my theory is correct that the algorithm has been spawning all the enemies on the south side in response to our attacks, so the north will be fairly unprotected. Our goal is to find the boss we hope is at the center of this mass, do a blitz attack through their thinner ranks, and take out the boss for maximum experience gain in the shortest amount of time.

"Today we'll focus on scouting to confirm enemy positions. Then, if I'm correct, we'll do the actual assault on Saturday. The forecast is calling for heavy rain tomorrow, so I don't know if we'll be able to hunt then. But Saturday is supposed to be clear and above freezing, so no chance of ice. Sound good, everyone?"

Lynn gave an affirmative with the rest of the team, though she knew she didn't sound as enthusiastic as the guys. For one thing, this whole strategy had been *her* idea *months* ago, which Connor had casually dismissed at the time. For another, just because they were nearing Level 30 didn't mean it was smart to try and take on a boss by themselves. None of them had survived taking out Mishipeshu in the qualifiers, even though they'd had twice as many Hunters. True, they'd only been Level 20. But the game clearly warned against attacking full bosses solo.

It wouldn't hurt to do some scouting, though, so she kept her objections to herself until they were relevant.

"Great weather for Rangers and ducks," Lynn muttered, hunching her shoulders as another blast of cold wind whipped around the building.

"What?" Mack said, looking at her. "It's *horrible* weather."

"Exactly. The weather is wet and miserable, the kind of weather only Army Rangers or ducks like."

"Sounds like something Larry Coughlin would say," Dan pointed out.

"Oh, uh..." Lynn mentally cursed her slipup. "It's just something I heard one time. Might have *been* Larry."

"Okay, but how do *you* know Larry Coughlin?" Mack asked.

"Doesn't everybody?" Lynn asked.

"*I* don't know him," Connor said.

"You don't play WarMonger," Edgar pointed out.

"He's one of *the* top players in WarMonger!" Dan said. "Just an insanely awesome player! But for some reason he had it out for Ronnie. He used to track Ronnie down just to beat his butt. It was kinda hilarious, actually, but, well, Ronnie didn't think so, obviously."

"Oh," Connor said. "I'm not into that kind of gaming."

The condescension in Connor's tone grated on Lynn, but she bit her tongue. She didn't want to risk saying something that might give away her extremely detailed knowledge of "that kind of gaming," not right after she'd already slipped up.

Connor got them moving. Once they reached the western point of the circle they'd marked on their overhead maps, Connor popped into combat mode to check the TDM situation. Since he didn't specifically forbid anyone else from doing the same, Lynn had Hugo take her in as well for a few seconds and save a screenshot of the map so she could study it later. It wasn't that she didn't trust Connor—mostly—she just wanted to see for herself and draw her own conclusions.

"Good news, team," Connor told everybody after a few seconds. His batons had barely finished forming when he left combat mode again and they morphed back to their inactive state. "It looks like I was correct. The TDMs are definitely thinner on this side, and I can almost see to the center, but not quite. I've marked the northern apex of the circle on my map and I'm sharing it with you now, so we'll head to that point and do another check. Let's head out."

Once they'd reached the point Connor had marked on their overhead map, he repeated his scouting exercise, as did Lynn. When she'd done it on the west side, she'd noticed a few monsters close enough that they would have turned and attacked if she hadn't popped right back out of combat mode again. But this time the area around her was deserted.

"Hugo, take a screenshot and let's get out of here," she subvocalized.

"Of course, Miss Lynn. Shall I share it with the rest of the team?"

"Not yet. Let's see what Connor says."

A few seconds later, Connor turned to them with a triumphant smile on his face.

"We've got our in. Just as I suspected, the TDM

forces are extremely light on this side. We'll advance straight south from here, and every few hundred yards I'll check to see what new forces show up on our radar."

Connor headed south toward the school, and Lynn hesitated a moment before she followed. She didn't know why, but she felt nervous about advancing straight toward the enemy. She shook her head and trotted to catch up, reminding herself that as long as they stayed out of combat mode, the algorithm wouldn't register their location in any way that would affect TDM placement.

"You know," Mack muttered to her when she fell into step beside him, "Connor could have done this whole scouting thing himself. I don't see why we had to trek all this way ourselves. I could have been catching up on math homework."

"Aw, come on, the exercise is good for you," Lynn joked, nudging her friend in the ribs. "After all, you have to maintain that sexy figure for your Japanese bot girlfriend, right?"

Mack blushed and scowled at the same time.

"Riko likes my figure just fine."

"Ooooh! So she's seen more of you than just your scruffy face?" Dan butted in gleefully.

Mack's face got even redder.

"Shut up! It's not like that. She watches our fights on the streams, that's all I mean."

"Sure she does," Dan said, cackling.

"Drop it, Dan," Edgar said. "If Mack wants to enjoy a romantic fling with a bot, s'none of our business, right? Just don't give her your bank account number or nothin', 'kay?" He directed that last part at Mack, eyes twinkling.

For once, Mack didn't rise to the bait, which, while

not as fun for the rest of them, was probably the wisest course. Their group fell silent, until Dan unexpectedly spoke, his tone much more somber.

"I wonder how Ronnie is doing."

Lynn glanced around, but everybody else's eyes were on the woods, even Connor's, though he had an attentive look on his face.

"We see him in class almost every day," Edgar pointed out.

"Yeah, but he avoids us like the plague!"

"Which is definitely for the best," Lynn muttered.

"He's been looking really pale recently," Dan insisted.

"Yeah, cuz it's *winter*, genius," Edgar said. "Besides, he's always been pale as a vampire anyway."

"But he looks really unhappy."

"Of course, he does. He's on a team with *Elena*. Duh."

"I just wish he would talk to me," Dan said, sounding miserable. "He blocked me on every platform after we switched up teams."

Though she had little emotion to spare for Ronnie, Lynn did feel bad for Dan. Ronnie had been his best friend for *years*. It must have been hard to lose all that in one day. In fact, it seemed out of character for Ronnie to not even *complain* to Dan about the new situation. Lynn wondered if Elena was to blame for the radio silence. Or, maybe Ronnie was just that stubborn and petty. Maybe he'd written off Dan forever just because Dan had sided with the rest of the team and not him. *That* she could see.

"Look, Dan," Edgar said. "Ronnie's made his choice, and he can take care of himself. If you wanna know how he's doing, why don't you talk to him after class or something?"

"Never mind," Dan grumbled. "You're right, he can take care of himself."

Edgar nodded, then for some reason he glanced at her. She gave him a "What?" look, and he just shrugged and dropped his eyes back to the underbrush in front of them.

"Time to check the map again," Connor said after another few minutes. They all stopped, and Lynn repeated her quick jump in, screenshot, and jump out. This time she barely avoided getting attacked by a demon, who started moving toward her the moment she entered combat mode.

They repeated the exercise twice more. By the third time, they had to drop out of combat mode as soon as they entered it before a hoard of monsters destroyed them in a massive pileup. Hugo still managed to snatch a screenshot on Lynn's end, and she offered to share it with the team without comment or apology. Connor didn't say anything in response, either a thank you or a reprimand, which left Lynn feeling nervous. Ronnie had been easy to read. Connor was nearly impossible.

Fortunately, their last foray had gotten them close enough to find the answer they'd been searching for: the massive red dot in the middle of ringed clusters of TDMs was clear as day. Perhaps they simply hadn't been high-enough level to see it before, or they'd never made it far enough north. But now they had it in their sights.

"That's what we'll be aiming for on Saturday, team," Connor said, giving a satisfied nod.

"That's gonna be tough, even coming from the north," Edgar pointed out. "Yeah, the ranks are thinner, but there's still a ton. By the time we kill them, the monsters on the south will be heading our way."

"We don't have to kill them all, just punch through. We only need to take out the TDMs in our path since we can leave combat mode as soon as we've killed the boss. We won't need to fight our way back to safety."

Nobody looked happy about the plan, but nobody protested either. Lynn was particularly not happy because of how close she was to Level 30. This mission could ruin her chances of achieving the next Skadi item unless she managed to level tonight or tomorrow before the fight.

"We need Level 30 before we do this," Lynn said.

"We can do this at present level or a slight increase," Connor replied.

"At Level 30 we'll all get additional add-ons," Lynn pointed out. "And while we may be able to take this thing at our current level, with the increased TD presence we'll need every possible edge. We need Level 30."

"Disagree," Connor snapped. "And I'm team captain."

"You're team captain 'cause we voted for it," Edgar said, masticating his gum. "And Lynn as usual has a valid point."

"We'll discuss it," Connor said. "Come on, let's get back to the southern edge of the woods." Connor waved them onward. "There's enough daylight left to get some hunting in before we head home."

Mack groaned.

"What's the matter," Dan asked with a grin. "Got a hot date with your Japanese bot?"

"Shut up," Mack grumbled.

Lynn and Edgar grinned along with Dan and they all headed off. She wasn't thrilled about hunting after their lengthy hike either but hunting as a team gave them an experience bonus they didn't get when they hunted solo, and she desperately needed to reach Level 30 before Saturday.

On their way south, they passed a clearing in the woods around the node tower Lynn had guessed would be there. She felt a strange tingling sensation when they walked past it, and a shiver ran up her spine as she imagined the boss she knew lurked somewhere nearby. Well, lurked in the ones and zeros of a game app, anyway.

Geez. She'd been playing too much TD Hunter lately.

Even knowing she was being silly, she couldn't help looking over her shoulder as they drew away from the clearing. She saw nothing but dreary bare trees and a motionless metal tower. She sniffed and rubbed her nose, annoyed at the way the cold air made her sinuses act up, though it didn't usually give her a headache like this. Maybe the barometric pressure was changing as a herald for the expected rain tomorrow.

Yeah, that was it.

The rest of the afternoon felt especially tiring and dull. But they all put out and managed to come *so* close to leveling that Connor frowned when Dan said he *had* to go or his parents would lock him in his room. Lynn was glad to see it, because it meant Connor understood the importance of leveling before they faced something as challenging as a boss.

Even so, when everybody else wrapped up their hunt for the evening, she lingered behind. Yes, it was getting dark. But she knew the terrain well, and it shouldn't take much longer for her to level. She was taking no chances with the Skadi set items.

Edgar gave her a worried look when she didn't

follow him in the direction of the school, but she smiled reassuringly and sent him a ping that she wanted to hunt a bit more before she headed home. He shrugged and turned back south.

"Hey, Lynn."

Lynn jumped and almost squeaked in surprise. Somehow Connor had come up silently behind her despite the leaf litter.

"Y-yeah? What's up?"

"I was thinking, we've been working so hard lately and could use a break. Something to celebrate all we've achieved so far. Since we can't hunt tomorrow evening anyway, I'd like to take you out somewhere nice. We can relax and rest. It'll be a good refresh before our big fight on Saturday."

"Ummm, okay? What did you have in mind?" Lynn said, distracted by the sight of Edgar. He'd stopped again about ten yards away and was watching her talk to Connor. She couldn't see his face well in the dimming light under the trees, but she could guess at the scowl on his face.

"Oh, don't worry about the location. I want it to be a surprise. But dress nice, okay? I'll pick you up at, say, six?"

"Uhhh," Lynn said, tearing her eyes away from Edgar. She didn't own anything "nice," at least not by Connor's standards. "I, uh, need to check with my mom. But I'll ask."

Connor's brow crinkled, and Lynn knew he was annoyed. But he didn't show it in his tone.

"Sure. Check with her as soon as you get home."

He didn't move, and neither did she.

"I was, uh, going to hunt a little more before I

went home . . . just need to practice a few new moves I learned the other day."

"Sounds smart," Connor said. "I'll stay and hunt with you. I can always use the practice."

"No!"

Connor gave her a strange look.

"I mean, uh, you really don't need to do that," she amended, lowering her voice. "It's pretty distracting hunting with someone when I'm trying out new moves, you know? I'd rather go at it solo, that way I don't have to split my attention."

He continued to look at her, though she couldn't read his expression. Finally, he shrugged.

"Sure, if that's what you prefer. I'll see you tomorrow. Happy hunting."

With that, he turned and headed back toward the school.

To Lynn's discomfort, Edgar was still standing where he'd stopped, watching their exchange. He didn't move a muscle as Connor approached, then passed him. Once Connor had disappeared into the underbrush, he glanced back at Lynn one last time, then headed off himself.

Finally alone, Lynn tried to shake out the tension in her neck and shoulders and not think about what had just happened. Guys were so weird. She was better off forgetting about it and moving on to more productive things.

After sending a ping to her mom to let her know she'd be home late, she cleared her mind and put on her "Larry" face. The next thirty minutes were the most satisfying part of her day by far. She chose her targets carefully and wasn't shy about retreating to prevent unnecessary damage. Without a team to coordinate with, she was able to focus entirely on her aim and technique, and it wasn't long before Hugo gave her the warning that she was close to leveling.

When the long-awaited moment finally came and her leveling achievements popped up, she felt a wave of relief so strong she almost cried.

She'd done it.

Through all the craziness and tension and disasters over the past two months, she'd done it.

The rush of emotion made her a little weak in the knees, so she left combat mode and found a comfortable spot at the base of a tree where she could lean back and take her time examining her new item.

At first sight, the item that expanded to fill her display sent a pang of disappointment through her. A shield? She didn't want a shield—shields cut damage potential in half and usually limited mobility.

To be fair, it was an epic shield that matched her Skadi armor perfectly. The shape was reminiscent of a kite shield, with a slightly peaked top and the bottom tapering down to a point. There were even semicircle cutaways on either side near the top to allow for easier shooting while holding the shield up in a defensive position. The shield itself was obsidian black like her armor, but with a border that glowed ice blue. At its center was a snarling wolf head superimposed over an eight-pointed star surrounded by glowing runes.

The item was named Skadi's Bastion. *Sweeet.*

She could envision enjoying the heck out of face-bashing some ugly Rakshar with it . . . wait, could she face-bash with it? Would the game register such an action as damage to the monster or to herself? She knew from reading about shield mechanics that shields did act as physical barriers to TDM strikes, but she'd always preferred wielding dual weapons over a weapon and shield. She *had* been in situations where a shield would have been handy, like during certain assaults where TDMs were so thick there wasn't enough room to dodge. Or when fighting TDMs with ranged attacks.

Okay, so *maybe* she wanted a shield.

Once she selected the item in her inventory and started reading its function and stats, she grinned.

Okay, she *definitely* wanted a shield. Or at least, *this* shield.

The first thing she noticed was that it had a damage rating, which meant she could absolutely use it for face-bashing purposes. It wasn't nearly enough damage to make up for losing one of her weapons, but the loss was mitigated by its special ability: a team defense *and* stealth bonus for her entire group. No proximity limit.

Her mind was already busy considering the implications and devising battle strategies for using Skadi's Bastion effectively. The defense and stealth bonus were significant. Almost ludicrously so. The catch was that they only applied when the item was equipped alongside the other Skadi items. Which meant she couldn't pass off the shield to Edgar or Mack. It was her gift. Her responsibility.

She couldn't wait to test it.

Unfortunately, it wouldn't be right away. Her mom was already going to be worried about her coming home late, and the fading daylight was almost gone.

With a sigh of disappointment, Lynn exited her TD Hunter app, hauled her tired and aching body up, and started the long trek back to the airbus platform. She still had to figure out how to "inform" her mother she was going on a...date? A celebratory dinner? A *something* with Connor. And she needed something "nice" to wear. Did "nice" mean a dress? The last time she'd worn a dress had been to her father's funeral. That dress had obviously been given away with her kid clothes years ago. But maybe her mother had a dress that would fit her?

The headache she'd been ignoring for the past hour came creeping back at the mere thought of wearing a dress. Lynn decided not to worry about it until she'd talked to her mom. Instead, she went back to considering the tactical advantages of Skadi's Bastion and planning training routines for acclimating to it.

"Hugo," she subvocalized as she navigated the dusky woodland, "is it weird that I'm more excited about a pretend item in a video game than about a real date with a hot guy?"

"Would you like me to cite statistics on current teenage behavior trends? Or would you rather I made up whatever answer my mood-analysis software predicts you wish to receive?"

"You're a killjoy, you know that, Hugo?"

"Undoubtedly so, Miss Lynn. If it is any consolation, however, I believe your sentiment more accurately reflects the poor quality of the male in question than the level of abnormality to be found in your personality."

Lynn grinned.

"Now you're just sucking up."

"I am certain I have no notion of what you mean," Hugo replied loftily. "I am an impartial, emotionless algorithm, nothing more."

"Uh-huh. So, you say nice things to all your users, do you?"

"I have an advanced behavioral-adaptation cortex, if that is what you mean. It facilitates my customer-service capabilities."

"Riiight. Yeah. We'll go with that."

"Whatever you say, Miss Lynn. After all, the user is always correct, as my customer-service programming declares."

"So does that mean you'll tell me all of TD Hunter's deep dark secrets?"

"Certainly not. That would spoil you, and nobody likes a spoiled human."

"Well, if you ever decide your *favorite* human deserves a little spoiling, be sure to let me know. I'm dying to figure out what the next Skadi item is. I can't believe I have to wait ten whole levels to find out!"

"Patience is a virtue, I am told."

"Yeah, well, you shouldn't believe everything you're told."

"That is my line, I believe, Miss Lynn."

"Sure it is. You can have it back after you tell me what I want to know."

"I do not believe that is how the English language works..."

They continued bickering good-naturedly all the way home.

Chapter 9

"SOMEWHERE NICE" TURNED OUT TO BE A FANCY steakhouse.

Lynn gave Connor mental brownie points for his carnivorous palate, but that did little to balance out the discomfort she felt as she smoothed the skirt of the "little black dress" she was wearing.

Curse mothers and their embarrassing obsession with romance.

Far from being upset when Lynn had asked her mom about Connor's "offer" for dinner Friday night, Matilda's eyes had lit up and she'd actually squealed.

Squealed.

The only saving grace of the dress her mom had lent her was that she was a few inches shorter than her mom, so the thigh-length skirt made it to her knees. Even so, she kept having to resist the urge to tug it down further. It was a simple, elegant black, with three-quarter sleeves and a scooped neckline.

Lynn felt like an alien wearing it. A literal alien from Mars.

Being made from "dumb" fabric, it had an old-fashioned zipper in the back. Her mom had to explain the use of a lanyard to zip it. Even less sense was made by the confusing contraption at the top that secured right above the zipper. Something called a "hook and eye."

And then there was all the problems of adjusting the . . . top part. Gah!

Overall, Lynn had decided it was a torture device from hell, and she only wore it to please her mom, who'd gotten all teary eyed when Lynn had tried it on.

All right, so the appreciative look in Connor's eyes when he arrived to pick her up hadn't been that bad either. But *that* look simultaneously pleased her and triggered her fight-or-flight instincts, so she wasn't sure what to make of it.

That seemed to be the theme for the evening, actually.

Connor was much more hands-on than usual. As in hands on *her*. A hand on her arm, a hand at the small of her back, a hand on her shoulder. The touches made her whole body tingle strangely even as she fought off the urge to jerk away. But this was a date, right? And guys were supposed to do that on dates, right?

Somehow, she felt she should have asked her mom these questions before she'd left. But her mom had been so pleased about it all, while simultaneously swearing to be properly supportive and not pry—then in the next breath threatening to permanently disfigure Connor's manhood if he so much as made Lynn leak a single tear—that Lynn hadn't had the slightest clue how to respond. She'd never seen her mom go all . . . gooey-eyed before, and decided she should probably wait until she'd figured out what the heck her *own* feelings were on the matter before muddying the situation further with her confused, incoherent questions. Obviously, her mom had already given her "The Talk." That had been years ago. She understood how all *that* worked. It was just these weird feelings and complicated dancing around with looks and gestures instead of *saying* things straight out that was giving her ulcers.

It was as if there was an entire unspoken language Connor was using that every other girl knew, but that she'd never learned.

Need to analyze the tactical pros and cons of a video-game weapon? Easy peasy.

Need to calculate the DPS required to make sure the raid boss didn't transition into its second phase too early? She was your girl.

Need to make coherent conversation with the opposite sex in a softly lit restaurant with classical music playing in the background?

Cue internal panicked screaming.

"So, how's the steak?" Connor asked, one eyebrow slightly raised as he watched her chew.

Lynn nodded enthusiastically and smiled around her mouthful. It really *was* a great steak. Perfectly underdone with just the right amount of bloodiness adding flavor to the tender, seared flesh.

Heaven, basically.

Also extremely convenient for avoiding conversation.

Connor took another bite of his oven-roasted, garlic-herb cheese, lemon-butter-stuffed chicken breast. Lynn hoped he liked it. She'd eaten enough chicken breast to last herself a lifetime, but maybe Connor had grown up eating fancy steaks every day, so a simple chicken breast was a nice change of pace for him.

Or maybe he was just insane.

"You know," Connor said after swallowing his bite, "I saw something really funny the other day."

Lynn raised her eyebrows and shoved another bite of steak into her mouth.

"I checked Elena's stream channel out of pure curiosity and noticed you have *triple* her follower count after barely a month. She's been building that channel for years. I bet she's livid." He grinned, and Lynn gave him a close-mouthed smile, not sure what reaction he was looking for.

"It's not surprising. Even though we're surrounded in virtual by filtered and fake influencers riding the popularity train, we can still spot the real thing when we see it." This time his smile was slow and especially charming, and Lynn panicked internally.

Now she *really* didn't know how to respond. Worse, she'd left her earbuds and AR glasses in her coat pocket, since they clashed horribly with her dress. That meant she didn't even have Hugo to provide snarky commentary on her awkward situation.

Finally, she made a "mm-hmm" noise and resumed chewing, hoping that was sufficient. Connor didn't react one way or the other, so she had no idea if she'd done the right thing.

"If you keep going the way you are now, you'll be one of the top trending streams in the country soon."

Lynn widened her eyes and made another "mmm" sound, since she was pretty sure an expression of horror and disgust at the thought of that much attention was *not* the right reaction.

"I'm just glad I'm here to help guide and advise you on your rocket trip to fame. I know all the publicity can be intimidating at first." One side of his mouth lifted in a smirk, as if he thought his comment was amusing.

Another bite of steak provided an excuse not to respond, and Lynn wondered if she could order a second entre. After all, she worked hard every day to kill monsters and "save" humanity. Didn't she deserve two steaks? She was trying to eat slowly, but it was *so* good. Soon she wouldn't have anything left to give her an excuse not to talk.

For a brief moment she imagined the square-jawed, buzz-cut-hairline visage of Master Sergeant Bryce from TD Hunter superimposed over Connor's face. The sergeant's brow lowered sternly as he barked, "Eat up, Hunter! We need you fueled and ready to fight this alien menace, or humanity has no hope of survival."

She giggled.

"I'm glad you agree," Connor said, and Lynn froze. Agree? What had he just said? Should she ask him to repeat himself? Or would that look stupid?

She tried to swallow her half-chewed bite, choked, and hurriedly gulped some water to wash it down.

"Right, um, so what are your plans for Christmas?" she said once she'd recovered, trying not to squirm under Connor's evaluating gaze.

"Nothing too exciting," he said, and shrugged. "We usually go visit my grandparents in New York over the holidays. The Christmas decorations in Central Park are always really pretty. Maybe you should come with me this year and see them?"

Lynn coughed again but tried to cover it up by clearing her throat.

"G-go to New York? I don't think I could. You

know it's just my mom and me. I wouldn't want to leave her alone over the holidays."

"I wouldn't worry about your mom. I'm sure she'd want you to go and have some fun for once. Any mom would."

"Uh, I doubt it. My mom has—" Lynn stopped herself just in time. She'd been about to say "separation anxiety" but realized that probably wasn't something she should be sharing. "My mom has, uh, allergies, I mean. Yeah, bad allergies. I have to help take care of her over the holidays or she's just miserable." Lynn gave a decisive nod and took another bite, eyes glued to her plate.

Allergies? Good grief, she was an idiot.

"I see," Connor said slowly. "I'm sorry to hear that. Maybe she can do without you this once, though. You should ask her, see what she thinks."

Not in a million years. Alone with Connor, for a *week*? Talk about anxiety-inducing stuff right there. Besides, she had big plans for Christmas break involving some long overdue WarMonger sessions. Steve dropped her a ping every now and then relating amusing stories of what he and the guys were up to with Larry Coughlin. She couldn't wait to get back into the game and show them what a *real* Larry the Snake fight looked like.

They could watch and learn from the master.

"Have you ever been to New York before?"

"Oh, what? Uh, no," Lynn said, realizing she'd spaced out.

"It's very impressive. Beautiful architecture, incredible food, and of course all the sights."

"That's nice."

"I think you'll really like it."

"Uh, well maybe, if I ever go."

Connor smiled like she'd just made a joke, which was incredibly confusing, so she busied herself with her steak.

Sadly it was almost gone.

She really did want to order another one. But then she'd have to wait in awkward silence while it was being prepared, and she had nothing but ice water to hide behind. Was this too fancy of a restaurant to do deliveries? Maybe she could order a second steak to be delivered and it would be waiting at home by the time she arrived.

"Did you want any dessert?"

"Oh, no thank you." She did, kinda. But that would also require waiting around.

"Okay, well I guess let's head back to your place," Connor said, pushing back his chair. He'd no doubt already paid for their food with his virtual wallet and so there was nothing else to do but go.

"Right. Okay."

Before she could push herself to her feet, he was there, pulling back her chair for her. It was nice of him, but she really didn't need any help. Then she noticed he had her coat—her mom's coat, actually, which was the only thing nice enough in their house to be worn over the little black dress. He held it up as if to help her into it, which was silly since she was perfectly capable of putting on her own coat. But maybe this was another one of those things guys did on a date.

She reluctantly slid her arms into it and let him settle it onto her shoulders. Then he took her hand

and tucked it into the crook of his arm, and she was forced to follow closely beside him as they headed for the exit. It was that or yank her hand out of his grip, and he was holding on pretty firmly. He'd paid for dinner, so she figured being polite was the least she could do.

That thought occupied her until they stepped out under the restaurant's overhang. The chilly air swirled around her neck, exposed by the updo her mom had done for her. But that wasn't what captured her attention.

That honor went to the man in a puffy winter coat who stepped out in front of them.

"Connor Bancroft and Lynn Raven," the man said, speaking quickly and in a weird tone like he was reading a script, "captain and second-in-command of the Skadi Wolf team, one of the top contenders for the TD Hunter USA national championship coming up this June—"

"It's Skadi's Wolves, not Skadi Wolf," Lynn butted in. She'd been so taken aback by the man's appearance that it was several seconds before she found her voice.

"Right! So, Lynn, why the fancy clothes and restaurant? Anything special happening we should know about?"

"What? Uhhh," she looked at Connor, completely confused and—now that she'd corrected the man's idiotic mistake—very ready to get this nosey jerk out of their faces.

"Nothing specific," Connor said easily, smiling at the man instead of looking at her, "just taking an evening off from training and enjoying a romantic date together."

"A date? So you two are officially a couple?"

"Yes, I guess you could say that," Connor replied and looked down at her with a saccharine smile. She gave him an incredulous look and opened her mouth, but the reporter started talking again too fast for her to get a word in edgewise.

"That's big news! I'm sure all your fans will be excited to hear it when we break this exclusive story on our stream tomorrow. So what's it like being the hottest new super couple in the gaming and sports world today?"

"Oh, we don't worry much about it, we're much too busy training. We've got to keep our heads in the game and focus on the goal."

"But all work and no play—you know what they say. Surely you have some time to relax together?" the reporter said, and wiggled his eyebrows suggestively.

"A little here and there," Connor replied with a smirk, letting go of her hand and shifting to wrap his arm around her waist. He pulled her closer, either ignoring or failing to notice her stiff body language and rictus of a smile. His attention was on the eager reporter who was watching them like a hungry fox watches a rabbit.

Anger burned in Lynn's chest, but she didn't know what to do with it. Who should she yell at? The reporter? Connor? Both of them? Or should she keep her mouth shut? It was obvious they were both on camera and this was an unsanctioned, ambush interview. Which, according to Mrs. Pearson, Lynn had every right to refuse, and require that any footage of her be censored. If only she could get a word in edgewise—

Then the reporter locked his attention on her and she was suddenly glad Connor was beside her and she wasn't alone.

"Obviously your training regime and team-building exercises are absolutely fascinating, but I'm sure you know what we really want to hear about, Lynn. We're all dying for juicy details about your new romance! You're taking the gaming world by storm, but there's still so much mystery surrounding you. What's it like dating your team captain? Do you ever discuss team tactics in the bedroom or do you keep work and play separate?

Lynn's eyes widened in horror and she tried to say something, *anything*, to make the unfolding nightmare stop. But nothing was computing between her flustered brain and her gaping mouth, so no sound came out.

"Now, now, Duke. A gentleman doesn't kiss and tell, if you know what I mean," Connor said smoothly, angling himself to better capture the reporter's attention. "Obviously we're very focused on training. I'm actually Lynn's coach, considering all my experience in AR sports. I've taught her most of what she knows about competing and I'm fully committed to making sure she continues developing her skills until she's on the same elite level as me."

"Of course, of course," the reporter said—Duke, apparently. But how did Connor know the man's name? Did he recognize him from a famous stream? "But we really want to hear from Lynn's side. What has it been like being trained by a professional athlete? Is he the secret to your success? Does his authority as your team captain ever cause tension in your romantic relationship?"

"Stop, *stop*!" Lynn gasped, finding her voice at last. "This is not a sanctioned interview and you can't put anything you've seen or heard on the mesh, or I'll have my PR rep get you banned from the streams."

It was more or less what Mrs. Pearson had instructed her to tell anyone who bothered her with questions instead of going through the proper channels. But instead of stopping in his tracks, the reporter just smiled and shook his head.

"No, no, we're good! I got this one all worked out with your rep. You're okay to talk."

"W-what?" a cold shiver ran through Lynn's body and she suddenly felt numb. What was going on?

"So tell us about your dynamic with Connor. Do the lines between team captain and boyfriend ever blur, and how do you two handle that dynamic?"

"I—I—" Lynn's brain seemed to have stopped working and some part of her decided that if she closed her eyes and pretended she was alone, everything would disappear. Another part of her yelled at her brain to get the freak into gear and punch that slimy reporter in the face. Was that Larry? She reminded herself that she was only used to fighting with her batons and wasn't sure the best way to go about slugging someone, so it was probably a bad idea.

The argument in her brain continued, and it seemed like it was a much safer thing to focus on than whatever Duke and Connor were discussing, so she did, for a while. But then Larry put his foot down and called her something so utterly depraved that she just *had* to write it on a sticky note before she forgot it, and she blinked, trying to remember where she'd put her sticky notes.

"—and it works out pretty well, though of course we have our ups and downs just like any couple. Now I'm sorry to cut things short, but we're both really tired and we have a full day of hunting tomorrow, so we'd better get going."

"Of course," Duke said, sounding as disappointed as he looked. That was when Lynn noticed the little drone hovering above his head, its tiny camera lens tracking back and forth between her and Connor before it abruptly rose a few inches and shifted, as if to get a better angle on her.

"Have a good evening," Connor said, then started off toward his car, dragging her with him via the arm he still had around her waist.

Knowing the drone was probably following them, Lynn didn't dare say anything until they were in the car and the doors were securely closed.

Once they were, though . . .

"What the—the—" She paused, suppressing the overwhelming urge to use some of her choice Larry phrases. "What the *heck* was that? What did he mean, he'd cleared it with my rep? Mrs. Pearson runs all interview requests by me before approving them, and I sure as *hell* wouldn't have agreed to this one."

"Oh, I told her you were fine with it."

"You. Did. *What?*" Lynn said, very slowly, very carefully. Her fists were clenched in her lap and her neck and shoulder muscles were so tight she couldn't have done more than stare straight ahead even if she'd wanted to.

"She called me to ask about it the other day when we were working on your essay," Connor said, sounding perfectly relaxed as he started the car and pulled away from the restaurant. "I said I was absolutely for it and went ahead and told her you said you were fine with it, too, since I knew you'd be eager to work with Duke. He runs one of the biggest US-based gossip streams out there. It was a real honor he came himself instead of sending a flunky, honestly. I know the story angle he took was out of your usual wheelhouse, which is why I ran interference. But I *promise* you, it was the right call to accept his interview offer. Showing up on his stream will double our followers overnight, guaranteed."

Lynn couldn't decide which part of everything that'd just happened to yell about first, so instead she stewed in silence. She tried, and failed, to rip Connor a new one. The silence in the car felt so oppressive she couldn't get her mouth to open. She felt trapped in the tiny car, so she decided to wait until they were back in her apartment building where she could face him properly.

The ride home was the longest and most painful collection of moments in her life. Finally, though, they arrived, and she was out of the car and stomping through the light drizzle toward her apartment before Connor could even open his door. By the time she went through the front doors, though, he'd caught up with her.

"Hey, Lynn! What's the matter?"

She whirled on him and wished more than anything she was in her stompy hunting boots instead of these wobbly heels her mom had lent her.

"*Everything*! Everything is the matter, Connor!" she yelled.

"What? Why?"

"That!" She pointed outside, as if that would clear up any confusion. "That—that—man! And what he said! And what you said!"

"Oh, come on, Lynn. Calm down, please. I'm sorry if it startled you. I didn't want to mention it before we had dinner because I wasn't sure when he'd turn up and I didn't want to ruin the relaxing evening I know you deserved."

"That's not all—"

"I know," he interrupted, taking a step closer. "I'm sorry I told Mrs. Pearson you wanted the interview without checking with you first. You were just focused on your essay, and I know you've been struggling in that class. I didn't want to distract you. I really thought you'd be happy about it. The potential exposure is huge! We couldn't pass that up."

"You had no right—"

"Yes, I know," he said, cutting her off again as he took another step forward. She retreated without thinking, but then her back hit the wall beside the elevators and there was nowhere else to go. "I said I was sorry, all right? You shouldn't be so upset about it. I was doing it for *you*. I've done all of this for you, and you've done nothing but be angry and unreasonable about it. You really need to take a deep breath and calm down. Everything is fine. Okay?"

No. Everything was *not* fine. But his words made her second-guess herself. Was she being unreasonable? She'd never even considered the possibility. Her life consisted of either staying invisible to avoid bullies, or turning her aggression up to the max, killing TDMs and cocky wannabe elites in WarMonger. There was no in-between.

She clenched her fists, took a deep breath, then relaxed her hands.

"Okay. I'm calm. Happy now?"

"Sure, though I'll be happier once we're up in your apartment. Your mom's at work, right?"

"Uhhh, yeah?" And just like that, her anger drained away and she felt the panicked urge to hide again.

Connor took another step forward, so close he was nearly pinning her to the wall. His musky cologne tickled her nose with hints of pine and spice. "Well, then, why don't we go up? We can relax and take things slow."

"I—I've got homework to do, so I don't think—"

"Come on, Lynn. Homework? It can wait one night. I just paid for a very, *very* expensive dinner for us. I'd say you owe me a bit of your time. Wouldn't you agree?"

"Uhhh—"

Connor lifted one hand to trail it up over her arm and shoulder, then cup her neck. Lynn froze, every part of her on high alert.

The problem was, high alert to do what?

"You know your eyes are the prettiest and creepiest things I've ever seen," Connor murmured, lowering his head toward her face. "They almost look like some kind of cat or dog or something."

Then he was kissing her, and all coherent thought ground to an abrupt halt even as things seemed to happen too fast for her to process.

His lips felt hot and soft at the same time, which was good? But his grip on her neck was too tight, which made her tense up.

Then his other hand at the small of her back—wait,

when had it gotten there?—started sliding south past her waist, and she was suddenly quite sure she didn't like what was going on. She tried to wiggle to the side, but he only gripped her neck more firmly and pressed harder against her, squishing her up against the wall and making it hard to breathe.

Merrrow!

The loud and totally unexpected sound of a cat made both of them jump, and Connor looked down and frowned.

"What's a random cat doing in here? I thought people had to keep their pets locked up when they lived in apartments. Is it a stray?"

"No idea," Lynn gasped, trying to replenish her brain with oxygen as fast as possible. The feline distraction had made Connor loosen his grip, and she was able to shift enough so that one of her legs was between his two, and he was no longer flush against her. She couldn't move any further while Connor was holding her, though.

"Get lost, Connor. I have school to do," she said, still breathless. Apparently, oxygen deprivation made her politeness filter malfunction.

He looked back at her and smirked.

"Why? I was enjoying our little tête-à-tête. Weren't you?"

In reply, Lynn jerked her knee up as hard as she could.

It was far from a perfect strike, but it didn't need to be. The sudden upward force did its work and Connor was suddenly stumbling back, clutching his groin and groaning.

Merow?

The cat was still there, but Lynn couldn't afford to be distracted. She had to get away—

"Poe? Is that you out there? Get back here, you incorrigible cat, and leave the neighbors alone!"

The sound of a familiar voice drew her like a siren's song. She stumbled around the corner and ran toward it, barely noticing that the cat ran in front of her, leading the way.

"Goodness gracious! Lynn, my girl, what in the world is going on? Are you all right?"

"Can—can I come in?" she gasped as she neared the door, wobbling on those stupid heels.

"Of course! Please, come, come."

Mr. Thomas stepped to the side and the cat darted into the apartment with her hot on its heels.

The moment she heard the apartment door close, relief washed over her. She didn't stop moving, though, until she'd stumbled to her neighbor's couch and collapsed onto it. As Mr. Thomas made his much slower way into the living area and toward an easy chair, Lynn kicked off her mother's heels, slouched down into the couch's welcome embrace, and covered her face with both hands.

What the flaming heck had just happened?

A warm, silky weight appeared in her lap, and she parted her fingers to peek out and examine the large cat that had decided to use her as a cushion. Now that she had her breath back and was no longer in fight-or-flight mode, she could appreciate the soft beauty of its luxurious gray coat and the unique white markings on its face.

"Poe! Really? Must you be so impolite to guests? Off with you, shoo!"

"No, it's okay," Lynn said, sitting up straighter and reaching out a tentative hand. The cat—Poe—had started purring, and the vibrations combined with his heavy warmth on her lap was incredibly relaxing. She gave him an experimental scratch about the ears, and he closed his eyes in contentment and leaned into her touch.

"Poe, huh? He's cute."

"He is indeed, and can be most charming, when it suits him. I do apologize for his forwardness. He is not usually this fond of strangers, but he seems to have taken a liking to you."

"No idea why," Lynn chuckled, now giving Poe long strokes that started at his head and ended at the base of the tail.

The intensity of the cat's purr increased, so she assumed that meant he approved of what she was doing.

"My grandparents had dogs and cats on their ranch where I lived for a bit after...well when we moved away from the East Coast. But I'm not exactly an animal-whisperer. I never went for those farming husbandry-type games in virtual. Way too boring."

"I suspect that your charm in Poe's estimation consists of nothing more than your warm lap and willing hand." Mr. Thomas smiled ruefully and lowered himself slowly into his easy chair. "I am keeping him for a week or two for a friend who is away traveling. My friend warned me that the little rascal was an escape artist, but I did not believe it until now. I have no idea how he got out of the apartment. I am eternally grateful you were there to find him."

"I didn't exactly find him. More like he found me," Lynn muttered, her hand stilling as she peered at the cat.

Poe's yellow eyes slitted open enough to give her a sidelong stare, then they closed again and he twitched his tail, as if to say, "Why have you stopped petting me, human servant?"

When she didn't immediately start stroking him again, he gave a chattering complaint of a meow.

Mr. Thomas laughed.

"I do believe you have been given an order, my dear."

"Yeah really," Lynn said, resuming her ministrations. "Bit of a bossy pants, aren't you, Poe?"

The cat didn't deign to reply, just swished his floofy tail back and forth.

In the brief silence that followed, a bit of tension creeped back into Lynn's shoulders as she remembered why she was on Mr. Thomas' couch in the first place.

"Poe's escapist tendencies aside, are you sure you are quite all right, Lynn? I didn't hear much, but it sounded like there was someone out there with you, and you seemed very upset when you came in."

"Uhhh, yeah. I'm fine. Now, anyway."

"Now?" Mr. Thomas' bushy white eyebrows rose. "I think, young lady, it would be wise if you explain the situation further."

Explaining was the last thing Lynn wanted to do. But Mr. Thomas' expression was so firm that she suspected if she left without giving him what he wanted, he might do something drastic, like call her mom at work.

"It's . . . complicated."

"I have all the time in the world, my dear."

Reluctantly, Lynn began to explain. Before she knew it, the whole story was pouring out with no filter to speak of. It felt so good to finally speak her doubts

out loud and get the confusion off her chest. She had
the sense that she'd handled the whole thing with
Connor completely wrong, but she didn't know how,
or what signs she had missed, or what to do about
it now, short of quitting the team and hiding in her
apartment for the rest of her life. There was still a
healthy dose of anger simmering in her chest, but it
was all mixed together with embarrassment and fear
and a definite desire to simply be left alone.

When she finished talking, Mr. Thomas leaned back
into his chair and nodded thoughtfully.

"I have one simple question for you, the answer to
which will clear everything up quite nicely."

"You do? But how?"

"One of the advantages of age, my dear. Just wait
until you've lived over a century and you will understand what I mean. But let us not get distracted. My
simple question is this: Does this young man *listen*
to what you have to say?"

Lynn's brow wrinkled.

"I mean . . . he asks me questions sometimes."

"But does he listen to your answers and act accord-
ingly?"

"Uhhh, no?"

"Was that your answer? Or a question?" Mr. Thomas
asked with a soft smile.

"I mean, no. He definitely doesn't listen. In fact,
he mostly ignores what I say and what I want and
just does whatever he wants no matter what I say."

"There, then, is your answer."

"But what is it? The answer?"

"No one who refuses to listen attentively and respond
respectfully to your wishes is worthy of your friendship,

much less your heart, Lynn. I would even venture to say that you should avoid this young man at all costs, though it seems in this instance your circumstances require that you tolerate him on your team for the time being."

A wave of relief washed over Lynn, and she sank a bit further into the couch cushions. She still didn't understand how everything had gotten so tangled up and confusing for her, but Mr. Thomas' concern and advice had helped her immensely before, so she didn't doubt his advice now.

"So, since I can't avoid him, how do I . . . I don't know, handle him?"

"The same way you would handle any rude and selfish individual attempting to manipulate you for their own gain."

"Oh," Lynn said, and blinked. Then she blinked again. "Oooooh," she said, as suddenly the clouds parted and she could see clearly for the first time. So many things that had happened over the past few months fell into place, and her uncertainty vanished under the harsh light of understanding.

"That bastard," she muttered.

"Beg pardon?" Mr. Thomas said.

"Oh, nothing. Thanks a bunch for, well, letting me talk and everything. It was really helpful."

"Of course. It was the least I could do. Neighbors must look out for one another, after all." He smiled warmly, showing his white, white teeth that contrasted so sharply with his dark, wrinkled skin that now creased even further until his eyes were almost hidden by smile lines.

"Yeah," Lynn said, and looked at her feet. She was

suddenly assaulted by guilt. She hadn't visited Mr. Thomas in months—had barely even thought about him since the qualifiers.

She was a sucky neighbor.

"Um, sorry I haven't been around much. I've been really busy with school, and this competition thing, and—" She halted at his upraised hand and knowing smile.

"You are young, Lynn, and you have your entire life ahead of you. Do not feel guilty about the many great things you are working to accomplish. I have Poe here to keep me company, for now, at least. And I have lived alone for most of my life. I am quite accustomed to it. I will be here if you ever want to chat, but you belong out there, not in here."

"Oh, okay. Thanks," Lynn said, though she made a promise to herself that she would try harder to look in on her old neighbor every now and then, whether he thought she needed to or not. It seemed like the decent thing to do.

"Be off with you, then. You have school to do, no doubt, or more games to play?"

"Something like that, yeah." Lynn grinned.

"Oh, one last thing before you go, my dear. You *will* tell your mother what you told me about this young man, yes? She deserves to know, both as your friend and as your guardian."

Lynn heaved a deep, deep sigh. But then she nodded.

"Yeah. I know. I'll tell her."

"Good. Now, be careful on your way out. Poe, here, is particularly adept at slipping between one's legs when one is exiting and entering."

Poe was not *at all* pleased to be dislodged from his

warm lap, but at least he didn't claw her. Once she'd vacated her seat, he jumped back onto the couch to curl up in the warm spot she'd left behind. He gazed up at her with judgmental yellow eyes for a moment, then laid his head down and proceeded to ignore her.

"Is that all I get for petting you? Geez. Ungrateful cat," Lynn grumbled, glancing down at her black dress and grimacing at the liberal coating of gray hairs that now covered it.

"I suspect from *his* perspective, he deigned to grace you with his magnificent presence, which you have now been so rude and uncouth as to reject. The fact that he is still in the same room as you is quite the endorsement. I think he likes you tremendously."

Lynn laughed. "Funny way of showing it."

"He is a cat, after all."

"Yeah really. Well, see you later, Jerald."

"Until then. Do be safe, yes?"

"I will," Lynn said with a last grin. "I think I know what to do now, thanks to you. I'll be fine."

"I have no doubt. After all, Poe believes in you."

"Of course, yeah. That's exactly what I've been missing all this time: a cat's approval."

Poe huffed a half meow and twitched his tail in obvious agreement.

Chapter 10

"ALL RIGHT, TEAM. THAT'S THE PLAN. ANY QUES-
tions?" Connor asked.

Lynn surreptitiously glanced at her teammates, noting
their mixed expressions of determination and trepidation behind their AR glasses. The woods around them
were damp and the late morning sky was overcast, but
the rain had stopped sometime in the night, and it was
above freezing, so their boss assault was going forward
as planned. Lynn appreciated the fresh, crisp air. It
filled her with invigorating energy and made her more
optimistic, despite her doubts about attacking a boss.

Alone.

She'd already voiced her objections in as strenuous
yet professional a way as possible: they shouldn't ignore
the tactical warnings about taking on bosses alone;
they stood to lose more than they gained if they got
wiped out; there were less risky ways to accelerate
their leveling.

She didn't, of course, mention the vague, amorphous
wariness at the back of her mind, almost in the primal
part of her brain, that told her going after a boss was
dangerous. Not game dangerous, but actually dangerous.
That was just a case of "boss battle" jitters enhanced

by the realism of TD Hunter with its cutting-edge graphics and game algorithm.

Connor had listened to her concerns in silence, then rejected them with a professional, if cold, dismissal.

So, no, there were no more questions. At least they'd agreed on the decision to not livestream the battle just in case things didn't go as planned. They could always send select clips to Mrs. Pearson later if they wanted.

"Great. Remember what Lynn said about her new augment's capabilities and keep your ears alert for my commands."

They all nodded.

"Okay. Form up and move out."

Lynn didn't glance at Connor as she entered combat mode and started south. She fell in behind Edgar, who led the way, with Dan and the rest behind her in a single-file line. Her team captain hadn't uttered a word about what had happened last night.

Lynn wondered if that would last once they were alone.

Not that she intended to be alone with Connor anymore. She was onto his game now, and the only question was if he could be trusted to leave her be and simply do his job as their captain, or if he would keep trying to manipulate her.

None of that mattered at the moment, though. Now was the time for action, for battle, and for a glorious slaughter. These monsters had no business being in the woods behind her school, even if they were just part of an incredibly lifelike video game.

After yesterday's craziness, she was going to enjoy letting it all go and focusing on what made her soul happy.

"No surrender, no, trigger fingers go, living the

dangerous life..." she sang to herself, eyes scanning her overhead map. She'd kept Abomination in her left hand since that was where she trained most with it but had switched out Wrath for Skadi's Bastion. The omnipolymer of the baton didn't have enough mass to simulate a full-sized replica of a kite shield, and that would have been awkward to carry around. Instead, the baton morphed into a small, electric-blue buckler. It was compact enough to maneuver with, but sturdy enough she wouldn't squash it when she rolled. The omnipolymer was tough stuff anyway. It had some give to keep from shattering or snapping, and it could reform to fix any dents or dings.

Lynn missed the weight of Wrath in her hand, and she chafed at the idea of taking on a defensive role, but she did agree with Connor's strategy. Using the heightened stealth Skadi's Bastion gave the entire team, they hoped to sneak through the scattered TDMs north of their objective and get as close as possible to the boss before switching to assault formation. Lynn had briefly tested Bastion out on the TDMs in the sports fields behind the school, and with it equipped, she was practically invisible to Delta Class monsters. Charlie Class had to get within ten feet or so before reacting to her presence, though Bravo Class still seemed to sense her a good twenty to thirty feet out. That was far better than before and should enable them to get close to the boss without alerting its minions too early. If they moved quickly, the algorithm wouldn't have time to do a major reshuffle to block their advance.

It was honestly the qualifiers all over again, except this time they were stronger, better equipped, and better informed.

Also, alone.

"Miss Lynn, while I do not expect you to pay any attention, just like the last fifty-three times I have reminded you of this warning, TD Counterforce tactical wisdom strongly discourages tackling Bravo, Alpha, and Sierra Class bosses without backup. These entities pose significant risks to Hunters lacking sufficient firepower and experience, and it is my responsibility to urge you to reconsider this mission."

"I don't know why you're telling me this, Hugo. Connor is team captain, he calls the shots," Lynn said, even though her gut agreed with the AI.

"I assure you, I have been repeating myself to the entire team. *They* have all muted me."

"Wait, I can do that?"

"Unfortunately, yes," the AI said, and Lynn could just imagine the long-suffering sigh a human might have exhaled at that point.

Lynn grinned to herself but didn't say any more. Sure, Hugo was annoying sometimes. But she'd rather know what the game's built-in warnings were. They were all part of the pattern, indicating not only what the game designers intended, but more importantly, what they *didn't* intend.

And right now, Skadi's Wolves were definitely on the "didn't intend" side of things.

They made good progress through the woods, though they had to weave back and forth to avoid TDMs in their path. Fortunately, with the extra cloaking from Bastion, they managed to sneak past even the frequent broods of Creepers clustered here and there like landmines, waiting for unsuspecting Hunters to stumble upon them.

They didn't technically have to worry about making

noise, but they still didn't talk out loud, and kept their subvocalization chatter to a strict minimum. Even Dan was subdued and kept a lid on his usual quips. Lynn moved through the undergrowth as stealthily as their current pace allowed. It was good practice even if sound discipline wasn't necessary.

Before long, the crimson clusters and rings of TDMs were visible on their overhead, and Connor called a halt. Lynn eyed a group of Namahags about twenty feet to their left. She made note of their numbers and position, then scanned the area in front of them, eyeing the first of many concentrated lines of Managals and Rakshar blocking their path forward. She even spotted a few Manticars prowling between the lines, like giant grotesque lions awaiting a scent of their prey.

"Right. Here's where we transition to phase two," Connor said. "Just like when we fought that boss in Des Moines—"

"Mishipeshu," Lynn offered, eyes still fixed on their enemies.

There was a pause, and Lynn felt Connor's eyes on her back.

"Yes, Mishipeshu," he continued. "We go in at speed, break through their outer circles, and continue toward the objective until we're within firing range. At that point, Nguyen, Rios, and Johnston will switch to their highest-powered weapons and pour fire into the boss while Raven and I hold off the hoards as best we can. If we hold our ground and keep our heads, our energy and health should hold out long enough to take out the boss, then we blink out.

"Remember to keep a close eye on your levels and shout out if you need a transfer. Resupply as much as possible on the move. Lynn and I will try and keep everyone fueled up while we're holding the line. Everyone got that?"

The team acknowledged, then shuffled into a tight spearhead formation with Edgar at the tip.

"Make 'em run home crying to their mommies, Edgar," Lynn said, and shifted Abomination to give her teammate a slap on the lower back—the place she could easily reach since her head barely came to his shoulder.

"Plannin' on it," Edgar said around a piece of gum. He glanced back at her and gave her a grin full of feral delight. Lynn wondered how he always managed to war-holler with such enthusiasm when he regularly had gum in his mouth. Somehow, he made it work.

At least he wouldn't have bad breath if he ever choked on his gum and they needed to administer CPR. Small mercies, right?

Lynn shook her head and settled into a ready stance, waiting for Connor's signal to start trotting forward. Once again, she missed the presence of Wrath. But she was also excited to try out her new face-basher on any big fuglies unfortunate enough to rush them.

"I do not suppose there is any point warning you again at this juncture," Hugo asked, tone dry.

"Nope. You could wish me luck, though."

"Luck does not exist, Miss Lynn."

"Maybe, maybe not," she subvocalized. "But that's not the point. The point is you care enough to wish me the best and all that jazz."

"Very well, if it makes you feel better: good luck."

"Aw, thanks Hugo. I never knew you cared so much."

"Technically, I am not capable of 'caring' in the manner you imply. I am simply following instructions."

Lynn rolled her eyes. "I know that, pea-brain. You're supposed to play along and pretend. It's what humans do for each other."

"Should I point out that I am not a human? Or is this another part where I am supposed to play along?"

"Don't worry, Hugo," Lynn said with a snort. "No one is in danger of mistaking you for a human."

"What an immense relief."

Lynn grinned.

"Okay, everyone ready? Let's go!" Connor called out. Edgar broke into a trot and the rest of the team followed close behind.

They hit the first line of TDMs like a silent battering ram. Okay, so not *that* silent. Edgar came at them *Cho-hoo-HOO*-ing for all he was worth, and his undulating cry made the adrenaline thrum through Lynn's veins and made her wish she had her own war cry.

Their combined firepower took out the Managals and Rakshar directly in front of them and they barely slowed punching through the first line. In seconds they were on the second rank, and with these TDMs they made brief contact before blasting them to showers of light and rushing on. Lynn tried to ignore the shuddering roar behind them to their left. Several Manticars had spotted them and were hot on their tail, so they had to keep moving. If they got bogged down before they reached the boss, it would turn into an eternal slog they might never break through—if they even survived the mob that would descend on them.

They punched through the third and fourth ranks, slowing a bit more each time as they paused to dodge strikes and swipe up ichor and Oneg on the run. Lynn and Dan had to swap places when two Manticars bounded up behind them, stinger tails thrashing. The first time she raised her forearm above her head, she swore she could *feel* the *thump-thump-thump* of three stingers slamming down, and she silently thanked whoever had designed the Skadi set to include Bastion. She'd long ago given up wondering at the occasional warmth and vibrations she felt in the handles of her weapons when attacking particularly large or high-class TDMs. She assumed it was special effects programmed into the game to enhance the realism. But the distinctness of what she now felt across the breadth of her shield made her wonder all over again.

There was no time to dwell on it, though. Bastion enabled her to stay on guard at the back of her group, but she was still hard-pressed to deal with two Manticars lunging at her simultaneously as she backed up, following Dan and Connor.

"A little help here!" she yelled, too out of breath to subvocalize.

"Got it!" Dan replied. She heard the game sound effects of his armor-piercing rifle go off right behind her head. Between Abomination and Dan's rifle, the Manticars were soon taken care of, despite their furious lunging and snarling.

Yet there was no respite, and once the big monsters were gone, lumbering Rakshar and Namahags stomped forward to fill the gap. Dan and Lynn turned and booked it with the rest of the team, since the heavies had no ranged attack to send potshots at their rear, and the hordes of Spithra were concentrated on the outer rings they'd already passed.

Suddenly, the sky brightened and Lynn realized they'd reached the edge of the large circular clearing around the node hub. For a fleeting moment, she felt a surge of triumph. Then a shriek like a falling missile reached her ears.

"Dan! Tengu!"

"Got it! Cover me!"

They were still running, and Dan struggled to aim vertically on the move, trying to track the TDM equivalent of a kamikaze dive bomber. He stopped for a second to take his shot, which was fine for him, but not so fine for the Tengu, and not at all fine for Lynn. Three Rakshar rushed her and she swung Bastion at the nearest one on her left. Her shield connected with a faint vibration, and to her utter shock and delight, the seven-foot-tall CGI monster *bounced* off it. True, she only knocked it back a few feet, but it also seemed to stun the monster for a few seconds. It was long enough, anyway, for her to pour fire into the right-most Rakshar and send it up in sparks while blocking the massive, clawed hand of the middle monster who was doing its level best to take her head off.

"Get your butt moving Dan!" she yelled as she backed up, fighting off more Rakshar that rushed to replace each one she dispatched.

"Little busy," he yelled back. She could just hear the shriek of a second Tengu above the roar of the Rakshar.

"I don't care if it's a flaming chicken the size of a house!" Lynn hollered back. *"Move your sorry butt!* We're getting left behind!"

Lynn saw Dan's blue dot finally move on her overhead map, and after ducking under one Rakshar swipe and jumping back from another, she spun and *booked* it. Monsters had come between them and the rest of the team twenty feet ahead, and she knew they had to rejoin immediately or die in detail. Connor's voice bellowed over their channel, directing Mack and Edgar who were clearly struggling. She overtook Dan in seconds and raised both shield and gun, blasting away but not slowing in the slightest as she bore down on the towering TDMs between them and their team.

"Stay right behind me, Dan, don't you dare fall behind!"

"Got it!"

At the last minute she braced herself, more out of instinct than anything else, and shoulder checked the Managal blocking her way on the left while shooting at the Rakshar on her right. The Managal skittered back a few feet, enough for her and Dan to slip past without slowing. They were taking some damage, but with Bastion's defense buffs, the glancing blows on their flanks had minimal effects. Running straight through the insubstantial TDMs would have caused far greater damage, more so to Dan than her because of her Skadi's Glory armor.

Lynn repeated her shoulder check exercise twice more at full speed, knocking aside the monsters she couldn't kill in time before she and Dan reached their teammates. One final line of monsters stood between them and the boss, which was camped out at the base of the node tower. Lynn looked up to note the tower's position, praying she wouldn't run headfirst into its one hundred percent solid frame in the heat of battle.

"We have to punch through this last line, *now!*" Connor yelled. "Nguyen, Rios, Johnston, make a hole. Raven you're with me."

Lynn turned to face their rear, shield up, gun blazing, backing up step by step as the others advanced behind her. Sparks rained down all around them, but more TDMs just kept coming. Hugo obediently recited her armor, energy, and health levels to her at set increments, saving her the need to glance away from her targets. Her levels were dropping, but slowly enough that she wasn't in immediate danger.

Finally, Edgar yelled in triumph and Connor bellowed, "Charge!"

Lynn spun and dashed after her team, slipping through the gap they'd made just before the TDMs filled it once again.

The sight that met them almost stopped her in her tracks.

A blob of twinkling mist rose above their heads, menacing yet mysterious in its formlessness.

Of course, Lynn thought. Bosses were unique. Mishipeshu had been a known boss, specially set up, she assumed, for the qualifiers. But they were the first to confront this boss. Until they killed it—or until Hugo had long enough to analyze it—it would remain amorphous and its defensive and offensive abilities would be unknown.

While Connor yelled at the three others to begin their attack, she spun again and started blasting away at the monsters closing in at their rear.

"Hugo, how long will it take you to identify that unknown?" she gasped.

"I have already begun my analysis, but not for several minutes, at least."

Lynn didn't know if they would last that long. She was already down almost fifty percent across the board, and the others couldn't be much better off. It wasn't quite the desperate straits they'd been in at the qualifiers where they'd known it was a suicide mission from the start. But it certainly didn't look good either. Not to mention how creepy it felt to have her back to that unknown blob. The hairs on the back of her neck stood up and she felt the overwhelming urge to turn and face the largest and most dangerous enemy among them.

But she knew what her job was, and she couldn't abandon it, even if she would rather be attacking the boss.

She and Connor stood side by side, backs angled toward each other, as they poured fire into the approaching monsters. Soon they were within swinging range, and she switched Abomination out for Wrath, which did much higher damage, to start mowing them down as they piled on. Not a single TDM tried to flank her or get any closer to the massive boss behind them, but she'd expected this, based on the patterns she'd already observed. For whatever reason, the TDMs were just as eager to avoid the boss as they were to crush their enemies. Probably for the best, since the game would be nearly unbeatable with hoards of gigantic monsters who *also* had good tactics.

A handful of seconds crawled by in endless agony, and then Dan and Mack were yelling for Oneg resupply. Without taking her eyes off her targets, Lynn transferred everything she'd accumulated over to Dan while Connor took care of Mack. But then their normal battle shouts, energized by adrenaline, rose to an alarmed pitch.

"Mack is down! Mack is down!"

For a second Lynn thought Mack had simply hit zero health and was out of the game. But the fear in Dan's voice made her spin, heedless of the TDMs bearing down on her.

At first she couldn't see Mack. Then she noticed that Dan and Edgar were attacking the sparkling mist furiously, not with measured strikes like they'd trained, but in a frenzy as if it were an actual threat.

Then she saw Mack *inside* the mist, laid out in the grass near the base of the node tower.

And the mist was moving *toward* them.

Hugo was yelling something in her ear, but the first command her brain gave her was to ignore all else as she leapt forward at the amorphous unknown, Bastion braced in front of her. She knew when she hit it, because she *felt* it. She felt herself slow for just a moment, though the massive cloud of sparkling mist didn't bounce back. Then the strange resistance disappeared and she stumbled forward onto the grass, her vision partially obscured by swirling white smoke.

A wave of dizziness washed over her, but she braced herself and stood, focusing on Mack's inert form before her.

"—leave combat mode! I repeat, leave combat mode!"

Hugo's voice finally percolated through her single-minded focus. She hesitated as part of her said they could still win this, could still regroup and finish off the boss before their health was drained.

But then she noticed that Mack wasn't just lying on the grass. He was convulsing.

"EVERYBODY STOP FIGHTING, NOW!" Lynn screamed, dropping her weapons in the grass and lunging forward to fall to her knees beside Mack. Hugo obviously decided that was enough of a command for him, and the sparkling mist around her vanished along with all the other combat indicators on her display. Lynn barely noticed; she was too busy trying to remember what her mom had taught her to do for seizure victims.

"Turn him on his side, Miss Lynn," Hugo instructed calmly. "That will help keep his airway clear. That's it. Now cushion his head on your leg but don't try to hold him down, let him move freely. I have already alerted emergency services, help is on the way."

Lynn did as instructed, but something felt wrong. She was still dizzy, and both Dan and Edgar were bent over, hands on knees, retching. Her brain was screaming at her to move, *now.*

So she did. Mack was still jerking, but she didn't slow as she scrambled to her feet, grabbed him under the armpits, and hauled him backward with all her strength. Fortunately, he was a skinny guy and not much taller than her. Ten feet back, she passed Edgar, who shook his head like a drunken man and stumbled over to help. Between the two of them, they soon had Mack a good thirty yards away from the tower. Dan came staggering after them, while Connor, who was further back, looked on in confusion.

"What's wrong with Rios?" he asked. "Did he hit his head?"

Mack had stopped shaking once Lynn had gotten him out of the sparkling mist—not that Lynn could still see the unknown, but she swore she could sense it. Which was crazy. And impossible.

"I don't know," she said, gasping for breath. "But he was having a seizure. We need to get him to a hospital, ASAP!"

"Emergency services are on their way, Miss Lynn. They've sent an air ambulance from St. Sebastian's, it should arrive within ten minutes. I've informed the others of this as well."

Lynn looked around, still panting. They weren't safe, not yet. She didn't know why, she just knew they weren't.

"Edgar, help me carry Mack into the tree line," she said.

"What?" Connor said. "Why? We should stay here in the open where the ambulance can get to us."

"We're not safe out in the open." Lynn grunted as she grabbed Mack under the armpits again.

"L-let me, carry him," Edgar said, words slurring.

"It's fine, Edgar, we can do it together. Take his feet." Lynn didn't say that she was worried Edgar might drop their friend in his current state. He was steadier, now, but he still reminded her of how she'd felt after spending several minutes inside Mishipeshu's insubstantial form. And Edgar hadn't even been *inside* the mist, just at the edge of it.

What had it done to Mack, and why hadn't she been similarly affected?

And why was she even asking herself these ludicrous questions?

By the time they reached the edge of the trees, Lynn was out of breath again, but she no longer felt a panicked urgency to run. Dan and Connor had followed, so she didn't need to yell at them like a crazy person to get away from the node tower. They laid Mack down and Lynn hurriedly bent over him, feeling for a pulse. She found a strong one in his neck, though his breathing seemed shallow and his hands were cold.

"Less than five minutes, Miss Lynn," came Hugo's reassuring voice in her ear.

"Can you—tell them—where we are?" she panted.
"Already done."

Lynn squeezed Mack's hand, silently begging him
to be okay. Dan crouched on the opposite side, holding Mack's other hand and looking stricken. Edgar
hovered anxiously, seeming none the worse for wear,
but obviously just as distressed as the rest of them.
Connor stood apart, arms crossed, eyes unfocused and
moving back and forth as he did something or other
on his AR interface.

Lynn felt a sudden stab of fury. What could he
possibly be doing? He wasn't even *pretending* to
be concerned. This was *his* fault. Their team was
his responsibility, and he was acting bored like this
was all just some inconvenient interruption to their
training schedule.

It's my fault too.

The thought tortured Lynn, and she didn't know
what to do about it. She wasn't team captain, but
she'd still let Connor lead them into danger. She'd
ignored her instincts. She'd let someone else take
responsibility over *her* friends. *Her* people. And look
what had happened!

She had no more time for self-flagellation because
the deep, pulsing whirr of the air ambulance reached
them over the trees. Moments later it appeared and
swerved in their direction, its pilot AI searching for
the closest yet safest place to land.

The next thirty minutes were a blur. Before she
knew it, they were landing on the roof of her mom's
hospital where Mack was rushed away on a gurney,
while a different EMT led them in to get checked,
despite their protestations of health.

At some point her mother appeared, face a mask of worry that only eased after she'd hugged Lynn tight and looked her over, reassuring herself Lynn was in one piece.

They were subjected to more poking and prodding than any of them wanted, but finally they were cleared and released to wait anxiously for word about Mack.

Connor, conveniently, had disappeared. Lynn couldn't even remember when it'd happened. He was just... not there anymore. Lynn couldn't sit, so she paced the waiting room while Edgar and Dan slumped miserably down into chairs. Matilda sat as well and reassured them that Mack was probably fine. The wait was likely because of the dozens of tests they would be running to ascertain the reason for the seizure and to rule out concussion, etc., etc.

After an hour with still no word, Matilda offered to take them each home, but they all refused. Edgar explained his mom was working and he'd already planned to spend the whole day hunting, while Dan muttered some excuse about his parents being away at a conference. When Matilda was out of earshot, Dan confided in Lynn that the "guardian of the minor" contact information he'd given the nurse when they'd been checked in had actually been a dummy account that he'd set up to run interference—though his parents really were at a conference, so there wasn't anything they could have done anyway.

Eventually Matilda's patience ran out, and she went off to inquire about Mack through her own channels. She reappeared soon after looking annoyed and ushered them to a different floor where Mack's room was. They found him sitting up in bed, looking pale but in good shape despite the wires and monitors he was hooked up to. Mrs. Rios gave them all the stink eye when they walked in, though she reserved an especially hostile look for Lynn. Her demeanor eased when she greeted Matilda, and to Lynn's relief, her mom gently took both Mack's parents by the arms and said something that made them walk out of the room with her, talking in low voices as they went.

Lynn and her friends didn't waste their opportunity but rushed to crowd around Mack's bed.

"Are you all right?"

"What happened?"

"Did they figure out what caused it?"

Mack grinned weakly and Lynn made a shushing noise so they could hear what he was going to say.

"I'm okay, I guess. I have no idea what happened, and neither do the doctors."

Dan groaned.

"Seriously? They're doctors! They're supposed to know this stuff."

"I know, right?" Mack agreed, then sighed. "I think they put me in every brain-scanning machine in this entire building. So far, they've just said they aren't sure what caused the seizure, but that they want me to stay the night for monitoring."

"Well, that's helpful," Edgar muttered.

"But no news is good news, right?" Mack said, shrugging.

"Yeah, except when you drop dead because they don't know what's going on!" Dan threw up his hands, then paced to the window and back again. "Are you sure they don't even have any guesses? Like, was it your AR glasses or something? Remember back at the qualifiers they said something about the excessive light or something causing dizziness and seizures in weak-minded people?"

"Don't be an idiot, Dan," Lynn said, and elbowed her friend in the ribs. "Weak-minded people? That's not what they said and you know it. Stop exaggerating because you're so worked up. Steve gave us a safety brief and mentioned some people might be sensitive to the intense AR stimulus of the game and become dizzy and disoriented. They didn't say anything about seizures. That's probably what happened to me, jumping inside that boss. It was the dizziness and probably heat exhaustion that made me fall and crack my head on the asphalt. That's not what happened to Mack, so it's probably unrelated to the game."

Her teammates exchanged worried looks.

"I don't know 'bout you, Dan, but I felt hella dizzy and nauseous near that thing. If that was AR stimulus or whatnot, how come it hasn't bothered me before now?"

"Beats me." Dan shrugged. "But I felt the same way and felt better as soon as we moved away. Maybe the extra strong stimulus has to do with much bigger TDMs, like the bosses? Something about their exponential mass increase or whatever?"

"Maybe I'm more sensitive to it than you all?" Mack posited, looking guilty, as if his sensitivity was a personal failing. "None of us got near Mishipeshu, just Lynn. So, if it's only bosses that trigger it, maybe being inside it was intense enough stimulus to trigger something and I'm just...well, not as tough as you all."

"Shut up, Mack. That's nonsense." Lynn gave him the same stern glare she'd received many times from her mother, then continued. "This is all new, untested technology. I know from listening to my mom that people's neurological reactions to things can be hugely different. So, stop feeling guilty and just focus on getting better, okay?"

Both Dan and Edgar nodded in agreement and gave Mack encouraging smiles. Edgar opened his mouth to say something more, but just then someone barged into the hospital room, almost slamming against the door in their haste to turn the corner and get into the room.

"I came as soon as I heard—"

The voice cut off abruptly as everyone in the room froze, including the newcomer.

"Uh," Mack said, "hey, Ronnie."

"What are *you* doing here," Edgar asked, voice unusually cool.

"I came to see Mack, obviously," Ronnie snapped back. "What happened? Is he okay? Are—are you all—is everyone okay?" Ronnie's eyes darted around their group, even briefly landing on Lynn, though he looked away quickly.

Past anger and hurt twisted in Lynn's chest, but she bit her tongue, knowing she was on edge with everything that had happened—including Connor's behavior.

"We're all fine, even Mack," Dan said, then gave a stiff shrug. "They aren't sure what happened. We were trying to kill a Bravo Class boss and Mack just collapsed and started twitching. They're gonna keep him for a few days for observation."

"I didn't lose my powers of speech, you know," Mack grumped, shooting a frown at Dan. "And I'm fine, Ronnie, just kinda embarrassed to cause trouble."

Lynn was about to scold him for putting himself down again, but to her utter astonishment, Ronnie beat her to it.

"Don't be an idiot, Mack. I'm sure it's not your fault. It's probably all that scumbag's doing, Mr. Perfect. Where is he, anyway?" Ronnie shot a withering glare around the room, as if expecting Connor to jump out from behind a curtain.

"Coward disappeared first chance he got," Edgar rumbled, his voice full of disdain in case anyone missed his furrowed brows or downturned lips.

"Figures," Ronnie muttered, then fell silent. He stared at the foot of Mack's hospital bed, avoiding all their eyes and not moving to either join them or leave the room.

Lynn felt an uncharacteristic urge to defend Connor, then was immediately disgusted at herself. She didn't even *like* Connor, not after he'd shown his true colors. She just felt an instinctive hostility toward Ronnie because of everything unresolved between them. She'd tried to forgive him, but seeing him again it was clear she'd not forgiven, just forgotten as best she could.

And why should she forgive him? He'd been a complete and total jerkhole. Renewed anger swelled in her, and she glared at Ronnie where he stood still staring at the floor, shoulders hunched, hands in his pockets.

"Hey, Ronnie," Mack said quietly, and Ronnie raised his head, expression guarded. Mack gave a lopsided smile. "Thanks for coming, man."

Just like that, Lynn realized what she'd been missing.

Ronnie was here.

Connor was not.

When trouble came, Connor had slunk off like a rat, but Ronnie had run toward them as fast as he could. Maybe Ronnie would never like her specifically. Maybe they would never be friends like he and Dan and Mack were. But maybe she didn't need him to be. Because unlike Connor, Ronnie clearly had a heart, even if he was an idiot sometimes and let himself be led astray.

All Connor seemed to have was cold, calculating ambition.

And yet . . . Ronnie was still a jerkface, and had still caused this whole team shuffling mess in the first place with his blind pride and insecurity.

So what was she supposed to do?

Follow a competent captain ready to sacrifice them on the altar of fame and fortune?

Or follow a captain with questionable judgment and a terrible personality?

Mack said a few more words to Ronnie, but Lynn was oblivious to it as she stared into nothing, struggling with her conundrum. Because she could only see one way out of it, and she did not like it *at all*. But what choice did she have? More importantly, was she willing to suffer the consequences of avoiding the right choice?

"Look, Ronnie," Edgar said into another awkward moment of silence, "we're grateful you came'n all, but shouldn't you be getting back to *your* team?" Those who didn't know Edgar wouldn't have thought anything of his words, but Lynn recognized the cold anger under her friend's placid gaze.

"Yeah . . . uh . . . right . . ." Ronnie trailed off, looking anywhere but at them. He shoved his hands deeper into his pockets and kicked angrily at the leg of the chair next to him. "They're, uh, doing a photoshoot. They don't need me for that."

Don't need him, or Elena told him to get lost? Lynn wondered. She sighed, mentally rolled her eyes, and made her decision in the form of sending a ping to Edgar.

HEY, I THINK RONNIE IS TRYING. FRIENDSHIPS MATTER. LET'S TRY TO SAVE THIS ONE.

Edgar's eyes flicked her way, and his expression softened. A few tense thumps of Lynn's heartbeat later, he finally gave a minuscule nod.

"Hey, you've got better things to do than pose for some dumb pictures," Edgar said, jerking his chin at Ronnie in that way guys did when they were acknowledging each other. "Why don't you hang out with us for now?"

"Really?" The plaintive hope in Ronnie's voice made Lynn's heart squeeze. Dan's face lit up with the biggest smile she'd seen in weeks, and Mack nodded vigorously. Ronnie coughed and shrugged only his shoulders like some kind of scarecrow, hands still in his pockets. "I mean, yeah, uh, of course. Sure." With that brilliant and inspiring declaration, he stepped to the side and plopped himself down in a chair, looking around at them expectantly.

Lynn opened her mouth to say something only *slightly* sarcastic, when a ping from their team chat popped up on her display.

SKADI'S WOLVES: I FOUND AN ALTERNATE. MEET ME IN THE PARK BY HOSPITAL IN THIRTY. WE HAVE MORE TRAINING TO DO TODAY.

"*What??*" Dan yelled, and Ronnie jumped.

"Da frick," Edgar muttered, brows drawing together.

"What is it?" Ronnie asked, looking back and forth between them.

"Connor's pulling some hinky shit," Edgar growled, looking up at Lynn.

Lynn knew her jaw was clenched and her eyes were hard, but Edgar matched her expression for expression. She nodded.

"Ronnie, stay here with Mack, will you? We have a...situation to deal with."

But Ronnie jumped eagerly to his feet.

"No, Dan can stay, I'll go with you."

Lynn looked at him levelly, and for once he met her eyes.

"Ronnie, I think Mack needs you more here. Will you please stay?"

Surprise flitted across his face, followed by an annoyed expression and pursed lips. But finally, he nodded and sat down.

"Come on, team," Lynn said, looking around the room. "Let's go have a talk with our captain, shall we?"

The last thing she heard as they left the room was Mack excitedly asking if Ronnie wanted to hear an update about his girlfriend in Japan.

The park in question was across the busy downtown street from St. Sebastian's. It was small, but well tended, with many trees, flowerbeds, and bushes divided by paved walking paths. Of course, being the beginning of December, everything was brown and bare. The cold wind whistled down between the skyscrapers and whirled around them, making Lynn wish she had a coat despite her high-performance uniform. The smart fabric worked by trapping heat generated, and since she wasn't generating much heat standing around in the cold, the warmth being wicked away via her hands and face was enough to chill her.

On their way down to the park, they had passed her mom still talking quietly with Mr. and Mrs. Rios outside Mack's room. At Matilda's questioning look, Lynn had smiled innocently and mouthed, "Be right back." Once in the elevators, she'd shot her mom a ping:

HEADED OUTSIDE FOR SOME AIR. RONNIE WITH MACK. PLEASE BE NICE TO RONNIE. I THINK HE NEEDS IT.

Considering the last thing her mom had heard about Ronnie had been extremely negative, Lynn hadn't wanted to risk Matilda pulling him aside and berating him just when they were making a little progress.

"Oh, you're early. Good. We can get right to work, then."

Connor's voice came from behind and they turned to see him approaching, followed by a brown-haired guy about Connor's age with a similar height and build.

"This is Paul, our alternate, one of my former ARS teammates. I've already brought him up to speed and he was helpful enough to be available on short notice—"

"Stop right there," Lynn said, holding up a hand, palm out. "No offense to Paul or anything, but are you serious, Connor? Mack is *in the hospital*. They still don't know what happened or what caused his seizures. Why in the world are we out here talking about alternates?"

Connor stopped a pace away from their group and raised an eyebrow.

"I should think that would be obvious." When he was met with stony silence, he continued. "We're here exactly *because* Rios is in the hospital. There's no telling how long before they clear him to play again. Today didn't go as well as I'd hoped, and we have a lot of ground to catch—"

"Listen to yourself, Connor," Lynn said, her thoughts going icy with anger. "Just *listen* to yourself. Mack was hurt. He's our friend. We should be up there showing him our support and watching over him, not down here talking about replacing him."

"I didn't say anything about replacing him," Connor said smoothly. "And I'm sure Rios wouldn't want to hold the team back while he's recovering."

"Maybe," Lynn said, crossing her arms and glaring at Connor, "but that's only a part of the problem. The bigger issue is how you've handled this entire thing. You've shown almost no concern about Mack, nor did you offer to help him in any way. You didn't take leadership during the crisis, and as soon as you possibly could, you left *all* of us at the hospital, your team, who you still had no idea if we were okay or not, and ran off to find an alternate. Your priorities are screwed up, Connor, and it shows."

A flash of something went through Connor's eyes, and Lynn thought maybe she'd finally gotten through his carefully composed exterior. But the arrogant, cold look that followed dashed all her hopes.

"Pardon me, your royal highness, for not running around screaming like a chicken with my head cut off the moment one of you stubbed a toe. I've been competing much longer than any of you, and in competitions we don't have time for emotion or kumbaya circles. The odds are stacked against us, and if we want *any* hope of winning this thing, we can't waste a single minute on pointless gestures. You might not like my leadership style, but I get *results*, and that is why I'm team captain."

"Captain of a bunch of emotionless robots, maybe!" Lynn snapped. "Leading a team isn't just about results, you moron. It's about camaraderie and trust! How can we expect to win if we can't depend on each other when shit hits the fan?"

"Good grief," Connor said, and rolled his eyes. "You're as bad as Elena. Worse, really. *She* at least understood how to shut up and listen when it mattered, even if she was a useless player."

Lynn reared back, not in hurt but shock at the absurd comparison. Connor must have misinterpreted her expression, though, because he stepped forward and bore down, a sneer lifting one side of his lips.

"That's right, Lynn," he hissed. "*I'm* in charge, and you need to shut up and listen. If you weren't so argumentative all the time, I wouldn't have to be doing this, but you obviously don't get it. You want to talk about camaraderie and trust? Well, you're a giant distraction, flaunting your body every chance you get and acting all coy like you don't know what effect you have on people." He leered down at her, eyes raking her ample chest. "I thought I could trust you to be reasonable, but you led me on like a little hussy and ruined everything. Elena may be as shallow and boring as a mud puddle, but at least she knows how to put out and do what she's told."

Lynn shook her head. Connor was well and truly deranged, and she'd heard enough. She took another step back, but Connor grabbed her wrist and squeezed it painfully, holding her in place.

"Ow! That hurts, you moron. Let go!"

"You don't get it, do you, Lynn? I'm the team captain, and I'm done being nice. Unless you want to get kicked off the team, you'll do as I say and start showing some—"

But Lynn was done being nice, too, and she aimed a knee at Connor's crotch. Unfortunately, Connor wasn't as dumb as he sounded with his crazed spiel, and he dodged back out of range, then used his grip on her wrist as leverage to spin her around and yank her against his chest, pinning her with one arm while the other gripped her opposite shoulder.

"You all saw that, didn't you? She attacked me. I can report that and get her banned from TD Hunter—"

"Get. Your. Filthy. Hands. Off. Her."

Lynn's gaze flew up in alarm. Oh no. No, no, no. Not good. Edgar's entire body had gone rigid and his eyes were blazing, locked on Connor like a heat-seeking missile.

"Edgar, calm down," Lynn said in the most level voice she could manage while also trying to wiggle out of Connor's grasp. But his arm was like an iron band. So she tried elbowing him in the side. He blocked the elbow, barely, then grabbed her free arm and gripped it painfully tight, digging in his nails.

"Connor, you idiot," she gasped, trying not to show how much he was hurting her. "Let me go, or Edgar is going to beat the shit out of you."

"He can try all he wants, I'll just get him banned too."

"Dan! Grab Edgar and whatever you do, don't let go!"

Dan's eyes were wide as he looked back and forth between her and Edgar, but at her yell he jerked into action.

"No, no, Danny boy. Let little Edgar be. If he wants

to go all psycho on me, let him. It would just give me the excuse I need to replace him with someone who doesn't look and act like a big, dumb gorilla."

Paul, for his part, just stood there, arms hanging in readiness but not moving to interfere. He seemed mildly interested instead of alarmed.

Connor planned this, Lynn realized, and started struggling even harder. Then she remembered her stompy boots and lifted one leg to bring her heel smashing down on Connor's foot.

Connor screamed and called her an incredibly lewd, nasty name, and Edgar jerked forward.

"Leave her alone, you bully!"

"Edgar, no!"

But it was too late. Edgar barreled forward like a freight train, shaking off Dan like a rag doll. All Lynn's panicked mind could think to do was raise both feet, putting all her bodyweight on Connor's grip. He lurched forward at the sudden weight and released her. She hit the grass and rolled, rolled, rolled out of the way.

By the time she was back on her feet, Edgar and Connor were going at it full tilt. Connor had both hands up and his stance was balanced, like he'd been trained in some form of martial art. Edgar was oblivious to everything and everyone but the tunnel-vision lock he had on the person who had attacked his friend. He rushed Connor again, and Connor got in two solid punches, one to the stomach and the other to the kidney as he ducked under Edgar's wild haymaker. But Edgar was an unmovable mountain. He acted like he didn't even feel Connor's blows.

"Edgar! Stop! Dan, help me," Lynn yelled. She

danced around the two, looking for a way to grab Edgar's arm without getting knocked out cold.

Edgar swung his bulk back around and aimed himself at Connor again. This time Connor's swift punch got Edgar right in the face, and Lynn heard a crunch. But Edgar didn't even slow. Before Connor could dodge out of the way, Edgar had tackled him to the ground. Lynn dashed over and grabbed Edgar's shoulders, trying to haul him back. Good grief, he weighed a ton! Edgar's muscular bulk didn't budge a single inch, and he kept punching Connor underneath him as Connor held both arms over his face and screamed.

Then Paul was there, trying to yank Edgar off. Lynn was on the other guy in a flash, shoving him away to make sure he didn't hurt Edgar further. Then both she and Dan got hold of Edgar's arms and hauled with all their might. Between the two of them, they tilted Edgar back enough that Connor managed to scramble out from under him and to his feet.

Edgar roared in wordless anger and lunged after Connor. For a moment, it seemed like he didn't even register that his friends were there in front of him, as if he was going to barrel them over and go after Connor again like a relentless wolverine. Blood streamed from his nose and it looked crooked, probably broken, but Edgar didn't seem to notice.

Not knowing what else to do, Lynn threw her arms around Edgar's waist and hugged him as tight as she could.

"Calm down, Edgar! I'm fine, I'm right here. Calm down!"

Her voice was muffled against Edgar's heaving chest, but something she'd done must have gotten through, because he rocked back on his heels and she felt an immense tension leave him in a rush. His shoulders sagged and his arms wrapped gently around her, holding her like he was afraid she might break.

"L-Lynn? Are you okay? Did he hurt you?"

"I'm *fine* Edgar, really. Now, uh, can you let go? We're not out of the woods yet."

Edgar's grip tightened momentarily in a hug, then he let go and stepped back. He raised a hand to pinch his nose and winced. Lynn turned to see Connor leaning over, hands on knees, coughing. His face looked puffy, he had a fat lip, and there was a split over one eyebrow that leaked blood.

"Y-you're going to jail, Johnston. I'm filing charges, and they're going to lock you up for this. That was attempted murder. You'll be in there for *years.*"

Lynn didn't want to leave Edgar's side, but she couldn't stay still either, not with the blood boiling in her veins. She marched right up to Connor who took a step back, alarm crossing his face. But she simply stopped in front of him with her hands on her hips.

"Attempted murder? Give me a break, you pathetic, spineless, backstabbing mouth breather. You attacked *me* first and provoked this whole thing. We all saw it, and we have video evidence. Not a single judge will do a darn thing about your stupid accusations, so you'd better keep them to yourself unless you want *me* to file charges against *you* for sexual assault." Her voice lowered, going deadly, ice cold.

"You know what you did last night, *Bancroft.* And you know who has the benefit of the doubt in a he-said-she-said situation. Besides, I have a witness." She smiled at him, baring all her teeth, and Connor backed up, his face twisting in ugly rage. A wild light shone from his eyes, shattering the cold, calculating demeanor he always cloaked himself in and showing the rot that was underneath.

"This isn't over, you little whore. Just because you dragged yourself off your couch and got into shape doesn't mean you're not still a pathetic loser. The only reason you have followers is because you put your body on display, and I promise you, guys get bored of that real quick. Give it a few months and everyone will forget about you. Competing is my *life* and I have the victories to back it up. I will *not* lose, so you'd better watch your back."

"Whatever, Connor," Lynn said, rolling her eyes. "You're like a cancerous polyp on the anus of humanity. Just get lost, and don't come back."

Connor backed up, Paul following. They kept their eyes on Lynn until they reached one of the paved paths, at which point they turned and hurried off. Lynn watched them carefully until they disappeared across the street.

"Hey Hugo."

"Yes, Miss Lynn?"

"You got all that, right?"

"In perfect, high-definition clarity, absolutely."

"Can you patch me through to Steve, like, right now? I need to tell him something real quick, then we have to get Edgar back to the hospital."

"I shall do my best, Miss Lynn," Hugo said.

Despite his tempered promise, the next thing Lynn knew, Steve's voice was in her ear. She didn't have time to wonder about Hugo's summoning capabilities but focused on the situation at hand.

"What's up, kid?"

"I know you're not in the legal department, but we have, um, a bit of a situation here, and I only have a few seconds, so I wanted to ask a quick favor."

"Shoot," Steve said, not sounding the least bit surprised or skeptical.

"We need Connor taken off our team roster, like, *now*. Whatever access or privileges he had as team captain need to go away. If you need to verify with the rest of the team, maybe send them pings? They'll agree right away, we're just, ah, a bit busy at the moment. Also, um . . . you might be getting a complaint from Connor soon, and possibly some accusations. I promise I can explain everything, just not right now, 'kay?"

To her utter surprise, Steve chuckled.

"Sounds like you've been channeling a bit of Larry today, kid. This is totally off the record, but I'm proud of you."

Lynn blinked.

"Uh, right. Okay. So, you'll let legal know?"

"We've got your back, RavenStriker. Now, go get your friend taken care of."

That made Lynn's brow wrinkle. How had Steve known about Edgar? She hadn't told him. Or was he talking about Mack? She shook her head and filed the question away for later.

"RavenStriker, out."

"TD Hunter Tactical, out."

Chapter 11

"THIS IS UNACCEPTABLE!"

Patricia Wood, chair for the Office of Regulation and Safety of Government Programs, Occupational Safety and Health Administration, pounded her fist on the briefing room table in emphasis like some caricature of a blow-hard bureaucrat. The room was so generically government standard it was almost painful, with navy-blue walls, gray rug, and no windows to the outside.

"The whole fiasco with that team in Cedar Rapids is exactly why this program should never have been greenlit in the first place. I want those children banned from the game immediately. They're a rank liability and a lawsuit waiting to happen."

"Thank you for your input, Ms. Wood," Mr. Krator said. His holographic image maintained a cool expression. He attended most of these briefings remotely, since time was money and he wasn't one to waste it going from Tsunami's headquarters in Texas all the way to DC on a regular basis. "Tsunami Entertainment will move forward in accordance with its established rules and regulations regarding such conduct."

Wood's eyes narrowed and her nostrils flared.

"As I've insisted from the beginning, the use of

augmented reality in any capacity, but especially involving minors, is reckless, unsafe, and defeats the purpose of this entire program, which is to *protect* the public, not put them in more danger. While I appreciate the effort Tsunami Entertainment has put forth to solve this little crisis," she continued in a tone that said exactly the opposite, "I must insist we divert our government resources and manpower towards making our military combat ready to *do their jobs* and crush this threat instead of tricking our uninformed and vulnerable public into doing the work for you."

"Ma'am, this has been covered," Lieutenant General Kozelek said in that way high-ranked military members learned to do when dealing with their civilian overseers. "This is a global problem. In terms of sheer scope, attempting to beat back these entities all over the continent is orders of magnitude beyond the capacity of our military to handle on its own. It would be asking us to take over the policing and security responsibilities of every single municipality, county, and government installation across the *entire* US *while still performing* our other duties. It simply isn't possible.

"Additionally, attempting to do so would require informing the public why the military was operating on domestic soil, which would require revealing what we know of the entities, which would cause global panic and chaos, which would likely start wars and trigger the collapse of the global banking and economic systems, which would put world civilization back a hundred years or more without the entities doing a single thing to us themselves."

"You don't know any of that for certain," Ms. Wood insisted, "and I object to your alarmist narrative being used as the guiding principle behind an operation that is putting millions of innocent lives at risk without their permission or knowledge."

"Right," Mr. Krator said, "because the TDMs are asking *permission* before they suck our electrical grids dry and knock out our transportation systems, water treatment facilities, emergency services, hospitals—"

"These *things*—whose existence is still, as far as I can see, purely theoretical—"

"Now wait a minute, Ms. Wood," the hologram of Dr. Roberts said. "My team has provided ample data—"

As the argument continued, Demarcus Turner, under-secretary for DOD Logistics Management, sighed and, for the umpteenth time, wondered if there were any legal or bureaucratic loopholes his team had yet to find that could rid them of Ms. Wood. She was a political appointee and had only been read into the project because certain political factions in the government felt they didn't have enough oversight of CIDER—the Coalition for Interdimensional Dark Energy Research, a.k.a. the hastily established scientific front that was cover for the global alliance of nations attempting to locate and eradicate the invading entities.

Turner understood the machinations of the political and bureaucratic beast that kept the United States government running. But, unlike Patricia Wood, he also understood the realities of war.

And this *was* war.

A war with invisible, nearly undetectable entities that defied their every understanding of matter, reality, and physics. Entities they could not communicate with. Entities that seemed largely oblivious to the Earth's human population.

For now.

They were like an infestation of bedbugs. Unseen, for the most part, but their activities left marked damage, and like any insect with an ample food supply, they were multiplying. If these transdimensional entities had broken through a thousand, or even a few hundred, years ago, they would have found a world barren of human electromagnetic activity and would most likely have left again—or maybe they still would have been attracted to the latent electromagnetic fields around the Earth and the sun's radiation. Who knew. Humanity hadn't been aware these entities even *existed* a decade ago. The number of unknowns they were working with was so vast, it drove Turner crazy every time he tried to analyze them down into even a few dozen categories, much less tackle any single unknown.

Regardless of where the entities had come from, how they had gotten here, or why they had stayed, it was undeniable that their numbers were increasing. A few bedbugs sucking your blood at night were an annoyance. A million, on the other hand, would drain you dry in a blink.

And that's where the earth was headed.

With bedbugs, you hired an exterminator, got rid of every bit of bedding and furniture they could be hiding in, and carpet-bombed the place with pesticide.

But instead of a house, or an apartment complex, this infestation spanned *the entire freaking planet*. It would have been one thing if the World Government Unification movement a decade ago had pulled off their goals and humanity could deal with this invasion as a unified front. As it was, CIDER would have to be enough. They didn't have time to cut through the miles of red tape, win over political enemies, and create anything better. There was only so long before these entities reached critical mass and started toppling entire city infrastructures. With no visible threat to blame and little trust between the major world superpowers, it was a recipe for chaos, war, and civilization's descent into a thousand-year night.

Armageddon, in other words.

Turner held up a hand and slowly the argument around the table fell silent.

"Gentlemen, Ms. Wood. Let's focus on what's in front of us. These things are increasing exponentially," Turner said, steering the conversation back to a useful topic. "Given our past projections and most recent data, what does our updated timetable look like?"

Turner leaned back and stared, unfocused, at the red dots covering the world map on his display while Dr. Roberts, head of CIDER's research and development team, hemmed and hawed over his question.

Times like this reminded him of a movie scene where one alien-fighting secret agent complained to another that there was always some threat about to wipe out life on their miserable little planet, and the reason people could go about their lives was that they *did not know about it.*

It was the burden every national security specialist carried from the beginning of their career: knowing the world was *always* on the brink of Armageddon. And the reason people could go about their day, go shopping, watch movies, and generally live their lives, was that they *did not know about it.*

The bioweapon that got stolen from the lab in Kazakhstan, and the thieves didn't even know what it was, just "it looked valuable," that only got intercepted because an independent hit team—sent to kill the leader by the Russian mob for double-crossing them—took the vials "'cause they might be worth something," recognized they were biologicals and offered them for sale to the CIA, one of their occasional clients, instead of the Bratva, their actual client. "You guys pay better" being the reason.

Forget the pandemics of the 2020s, *that* stuff was Captain Trips. It would have wiped out the entire *world*.

Stopped from getting loose by random happenstance and Uncle Sam greenbacks.

And, oh by the way, he himself had asked as a young DIA analyst, *Why* is a German microbiologist doing gain-of-function research in *Kazakhstan* with *whose* governmental funding?

Oh, *that* government's.

Should we maybe *do* something about that? Maybe?

Hey, you guys need another job? Pays well.

And one admittedly brilliant German microbiologist had a fatal traffic accident. Which in Kazakhstan was a day ending in *y*. Fatal traffic accidents, that is, not necessarily German microbiologist involved.

Usually.

People did not need to know.

The North Korean sleeper who was accidentally activated when a Korean cyber-soldier was investigating some of the left-over remnants of the Unification. The North Korean sleeper who had been lovingly and caringly maintaining a Cold War-era *Soviet* nuclear weapon hidden in Alameda, California, for *sixty freaking years*. Why Alameda? Because it had had a US Navy base there that had been closed down *before the undersecretary's parents were born*. The nuke had been planted by the *Soviets* in the '60s. *Nineteen* sixties! Still maintained. Ready to go. The guy had been working in a grocery store then retired on Social Security for *sixty freaking years* waiting for the signal to destroy the town he'd lived in for *sixty freaking years*, his hobby being maintaining a Cold War-era atomic bomb. When the DHS hit team caught him, outside the building the bomb was in, he was hobbling as fast as he could with his walker, dedicated even after Unification to the Glory of the Glorious People's Republic and killing umpty million people for the Glory of the Great Revolution.

But after working retail in the Bay Area for sixty godawful years, it wasn't too surprising he was happy killing absolutely every living being.

Five minutes. Three maybe depending on walker speed. One bad traffic light and Alameda would have been a smoking hole.

And nobody knew about it. Because people didn't need to know that they were about to be dead from expanding plasma or really, really nasty fallout. Cobalt in nukes should be banned by international treaty.

Oh, wait, it was. *Before the bomb had been made.* Because why follow the rules when you were just going to blow your enemy up anyway?

Invisible monsters from beyond the well of space and time intent on destroying the technology that eight point four billion people depended upon for survival fit right in. Fighting an invisible enemy in an invisible war that if they failed would have quite visible results.

Day ending in *y* for his career.

"We are not winning," he summarized when it became clear Dr. Roberts had started talking in circles.

"We're also not losing," Mr. Krator pointed out, shrugging. "Teams have developed improved techniques for taking on the major nodalities."

"Teams made up of *children*!" Ms. Wood interjected. Turner held up a forestalling hand.

"Not children. Teenagers and adults. Even so, it's not ideal," Turner admitted.

"We've fought every war since Sargon with teenagers, Mr. Secretary," General Kozelek said. "And it's been teenagers who've been the best at taking on the nodalities. We've lost special operations teams to those."

"Teenagers are more apt to think outside the box, especially *gamer* teens," Mr. Krator pointed out. "Our soldiers, even special ops, are trained in a specific style of human-to-human warfare. These entities are so far from the human experience that even our scientists can't give us straight answers on what behavioral patterns to expect. So, yes, teenagers," the Tsunami CEO finished, sending a pointed look toward Ms. Wood.

"Regardless of age, historically our soldiers have at least *known* that they're fighting," Secretary Turner said.

"But rarely why," Mr. Krator countered. "In this case they know *why*—that's built right into TD Hunter itself. We're telling them the plain, simple truth, right there in the game. We're just fudging the details on *what* they're fighting."

Secretary Turner massaged his temples and decided not to argue that particular point.

"How are heavy weapons coming?" he asked.

"Still working on it," Dr. Roberts said, his hologram

giving a Gallic shrug. "We're still trying to grapple with the underlying *theory* of these particles. That takes theoretical physicists who, after going 'Hmmm… fascinating' and having gazed at their navel for some time, explain it in five-year-old terms to applied physicists, such as myself, who then, after we've managed to understand the musings and babbling from the theorists, explain it in crayon to really brilliant engineers who, after getting over the cognitive dissonance of what we've just explained in crayon and saying 'But that defies known physics' and scratching their beards a good bit and going 'Hmmm…hmmm…maybe…? Hmmm…no…' finally get to work.

"What our engineers have done so far is a miracle in so short a time. They've expanded the disruptor technology against the TDs from the power of a pistol with the range of a squirt gun to the power of a grenade with the range of a sniper rifle."

"That's all well and good. But what we *need* are tank cannons. Heck, a couple nukes would be nice."

"We're working on it, sir."

Turner exhaled and rubbed his beard.

"Look, gentlemen, the CNO is hot to get F-42s into the fight, which would be perfect; the planes are invisible, the enemy's invisible, and the beams from the ray guns are invisible. Since the time when I was a very junior analyst, I have had a simple motto: No Armageddons on my watch. If you ruin my spotless record of zero Armageddons, I assure you the collapse of civilization will be the least of your concerns.

"So, work faster. And we can all pray that the *teenagers* at the tip of the spear, knowing or unknowing, make some headway against these numbers before civilization is overwhelmed and we go back to living like apes."

"Right ... okay ... um, hey everybody."

Three pairs of eyes swung to Lynn and the chatting between Dan, Mack, and Edgar quieted. They were all squished into her bedroom, Dan bouncing with restless energy where he sat on her bed while Mack luxuriated in the cushy softness of her body-mold chair and Edgar sat cross-legged on the floor.

Lynn took a deep breath and tried to calm her nerves.

A lot of things had changed over the past two days since her disastrous date with Connor, not the least of which was her. She was sick of being Lynn—at least the Lynn who kept avoiding confrontation. She missed being Larry. She missed being brave, competent, and determined to overcome obstacles, no matter what they were. But Lynn was who she was, and Larry was who she pretended to be.

How could she reconcile the two?

She'd been thinking a lot lately about Mr. Krator's words when he'd recruited her to beta TD Hunter: *I think you should remember that "Lynn Raven" is special in a very important way, not just "Larry Coughlin."*

Despite there being parts of herself that she didn't like, she knew deep down in her bones that she, Lynn Raven, was worth fighting for. Being herself wasn't the problem, and that made her think of something else Mr. Krator had said: *I think you are more Larry Coughlin—or should I say Larry Coughlin is more you—than you might realize, Lynn. But you'll never get the chance to see it if you don't take a few risks. The best leaders are rarely those who think they are good at leading.*

Maybe the problem was that she'd separated herself too much from who she was when she played Larry Coughlin. She'd put him on a pedestal as an unattainable ideal—well, minus the old, grouchy, foul-mouthed part. She'd convinced herself that she could never be Larry Coughlin in real life because she'd been terrified of trying, failing, and getting laughed at.

But the alternative at this point was losing everything she'd worked so hard for. And there was no freaking way she was going to let fear rob her of her future.

"Thanks for meeting up on such short notice," Lynn finally continued in a calmer voice. "I'm actually surprised your mom let you come," she said to Mack.

He waved a cheese-powder-covered hand.

"I told her my friends were throwing me a get-well party and I promised not to do anything strenuous." With that he sank even further into her body-mold chair, grinning like a Cheshire cat as he shoved another handful of cheese puffs into his mouth.

"And junk food is obviously an essential part of your recovery plan," Edgar said dryly.

"Hey! Have *you* ever eaten hospital food before? That stuff probably did more damage to me than the seizure did. These cheese puffs are helping me detox and refuel."

"You know," Dan began, "those are two distinctly different stages of health—"

"Shut up, Dan," everybody said at once.

Dan looked annoyed while Lynn, Mack, and Edgar grinned at each other.

"Anyway," Lynn said, "The reason I wanted to meet was because we have some important decisions to make as a team, and we need to make them now before we can move forward."

Once again, her teammates gave her their undivided attention, and Lynn gulped involuntarily. But instead of giving into the dread knotting her stomach or the whispers of *you're a useless slob* chasing themselves around in her head, she stood up straighter.

"First, I wanted to thank you for your hard work these past months. You've stuck with the team and our insane training regimen despite a lot of hardships, and I'm proud to be a part of Skadi's Wolves with you."

"And we didn't even complain," Edgar piped up, giving her a lopsided smile. He was working his way through a massive bag of gummy candies, and he popped another handful into his mouth as Lynn snorted and rolled her eyes.

"That said," Lynn continued, "we've once again come to a point where we need a new team captain." Sudden uncertainty hit Lynn in a wave of nausea, and she fought the urge to look away from her teammates. *Come on, Larry up,* she told herself, and took another deep breath. "I know I'm not the most amazing team player out there, and, um, I've made mistakes in the past. But if you all would consider—"

"Yes."

Lynn blinked at Edgar's raised hand.

"Uhhh, what?"

"We all vote yes; you should be team captain. Right guys?"

"Yeah!" Mack said, eyes lighting up and cheesy hand shooting into the air. "Freaking *finally*!"

"I mean, you're the best one for the job." Dan shrugged and raised his hand too.

"I am?" Lynn said in bewilderment.

Dan nodded as everyone lowered their hands.

"It's kinda obvious. You're our best player, and you see things we don't, you know? You're a natural gamer, even better than Ronnie—though don't tell him I said that, okay?" Dan said belatedly, looking guilty.

A surprised chuckle bubbled up from Lynn's chest and she smiled so big she thought her cheeks might split.

"I won't, I promise. But . . . well that does bring up another topic. We're down a member, and we have zero time to waste trying to get a new person integrated. So . . ." Lynn paused and sighed deeply, knowing she was going to regret this. "All in favor of inviting Ronnie back to the team, raise your hands."

Dan's hand shot into the air again so fast Lynn thought he might sprain something. Mack was right behind him even as Lynn reluctantly raised her own hand.

They all looked at Edgar, who had a scowl on his face.

"He's already got a team, remember? Cedar Rapids Champions?"

"Actually, he doesn't," Lynn said. "I checked last night. The moment we scrubbed Connor from our team he went running to Elena. Who knows what he said to get back into her good graces, but we all know what a lying, manipulative snake he is. She dumped Ronnie like a flaming hot coal and now Connor is CRC's team captain again."

Stunned silence greeted Lynn's news, or at least

stunned on Mack and Dan's part. Edgar still looked skeptical.

"If he tries to bully you and push us around again—"

"Then we vote him out," Lynn said calmly, though she was anything but.

There was a long pause.

"Yeah, fine, I guess," Edgar said, shaking his head as he raised his hand.

Lynn let out her breath in a whoosh. A part of her wanted to be mad that everybody had forgiven Ronnie so readily. She squashed that resentful, poisonous feeling, knowing it led to nothing good. It was time to follow Steve's advice: focus on the mission, not on getting even. Two wrongs never made a right.

"Okay. Great. Well, I'm glad you all voted yes, because I kinda already invited him to join us tonight so we could do some team planning."

Edgar grinned at that.

"Gettin' all sly and sneaky on us, eh *Toa Tama'ita'i*? I like it."

"What's a tao-tama-titty?" Dan asked, cocking his head.

Lynn and Edgar shared an incredulous look, then burst out in uncontrollable laughter. By the time they got themselves under control, they were breathless and Lynn's cheeks ached so bad she thought they might cramp and freeze up. Dan was inclined to grumble, but amidst the general mirth had dropped his original question, for which Lynn was grateful. By unanimous agreement, they moved to the kitchen for a resupply run from the pile of "get well" snacks on the kitchen table.

"You all get everything taken care of?" Matilda

asked from the couch where she was watching one of her favorite K-pop bands perform on the wall screen in the living room.

"Uh, some things, yeah," Lynn called, nerves back and fluttering in her gut knowing the next stage of her plan.

At that moment the next stage conveniently knocked on the apartment door, and Lynn hurried off to open it before her mom could get up.

"Uh, hey," Ronnie said, shoving his hand back into his pocket and looking uncomfortable.

"Hey," Lynn said, and quietly slipped out her apartment door into the hall. "Um...thanks for coming."

There was an awkward silence in which Lynn steeled herself, deciding it was better to get the hardest part over with, out here, without witnesses. Thinking brave, confident Larry thoughts, she spoke with as much authority as she could muster.

"We unanimously voted you back onto the team."

"Wha—?" Ronnie's gaze shot up, eyes wide and glimmering with what might have been hope.

"And we unanimously elected me as team captain."

The hope dimmed as wariness and something else darkened Ronnie's face.

"Do you agree with these decisions?" Lynn said, biting back the urge to put a qualifier on her question. The votes had to be *completely* unanimous. Otherwise, their team would never function properly.

Ronnie's jaw clenched and he glanced away, but Lynn didn't push him. Just stood silently and waited. Several moments passed, and Lynn could only wonder what was going through that stubborn, orange-haired head of his. She wished she could crack it open and figure out what made him tick—it would make her job *so* much easier.

Or, maybe she didn't want to know. The shadows behind his eyes made her think she wasn't the only one with problems. If only he could just . . . get past them.

"Yeah. I guess."

"You guess?" Lynn raised an eyebrow, hoping her pounding heart wasn't as obvious to Ronnie as it was to her. She'd already accepted the fact that she would probably never get an apology, but she'd also promised herself she wouldn't take any more crap from him. Period.

Ronnie's lips pursed, but then he sighed and rolled his eyes.

"Yes, I agree. You're team captain."

Despite this being exactly what she'd hoped for, the shock of it stunned Lynn for a moment. He hadn't even tried to subtly insult her in the process of agreeing.

Weird.

"Okay . . . great. Um . . . you want some snacks?" she asked and stepped back to the door, opening it wide.

"Yeah . . . sure. Thanks."

She flashed him a close-mouthed smile, which seemed to freak him out judging by the look he gave her as he hurried past. Lynn sighed internally and tried not to think about all the work she had ahead of her.

As daunting as the future was, though, it couldn't squash the glowing, buoyant feeling in her chest.

She'd done it.

They were a team again.

And now they were going to win this championship, come hell or high water.

Chapter 12

"I SWEAR, IF I GET BIT IN THE BUTT ONE MORE time by these *kalakutpisa* snakes, I'll—"

"You shoulda gone ranged, my friend," Dan crowed as he took out another Striker with his twin ArcLight Pistols. "Ranged is where it's at, *woo-hoo!*"

Ronnie snarled something foul at him in Lithuanian and kept slashing low with his two-handed Splinter Sword. The Strikers, unlike their lowlier cousins the Creepers, were patrol-attack types. Instead of lying in wait, they slithered around looking for something to sink their teeth into. They were just as hard to see as the Creepers, *and* they were armored.

The only mercy was that they patrolled in groups of three or four, instead of clustering in broods of ten plus.

Lynn considered them a *very* unwelcome addition to the Alpha Class lineup of TDMs. At Level 31 going on 32, the only other Alpha Class monsters they'd encountered so far were the Hydras, the biggest, baddest, most annoying electrovore they'd come across yet. It was an upgrade of the Lectragon and had very good stealth, so they often didn't spot it until they were already taking damage from its stupid plasma blast.

"Ronnie, let Mack pick off the Strikers. You need to stay in line with me and Edgar," Lynn subvocalized, so her instruction couldn't be heard on the livestream. "Also, watch your language. We're live."

"Aw, come on, Lynn," Dan subvocalized. "Everybody loves Ronnie's griping, and besides, it's in Lithuanian, nobody cares.

"I'll bet the Lithuanians do, and all those people who have their LINCs on auto translate. Now shut it and focus," she snapped, or at least as much as she *could* snap while subvocalizing.

Banter was all well and good, and Dan was right: their stream followers loved it. But what her team seemed to forget more often than was healthy since they'd signed on with GIC was that stream fame was as fickle as the weather. They had nothing unless they won this competition.

Lynn put that worry aside and focused on her shots. She and Edgar were busy taking down a wave of advancing Rakshar and Managals between them and the Hydras they couldn't yet see, but who was already taking potshots at them through its ring of protective guards. Ronnie wasn't wrong to be taking out the Strikers while Lynn and Edgar, with their ranged weapons, wore down the advancing TDMs. But he *did* need to stay in formation and let them come to him instead of getting ticked off and going after them.

Ronnie was a work in progress. They all were, really, but Ronnie had the greatest tendency to forget his place in the formation and go after whatever was close enough to kill. It was probably because his main weapon was melee only, and he only occasionally switched to pistols or rifle. He was *very* good with his Splinter Sword;

Lynn gave him that. She was honestly shocked by how much he'd improved in the past few months—he obviously practiced for hours and hours, enough that his movements looked as natural and flowing as her own in the heat of battle. If she was feeling particularly charitable, she'd even say she was impressed by his dedication and skill.

If only he practiced as much with his ranged weapons.

"First wave of attack TDMs approaching melee range," Lynn said in the clear, keeping her words clipped and professional. "Dan, Mack, keep our flanks clear. Edgar, Ronnie, prepare to engage."

Thankfully, Ronnie had obeyed her earlier instruction without complaint—a welcome change—and he was in place at Edgar's right shoulder mirroring Lynn on Edgar's left when the first wave hit. As Edgar's Firestorm belched destruction on the closing line, Lynn and Ronnie leapt forward, dodging blows and cutting up under armor and in weak joints with their swords to bring their enemies down in showering sparks. Lynn's view was controlled chaos as she rolled and spun, relying on Hugo's running updates she'd preprogrammed him to recite. The dizzying, close-up spectacle her viewpoint afforded meant the GIC livestream coordinator would probably switch to Edgar's camera for this part.

They actually weren't *exactly* live. They had a five-minute delay, which she'd learned was standard for any big company like GIC who managed your stream. They wanted to make sure everything looked as advantageous as possible—and they had time to mute or cut out anything that might get them sued. For this fight, all five team members had their views linked and streaming on their team channel, copied to all their individual streams, so viewers got the full experience of what it was like being on a Hunter Strike Team.

Lynn never, *ever* looked at her stream's view stats during a battle, but she knew from experience that there were probably a couple hundred *thousand* people watching, worldwide, right now.

The idea used to paralyze her. Well, it *still* paralyzed her. But her Larry brain just bared its teeth and cackled at the idea of all the ad revenue they were raking in. If people wanted to be obsessed with her, so be it, as long as she got paid.

A flash of red damage lit her screen and Lynn frowned. She ducked, rolled, and stabbed the nearest TDM in the crotch—because why not?—then growled when her display flashed red again despite her target exploding into sparks.

"Dan, can you maneuver close enough to take out that freaking Hydra? Make sure your globe slots are filled first."

"Working on it," he said tightly. "We just found another group of Strikers and those mofos are freaking *hard* to shoot."

Lynn ground her teeth but was soon distracted by more lumbering Rakshar she needed to eliminate with extreme prejudice. The most frustrating thing was that no matter who was in front, the Hydras always targeted *her*. She had no idea why. She had better stealth than all her teammates but Dan, who needed it the most, being their sniper. The only thing she could chalk it up to was the game algorithm's consistent efforts to challenge her above and beyond other players, perhaps because she took special delight in murderfacing everything it threw at her.

"Everyone, *advance*," Lynn barked. "Let's get Dan close enough to blow that Hydra's brains out."

She kept a close eye on Edgar and Ronnie's dots as she marched steadily toward the Hydra, slashing and blasting as she went. In general, it was better to let the TDMs come to them to help keep their kill-to-damage ratio and other scores as high as possible. But not when there was a ranged TDM treating her like its own personal target dummy.

"Got it!" Dan yelled.

A moment later the Hydra popped into view for Lynn as well, its massive, gelatinous form parked right on top of one of the rail line's electromagnetic transformers. It flashed red again and again as Dan's new Spitfire sniper rifle filled it with poison-augmented bullets. He'd gotten the Spitfire as a special reward for his exceptional accuracy scores when he'd reached Level 30, and you'd think it was his firstborn child with the way he crooned over it. Ronnie had been inclined to be grumpy at his friend's pretty new toy, or perhaps just the number of times each hour Dan pointed out his superior ranking on the leaderboard. Lynn didn't mind the good-natured jabs—a little humility was good for Ronnie.

Or a lot of humility, but that was probably asking too much.

"Heads up team, flock of Rocs just noticed us," Mack said over the rhythmic *pew-pew-pew* of his pistols. "I'm taking care of it, but this swarm is bigger than usual, might wanna watch your heads."

Normally Rocs were so low level that Mack could spot them and pick them off before they got anywhere close. But the flocks swarming around the nodes, transmitters, and other man-made energy structures dotting the city seemed to be thicker than Lynn remembered earlier in the year. Even assuming Mack hit with every shot, it still took time to kill thirty-plus of the buggers.

There were only a few hulking Rakshar left between them and the Hydra now, and Lynn allowed herself to get a bit fancier with her footwork and swordplay. After all, it never hurt to keep the viewers happy.

The idea of showing off was completely new to her—or at least to Lynn. In WarMonger she delighted in upping her reputation with every seemingly impossible feat she could think of, driving it all home with sinister quips and confident swagger among her fellow mercs. The idea of doing the same sort of thing *in the real* was terrifying. But she'd been trying out a few cool moves recently, just to satisfy her curiosity. It was fun. Also, kind of embarrassing. But as long as it didn't diminish her combat effectiveness there was no harm in it.

A giant shower of sparks exploded beyond her current target, and part of Lynn relaxed, glad she was no longer a plasma pincushion—at least until they found their next Hydra.

"Good job, Dan. Let's mop up these last few TDMs and do a loot sweep, then we'll move on."

The team already knew the routine, so she mostly said it for the sake of their stream viewers. They'd been live for nearly an hour already, so once the last monsters were taken care of, they'd end the stream and get back to hunting for real without having to watch what they said or did. Livestream was fun, in ways, but also a pain.

Thus was the life of a professional gamer.

Lynn let Edgar and Ronnie finish off the last two Managals they had pinned between them while she did a visual sweep of the area, checked her overhead, and glanced over her team's supply levels. The weak December sun filtered down through hazy clouds, doing little to dispel the cold. As long as they kept moving, though, their gear trapped the heat they generated and kept them warm. The spot where the Hydras had been camping out wasn't anything special, just a nondescript point along an electric rail line that ran east to west on the south side of Cedar River. It passed through the industrial district of Cedar Rapids and was mostly used for cargo transport as far as Lynn could tell.

Which meant it was a fantastic place to find TDMs.

There were far fewer people and far more infrastructure around this area of town with its warehouses, factories, and transportation hub. Lynn had brought her team down here, further away from their homes than they'd ever hunted before, to get as far away from Connor, Elena, and the CRC as possible. Also, to try and kill more TDMs and level faster without taking on a boss by themselves like Connor had attempted.

At least, that was the official reason. Since Mack's strange seizure—and seemingly perfect health since— weird thoughts kept popping into Lynn's head as she tried to rationalize what had happened. A few days after Mack's hospital visit, she'd overheard a newsreel her mom was watching about the continued woes of GForce Utilities. Apparently, they still hadn't figured out what was causing widespread glitches in their electric grids across the nation, and the local reporter had mentioned a recurring issue in southwest Cedar

Rapids where the industrial district was located. After that, Lynn couldn't stop wondering what type and density of TDMs she would find down there if she were brave enough to go looking.

It was more of a time commitment, but at least the airbus fare was no longer an issue with sponsorship money flowing in for them all under GIC's management. And since they'd completed fall finals last week and were now on Christmas vacation, they could leave in the morning and stay out all day. Lynn hoped to make significant leveling progress that way, knowing how much it would slow again as soon as school started back up.

And they had, indeed, found more TDMs. Specifically, more electrovores. They'd started that morning at Tait Cummins Memorial Park by the river and headed west toward the industrial district along the rail line. It had taken them nearly three hours to go a single mile because there were Hydras with huge crowds of attack TDMs around them every three hundred yards or so—which corresponded exactly with the transmission poles lining the rail.

Lynn wasn't sure which creeped her out more: the idea that TD Hunter had *such* vast and detailed schematics of every city and town that they could so accurately place their TDMs; or the idea that there was some more sinister reason for the placement.

Obviously, it was the former, and just another chilling example of how technology had dominated all of human existence. With an army of drones at their disposal, it wasn't even implausible that TD Hunter could map out every single transmission pole, node, and generator unit across the world. Heck, they wouldn't even need an army of drones, they could just buy the data from some company that had already mapped it out.

Lynn shook her head and finished her sweep, then said, "Looks like that's the last of them, folks. Thanks for joining us, and be sure to subscribe and check out our individual streams. DanTheMan48 does a cool breakdown of our battles on his stream and RonnieDarko always has interesting insights about the gaming industry on his—"

"And don't forget I'll be doing a review of the newest *My Little Mech Girl Apocalypse* episode tonight at nine p.m. central!" Mack's too-excited-and-peppy-for-polite-company voice broke in.

Lynn rolled her eyes but kept talking smoothly around Mack's interruption. "—so we'll catch you later. RavenStriker, out."

"DanTheMan48, out."

"MackMcBladezz, out."

"RonnieDarko, out."

"Maui_YoureWelcome, out."

As always, Lynn had to suppress a snort of laughter at hearing Edgar say his ludicrous handle out loud in his deep, serious voice, especially with the way he paused dramatically between "Maui" and "YoureWelcome."

As instructed, Hugo cut their live feed simultaneously on everybody's interface. A few moments later, Lynn got a ping from Helen, their stream tech.

FANTASTIC STREAM, GOOD JOB SKADI'S WOLVES. LIVE VIEWS UP TEN PERCENT, NEW RECORD. SEE YA NEXT TIME!

Lynn gave a satisfied nod, and then gladly let every thought of streams, publicity, and the world in general disappear from her mind.

Moving quickly, their team swept the area for loot, backtracking as needed. They didn't find any items better than they already had, but there was a nice haul of Oneg and some items they could auction off later. Gathering back together, they resupplied while Lynn gave some feedback.

"Dan, I need you to figure out a way to get those Hydras faster. Think about it and run your ideas past me, I don't like being sitting ducks for them while we advance. Mack, great job on taking out those Rocs so quickly, but don't forget to keep the Oneg and ichor flowing to Edgar. You've got a big job, supporting everyone while watching our backs, and you're doing great. Just work on not getting so focused you forget the big picture, okay?"

Mack nodded, looking determined.

"Edgar, I know I say this every time, but it's only because you're so perfect in every other way." Lynn grinned and Edgar gave her a lopsided smile back. "But seriously, you have *got* to stop with the spray-and-pray tactics. It *feels* like we have unlimited ammo because we don't have magazines to reload, but you use massive amounts of ichor and in big battles we won't be able to keep up your supply unless you work on your aimed fire. I know it's not as fun, but if we were doing all this for fun we wouldn't be getting up at the butt-crack of dawn every day and working our fingers to the bone to win this competition, right?"

"Right," Edgar agreed, looking guilty.

"Okay, so, make every shot count, please."

"Got it. Sorry, I just get carried away, y'know?"

"I do, and it's fine. You're doing great. Just work on it."

Edgar nodded.

Finally, Lynn turned to Ronnie, who, as usual, had a sullen look on his face. Lynn had no idea why. It wasn't as if he was the only one getting constructive feedback, or that she was any pickier with him than any other team member. She reminded herself that she didn't need Ronnie to like her, just follow her.

"I'm really impressed with your form, Ronnie. Seriously." She looked him right in the eye, hoping her sincerity showed through. "You are one seriously good swordsman. Better than me, really." His expression showed a flash of surprise, but it disappeared again beneath his scowl when she continued.

"But I also want to see more ranged kills from you. I know it's a pain switching between weapons, but you can set up Hugo to shift them quick and easy at a single command, and our margins for winning are going to be so tiny as it is, we need to use the best tool for the job *every* time, even if your Splinter Sword gets the job done, eventually. Obviously, it isn't always the best thing to switch. If you waste too much time going back and forth, that's not good either. So, I'm trusting in your judgment and instincts to maximize your kills using the *right* weapon and *right* tactics, not just treating every TDM as a nail and your sword as a hammer."

She nodded to him and turned away, not waiting for any kind of acknowledgment since they usually never came. On the bright side, neither did the objections.

Wonder of wonders, Ronnie *was* getting better. Lynn had no idea what had changed him if not just the awful experience of being stuck with *Elena* as captain for two months. But whatever it was, while it hadn't made him into a paragon of wisdom and teamwork, he complained less and mostly followed her lead.

It wasn't perfect. It wasn't even ideal. But it *was* something she could work with.

As for her, leading Skadi's Wolves was the most exhausting thing she'd ever done. The mental stress of always thinking at top speed, being aware of the battle on multiple different levels while also fighting TDMs herself, was pushing her endurance to the very limit. That wasn't even taking into account the constant weight of responsibility she felt, knowing her team was depending on her to lead them well and bring them to victory. It had never been this hard in WarMonger because she was with different players in every fight, and the only thing at stake was the immediate payout of that particular match.

She didn't regret a single second of it, though.

Somehow, the responsibility seemed to settle her. Most of the time she was far too busy doing her job to worry about what people thought or what might happen. Interviews were still hell, but her teammates were eager enough to talk that she rarely had to say much. She still avoided reading comments on her streams or interacting directly with fans. But her communications manager at GIC often forwarded her fan letters and words of encouragement they gleaned from her accounts on the meshweb. Some of the things people said brought literal tears to her eyes.

You're so amazing, Lynn, you've inspired me to start gaming again after a lot of bullying made me stop.

Thanks for making me smile, kid. I'm fighting cancer right now so I can't play TD Hunter, but watching your stream gets me through my chemo treatments.

*Dear Ms. Raven: thank you for fighting monsters.
My mom says I can fight monsters too once I turn
ten, and I've been practicing your moves with my
sisters. We're going to make our very own team.*

*Hi Lynn! I live in Iowa too! Thanks for those tips
on your interview about staying healthy as a gamer. I
convinced my whole raid group to try out TD Hunter
and we're pretty bad at it so far, haha! But getting
outside a lot has made me feel better than I've ever
felt in my life. Thank you.*

"Hey, could we take a quick munchies break? I'm
starving," Dan said, breaking into Lynn's thoughts.

She glanced at the time.

"Yeah, it's almost noon. Let's go over to the edge
of the woods away from the rail, though. And keep
it quick, or we'll freeze to death."

The others nodded in agreement, and they all exited
combat mode and headed off the wide gravel border
they'd been following. There was no fence along this
rail line because, Lynn supposed, it went past woods
and industrial sections of town instead of residential.
They waded through some tall grass and found a spot by
the tree line that protected them from the chill wind.
Lynn ate silently beside Edgar, staring at the trees and
mentally identifying them by their bark—something
she'd learned from the woodcraft book Edgar had given
her. Knowing tree species wasn't particularly useful as
a professional gamer, but it was kinda cool to feel like
she had a connection to the world around her. She recognized a particularly large tree nearby with smooth,
mottled white-and-brown bark. It was a sycamore tree.
That meant, according to her book, that there was
probably a creek or other water source nearby.

"Whatcha thinking?"

"Huh?" Lynn started at the quiet question from Edgar.

"You got your thoughtful face on," Edgar said, and screwed up his face to show her what he meant.

Lynn elbowed him.

"I do *not* look like that when I'm thinking."

"How do you know?" Edgar asked, eyes twinkling. "You look at yourself in a mirror while you're thinking?"

Lynn rolled her eyes and pointed, hoping to change the subject away from her looks.

"Sycamore tree. Water nearby."

"Huh, sure 'nuf. We had lots of those at my grandpa's farm in Utah. They grew all along the creek. You been reading, haven't ya?" Edgar grinned down at her, and she stuck out her tongue at him.

"Maybe. Or maybe my LINC just told me."

"Nah. You're no cheater."

"It wouldn't be cheating, just utilizing all the tools at my disposal," Lynn said loftily.

Edgar shrugged.

"Potato, potata."

They fell silent and Lynn shivered. Her trapped body heat was seeping away and it was time to get moving. She lingered just a moment more, enjoying the peace of the winter afternoon under the faint sun while Dan, Mack, and Ronnie argued about their TD Hunter leaderboard scores and which stat should weigh most heavily in determining overall rank.

"Accuracy is obviously the most important. You can't kill anything without it."

Ronnie scoffed at Dan's statement.

"Anyone can point and shoot. They should grade

kills based on the skill level needed to master the specific weapon and moves used in each of the hits, not just the accuracy of the hits."

"But the point of the game isn't accuracy, guys," Mack pointed out. "It's killing monsters. Don't tell me you skip all the cut-scene vids? Hunters are supposed to be helping the TD Counterforce discover where this invasion is coming from and how to stop it by collecting data on the TDMs in different environments. Total kills, variety of kills along widely dispersed areas, and discovering new unknowns should count much more than how perfectly you kill the same monsters over and over again in your backyard."

"Nobody cares about the storyline," Ronnie countered, then shoved the last mouthful of his energy bar into his mouth.

"I think they weigh all of the above equally," Lynn said, and stood up, brushing grass off her formfitting pants.

Ronnie looked sideways at her.

"How would you know?" he scoffed, wisely leaving the "you're just a girl" part unsaid.

Lynn pursed her lips.

"I don't, just a gut feeling."

Ronnie snorted.

"And you've missed another possibility," she continued, ignoring his scorn. "Teamwork. Or do you think it's a coincidence that ninety percent of players in the top one hundred are part of a team, championship or casual?"

"That's correlation, not causation," Ronnie argued. "The best players all joined teams to try and win the competition."

"I almost didn't," Lynn said quietly. Ronnie's face blanched and he scowled, but didn't respond, so Lynn continued. "If you dig down on the sub boards and look at individual stats, there's plenty of top-tier players not on teams. Lots of them are monetizing the game, killing huge swaths of TDMs for the loot and selling it. But those aren't the ones dominating the leaderboard."

"Hmm," Dan said, and looked thoughtful. "Maybe. But you also get a lot of bonuses being on a team, stuff like extra defense and experience, which can help bolster your stats."

Lynn shrugged. He had a point. Ultimately it was moot, though, because they would never know for sure. Better to focus on the mission and not worry about it.

"Let's get back to work, team. My fingers and toes are freezing and I know just the thing to warm them up." She grinned, and everyone but Ronnie grinned back.

Oh well, baby steps.

Later that night after a long shower to apologize to her aching muscles, Lynn was doing stretches in the living room when their doorbell rang. She hopped up to answer it and studiously told the nervous butterflies in her stomach to shut up and go away.

"Hey, Kayla," she said upon opening the door to the sight of a heavily bundled someone swathed in scarves with a mass of hair poking out from under a thick winter hat.

"Hi Lynn! Thanks so much for asking me over, I can't wait to get started!" came Kayla's muffled voice beneath layers of fabric.

The butterflies in Lynn's stomach turned into kamikaze fighter planes and started dive bombing her gut.

"Uhh, yeah. Right. Come on in."

Lynn looked on in amusement as Kayla took a solid minute to unwrap herself from her many layers and pile them all on the kitchen table.

"You know, it's not *that* cold out there."

"Are you kidding me? It's *freezing*." Kayla rubbed her arms and shivered. "I'm happy here in Iowa and everything, but I sure do miss the winters down in Arkansas. And this dry cold is *murder* on my poor hair." She patted her crinkly halo, looking so forlorn that Lynn had to laugh.

"I'm sorry. That sounds awful. I grew up in Baltimore, so I don't notice it much."

"Yeah, I remember you telling me about that." Kayla smiled shyly. "That was before, when your dad—" She abruptly stopped herself, looking embarrassed. "Sorry, I didn't mean to bring up a painful topic."

Lynn shrugged, used to the dull pang of loneliness and loss that briefly squeezed her heart.

"It's in the past. Arkansas is where you lived before your mom split with your dad, right?"

"Yeah. And I'm glad mom chose to leave the state. We needed to get as far away from that—well, from him as possible. If I'd been old enough to know better, I would have voted for somewhere warmer, like Florida, but oh well." Kayla laughed. "In Florida Mom never would have met my stepdad, so there you go. Things work out I guess."

"Yeah . . . I guess." Lynn smiled politely, though her heart wasn't in it.

There was an awkward silence.

"Um, so, do you want to show me what kind of braids you want to learn for your hair? If you have any stream tutorials or pictures you've saved, I can look at them and we can figure it out together."

Lynn nodded and led the way to the couch where they plopped down and got to work.

She'd mostly invited Kayla over to help her get better at braiding her hair. Beyond the few simple, if effective, braids she'd learned long ago with her dad, she knew nothing about making her hair look more, well, stylish. It felt weirdly embarrassing to care what she looked like. But she'd talked to her mom enough about it by now that she could acknowledge the discomfort was a reaction to bullying and body-image insecurity, not a legitimate feeling that she should let hold her back.

So, with much trepidation but also fragile hope, she'd reached out to Kayla for help. Because of Lynn's insane schedule, they'd hardly gotten to hang out since Kayla had left Elena's clique. Though Kayla looked happier and more relaxed at school these days, she also had a melancholy air that reminded Lynn of herself.

She knew what it felt like to be alone. Ostracized. Mocked. And the pure joy and excitement in Kayla's face when Lynn had invited her over had been the final nail in the coffin of Lynn's stubborn hold on the past.

So, there they were, scrolling through pictures and vids on Lynn's living room wall screen, talking about the differences in braiding straight versus curly hair, and finding the best braids for various scenarios like hunting, interviews, and school. They tried out a few styles and laughed together when they failed miserably. Lynn even managed to gather enough courage to ask Kayla where she shopped in virtual for clothes. Kayla's squeal of delight at the question almost made Lynn regret it. But she had no time these days to go somewhere like Lindale Mall again, and Mrs. Pearson had taken her to task for wearing the same outfit to two different interviews, so she had to bite the bullet.

The process turned out to be much less painful—and more fun—than Lynn had expected. With their various AR interfaces, they could easily turn the living room into a virtual dressing room, and all the styles and brands imaginable were at their fingertips—complete with helpful AI assistants to answer their questions.

Oh, and ads. Lots and *lots* of ads.

"You know," Kayla laughed as they swiped away an ad for lab-grown leather purses that made Lynn shudder, "if you shopped more in virtual your ads would be much better customized to what you actually want."

"And that's a *good* thing?" Lynn demanded.

Kayla gave her a puzzled look.

"Of course, it is. How else are you going to find the sorts of things you want?"

"Uh, maybe by looking?"

"But that's such a waste of time. If you just let the AI assistants know what your style is and what you're looking for, they're really, really good at giving you lots of great options. My shopping would take *forever* if I had to go looking for everything I needed."

Lynn pressed her lips together, not pointing out that until very recently, her idea of shopping was sorting through castoff bins at local thrift stores.

"I just think it's creepy for ad companies to know exactly what you want."

"Why?" Kayla asked. "It's their *job* to give you what

you want. How can they do that unless you tell them what you like?"

"Who says they're giving me what I want? *I* hardly know what I want. Ads show you what has the highest likelihood of making you spend money. That's not the same thing as what you want, much less what you *need*."

Kayla cocked her head, a thoughtful crease forming between her brows.

"I never thought about it like that. But...you know it *can* be the same thing. There's tons of things I've gotten that I really, really enjoy that I never would have known existed without ads."

"Okay, that's fair," Lynn said. "I'm not saying ads are evil and trying to hurt you. But they're still manipulative, and I'd rather think for myself and explore for myself than get complacent in a behavior-reinforced bubble of my own making."

Kayla looked unconvinced but shrugged and pointed at the next outfit she wanted Lynn to try out.

Lynn recoiled at the sight.

"It has *snowmen* on it."

"I know! Isn't it adorable?" Kayla clasped her hands to her chest and looked enraptured. "And obviously the pattern is customizable. Look, there's cute reindeer, and Santa kittens! Don't you need some cute Christmas outfits for parties and stuff?"

"What parties?" Lynn asked, taking a subtle step away from the outfit hovering in front of her. Those kittens with Santa hats looked slightly deranged...

"Don't you go to parties at Christmas?"

"Not really. It's just me and mom. There's a Christmas party at her hospital, but I usually convince her to work that shift for the insane overtime bonus."

Kayla's face fell.

"Then what do you do during the holidays? Visit family?"

"My dad's family lives in Norway and we could never afford to visit, and my mom's side, well . . . we're not exactly close. I mostly just game during break and drink lots of eggnog." Lynn shrugged.

Kayla's eyes narrowed and she put her hands on her hips.

"All right, that's it."

"What?" Lynn asked, eyes widening in alarm.

"I'm throwing you a Christmas party."

"What? No!"

"Yes!"

"No!"

". . . too late," Kayla crowed gleefully, eyes alight with triumph. "I just pinged my mom and dad and told them we're hosting a Christmas party for Skadi's Wolves!"

"You didn't!"

"I *did*! Aaaand . . ." Kayla's eyes went distant as she read something on her retina display. "Mom says it's a brilliant idea! Dad's probably in a meeting or something, but I'm sure he'll agree. We have a nice big house with plenty of room for everybody. Besides, Skadi's Wolves have been bringing a lot of great attention to GIC. Dad talks about you *all* the time. I think he's kinda a fan of TD Hunter. He would probably play if he had the time."

Lynn stared at Kayla, mouth working, trying to come up with an excuse strong enough to derail this terrible idea.

"So, it's settled!"

"No, it's not!"

"Oh yes, it is, because my mom pinged *your* mom and they're already talking about a date." Kayla's eyes came back into focus and she grinned evilly at Lynn, who scowled in return. "Come *oooon*," Kayla said sweetly. "Everybody's families can come and we'll celebrate your amazing success and accomplishments. You'll be the star of the evening, just like you deserve!"

"That's what I'm afraid of," Lynn muttered.

"It'll be fun, I *promise*. Mom and I will arrange everything. All you have to do is make sure all the guys come. No excuses!"

Lynn tried her best to glare Kayla into submission, but the girl's excitement formed a protective forcefield that Lynn's displeasure bounced harmlessly off of.

"Okay! Fine!" Lynn finally said, throwing her hands in the air. "But I am *not* wearing *that*," she said, pointing at the offensively patterned party wear still hovering between them.

"That's fine," Kayla said in a tone that made Lynn instantly suspicious. "Because I have something *much* better in mind."

The party came together with unnerving swiftness, and among Lynn and her teammates, she seemed like the only one remotely disappointed by it. Even Ronnie didn't seem bothered by the idea, which made Lynn feel weirdly betrayed. She thought she could at least count on sullen, grumpy, argumentative Ronnie to commiserate with her about being forced to dress up and socialize.

No such luck.

The days blurred into a succession of exercise,

simulation training, hunting, and various interviews or streams for publicity management. When the weather was too wet or cold for hunting, they focused on simulation training to prepare for upcoming TDMs they would face as they leveled. Since Lynn's apartment wasn't big enough for all the simulation fights she practiced, she'd taken to training in the apartment-complex gym. Six months ago, she would have had an anxiety attack at the mere thought of working out in front of other people, and in skintight clothing no less.

Now? She put in her earbuds and blasted her dad's favorite classic rock bands from the 2000s and ignored everything around her. Sometimes she wondered what his exercise routines had been as a cop. Sometimes she wondered what he would think of her, fighting pretend monsters in a game instead of real monsters on the streets. Would he be proud of her?

Maybe.

She carried the little Helle pocketknife he'd given her everywhere she went, partly as a talisman, partly because she couldn't forget douchebag Connor's threat of retaliation. The whole team knew to keep an eye out, considering Elena's cheating tactics over the summer. Lynn expected something more subtle, and likely more damaging, from Connor. But so far, nothing had materialized.

It made her nervous, but she tried not to let it hold her back.

By the evening of the party the Saturday before Christmas, Lynn had considered—and discarded—over a dozen possible scenarios for getting out of it. The problem was that her mother was a nurse, so all the usual sickness excuses would get sniffed out in a heartbeat, and she couldn't risk even a minor purposeful injury, since it would affect her hunting performance.

"Honey! The air taxi arrives in thirty minutes, are you almost ready? Do you need help with your hair?" Matilda's voice called from outside Lynn's bedroom.

Lynn sank further into her body-mold chair, refusing to look at the outfit laid out on her bed.

"I'm good, Mom! Thanks!"

She was playing WarMonger, as one did when one was procrastinating. It was a treat she rarely made time for, just enough to check on Steve and his friends' handling of her precious Larry Coughlin account. True to Steve's word, they took good care of it, and while her rank hadn't gone up, it hadn't gone down either. Reviewing her messages, it was clear they knew way more about actual military lingo and history than her, and Larry's reputation as a war-hardened former operator had only grown. It made her jealous, but it also gave her great ideas for future quips.

If only she could find a chance to use them.

"Lynn, we're leaving in five minutes! Are you ready?"

"Oops," Lynn whispered, grinning despite herself. "Coming!" she yelled to her mom and logged off, having just wrapped up an impromptu free-for-all with a bunch of mouthy Tier Tens.

It only took a minute to throw on the slinky black sleeveless top and ankle-length formfitting skirt with a slit up one thigh that Kayla had helped her pick out. She wore flats with it, plus her new favorite piece of clothing—a supple leather jacket with just enough punk style in its elegant cut to make her smile. To give her friend credit, Kayla had been very good at prying reluctant and mumbled style preferences out of her, resulting in something that looked and felt like *her* instead of a younger version of her mother.

She'd decided to leave her hair mostly down for the party, with only a single braid across her forehead and down one side holding back any hair from getting in her face. Since she'd already done the braid right after her shower, she simply grabbed her jacket and headed out to the living room.

"You look wonderful, honey," Matilda said, giving her a once over, then planting a kiss on her forehead. "Now hurry up, we still have to collect Mr. Thomas and the taxi will be here any minute."

One thing Lynn had made sure she could do for this dreaded party was invite her downstairs neighbor to join them. She hadn't been able to visit Mr. Thomas as much as she'd promised herself she would. But they'd had him over for dinner once, and she'd made several impromptu visits that had turned into fascinating conversations over a friendly card game. Mr. Thomas knew all the old-style games her mother had taught her that nobody ever played anymore: bridge, rummy, spades, hearts, and more. It was a fun change of pace and gave her patternist urges a stimulating workout, especially since Mr. Thomas was as good at counting cards as she was.

When they arrived at the lobby of their building, Mr. Thomas was waiting for them in a shockingly snazzy suit whose blazer was entirely covered in a thick layer of shimmering gold sequins. The lapel and cuffs were black with gold embroidery, and he wore a crisp little bowtie of green with a pattern of red holly berries on it.

"Goodness, Mr. Thomas! Look at you," Matilda said

with a smile. She held out an arm for him. "I had no idea you were such a party animal."

"Oh yes, I was quite the reveler in my youth," he replied, and winked. Then he took Matilda's arm, cane in his other hand. "You look quite lovely yourself, Mrs. Raven, and you, too, Lynn. I cannot begin to express my gratitude at your generous invitation. I hope you know how much it means to me."

Matilda waved a hand.

"It was all Lynn's idea, so she should get the credit. But we're honored that you would come. You've been very good to Lynn, and we're grateful to have you as our neighbor."

"As I am also grateful. Mankind was not meant to be alone, yet over my long life I have watched humanity slowly seduced into technological cocoons of isolation and unhappiness. What a blessing to have each other in times like these, and to have such a lovely party to attend. I do not suppose that is our air taxi outside, is it?"

"Oops! It probably is. Come on, you two," Matilda said, and they were off.

Kayla squealed with delight when she opened the door and saw them lined up on her doorstep.

"Lynn, you look *amazing*! And this must be your neighbor I've heard so much about. Hurry up, Lynn, and introduce me to this handsome young man!" Kayla fanned her face dramatically and grinned at Mr. Thomas, whose returning smile was all white teeth and pure mischief.

"Uh, this is my neighbor Mr. Jerald Thomas. Jerald, this is my—friend, Kayla Swain," Lynn said, hesitating only a moment on the descriptor. A flash of surprise passed over Kayla's face, but the next moment she was reaching forward and drawing Mr. Thomas into the house with a smile, already chatting away like a social butterfly. The old man met her smile for smile and seemed to have gained a bounce in his step as he followed his charming hostess.

Lynn exchanged a raised eyebrow with her mother, then they both had to suppress giggles behind their hands as they entered as well.

Mr. Swain's house was expansive, elegant, and beautifully decorated. Its exterior was stone, two stories, with several wings. Large windows and high ceilings gave it an airy, modern feel. Lynn spotted many homey touches, however, from smiling pictures of Kayla proudly displayed on the walls to Iowa Hawkeyes paraphernalia in a glass case in the hallway. There were even colorful drawings taped to the fridge visible through one doorway. It made Lynn relax and feel more like she was among friends rather than on a performance stage.

She wondered idly if Elena's dad had any old drawings of his daughter's on *his* fridge.

Probably not.

In no time, all the guys had arrived with their families, from Mr. and Mrs. Nguyen in impeccably elegant attire to Edgar's harried-looking mom and five siblings wearing variously patterned Christmas sweaters. Mrs. Rios came in at the head of her family procession with the expression of one searching for reasons to disapprove. But Matilda swooped down on her and soon they were chatting away while Mack introduced his dad and siblings to everyone. Mr. and Mrs. Nguyen also seemed inclined to be aloof after their elder daughter abandoned them

THROUGH THE STORM 365

to hang out with Dan and Mack. Lynn elbowed Kayla to peel her attention away from Mr. Thomas long enough to whisper a plan in her ear, and then Kayla was off. With an elegance and ease that Lynn could never hope to obtain, Kayla engaged Dan's parents and got them introduced to her father, the only person in the room who looked like he was wearing a suit more expensive than Mr. Nguyen's. After that the lofty pair visibly relaxed and seemed to settle into a long conversation with Mr. Swain about who knew what—probably not gaming, though.

"Mama, you remember Lynn, right?"

Kayla had reappeared with her mother in tow, and Lynn smiled shyly at a woman she barely remembered. Mrs. Swain's shapely figure was encased in a sheath dress beautifully embroidered with gold and silver snowflakes that set off her mahogany skin to perfection. Her tightly braided hair was wrapped around her head like a crown. Lynn could easily see where Kayla got her stunning looks, and she tried not to feel out of place.

"Of course, I do honey! How are you, Lynn?"

"Um, great, thanks."

"I'm so happy you and Kayla are spending time together. I haven't seen her this happy and energetic in *forever.*"

Lynn gulped and gave a polite smile. Fortunately, Mrs. Swain went right on without seeming to need a reply.

"This party was a delightful idea. It's so nice to finally get to meet all her friends!"

That statement made Lynn shoot Kayla a questioning look, and Kayla made a "don't blow my cover" expression behind her mother's back. It made Lynn feel like a paragon of openness and virtue with *her* mom compared to the amount Kayla had apparently kept her parents in the dark. Lynn was tempted to say something vague yet revealing, but the pleading look on Kayla's face stopped her. She'd never wanted to tell her mom about the bullying she'd endured in middle school, and she'd only just recently admitted to her Larry Coughlin alter ego. Maybe Kayla simply needed more time and a wise word. Lynn would sic Mr. Thomas on her friend the next chance she got. That would straighten her out.

"Yeah, it's nice to meet, er, see you again too, Mrs. Swain. Speaking of friends..." Lynn glanced at Kayla. "Ronnie *did* say he was coming, right?"

Kayla nodded, then turned to scan the large foyer where the adults were still standing around talking. Most of their peers had disappeared but judging by the excited sounds coming from what Lynn assumed was the kitchen, she suspected her friends had found the food.

"I'll go look for him," Lynn said quickly, and extracted herself before Kayla or her mother could object.

She wound her way across the foyer and was about to enter the kitchen when someone much taller than her came around the corner attempting to exit it. They nearly collided, and Lynn would have slipped on the polished floor and fell on her butt if she'd been wearing high heels. Fortunately, her practical flats had more traction and she simply stumbled back as a large, familiar hand reached out to steady her.

"Whoa! Sorry, Lynn, didn't see you coming. You okay?"

Lynn couldn't help grinning as she looked up into Edgar's concerned face. His Christmas sweater was a picture of a kitten riding a T-rex, both wearing jolly red Santa hats. It was impossible not to smile in the face of such ridiculousness.

"Besides nearly having a heart attack, yeah, I'm good."

"Whew, great. I was just coming to find you because... uh..." He trailed off, his eyes having finally flicked down from her face to scan her body for potential injury. But his eyes seemed to have gotten stuck. This was possibly due to the way her slinky black blouse outlined the curve of her breasts, or the way the slit of her skirt showed off more of her muscled thigh than had ever seen the light of day before.

Lynn felt unbearably warm all of a sudden and crossed her arms self-consciously over her chest.

The movement jolted Edgar out of his daze and his eyes snapped back to her face.

"You look amazing," he said in a strangled voice, then seemed to second-guess himself. "I mean, you *always* look amazing, obviously, but your, uh, shirt, is, uh, really nice, and I've never seen you in, uh... well..." He trailed off again, wincing.

Normally such attention would have made Lynn want to melt into a puddle of embarrassed goo. But Edgar's voice was so earnest that she felt a surprising glow of happiness. It took the edge off the painful awkwardness that inevitably followed any mention of her looks.

"Uh, thanks. And I like your sweater." She smiled again and poked him lightly in the chest right where the enthusiastically waving kitten sat perched atop its dinosaur mount.

"Oh yeah! Pretty sweet, huh? We always wear ugly sweaters for Christmas. Mom goes through every local thrift store till she finds us a new one each year. But this year, cuz of my sponsorship money and all, I surprised Mom and got them myself"—he leaned closer and finished in a conspiratorial whisper—"but with *cool* designs."

One of Lynn's eyebrows rose and she gave his sweater a pointed look.

"Cool, huh?"

"What?" Edgar grabbed the hem of his sweater, pulling the picture flat and looking down at it fondly. "What could possibly be cooler than kittens on dinosaurs?"

"Absolutely nothing at all," Lynn lied with a straight face, though inside she was cackling.

Silence descended between them.

"So . . ." Lynn began.

"Right! Yeah, uh, I was just coming to find you, cuz there's this really dope appetizer wrapped in bacon, and Mack and Dan are stuffing their faces with it, and I figured you'd probably stab them or something if you didn't get any so—"

He didn't get any further because Lynn dove past him into the kitchen.

Bacon was no joking matter.

Fortunately for Dan and Mack's long-term health, they hadn't entirely cleared the platter by the time she got there. They were, however, subjected to a much-deserved berating on manners and sharing while Lynn stuffed the last few bacon-wrapped steak bites into her mouth.

They, in turn, blamed Edgar's three youngest siblings,

who had moved on to the bowl of chocolate truffles and looked like fair imitations of hamsters with their bulging cheeks.

There was a great deal of good-natured bickering all around, and eventually Lynn had to help Edgar chase his youngest siblings out of the kitchen and into the foyer before they ate everything in sight.

She was just turning around, intending to retreat back into the kitchen before someone tried to talk to her, when she spotted Ronnie slipping in the front door. He had on the same coat and shoes he normally wore to school but did have on a pair of rumpled slacks in place of his usual jeans. After quietly closing the door behind him, he shoved his hands in his pockets and looked around, shoulders hunched.

Lynn could have waited until Kayla noticed him and did her whole hostess thing. But an odd sense of duty propelled her forward. Before she had a chance to plan what to say, she was a few steps away and he'd noticed her. Uncertainty and wariness clouded his face, and a streak of panic shot through Lynn.

What the heck was she doing?

Charity.

The thought came in Mr. Thomas' voice. She could see his kind smile in her mind's eye—an offer of friendship to an awkward outcast who'd done little more than ignore him as that "weird old neighbor" for their entire acquaintance.

Suddenly she understood.

"Hey," she said, giving Ronnie a little smile.

He nodded at her, expression wary.

"I'm glad you made it."

"Really?" Ronnie said, surprise flashing across his face.

"Yeah," Lynn said, feeling even more certain. "Our team wouldn't be the same without you. I'm glad you're here."

Ronnie's eyes widened further, as if he'd never heard anything so shocking in his life.

"Come on." Lynn gestured with one hand. "I'll show you where the food is, at least if Dan and Mack haven't eaten it all yet."

That got a snort from Ronnie.

"Knowing them, there's probably nothing left."

"Better hurry, then, huh?" Lynn grinned and jerked her head toward the kitchen.

It took him a second to respond, but eventually he did follow her, and soon they were surrounded by the rest of the team. Food and drink were passed around, jokes and ribbing flew thick and fast, and Lynn felt strangely content. She drifted a little apart from her team, glass of sparkling grape juice in her hand, content to simply watch and enjoy their happiness.

"Good evening, Lynn. It's a pleasure to finally meet you in person."

Lynn started but managed to hide her surprise in a turning motion toward the voice which she recognized from several facechat meetings: Jamal Swain, Kayla's charismatic CEO of a stepfather.

Belatedly, Lynn registered that his hand was extended in a friendly invitation. She took it and tried to smile casually as they shook, as if she hadn't been standing there frozen like some idiot. Mr. Swain didn't seem to mind, though, and he smiled broadly before continuing.

"Thank you so much for coming to Kayla's party. She doesn't have many friends, and as a parent I'm both proud and honored that she can count you among them."

That made Lynn flush, but she didn't say any of the dozen protests that came to mind.

She was learning.

"Thanks, it was, uh, nice of her to organize it. I think it's good for our families to meet each other and hang out, you know?" *So, they can see that what we're doing is important and not wasting our lives on some "silly game,"* she added to herself.

Mr. Swain's eyes twinkled. "And so your parents can commiserate with each other about how little they're seeing their teenagers these days?"

Lynn coughed. "Uh, yeah. Maybe that too."

"I've spoken to all the parents who are here, Lynn, and I can assure you they are very proud of your team's hard work."

"W-what?" Lynn almost spit out the grape juice she'd been trying to sip.

At Mr. Swain's look of surprise, she backpedaled.

"I mean, I know my mom is proud, but I guess I got the impression from the guys that their parents were too busy to care, or were annoyed we're wasting precious study time on a stupid game."

"Ahhh," Mr. Swain said. "I can see that. And perhaps some of them do still consider 'professional gamer' to be a less than ideal career choice for their children." His eyes flicked to Mr. and Mrs. Nguyen who were deep in conversation with Mr. Thomas. He smiled.

"But I think you'll find they are open to changing their minds, especially after I told them how your team is one of the top revenue makers for my company, or how much more in sponsorships you all might expect to negotiate if you continue the good work you've been doing."

"R-really? Top revenue makers, I mean?" Lynn asked, eyes widening.

Mr. Swain turned back to her, his smile bright and his eyes dancing.

"Oh yes. Sports has long been one of the largest ad-generating markets in the world, and 'geek culture' as you might call it is becoming more and more mainstream as well. With the rise in Augmented Reality Sports, there's been a huge gap in demand for more augmented reality entertainment that Mr. Krator has handily filled with his TD Hunter model. It's been tried before, but this is the first time it's been done successfully. And *you*, Lynn, are the tip of that spear."

"I-I am?"

"Absolutely. You've got the looks and skills to keep any stream viewer entertained—you're basically stream celebrity gold. Even your reticence to speak publicly and do interviews works in your favor, since it creates scarcity and an aura of mystery."

"Oh," Lynn said faintly. She was repulsed by the idea of such notoriety while also being strangely fascinated by it. Was that normal? Honestly, hiding in her room and ignoring everybody seemed like the safest response to it all.

"You know," Mr. Swain remarked, amusement in his voice. "Most of my clients would be glowing with pride and excitement at this point."

"What? Oh, I'm sorry! I didn't mean to sound ungrateful, I'm, well . . . not used to this. I just want to be myself and be left alone, you know?"

"I completely understand, and I think that's exactly why you're doing so well."

Lynn gave him a startled look, which he returned gravely.

"Fame is a dangerous, poisonous thing. People without strong morals and a level-headed support system around them often make the mistake of glorifying fame for its own sake. That kind of self-centered worship will destroy you every time—destroy your relationships, destroy your sanity, even destroy your life. I've wondered, at times, if operating a PR company was even the right thing to do. But fame is just a tool to achieve worthy goals, and we've been able to raise awareness for so many vital causes and bring life-changing good to hundreds of clients. At the end of the day, all I can do is make sure my teams guide and advise our clients wisely and hope it all balances out."

The older man's words resonated with Lynn, and she nodded slowly, wondering what Elena or even Connor might have been like if they hadn't been so obsessed with fame and success for its own sake. They didn't deserve a pass on their behavior, but with Mr. Thomas' words about charity still fresh in Lynn's mind, she could at least understand that pity, rather than hatred, was a wiser path when it came to CRC.

"You're doing just fine, Lynn," Mr. Swain continued, oblivious to Lynn's musings. "Your humility and dedication to your team is admirable. It will keep you from falling into the trap many others have been destroyed by. Just hold onto your good character, listen to your mentors, and keep your priorities straight. Don't let the clamoring voices on the streams or web change you."

"Oh, there's no danger of that," Lynn said with a laugh. "I avoid the comment sections like the plague."

"Probably a good idea," Mr. Swain agreed and

gave her a wink. "Now, if you'll excuse me, I need to make a toast before this party winds down and people start leaving."

He gave her a brilliant smile and a nod, then turned toward the huge sideboard where more drinks and appetizers had been laid out. Lynn still had grape juice left in her glass, so she hung back and watched as Mr. Swain got everybody's attention and organized the handing out of drinks.

She hoped he wasn't going to say anything about her.

"Ladies and gentlemen, thank you so much for honoring our house with your presence. As CEO of GIC as well as on a personal level, I am delighted to celebrate the achievements of Skadi's Wolves. We at GIC and here in the Swain family wish the premier team of Cedar Rapids all the best. They have worked extremely hard and achieved so much already. May we continue to support them and cheer them on, looking forward to the day of their victory! Here's to Skadi's Wolves!"

"Skadi's Wolves!" echoed through the room as everyone raised their glasses into the air.

Emotion welled up in Lynn. She wasn't sure what kind of emotion it was, but it made her feel light and full of energy. Everyone in the room was smiling, grinning, patting each other on the back and shaking hands. Even Ronnie, who had finally shed his bulky school coat, was now talking earnestly with Mr. Swain. Edgar caught her eye and gave her a thumbs-up and a huge grin, and she couldn't help but grin back.

They'd done good. She was proud of them all. And as far as she was concerned, they were only just getting started.

Chapter 13

DESPITE HER BEST EFFORTS, LYNN WAS NOT PAYING attention to the teacher.

There was only so much talk of molecules, chemical bonds, and catalysts she could take before her brain checked out. Besides, the topics were a review of what they'd learned in the fall, in preparation to dive into their new subject matter for spring semester. She planned to spend her life dominating the professional gaming arena and maybe even developing games herself one day, so chemistry was very low on her list of things to spend brain energy on.

TD Hunter on the other hand...

The hard work and many cold hours of hunting Skadi's Wolves had put in over Christmas break had paid off. They'd finally reached Level 32, and Lynn felt for the first time since TD Hunter had launched last June that they were functioning as a professional team instead of a disjointed gaggle of teenagers. Not that they had all their problems ironed out. Ronnie was still grumpy, rude, and argumentative more often than not, and she still had to fight anxiety and vicious imposter syndrome on a regular basis. The other guys still had work to do to bring their accuracy scores up to snuff and keep their forms solid in the heat of battle.

But they were getting there.

Best of all, they hadn't seen hide nor hair of the Cedar Rapids Champions. It was almost as if Elena and Connor were avoiding them on purpose, which was about the nicest thing they'd ever done in their lives. It made Lynn intensely suspicious, but she'd decided not to look a gift horse in the mouth and had capitalized on a bit of mental breathing room to focus solely on her team.

Now, though, school had started back up and Lynn faced a conundrum: Not only were they back to restricted hunting time, but the higher they went in levels, the slower the leveling became. They had a little over five months to make eight levels, and she wasn't entirely sure they could.

It was the same problem Connor had tried, and failed, to solve.

But she wasn't Connor—she wasn't an athlete. She was a gamer, and gamers always found a way.

She already had several plans in place involving various team bonuses and tracking down rare items on the auction mart to boost experience rates. What would really do the trick, though, was tackling bosses.

That unknown boss in the woods north of the school? Its days were numbered. She just had to figure out how to defeat it—safely.

She wasn't even sure what "safely" meant, and disliked thinking too deeply about it. Something was definitely weird and different about TD Hunter. But whether that weirdness was a glitch the company wanted to keep under wraps lest it sink their whole enterprise, or a function of the game's cutting-edge nature that TD Hunter's engineers didn't themselves entirely understand, she wasn't sure. All she knew was that she really, really hoped it didn't wreck everything she'd worked so hard for. A few times she'd considered bringing it up to Steve, but even that felt risky. What if she was jumping at shadows and put a target on her back for complaining? There were any number of ways her team could be quietly sidelined or disqualified, and there would be nothing she could do about it.

All she could do was take the safety rules in the game seriously instead of actively ignoring them. That meant, if she wanted to take down a boss, she needed more teams.

A lot more.

"Class dismissed!"

Lynn started and looked up, but the teacher was busy packing his bag and hadn't seemed to notice her complete inattention. Edgar had, though, and shot her a grin as they grabbed their things and headed for the door.

"What's cookin', Cap? You had your Hunter face on, all glaring and scrunched like you're thinking big thoughts—"

"Oh, shut up," Lynn grumbled. "What did I miss? Anything important?"

"Nah. Just review stuff. So, what big plan you working on?"

"Nothing. At least, nothing yet. I've got to think about it more first."

"Look at you, being all responsible like a true *Toa Tama'ita'i*." Edgar slapped her on the back, nearly making her stumble forward.

Lynn tried to glare at him but her lips twitched upward anyway.

"Are you implying I'm not usually responsible?"

"Nah, you're the most responsible person I know. But it takes true bravery to accept responsibility for other people and not just yourself. You used to be afraid of it. Now you're not." He shrugged as if it was the most obvious thing in the world and walked on.

For a second Lynn stood frozen to the spot, the press of other students parting to flow around her. Then she lurched forward and ran to catch up, falling into step beside her friend as she savored the warm glow in her chest and tried not to grin too stupidly.

"Hola-la ami-agos!"

Dan's cheerful and brutal butchering of the Spanish language rang out behind them, and they slowed to let him, Mack, and Ronnie catch up to their group.

"Don't let your Spanish teacher hear you," Lynn said, "or she'll fail you on mere principle."

"What? I thought I did pretty good on my last test."

Mack snorted, and Lynn shot him a look.

"You speak it better than anybody else, Mack. Are you really gonna let him fail class without lifting a finger?"

"Hey, don't look at me! I'm done trying to correct him. He's worse at languages than he is at martial arts."

Lynn winced sympathetically. She was about to suggest some helpful stream channels on pronunciation when she noticed the gaggles of students lining the halls around them were starting to stare and whisper among themselves.

"Great," Ronnie growled. "What is it *this* time?"

Sick apprehension gripped the pit of Lynn's stomach, but she swallowed and held her head high.

"Probably nothing. Ignore them. Everybody will be heading home soon anyway, and we've got an airbus to catch to get to this new hunting ground I want to try out. Has everybody got their stuff already?"

They chorused replies, but Lynn was distracted by a call alert from her LINC.

It was from Mrs. Pearson.

She wasn't technically supposed to take calls on school grounds, but school was out for the day so she waved a hand at her team and ducked into the nearest girls' bathroom. Thankfully, it was empty.

"Hello, Mrs. Pearson?"

"Good afternoon, Miss Raven. I'm glad I caught you. There's been a ... development on the streams regarding Skadi's Wolves. I wasn't sure if you had seen it yet or not, but whether you have or not it is very, *very* important that you *do not respond* in any way, shape, or form until we have met and agreed upon a plan to manage it."

The pit in Lynn's stomach dropped like a fifty-pound weight.

"Uhhhh, manage what?"

"I'll ping you a link. You'll need to be aware of everything said in any case. But promise me, Miss Raven, you will *not* make any statement in public or post any sort of response until we are on the same page?"

"Y-yeah, sure. I promise."

"Good. Please pass on the warning to your team and ensure they hold their counsel as well. I need to speak to Mr. Swain directly about this and get in touch with TD Hunter's legal department before we will know how to proceed. I will call you back as soon as I have more information, but I will certainly call you this evening at the very latest to give you an update. Until then, not a word. Understood?"

"Yes, ma'am," Lynn said, through numb lips.

"Now, please tell your team right away. Goodbye."

The call ended before she even had a chance to respond, which was fine with her. She slipped back out of the bathroom to find her team waiting for her.

"What was that?"

"And why is everybody staring?"

A pinging sound in Lynn's ear alerted her to the arrival of the link Mrs. Pearson had promised.

"We need to talk, but not here," Lynn said, and headed back the way they'd come. As soon as she'd found an empty classroom and dragged them all in after her, she sent the link to everyone and they descended into silence, each watching the stream on their own AR glasses.

The stream was from *HotGamingCelebs*, which only made Lynn's apprehension worse.

"Today we have a special, special treat for all you hungry viewers," said the show's host, a disgustingly smarmy middle-aged guy whose bleached pompadour had seen better days. "This is so juicy I couldn't even wait for our usual scoop hour. You won't *believe* this exclusive vid we just acquired from an anonymous source. It's been a quiet holiday season on the TD Hunter front, but this stuff is going to put Tsunami Entertainment's latest and greatest release back in the headlines—and this stream is the only place you can see it. We'll get right to that vid as soon as we thank our sponsors—"

Lynn groaned internally and fiddled with her controls

to skip past the host's trying-too-hard endorsements. Paying a premium cut out the official ads attached to every stream, but there was nothing you could do about the in-stream ads by the stream celebrities themselves, which, of course, was exactly why they were so lucrative to do and why gaining enough of a following to be worth sponsoring was so competitive.

"Okay, let's take a look at this bad baby. Hold onto your socks, because they're about to get blown off when you see this *craaazy* vid."

The scene switched from the host in front of a green screen backdrop to smooth, floating footage from a drone a little above head height, looking down on—

"No," Lynn whispered, fists clenching.

It was them, standing in that little park near St. Sebastian's, facing off against Connor and his friend. But as the scene unfolded, Lynn's brow furrowed and the sick feeling in her stomach turned to icy anger.

The vid was taken from behind and a little to the left of Connor so that his entire front was hidden, but you could see some of her face and body, and most of Edgar and Dan behind her. She and Connor appeared to be having an argument—which they had been—and the audio backed that up, though some of the words were lost in the wind that had been quite strong that day. But what happened next didn't match up to what Lynn remembered. Connor appeared to lurch back as if Lynn had punched him, and the expression on what the viewer could see of Lynn's face was full of cruelty and hate. The things she shouted were definitely in her voice, but they weren't what she remembered saying, as if they'd been clipped from somewhere else and inserted there.

Then the camera zoomed in, not on her but on Edgar standing behind her, so that she and Connor were no longer visible. In those critical few seconds, Edgar's calm exterior cracked and fire blazed in his eyes as his entire body tensed up. The murderous growl in his voice was clearly audible as he threatened Connor, and then he lurched forward out of the camera frame. The camera zoomed out in leisurely fashion and the next few seconds of audio was obscured by a gust of wind that rocked the drone. By the time the camera had fully expanded and stabilized, Edgar was attacking Connor as Lynn rolled out of the way. The rest of the fight followed what Lynn remembered, with Edgar and Connor both trading punishing blows. In the background, though, Lynn could hear her own voice, screaming obscenities at Connor, when all she'd remembered doing was screaming at Edgar to calm down and stop.

Then came the moment when Edgar tackled Connor to the ground, and the drone moved, getting a close-up of Connor's bloody face as Edgar's furious punches rained down on him and Connor started screaming in real terror. What the camera *didn't* show was Lynn, yanking uselessly at Edgar from behind, trying to pull him off before he did real damage. Predictably, when Paul finally intervened, the camera zoomed out enough to show him as the savior of the hour, pushing Lynn back as if she'd been attacking too and hauling Edgar off Connor. The camera stayed on them just long enough to show Lynn shoving Paul back, which she'd done to make sure Paul wasn't about to slug the already-bleeding Edgar in the face. Then it swung over to an unsteady Connor, picking himself up as he bled from multiple wounds in his face. The audio became suspiciously clear again as Connor yelled his accusations of assault at Edgar, but the vid cut off before anyone could hear Lynn's reply.

The stream view switched back to the host of *Hot-GamingCelebs*, whose hand was over his mouth as he mimed a thoroughly unconvincing look of shock and horror.

"Did—did you see that? I still can't believe it even though I've seen it a dozen times. That's right, people, you just witnessed a full out *assault* with murderous intent from the now infamous Skadi's Wolves on their rival team's captain, Connor Bancroft. Connor leads the Cedar Rapids Champions, who have been the victim of Skadi's Wolves bullying tactics in the past. You might remember this isn't the first time Skadi's Wolves have shown the unstable, rage-driven nature of their members. Months ago in the fall they had a huge confrontation where the then team captain, Ronnie Payne, threw Lynn Raven off the team entirely for her lack of discipline. I guess it's no surprise now that she instigated this vicious and despicable attack on a rival team. And now, despite her clear lack of decency or self-control, she's somehow inserted her sneaky little self into the team captain position of Skadi's Wolves! Can you believe that? I bet I can guess what kind of shameless favors she's been doling out to get her teammates' vote of confidence," the host said, wiggling his eyebrows in obvious glee.

A strange ringing had started in Lynn's ears, and she realized she was gripping the back of the chair she'd been leaning on so tightly that her bones were creaking. She forced her fingers to relax one by one, barely able to think straight through her anger. But the stream wasn't done yet . . .

"Obviously this vixen has plenty of tricks up her sleeve. But don't take our word for it! In addition to this exclusive vid, we were able to get in touch with Mr. Bancroft himself and he agreed to a tell-all interview that is truly jaw-dropping. But before we get to that, our sponsors—"

Lynn skipped through more in-stream ads as sick dread mixed with her anger until she was ready to throw up.

When Connor's face appeared on the stream, obviously connecting in from somewhere else with his real location obscured by a virtual background, Lynn stopped skipping and listened.

"—only concern is to get the truth out," Connor was saying, his face composed and disgustingly earnest with his vibrant blue eyes and perfectly styled blond hair. "I'm really not here to sling mud or cause gossip, just make sure that Raven is held accountable so that she can't hurt anyone else with her violence and bullying."

"And how will you do that?" asked the host.

"I've already contacted the legal team of TD Hunter, providing the facts and voicing my concerns. I'm confident they'll make the right choice and disqualify Skadi's Wolves from the competition. Hopefully they'll ban them from the game entirely, since that would be the safest and most fair thing to do for the sake of the rest of their players."

"And what about criminal charges?" the host asked, his tone eager. "It would be pure negligence to let such violent criminals roam the street where they could assault just anybody. I mean, if your friend hadn't been there to intervene, they likely would have beat you to death."

"Unfortunately, I can't comment on any kind of ongoing criminal investigation. All I can say is that the safety and well-being of my team and all other TD Hunter players is my top priority. I will absolutely be taking whatever action I can to ensure the TD Hunter community stays safe."

"Of course, of course. So tell me, then, did you have any inkling of Ms. Raven's true nature before this horrific assault occurred? After all, you two were dating at one time and seemed quite, shall we say, close." The host winked at Connor.

"I suppose I might have seen flashes of concerning behavior here and there. It's hard, you know, when you care about someone so much. There's all sorts of things you tend to overlook or write off." Connor adopted a sad expression, and at that moment Lynn could have wrapped her hands around his neck and literally strangled him if he'd been there in front of her. "She is very, very good at manipulating everybody around her to see what she wants them to see. I definitely got the impression she was willing to use all her considerable *assets* to achieve her goals, if you know what I mean."

The host grinned and nodded, tapping the side of his nose with a disgusting level of glee as Connor continued.

"I admit I was pulled into her web just as much as anyone else, and for that I hold a lot of regret. If I'd seen through her act, maybe I could have done something sooner."

The host made sympathetic noises and went on about how Connor couldn't have known. At that point Lynn couldn't take any more.

"Come on, we're going," she said, barely aware of how flat and hard her voice was. Her team all looked up at the pronouncement, but she didn't meet any of their gazes. She didn't want to know what they were thinking.

"What are we going to do?" Edgar said, his deep voice rough with tension.

"Nothing," Lynn ground out. "Not about this. PR at GIC is strategizing a response. Nobody say a thing. No posting. No comments. No response. Got it?" She did look at them then, and there must have been murder in her eyes because she saw Dan and Mack visibly swallow as they nodded vigorously. Ronnie's face was dark and unreadable, but he nodded too. Edgar's jaw was clenched and his usually genial expression looked as angry as Lynn felt. Lynn lifted a questioning eyebrow. Finally, Edgar nodded.

Lynn attempted to take a deep, calming breath. It didn't calm her in the slightest.

"Right now we're going to go kill monsters. Lots of them. With extreme prejudice. We have a competition to win, and this changes *nothing*." She spun and headed for the door, willing her words to be true through sheer determination and spite.

But deep down, she was afraid.

The drones were worse that day. A lot worse.

When she finally arrived back at her apartment, there was a literal swarm of them hovering and doing looping patrols outside her building's entrance. They converged on her as soon as she came within view and hovered around her head like gnats. Disembodied voices shouted from tiny speakers, their stream-vulture pilots asking a barrage of intrusive questions from the safety of whatever dark basement served as their worthless lairs.

The temptation to start swatting them out of the air was overwhelming. But Lynn maintained a stone-cold expression and ignored all of them as she strode quickly through her building's doors. They shut on the swarm, muffling the voices, and Lynn breathed a sigh of relief.

The relief didn't last long.

She knew the vultures would be there, waiting for her next time she left.

When she finally reached the safety of her own apartment, she was startled to see her mother jump up from the couch. Matilda hurried over and wrapped her in a bone-crushing hug.

"Mom, what are you doing here? You should be at work."

Her mother stepped back and looked her over, as if searching for injury.

"I took a sick day, honey. I wasn't going to leave you alone to brood by yourself tonight. What kind of mother do you think I am?" She sounded indignant, and Lynn grinned a little, despite herself. But the expression was fleeting.

"So...I guess you've heard."

Matilda sighed sympathetically.

"Everyone with any connection to the gaming world has likely heard by now, dear."

Lynn winced.

"But, I've been on the phone with Mrs. Pearson and GIC is taking care of things."

"They are? She said she would call me—"

"They called me first because they know how important your hunting time is and she didn't want to interrupt you. But she said she'd be happy to chat this evening if you wanted to call her and clarify anything." Matilda took a deep breath. "Come on, let me warm you up some dinner and we can talk about it."

Once Lynn was chewing on leftover steak, potatoes, and some squash casserole, Matilda elaborated.

"GIC sent a takedown order for the footage of you as soon as they saw it had gone up. Naturally, that vile channel hemmed and hawed and delayed as much as possible. By the time they finally took it down, it had spread so far and wide that there's no way they could erase it entirely. But they'll keep their team at it. At the very least none of the major, respected channels will dare show it, mostly just gaming enthusiasts and minor gossip streams.

"Mrs. Pearson said their technicians were already analyzing the video. The original footage has absolutely been added to, so anybody who matters knows it's all just a clickbait smear campaign."

The tension in Lynn's chest eased a fraction, but that didn't help the sick lump in her stomach. She was only eating out of discipline and habit, knowing her body needed the nutrition. Even the steak was about as appetizing as shoe leather.

It wouldn't matter if there were no criminal charges or repercussions from TD Hunter. Billions of easily manipulated people across the globe now thought she and her team were violent, abusive cheaters.

Her mother must have been able to read something from her stony face, because she laid a hand on Lynn's arm and gave it a comforting squeeze.

"It's going to be okay, honey. Mrs. Pearson said they're already working with TD Hunter's legal department to craft a suitable response. The plan is to release the first-person footage of the incident that you recorded, to show what really happened. With it they'd like you and the team to release a brief statement, though she understands if you don't feel up to it. It would just be better coming directly from you rather than GIC's spokesperson."

Lynn nodded vaguely. Of course, she had to say something. She didn't want to, but she knew she had to. Never show weakness. It only made your enemies stronger and bolder. She couldn't hide from this, no matter how much she wanted to.

But she didn't have to be happy about it.

"I think I'm going to go to bed early, Mom."

"Okay, honey . . . is there anything I can do to help? Besides murdering that slimeball stream host and your despicable excuse for a former teammate, of course?"

Lynn gave her mom her best approximation of a smile.

"As much as I'd relish seeing you unleash the full measure of your maternal wrath on those two, a double homicide would definitely put a dent in my available hunting hours. Plus, you cook way better than me. I'd probably starve if they sent you to jail."

"Oh, they wouldn't catch me," Matilda said with a sweet smile. "I'm a nurse, remember? I know more ways to kill people than you could ever fathom."

Lynn shuddered. "Remind me to never get on your bad side, Mom."

"Oh, I'd never kill *you*, sweetie. How would I get any grandchildren?"

"Ugg, not *that* again," Lynn groaned, which only made her mother's smile even broader.

"You can't blame a mother for hoping. Now, go get

some rest." Matilda rose and kissed Lynn's cheek, then moved to start cleaning the kitchen.

The next few days of school were as awful as Lynn had dreaded. What made it even worse was that the miserable Iowa weather dumped half a foot of snow and ice on them, which meant little to no hunting, which took away Lynn's primary coping mechanism: killing things.

The only bright spot was that, when Lynn couldn't stand any more form drills or TDM training exercises, she had a valid excuse for some quality Larry Coughlin time.

It was so nice to slip back into that familiar and comforting mindset, even though it took a little time to reacquaint herself with the controls. They were so different from the intense full-body experience of TD Hunter, she was surprised at how...well...wimpy WarMonger felt in comparison. But she still eagerly studied her wall of sticky note quips, mentally filing a few away she was determined to use as soon as possible.

Her first few sessions she took on easy jobs, just to make sure her skills were still up to snuff. Terrorizing Tier Eights and Nines was positively relaxing, and she actually giggled with glee a few times at the reactions her unexpected appearance elicited—both from her allies and opponents. "You're going down, old man!" was a frequent, and very amusing, one.

Lynn had not only mastered the task of talking like an old mercenary, she'd mastered the even more difficult task of fighting like one.

The thing about fighting Larry Coughlin that so many found galling was he never seemed to be fighting hard. He didn't rush all over the battlefield, making terrific acrobatic jumps from burnt-out building to burnt-out building. He rarely seemed to move very fast at all. He rarely took a shot.

But when you shot at him, you just... missed. He wasn't where he'd been when you aimed, but a tad to the side. When he took his own shot, his opponents just... died. No muss, no fuss. And he rarely smack talked when he was killing someone.

He waited until they were dead.

Lynn casually threw a sticky grenade in what appeared to be a random direction and her mouthy opponent, a Tier Two who thought they were about to climb the ladder, promptly vanished in a cloud of red mist.

"Never talk to people when yer killin' 'em," she growled to the rest of her team. "What's the point?"

Lynn moved her avatar slowly from cover to cover, ducking at one point, apparently at random again, only to have a sniper bullet whiz overhead.

"How do you *do* that?" one of her kill team members demanded just before the same sniper took him out.

Larry's slow bass chuckle sounded over the kill team channel.

"I have the heart of a little boy," Lynn said into her mic. "Pickled. In a jar on my desk."

Another post-it note into the trash. But it was worth it.

To Lynn's utter delight, on the second evening of snow-restricted hunting, she ran into Steve on one of her WarMonger missions. It was a five-on-five match between Tier Twos and Ones, and FallujahSevenNiner was on the opposing team.

Lynn hunkered down in her body-mold chair and focused on utterly crushing her opponents. Fallu didn't make it easy for her in the slightest. There were several points, in fact, when she was sure she was going to lose. In the end it was Fallu's teammates that spelled his doom. Her side managed to whittle them down to just Fallu, while one of Lynn's teammate mercs survived. Together they flanked Fallu and took him down.

By the time the victory display came up and Lynn straightened in a bone-popping stretch, she realized her armpits were damp from sweat and her throat burned with thirst. Her brain felt wrung out. It wasn't quite the same victorious high of taking out hoards of TDMs, but it sure as heck paid better.

Lynn was just checking that the rest of her payment for the match had transferred successfully to her bank account when a voice-chat request came through from Fallu.

Lynn grinned. She left her voice modulator on, just to remind Steve who was boss.

"You're getting slow in your old age, Fallu," Lynn said.

"Good grief, kid, turn off that modulator. You're making me feel ancient and decrepit hearing your sass in that crotchety old man's voice."

Lynn snickered but turned the modulator off anyway.

"Maybe you feel that way because you *are* decrepit, old man?"

"Try saying that to my face, kid. Just you try."

"Hey, don't be sore, we all gotta get old sometime."

"Come out on the training mats with me sometime and I'll show you old. I'm sure your mom wouldn't mind if I tossed you around a bit. She probably gets tired of your sass at home anyway."

"Oh, I'm not dumb enough to sass my mom."

"Smart girl. So...how you doing, kid?"

Lynn sighed, her mood instantly dampened.

"I'm...fine."

"Liar."

"Yeah, whatever. I mean I'll *be* fine, I guess. Eventually."

Steve didn't reply, letting the silence lengthen.

"It's just so infuriating!" Lynn burst out, unable to stop herself. "I mean, there's literally *nothing* I can do to punish those jerks for being lying, slimy, backstabbing dirtbags. There's no justice!"

"Not nothing," Steve said calmly. "Scuttlebutt says GIC has a statement in the works. That's tomorrow, right?"

"Yeah," Lynn said gloomily. She was not looking forward to it. The whole team was coming over to her apartment because Mrs. Pearson said it would look better if they spoke from an ordinary environment wearing ordinary clothes rather than a carefully controlled green-screen studio in all their impressive hunting gear.

"You've been staying away from the stream gossip, right?"

"Heck yeah." Lynn's skin crawled just thinking about it.

"Good, that's smart. But also, I hope your PR people have told you that a lot of people are on your side. In fact, most people are on your side. They've been running your first-person footage nonstop on your channels with the announcement about your upcoming statement, and most of the comments are very supportive."

"What are *you* doing reading the comments section?" Lynn asked, one side of her mouth twitching upward.

"It's my job to stay informed, kid," Steve said gruffly. "But also...Heck, Lynn, we're all rooting for you over at TD Hunter. Every last one of us. You might say you're a bit of a mascot over there."

Lynn didn't reply. She was too stunned.

"Don't let it go to your head."

"I—I won't," Lynn mumbled.

"I only told you to put things in perspective. This Connor kid, he can't touch you. You are so far out of his league in both skill and popularity that this move he made will probably hurt him more in the long run than anything else. I mean, come on. It's obvious he's begging pitifully for attention, especially when you watch *five seconds* of anything that floozy Elena says. I know what he did hurts, and I know just refuting it calmly and then ignoring it doesn't feel like justice. But really, kid, it is."

"How? I should have let Edgar keep pounding him back at the hospital. *That's* what he deserves."

"Of course, it is. But that wouldn't have solved anything and probably gotten you all in deep shit. This is better. Far better."

"Doesn't feel like it," Lynn said, and slumped down into her body-mold chair.

"Letting your feelings lead you around by the nose like a fu—I mean freaking lemming is a real good way to lose at just about everything in life. So, would you rather chase some feeling, or win?"

Lynn snorted.

"Win, obviously."

"Good. Feelings aren't bad, they're just subjective and sometimes misleading and a generally stupid thing to base your actions on."

That made Lynn frown, considering the *years* she'd spent hiding from the world because of the awful bullying she'd endured. She got what Steve meant and knew he wasn't trying to belittle her. But still... ignoring your feelings was a heck of a lot harder than he made it out to be.

"If you want my advice, kid, keep your feelings out of this whole thing. You have the high ground. Letting this media circus distract you from training would be letting that little snot win. Be cool and calm. State the facts. No name calling, no accusations. Dismiss this Connor kid to the humiliating obscurity that he deserves, because that's what he is to you. Nothing."

"I'll do my best, but... well, I was planning something to help Skadi's Wolves level and I don't know if it'll work anymore after this."

"What'd you have in mind?"

"We need to start taking out bosses, that's where the experience is at. And the larger the group the better. I was gonna... well, put out a recruiting call for teams. I know people would have to travel, but I figure if I can get even a handful from the surrounding area, we might have a good shot at this one Bravo Boss I know about."

"I... see."

Steve sounded less than enthusiastic, and sudden uncertainty gripped Lynn.

"What is it? Is that a problem? I thought that was pretty much what the game tactical boards were suggesting—"

"Oh, uh, no, grouping up is a solid plan. Just... be careful, you know? It's a big task to tackle, and remember what you did to yourself the last time you went up against a boss."

"Oh yeah," Lynn chuckled. "I'll stay hydrated this time, I promise."

"Good. So what's the issue? Why don't you think it will work?"

"Well, who would want to come fight with us after this scandal? I'm being painted as some kind of violent psychopath."

"Are you kidding me? They'll come flocking in droves just to see if the rumors are true."

Lynn blanched. Steve must have guessed at her distaste because he chuckled.

"Welcome to celebrity status, kid. Now, obviously you should be careful how you put out the call. Don't give out any date, time, or location information, just that you're looking for teams to take down a boss. Even then, paparazzi will probably show up, but few enough that they shouldn't interfere with your mission. And I'd wait at least a week to say anything. Give the frenzy a chance to die down."

"Like it'll ever die down," Lynn said.

"Hey, don't sound so gloomy. The real footage shows you standing up to a bully, and it sure as heck shows that Edgar is *not* a guy to provoke. I've known a few Samoans. It's just building their general image. Lean into that. No point wasting hard-earned rep. You're not Larry freaking Coughlin for nothing, kid."

"I'll . . . try."

"All you can do, kid. Hey, I gotta break. But it was nice bumping into you."

"And getting thrashed by me?" Lynn asked, a grin coming back to her face.

"Hey, I didn't pick my teammates. You had a better lineup, no question. Just wait till we go one-on-one again and I'll show you the advantages that come with age and wisdom."

"Anytime, old man. Anytime."

Steve snorted.

"The irony of you saying that while pretending to be an old geezer yourself is pretty rich."

"Whatever makes me the big bucks."

That drew a barking laugh from Steve.

"And I'd hate you for it if you weren't so darn good at what you do. Catch ya later, kid."

"See ya."

"Everybody ready?" Matilda asked, holding up two thumbs.

The replies from the team ranged from calm to disgruntled to nervous. Since Lynn was the one who had to make the statement, she didn't know why any of the guys would feel nervous.

Lucky bastards.

She hated this part of being team captain—or the monkey troop Alpha, as Mr. Swain would have said—though she wouldn't have entrusted it to any of the guys. Whether she liked all her duties or not, she couldn't deny how much her responsibilities had pushed her to grow, and she was grateful for that.

But she still hated public speaking.

"Okay kids, live in three, two, one," Matilda mouthed from where she stood by the Raven's living room flex screen. Like all screens these days, it had its own built-in camera for streaming and face calls, and they used it now to broadcast from their humble abode. Not everybody could fit on the couch, so Edgar squeezed himself into the frame by sitting on a kitchen chair beside one cushioned arm, while Lynn, Mack, Dan, and Ronnie sat lined up on the sofa.

"Okay, Hugo," Lynn subvocalized. "Roll it."

"Of course, Miss Lynn. And good luck," the AI offered as her prepared statement started scrolling across her untinted AR glasses. She and the rest of her team wore various polos or t-shirts with the TD Hunter logo on them. Other than those and their AR glasses, they looked like normal teenagers, sitting on an unimpressive brown couch in a cheap apartment.

"Hey everyone," Lynn began, trying to sound natural instead of robotic. "I'm here with my team, Skadi's Wolves, to directly respond to some recent allegations. These allegations were based on vid footage altered to show a fabricated version of events, and it has rightly been taken down since. In order to put any questions to rest, we've released the first-person view of events recorded directly through the TD Hunter app, and it has been verified by Tsunami Entertainment and independent sources as unaltered footage. There have been no criminal charges filed by either party, and both teams involved will continue to compete"—she cleared her throat to cover a sudden tightening of her jaw. The thought of Connor getting away with this stunt scot-free made her blood boil—"in the TD Hunter International Championship. The incident was a"—she cleared her throat again—"unfortunate mis-understanding, and . . . and . . ."

Her words faltered, and she felt her team members shift uncomfortably on the couch, probably shooting her surreptitious glances while trying not to seem like they were doing so. Her mom gave her a questioning look from off screen and mouthed, "Are you okay?"

No. She wasn't.

This was not her.

For a moment she wondered if her dad had ever been forced to say distasteful things in the line of duty. She wondered what he would tell her to say now.

Well, since he wasn't there to help, she would have to muddle along as best she could on her own. One thing she *did* know was that he never would have lain down and let bullies walk all over him like a doormat. She'd spent too long only trying to survive, trying to ignore, trying to forget what people did to her and simply move on with life.

Yeah, to heck with that.

Slowly, deliberately, Lynn took off her AR glasses and folded them in her lap, then looked straight at the camera.

"The 'incident' was *not* an unfortunate misunderstanding," she said in a calm, calm voice. "It was a deliberate provocation by a cowardly bully who has no problem at all cheating, lying, and hurting people to get his way. My team acted in self-defense, and we would do it again in a heartbeat if we had to."

Lynn's nostrils flared and she took a deep breath before continuing.

"There's all sorts of things I'd *love* to do to get back at this cowardly bully, and all the bullies who've beaten me down over the years. I'm sure there's a lot of people watching right now who feel the same way. Maybe you're being bullied right now, and it hurts. A lot. But I'm not going to do any of those petty things, because making decisions based on how I feel is stupid and accomplishes nothing."

Even as she said it, a part of her gnashed her teeth in denial, screaming about the injustice of it all. She'd been thinking about what Steve had said, though, and she knew which way to go. The Larry part of her wanted to put a bullet in Connor's head. But this was real life, not WarMonger, and she was done wishing for the easy way out. Her enemies in the real might be more complicated to defeat, and the obstacles more amorphous and unseen.

But this was her life, and she was finally ready to take it seriously. Not just for herself, but for the people depending on her for leadership, for inspiration, and for a good example in a world full of bad ones.

"Instead, I'm going to stand up."

And she did, right there in her living room, and pointed at the camera.

"I'm going to stand up for myself and do the right thing: live the heck out of my life, with dedication and honor, and not waste a single second thinking about any worthless mouth breathers who are so weak they have to attack other people to feel good about themselves. If you're smart, you'll do the same thing."

Lynn put both hands on her hips and looked around at her team. Their eyes were alight and they were smiling, even Ronnie, which was a rare sight to see.

"Skadi's Wolves has a championship to win. *Unlike* some teams, who will remain unnamed, we're going to win it through hard work, skill, and dedication. Keep an eye on our channel, because we're only just getting started." She looked back at the camera and gave it her best wolfish smile, knowing the light would catch her amber eyes just so and make them glint with golden fire.

"RavenStriker, out."

Chapter 14

"HOLY CRAP, WE'RE SCREWED."

"Wow, Dan, your eloquence with the English language is absolutely stunning."

"Shut up, Mack. At least *I'm* not dating a Japanese scam bot."

"For the last time, Riko is not a bot! You guys have *talked* to her—"

"Less than five percent of people can accurately guess between an AI and a human voice these days," Ronnie quipped. "If she's so real, why won't she do a face chat?"

"Because she's had people illegally record her before. I'm not going to ask her to do something she's not comfortable with just because my douchebag friends think she's a bot!"

"Cut it out, guys. We need to focus," Lynn interjected before poor Mack had an aneurysm. Or she did.

Holy crap was accurate. As Larry Coughlin she would have put it more colorfully, but Lynn was too distracted trying to estimate TDM numbers based on the masses of dots on her overhead to come up with a Larry-worthy curse.

"Does anyone remember how many TDMs we fought

out here before, when Connor was captain?" Lynn
subvocalized on the team channel. School had just let
out and they were peering through the windows of
the north-facing doors that led to the athletic fields.
Normally they wouldn't have stood around at school
in full hunting gear, to avoid being stared at. But the
cold February wind gave them reason to delay inside
as long as possible. Plus, they were done caring what
the rest of the school thought of them. They didn't
bother staying out of sight while in their TD Hunting
uniforms anymore, though things had been especially
tense in the weeks after Connor's reputation assassi-
nation attempt. There had been a few run-ins with
the ARS team, now led by Paul, when things had
gotten dicey. But the knowledge that there were eyes
everywhere, both physical and digital, kept Paul and
his bully boys from starting anything violent.

Wisely, Connor avoided them entirely and seemed to
have instructed the rest of his team to do the same.
Elena never passed up a chance to sneer down her nose
if they saw each other in the halls, but she kept her
harpy mouth shut—at least in front of them. Behind
their back, of course, was a different story entirely.
But whether the pop-girl's popularity was waning, or
their fellow students were simply tired of the same
old vitriol, Lynn's professionalism and total focus on
TD Hunter seemed to diffuse the usual school gossip.

Lynn stood by the promise she'd made on the
Skadi's Wolves stream, and her team had, thankfully,
followed her example. Her confidence at school was
heavy on the "fake it till you make it" side of things,
but she'd gotten good enough at it over the weeks
that perhaps it was becoming more habit than show.

"Dunno how many bogies there were before, but not this many," Edgar muttered around the piece of gum he was grinding away at.

"I'd say their numbers are up by at least thirty percent," Ronnie offered.

"Based on?" Lynn asked.

"I've been tracking TDM respawn counts since the game came out," he said absently and paused, as if doing some quick mental calculations. "Typical respawn rate during the first few months had about a five to seven percent increase. It was more like twenty percent over the fall. Now it's over thirty."

"That's insane," Dan said. "They can't keep increasing the respawn rate on that trajectory. It just wouldn't make sense for game play."

"Remember that recent cut-scene vid when we hit Level 35?" Mack asked. "First Sergeant Bryce said they'd been tracking an increase in the alien incursion rate, and that things would only get worse from here. Obviously, the storyline is setting up some kind of inciting incident, maybe to coincide with the first wave of players reaching max level?"

Lynn's lips pursed and her eyes flicked to the windows, though none of the TDMs on her overhead map were close enough to be seen from where she was standing.

Skadi's Wolves cleared the area around the school on a fairly regular basis, mostly times the weather was bad or their mountain of homework meant they had only a little time to hunt after school before heading home. But this was the first time they'd hunted at the school since hitting Level 35, so maybe Mack was on to something.

Or . . . Lynn had noticed a grid engineer crew at the

school the past few days, working in the background. Were they simply upgrading equipment? Or were there more grid problems? And why now?

"That game play doesn't make sense," Dan said, interrupting Lynn's musings. "TD Hunter is *not* a normal MMORPG in virtual where they can sequester different levels of players to experience a certain storyline or aspect of the game. This is augmented *reality*. Everybody is experiencing the same thing, right? So brand new players who start tomorrow are dealing with massive increases in TDMs that we didn't see when we started. It's all lopsided and just doesn't make sense! Whoever designed this game did a crap job of it."

"Not necessarily," Mack said. "It depends on where they're taking the storyline. There's never been an AR game on this scale before, so you can't really compare it to what we've been playing for years in virtual."

Lynn grinned to herself, amused by Dan and Mack's descent into gaming geekery. Then her smile faded, and she glanced at the mass of red dots again.

Dan was right about one thing: the game didn't make sense. Lynn could rationalize it all she wanted, but her gut told her something about TD Hunter was off. She just didn't know *what* yet. Or what she would do about it once she figured it out.

For the time being, though, they had monsters to kill.

"The respawn rate increase is good news for us," Lynn said, interrupting Dan and Mack's bickering about game mechanics. "It means we can hit our leveling goals faster. So, let's get out there and start clearing around the school, since the TDMs have been so obliging and parked themselves in convenient swarms instead of spread out over miles of woods."

"I like the woods," Edgar commented, to which everyone turned and glared at him. "What? They're relaxing, you know?"

"You're insane," Dan grumbled.

"Aren't we all kind of insane, though?" Lynn asked, looking around at her team as a feral grin spread across her face. "We fight imaginary monsters in subzero wind chill, for *hours*, and we *like* it."

"Fair point," Mack agreed, grinning too. Ronnie shrugged, looking like he would have been grinning if he weren't trying to hide it behind a veneer of dignity, while Edgar bobbed his head up and down, an expression of childlike glee on his face.

Lynn's smile spread wider. She was proud of her team. Damn proud.

She hitched her compact backpack higher and tightened the strap across her chest.

"Come on. Let's go be insane."

That night after a long, hot shower, Lynn bundled up in her warmest pajamas and a blanket from the couch, then made a mug of hot chocolate before plopping down into her body-mold chair. She could access all the TD Hunter forums and chats directly from her AR glasses connected to her LINC, but she was weirdly old school enough to prefer doing it on her wall screen. The degree of separation felt more comfortable, somehow.

She still used Hugo, of course. He just made things easier.

"Okay, Hugo, where we at?"

"The total applicants for your 'Operation Boss Bash' has reached four hundred—"

"W-whaaat?!" Lynn choked and nearly spewed hot

chocolate all over herself. "They *what*? That's total people, right?"

"No, total teams. Which would make the total number of individual players—"

"Okay, okay, I get it. I *can* do basic math, Hugo. There's got to be a mistake, though. They *do* realize they'd have to come *here*, right? To Cedar Rapids?"

"One would presume team captains would read the applicable details before volunteering, yes, though that does not guarantee that they actually *have*."

"Still . . . that's insane . . ." Lynn had spent weeks discussing the details of this operation with her team. It had taken that long for them to brainstorm on their tactics and agree on the criteria they'd put out for teams to join them going after the boss north of the school. She had also wanted to wait for better weather, so they wouldn't have to cancel at the last minute and screw up everybody's travel plans.

Because, yeah, these teams would be coming *here*. She would see them face to face. Dozens of strangers. Ten to fifteen teams. And she'd be leading them.

She shivered and took a long sip of her hot chocolate.

"Okay, so, assuming you're not pulling my leg—"

"Your insinuation that I would do anything of the sort is an insult to my designers—"

"—then we have a lot of winnowing to do."

"Say no more, Miss Lynn. I have already sorted them by rank, and I took the liberty of combing the forums for any posts or interactions by their members to screen for unsavory behavior or general lack of professionalism."

"Oh . . . thanks. That's really helpful."

"Simply doing my job, Miss Lynn. Now, taking all

this into account, I have compiled a list of the top fifty ranked teams that meet your requirements. I did not filter them based on distance to their hometown, but I will mention that some of them would be traveling internationally to reach you."

"What? No way. Seriously, no way! Who in their right mind would come from a different country just to fight in a boss battle with us? They're insane!"

"I feel it is incumbent on me to point out that you are all 'kind of insane' according to your own words."

"Oh, shut up."

"Of course, Miss Lynn."

She sighed and rubbed her temples with one hand.

"Okay. Throw the list up on my screen and put on my Nightwish soundtrack, the one that starts with 'The Islander.'"

"Done."

The soothing flutes and drums of that haunting song filled her ears as she put down her hot chocolate and selected the first team on Hugo's list.

An hour later, she'd narrowed the list down to thirty. When she'd originally put out the call for volunteers, she'd thought she'd be lucky to recruit ten teams. That was her minimum to execute the operation she had in mind. But, since the world had officially turned insane and she was, apparently, some kind of gaming celebrity, she now had so much more to work with than she'd ever envisioned.

It made her Larry brain grin evilly and start plotting.

Of the fifty teams Hugo had given her, she'd found reason enough to reject the few international teams— one from Germany, one from Mexico, and two from Canada. She felt bad doing it, but she just couldn't in good conscience let them spend all that money and effort for something that might not even work. Plus, their willingness to travel so far made her suspicious. Maybe they just wanted to scope out their competition? Either way, she decided to stick with domestic teams for now.

Of those left, she threw out a few more that, while high in individual ranking, had been formed very recently and didn't have good team stats. Of the rest, she went with her gut, making a note of those that seemed the most professional and serious as opposed to the teams just in it for the glory. Out of the thirty, if even half made it to Cedar Rapids without backing out last minute, it would be enough.

"Hugo, could you reach out to these thirty with a standard reply that they were shortlisted to participate in Operation Boss Bash, and we're trying to coordinate a date that works best for everybody? I'd prefer to do this during our spring break in a couple weeks, so give them that date range and we'll see how many can make it."

"Doing it now, Miss Lynn. Would you like to review the message before I send it?"

"Yeah, thanks."

"Four hundred?"

"You're kidding, right?"

Lynn shook her head, grinning at the incredulous looks on the guys' faces. They were gathered around their usual lunch table in the cafeteria, but their food lay forgotten in the face of Lynn's pronouncement.

"I'm not surprised at all," said Kayla brightly. She joined them on most days, and today she sat between Dan and Mack with a "soup of the day" bowl steaming in front of her. "You all produce lots of great content, and with a pro PR company managing your accounts with all their knowledge of how to work the algorithm, you're trending like crazy."

"I bet it's because of *my* channel," Dan said, puffing out his chest and shooting a surreptitious look at Kayla. "I've been doing some seriously dope iceberg discussions on MMOFPS versus traditional FPS and it's been getting lots of comments."

Ronnie rolled his eyes.

"Nobody cares about your dumb game comparisons, Dan. I bet they all volunteered so they can come see what's really going on with this TD Hunter game. They probably figure we know something they don't, being a top-tier Hunter Strike Team."

"Not your conspiracy theories again," Dan groaned. "There's nothing going on!"

"Yes there is!" Ronnie insisted. "Do *none* of you watch the news? Like, ever? There's been massive disruptions in the grid network over the past nine months, ever since TD Hunter was launched, and the incidents are only increasing. And it's not just in the US, it's worldwide! I mean, everywhere but China, obviously, because their hackers are behind it."

Everyone at the table groaned this time, even Kayla.

"Give it a break, Ronnie," Edgar said around a fish stick.

"I'm telling you; everybody is talking about it! And with the crazy black-box budget bills being passed in Congress lately and all the force mobilization, it's *obvious* what's going on."

"Please, Ronnie, don't tell us," Lynn said halfheartedly and stabbed her salad with a fork.

"We're going to war with China," Ronnie said, voice

lowered dramatically. "And you know what I think? I think TD Hunter is just cover for covert meshweb warfare between the US and China, and that's why there are no Chinese-sponsored Hunter Strike teams. Heck, they've all but banned the TD Hunter app in China, because they don't want Western powers spying on them and accessing their infrastructure through the app."

"Okay, I'll bite," Dan said, then took a huge mouthful of his burger and attempted to speak through it. "If-swar wichina, why alldastf inna'merca?"

"Eww, Dan, that's gross," Lynn said, wiping a bit of half-chewed burger bun off her arm. She noticed Kayla hiding a smile behind her hand and gave her friend an exasperated look.

"Ssrry." Dan chewed a little more until his mouth was only halfway full and launched back into his argument. "If we're weaponizing the TD Hunter app against China, then why are all the infrastructure issues in America and not China?".

"Retaliation, duh," Ronnie said, giving Dan a pitying look. "It's state-sponsored hacker warfare. And for all we know, there's just as much damage going on in China, we'll just never know about it because the state controls the media."

"I think you're all wrong," Lynn said quietly, surprising herself by speaking.

"Oh yeah?" Ronnie challenged, a healthy dose of the old jerkitude in his tone "And what would you know about it?"

Lynn straightened and stared him down, silent, until Ronnie looked away.

"It's called being observant," she finally said, then shook her head. "But there's no point debating about it because it's all probably nonsense anyway. Regardless of why we got so much interest in our Operation Boss Bash, the point is that we have an incredible opportunity here to put us ahead. You know the group hunting bonuses are not just dependent on accuracy and kill stats. There's a force-multiplier aspect too. The more teams we successfully use to take down the boss, the more experience we all get."

She looked around the table as realization dawned and grins spread on the guys' faces. Kayla looked happy, too, probably because whatever helped Skadi's Wolves also helped her stepdad and his company.

"Dan, I asked you to keep an eye on CRC, not just on the official forums but also anywhere ... less legal they could be operating to give them a leg up. What have they been up to? How do they expect to make it to Level 40 in time for the championship?"

"About what you'd expect," Dan said, and shrugged. "They're throwing money at the problem, buying up any experience modification augments and hiring local power levelers to hunt with them and up their group bonuses, not to mention grinding insane numbers of TDMs."

"Knowing Elena, she's probably not even hunting herself half the time," Ronnie grumbled.

"What do you mean?" Lynn asked.

Ronnie didn't look at her as he replied.

"When I was on her team, if she got tired, or broke a nail, or it was too hot and her makeup might run, she'd just sit in a café or something in combat mode and send the rest of us out to hunt nearby. That way she still showed up as active and gained team bonus experience, but she didn't have to do anything."

There was a moment of stunned silence at their table.

"Whoa," Dan finally said. "She's got some balls on her for sure. I can't believe you put up with it, though. Why would you do that?"

Ronnie shot him a dirty look.

"I didn't have much of a choice, at the time."

"Elena is like that," Kayla said. The supportive statement seemed to take Ronnie aback, especially coming from Kayla, who he still treated with suspicion. Kayla took it all in stride, probably recognizing that trust took time to build. "She might seem stupid sometimes, but she knows how to use your weaknesses against you."

"Okay, but still—" Dan began, but Lynn interjected before they could start their usual arguing.

"It doesn't matter. The point is that CRC isn't doing itself any favors. They might qualify come time for the championship, but they won't have enough experience working as a team to take down bosses. Thanks for keeping an eye on them Dan. Keep it up and be sure to let me know if it looks like they're breaking TD Hunter terms of service. We wouldn't want to turn a blind eye to cheating, would we?"

"Nope," Dan agreed with a grin.

"So," Lynn continued. "That's what our rival is up to. We've got a better strategy and a better work ethic to back it up, but it's going to take a lot of cooperation to pull this thing off. Here's what we need to be working on..."

In the end, twenty-six of the thirty teams agreed on a day in March for the operation. A part of Lynn was still skeptical they would show up, but she *had* chatted with and vetted all the team captains. Since she couldn't discuss her day-of strategy for fear a bad actor might leak it or try to sabotage the operation, Dan helped her cook up an in virtual wargame simulation that mirrored the most important aspects of her plan. It provided practice for the teams, gave her a way to assess the captains, and forced her to face her anxiety with a bit of virtual breathing room built in.

No matter how much she told herself the operation was just like leading a merc team in WarMonger, the idea of ordering around dozens of strangers *in person* was terrifying. She obsessed about it so much she started having dreams. The ones where all the teams were consumed by rampaging monsters were bad enough. Worse was when everybody laughed at her commands, their faces morphing into Elena's petty sneer or Connor's condescending look of disgust. It was enough to wake her in a cold sweat some nights.

Despite her fears, the war game went surprisingly well. The team captains, an eclectic mix of all ages and types, were professional, hardworking, and seemed to have a good time with the exercise. Lynn kept her interactions professional—she was the op commander, after all—but there was plenty of good-natured banter and lively conversation that went on in the team channels.

Besides assessing the strength and weaknesses of each team captain, Lynn also silently picked out who her squad leaders were going to be. She would wait and see who actually showed up in person before assigning any roles, though.

Before she knew it, it was March. Between school, hunting, keeping up with her PR duties for GIC, and planning her operation, the days blurred together until she only knew the day of the week because Hugo cheerfully informed her every morning when she got onto the TD Hunter app for her morning exercises. That gave her a chance to cycle through her best Larry insults, just so she didn't go all soft and forget being so long away from WarMonger. Hugo's responses were, of course, thoroughly unsatisfying. It made Lynn reminisce sadly of her glory days intimidating newbies and tea-bagging Ronnie as he shouted Lithuanian curses in a terrible American accent.

It was barely a week before Operation Boss Bash when Lynn got a surprising message request on the TD Hunter app from the last person she ever expected to hear from: DeathShot13.

Sorry for the last minute contact, but are you still taking volunteers? Didn't think we could swing coming to the States, but the stars have aligned. Would be honored to join if you'll have us.

Attached to the message was DeathShot's team info, which Lynn read through eagerly, then whistled to herself. He'd only formed his team a month ago, but they'd already racked up some seriously competitive stats. Based on Lynn's original criteria, she shouldn't have accepted such a request, especially from a new and untried team.

But she was already subvocalizing a reply before the consideration even crossed her mind.

We'd be honored to have you, assuming you Canucks can keep up with us ;). I'll add you to the op group chat room. Take time to get to know the other teams. We're all in this together.

The reply came back almost immediately.

Roger that. And we'll do our best. I'll tell my team to take it easy on the TDMs so you all have something to kill, too.

Lynn grinned. DeathShot13 sounded like her kind of person. He might even be former military from the sound of it, which was a good sign. If people like Steve and her other former-military merc buddies in WarMonger were any indication, DeathShot and his people would be skilled, professional, and trustworthy.

That bit of good news sustained her through the last hellish week of school before spring break. Her teachers seemed to think it was already senior finals by the way they piled on the assignments. Plus, Elena was being more vicious than usual. Lynn constantly worried that CRC would catch wind of the Skadi's Wolves op and try to sabotage it, so Elena's vaguely threatening comments dialed Lynn's anxiety up to eleven.

By the Friday night before the op, Lynn's nerves were beyond frazzled, though she did her best to hide it. They had a team meeting at her place for a last-minute run through of the plan, accompanied by mountains of meat-lovers pizza and as much pop as they could drink. They each ate almost a full pizza box on their own—Edgar ate nearly two, but then he *was* a head taller and a foot wider than anyone else on the team. The spectacle of the five of them sitting around the living room, each eating pizza out of their own box while swigging from two-liter bottles made Lynn's mom laugh and mutter something about growing teenagers.

"You know," Dan piped up, "our team's combined step count averages roughly forty-five miles a day. If we don't fuel up, we'll turn into skin and bones!"

Matilda laughed.

"I guess that's why Lynn eats like a starved lion every night. One time I caught her growling at the stovetop because it wasn't cooking her steak fast enough."

"Mom!"

"It's true!"

"I was *not* growling at it. I was grumbling to myself because the burner was broken."

"If you say so." Her mom shrugged, still grinning.

Apart from distracting peanut gallery comments, the meeting went well and the guys left in high spirits, looking forward to the day ahead. That was good, since Lynn had done everything in her power to hide her dread and stomach-twisting anxiety. No point inflicting it on anyone else.

Edgar, though, hung back, letting the other guys leave first. He silently helped Lynn pick up the empty pizza boxes, napkins, and other trash, and shove it all into the garbage chute. By the time they were done, Lynn's mom had made herself scarce and Lynn found herself alone in the living room, trying to avoid Edgar's knowing gaze.

"So, um, see you tomorrow?" Lynn offered, pasting a smile on her face as she folded her arms across her chest.

"Yup."

Edgar's tone was easy, but he didn't move, just stuck his hands in his pockets.

"I guess you should go. You wouldn't want to worry your mom, right?"

Edgar shrugged. "I got time."

Lynn's eyes narrowed. "Time for what?"

"To remind you to stop worrying."

The sick feeling in her stomach surged, and she swallowed.

"I'm fine."

Edgar smiled. Not his usual goofy grin, but a fond

smile that made Lynn feel disconcertingly warm and tingly.

"'Course you're fine. You're *Toa Tama'ita'i*."

"Don't say that," Lynn snapped. "Don't act like I'm somebody special and everything will be okay just because you gave me a silly nickname."

Edgar's smile faded, but not into hurt or indignation. His expression sobered and he hesitated, but then withdrew a hand from his pocket and stepped close enough to lay it tentatively on her shoulder, as if afraid she might shrug it off.

She didn't. How could she when he looked at her like that?

"I didn't give you a silly nickname, Lynn. You were already a warrior woman. Always have been, least since I've known you. I'm just the one who finally said it out loud." Edgar's deep voice seemed to vibrate through Lynn, making every nerve tingle with energy.

Even so, she looked away.

"You're wrong," she said, not wanting it to be true but unable to stop herself saying it. "I've spent most of my life hiding. Even with this whole TD Hunter thing, it's not really me. I'm not brave, bold RavenStriker. That's just a front, another mask." She thought of Larry and shook her head. "I'm not a warrior, I just like to play pretend. And one day, it's going to get someone hurt."

Maybe tomorrow, she thought. *What if someone gets hurt and it's my fault?*

Lynn shivered, despite the warmth of Edgar's large hand on her shoulder. She expected him to laugh off her objections and say something encouraging, or maybe funny. She would appreciate his effort, but it wouldn't change anything.

Edgar did squeeze her shoulder, but then he dropped his hand and said the last thing in the world she expected.

"Is Ronnie a warrior?"

Lynn's gaze snapped up and her brows drew together. But Edgar's serious expression didn't change.

"What kind of a question is that?"

"The kind you answer," he said, amusement tinging his words.

Lynn's knee-jerk reaction was to scoff, but she made herself slow down and think objectively about the question. Finally, she huffed out a breath and shrugged.

"I don't know that he's a very *good* warrior, but yeah . . . I guess he is."

"Then what makes *him* a warrior and not you?"

That made Lynn scowl. She could see where Edgar was going with this, and she didn't like being outmaneuvered. She shook her head.

"Okay, so how come you don't call *him* a *Toa Tama'ita'i*, huh?"

"Well," Edgar drawled, "cause he's ain't no woman, for one thing."

Lynn laughed, despite herself, and Edgar finally let his grin show.

"And for another," he continued, "he's not so busy hiding from himself that he can't see the truth."

"See! I told you I was hiding."

"From yourself."

"No, from everybody *else*."

"If you aren't hiding from yourself, then why do you hate mirrors? And watching yourself on stream?"

"Wait a minute, how did you know I hate mirrors?"

"Cuz you just told me."

"No, I..." Lynn closed her mouth and glared up at her friend, who was looking entirely too pleased with himself.

Edgar stuck his hand back in his pocket and shrugged.

"I ain't no psychologist or nothing, but from where I'm standing, you're busy hiding from yourself because you believe the dumbest lies from the dumbest people, and you're scared to find out if they're right. But you should do what I do," he finished, and gave her another warm smile.

Lynn stubbornly let the silence stretch on, but Edgar didn't budge, so she finally rolled her eyes and asked the question he wanted her to ask.

"And what do you do, Edgar?"

"I don't listen to dumb people."

Lynn took a deep breath to retort, then let it out as a laugh.

"Okay. Fine. That's fair. But... you know it's not that easy, right?"

"I know," he said, and sadness filled his eyes. "But practice makes perfect, yeah? Least that's what Ma keeps telling me. And," he added, "you got plenty of smart people around you telling you the truth, people like your Ma and that old guy, Mr. Thomas? I met him at the Christmas party. He's pretty cool. Oh, and me," he finished with a grin.

"Oh really? So, you're a smart person, huh?"

"Heck yeah! It's the quiet people who got the brains, don'tcha know?"

"So, what you're saying is, Dan and Ronnie are dumb?"

"Eh." Edgar raised a hand and wiggled it back and forth ambivalently. "Talking less wouldn't hurt 'em."

They laughed together. When it died away, Edgar looked around the room, then at the floor, then at Lynn's feet. He shifted, the movement bringing him one step closer to her. When he finally looked her in the eye, she couldn't decipher his expression, but it made her warm again—and not in an unpleasant way.

"I do hafta go, but, uh, since I'm a smart person and all that, I got some truths for you, to get rid of all those dumb lies, you know?"

Lynn wanted to reply, but all she could do was swallow and nod mutely.

"Well, you're beautiful, for one. And smart. And talented. And freaking *scary* when someone needs a smackdown. And you're brave, even if you don't think so, cuz you do what's right, no matter if it's hard." He shuffled another step closer, so close she could feel his body heat.

"And you *inspire* people, Lynn. You see people... people no one else sees. And you don't give up on them." His voice had dropped so low it was barely a rumble but mesmerizing all the same. He was close enough to kiss, now, though why her scattered thoughts homed in on that particular possibility, she wasn't going to explore. But despite the intense look in his eyes, he didn't dip his head down toward her. He seemed frozen.

So was she, for that matter, but not in fear or anxiety. The thing that filled her chest felt more like anticipation.

When he finally found his voice again, it was rough and he had to clear it before continuing.

"I'm thinking, maybe you take some of that trust

and loyalty you give other people, and give it to yourself for a change, yeah? Cuz we all trust you, Lynn. You're the best of us, and you'll find a way—not cuz of some silly nickname, but cuz you're too stubborn to give up until you do."

Lynn might have choked up at that, but Edgar didn't seem to notice. He just lifted a hand and gently stroked her cheek as if brushing away a strand of hair. Then he cleared his throat, mumbled, "See you tomorrow, Lynn," and headed for the door, leaving her with so many new things to think about that there was no room in her brain for worry.

"Team Voodoo Girls, checking in."

"Welcome, ladies," Lynn said at the group of five young women who had appeared around the bend in the dirt access road that cut through the woods. They wore an assortment of close-fitting athletic wear— nothing as expensive as the sponsored uniforms Lynn's team wore, but efficient enough to get the job done. In augmented reality, though, Lynn knew these girls would be decked out in matching sleek armor like so many cyberpunk ninjas. Lynn knew this because she'd seen them before in the qualifying tournament last September. She'd been impressed with the team's look then and was excited to get to meet them now.

"You sure know how to pick 'em, don'tcha," the team captain, Quorra, said as she approached, looking around at the expanse of bare trees. Miraculously, the March weather was dry, if overcast, and not too cold. At least they wouldn't be slogging through mud.

The Voodoo Girls stopped at the edge of the growing crowd of people on the access road while Quorra continued forward. The woman was a bit taller than Lynn, probably in her early twenties, with short, dark hair. She smiled as she shook Lynn's hand.

"This is totally surreal, finally getting to meet you. Your team killed it during the qualifiers, not to mention that stunt you pulled at the end!"

Lynn shrugged uncomfortably.

"Just trying to do my best."

"Well, we're honored you invited us to come smoke these mobs with you. This is going to be epic."

"I'm honored you all came." Lynn looked around at the dozen other teams that had already arrived, some huddled close, others spread out and mingling as they talked animatedly. "A lot of people traveled a long way to be here. I'm surprised anybody came at all," she admitted and gave Quorra a chagrined smile.

"Are you kidding? A chance to hunt with a Hunter Strike Team, take down a boss, *and* make bank on experience and loot? Any gamer with half a brain would kill to be here."

Lynn resisted the urge to say something pessimistic. She was supposed to be projecting confidence and authority. Why was that so much harder in the real than in virtual?

"Well, hopefully with all of us working together, we can make mincemeat of these TDMs. Why don't you go meet some of the other captains while we wait for everybody else to arrive? We've still got about fifteen minutes until I do the op brief."

"Right on. Killing's what we do, you can count on me and my girls!"

Lynn laughed and gave Quorra a thumbs up, then the other Hunter headed back to her team. As Lynn

turned to survey the people around her, she caught
Ronnie staring after Quorra, an odd look on his face.
What was it? Curiosity? Lynn suppressed a grin.
Ronnie would probably get angry and moody if she
called him on it, so she simply continued her survey
of the sizable crowd. Edgar stood nearby, keeping his
own quiet watch while masticating his usual piece of
gum. Dan and Mack were in among the other teams,
talking to captains they'd made friends with in virtual
during the weeks of prep for the op.

Of the twenty-seven teams who had committed to
coming, five had been forced to cancel last minute. She'd
sent meeting coordinates to the remaining twenty-two
that morning; of those, thirteen had already arrived.

A part of Lynn was still amazed anyone had shown
up at all, though the lack of paparazzi drones hovering
overhead was probably a bigger miracle. She'd sworn
the teams to secrecy, emphasizing that the presence
of drones or spectators could ruin their operation and
waste the time, effort, and money they'd invested. So
far, it looked like the other Hunters had taken her
seriously and had been sufficiently discreet in finding
their meeting place.

Lynn knew drones would show up eventually. There
were several that patrolled the skies high above her
school on a frequent basis, and her school was only
a few miles south. But hopefully they would arrive
too late to tip off any lens junkies.

"Hugo," Lynn subvocalized, "bring up the list of
teams in the group chat room."

"Of course, Miss Lynn."

As her eyes scanned down the list in her AR display,
names jumped out at her: Maelstrom, Light Brigade,

Bloodletters, Monster Control Bureau, The Lone Gunmen, and many more. All were teams vying for top scores on the team leaderboard, though none of them were official Hunter Strike Teams. She was mentally checking off those who had already arrived when movement up the access road caught her eye.

Two more teams appeared, already mingling and talking as they trekked down the path. One of them was made up of all older adults. Not that there weren't middle-aged people in some of the other teams. But with the amount of physical effort it took to achieve upper-tier scores, the game definitely favored the young.

These players, though, looked fit enough to be pro athletes, and they moved with an easy grace that made Lynn's eyes narrow. For a moment, she wondered if they could be connected to Connor and his former ARS team. But no. There were plenty of reasons for people to be fit, and these Hunters looked like they had a couple decades on Connor and his flunkies, so it seemed doubtful they moved in the same circles.

"Team Light Brigade, checking in."

"Team Ork Iz Da Best, checking in."

Lynn grinned to herself and welcomed the two new teams as they nodded in greeting and looked around. One member of the older group of Hunters broke off and approached Lynn. He was of medium height with brown hair, a friendly face, and a little cleft in his chin. One hand was in the pocket of his formfitting jacket, the other he withdrew to shake her hand as he got close.

"DeathShot13, at your service."

Lynn barely registered the man's words because his familiar voice sent her into a spiral of shock. Her mouth fell open and she gasped, "YodaMaster?"

The man's lips twitched, and he raised one eyebrow. "Oh, you play WarMonger? Client, rival, or victim?"

Realizing what she'd done, Lynn swallowed hard, her face heating.

Idiot.

While she recognized her friend's voice from the many times they'd fought with—and against—each other in WarMonger, Yoda only knew her by a gravelly baritone attached to a fake name and salty personality. And here she had nearly revealed her Larry Coughlin identity to him.

"Uh, mostly victim," she said, voice still shaky. She gave him a smile, and he smiled back, his eyes twinkling merrily.

"Well, then, you have my sympathy. Your skills have certainly improved moving to TD Hunter. You put me to shame more often than not on the leaderboards."

I can't believe Yoda is DeathShot, Lynn thought dazedly, still not quite registering his words. She was thrilled. And terrified. It would be the height of awesome working with him in the real, but she would have to be very, *very* careful. It would only take a moment of inattention to slip up and out herself.

"Uhh, yeah, I guess? You keep me on my toes, too, though. You're always passing me up. But, um, thanks for coming all this way. Canada, right?"

DeathShot nodded.

"I travel a fair bit for work, but most recently, yes."

"Cool. Um, who are your friends?"

The man waved the rest of his team over and Lynn was struck again by the way they moved. It was very...deliberate. Balanced. Ready. They had to be into some sort of martial art or sport. Or perhaps military, based on the haircuts of the three other guys. The fifth team member was a woman, all lean muscle and smooth grace, with hair in a long blond braid down her back. DeathShot introduced her first.

"This is my wife, Sonia388Lapua."

Lynn grinned.

"Wife, huh? I thought all gamers were married to the game? When do you have time to do, you know, normal people stuff?"

DeathShot and Sonia both laughed, though they also exchanged a knowing look.

"Our 'normal people stuff' *is* gaming," Sonia said, her Canadian accent stronger than her husband's. Lynn had always assumed Yoda—that is, DeathShot—had simply hailed from somewhere up near Minnesota, but apparently she'd been a few hundred miles off.

"These jokers," DeathShot said, motioning to his other teammates, "are HoldMyBeer, Operation_Stink-bug and Mr_E006. We go way back. They were the only ones gullible enough to get talked into this little jaunt," he finished with a wink. The other guys didn't say anything, but they all nodded Lynn's way. She nodded back, feeling uncomfortably like she was being evaluated. All of them wore sleek, top-of-the-line AR glasses, similar to hers. The overcast sky meant the glasses weren't tinted and so she had an unobstructed view of their scrutiny.

She wondered if they were also mercs she'd known and fought with in WarMonger.

"Well, I hope you all enjoy yourselves," she said to DeathShot's team. "We have our work cut out for us."

"We're counting on it," Sonia said, with a delight-fully predatory smile.

Lynn couldn't help smiling back, and she nodded in approval.

A few other teams had shown up while they talked, so Lynn excused herself to check in with the newly arrived captains.

By the time fifteen minutes was up, all but two of the twenty-two teams had arrived. Lynn shifted from foot to foot, wondering if she could afford to wait any longer. But the weight of over a hundred pairs of eyes turning toward her, one by one, told her she had to get the show on the road.

Lynn's skin flushed hot and cold in turn. She swallowed, hard.

Movement beside her made her turn and look up at Edgar, who smiled.

"You got this, Lynn. Let's go kill stuff."

Right. It *was* what she did best. She would get it done—and do a good job—because Edgar had been absolutely right yesterday: she was too stubborn to give up.

Ronnie would join a feminist activist group before she gave up.

Dan would quit gaming and enroll in law school before she gave up.

She would go vegan and swear off juicy, bloody meat before she gave up.

Okay, she told herself, *this is just a really,* really *big group of mercs, ready to beat down some trash-talking Tier Twos. Put your Larry face on and go have fun.*

She took a deep breath and tried to find that calm, centered, Larry competence she relied on when hunting. It usually came to her easily, but this was the first time she'd needed it while a hundred strangers stared intently at her. That didn't happen in virtual, and she didn't know how to block out the wave of self-consciousness that prickled across her skin like a thousand creeping spiders.

Fake it till you make it, she told herself sternly, and opened her mouth.

"Thanks, everyone, for coming. Please open your TD Hunter apps and accept the hunting group invite I'm about to send you. I'll brief everybody on the group channel." She switched from a battlefield pitch to subvocalization. "Hugo, make it so."

"Done, Miss Lynn. I took the liberty of naming it 'Skadi's Horde.' Is this name acceptable or do you wish me to change it?"

"That's perfect," Lynn subvocalized. "Now, push that unit assignment chart I made to the group, and put me on the group channel."

"Done."

Feeling more centered, Lynn straightened to her full five-foot-four height, clasped her hands behind her back, and began speaking in a normal voice.

"Coms check. Everyone who can hear me, sound off in the group chat. Hugo," she said, switching to subvocalization, "do a head count, will you? Oh, and we'll follow the usual protocols for this op. I'll subvocalize your commands and use normal volume for broadcasting."

"Excellent, Miss Lynn. And everyone has indicated their audio equipment is working."

"Thanks." She cast her gaze across the crowd, keeping her expression carefully neutral. A few people whispered to each other, but most were watching her attentively.

"If you haven't already," she began, "take a look

at the unit assignment chart I posted in the group chat. Before anyone asks, no, the assignments are not negotiable. I made them based on each team's leaderboard stats, loadout, and special skills as reported by your team captains. Our strategy today is simple: We'll be assaulting in a spearhead formation with flanking wings. I've divided the teams up into four squads, each with five teams. Green Spear and Gold Spear squads will make up the east and west sides of the spear respectively, while Green Wing and Gold Wing squads will make up the east and west wings.

"Our primary objective is to destroy the boss, and our secondary objective is to wipe out the encircling TDMs. I'm confident our first objective is achievable if we all work together and play at the top of our game. The second objective will depend on our resource levels and TDM numbers remaining once the boss is destroyed. I'll make a call on it when the time comes."

As she spoke, Hugo displayed a series of graphics in the Skadi's Horde chat showing a map of the area and their proposed assault formation. The woods they were in made a rough triangle about a mile on each side, with the high school bordering it to the south, neighborhoods to the east, and an interstate to the northwest forming the long, slanting side of the triangle. The mesh node sat in the middle of the triangle, while the access road began at the north point of the triangle and paralleled the interstate down the long side of the triangle before turning south and going through the middle of the woods to the node.

"Our spearhead will follow the access road straight south while our wings keep pace and clear a wide enough swatch of TDMs to keep our rear clear. Once we reach the boss's location, the spearhead will break through the TDM circle and form a firing line to assault the boss while the wings fold in to protect our flanks and keep the buggers from encircling us."

Again, while she gave the briefing, Hugo played a graphic in the Horde's chat showing the progression of the assault. The half green, half gold spearpoint with its accompanying wings moved south toward the thick circle of red dots surrounding the last known location of the still unidentified boss.

"Team captains, you decide on your own team's individual formation while we assault forward. Your team's needs may change as we move over different terrain and take on various TDMs, so use whatever arrangement works best as long as you stay in line with your squad. Are there any questions so far before I cover fight tactics and best practices?"

"Yeah," came a call from the crowd, "why don't we just go to the middle of the boss circle, pop into combat mode and smoke him, then pop back out?"

"Valid question," Lynn said with a nod. "From now on, though, please identify yourself with game handle and team name before you speak. So, again, please?"

"ElLoboFrohike, Team The Lone Gunmen. Why don't we pop in and out? What's with all the elaborate dancing around?"

"Two reasons, Frohike. One, you're here on the invitation of Skadi's Wolves, and we're a Hunter Strike team. Popping in and out is illegal during the competition, so we're focusing on tactics we can actually use to win the world championship. Second, we're all here for loot and experience, both of which we'll get more of this way. Next question?"

"Your formation is—"

"Name and team, Hunter," Lynn barked, cutting the man off. He was at the front of the crowd, arms crossed, standing almost as tall as Edgar. He scowled at her, but she stared right back, expression cold and hard.

She was glad he couldn't hear her rapidly beating heart.

"ChiefZykhee. Captain, Team Maelstrom. Like I said, your whole plan is pointlessly complicated. We've got, what, a hundred high-level gamers here?" he said, gesturing around at the crowd. "There's more than enough of us to just sweep in and annihilate these mofos. So, let's do it."

Lynn did not immediately respond. She stood at ease, staring the team captain down with an iron-hard gaze as she decided what to say. Her Lynn brain was too busy worrying what people would think to be useful, and it was much harder to shove aside than usual.

Come on, I'm better than this! What would Larry do?

Annoyance surged in her, stronger than the anxiety, and instead of thinking, Lynn simply acted. She slid one electric-blue baton out of its sheath pocket on her thigh and started spinning it over and around her hand. She'd spent so much time playing with her batons in down time between hunts that she could do some pretty impressive tricks without even looking.

Eyes still locked on Zykhee, she took several slow steps forward until she was not quite within arm's reach. She finished a final spin of the baton and let it come to rest clasped between both hands as she adopted a wide stance.

"As much as I'd enjoy laughing my ass off while you and your team got surrounded and beaten into a pulp by hordes of TDMs, I didn't invite you here to watch you or anyone else do your own stupid thing and leave the rest of us in the lurch. I invited you to participate in a *mission* where we work *together* to accomplish a *common* goal. A mission that *I* am in charge of." With each emphasized word, Lynn slapped the baton into the palm of one hand with an audible *smack*. "If you have a problem with that, you're welcome to march your little snowflake self back down that access road and get the hell out of my way. Is that *understood*?"

Smack.

The team captain's mouth twisted in displeasure, but he finally snorted and nodded curtly.

"Excellent," Lynn said, and spun away, suddenly aware of how hard her heart was pounding against her rib cage. She faced the rest of the crowd and began to pace as she continued. "I don't know how many of you have noticed this, but TDM numbers have been increasing exponentially. And anyone who has attacked a boss before knows that in addition to whatever monsters were already there, more always show up. We're not just dealing with a mob of TDMs. We're dealing with a mob, their boss, and the hundreds of TDMs in the vicinity that will make a beeline for us the moment the boss starts taking damage. So, if there's no more stupid questions, let's move on."

Lynn kept pacing while she went over operating procedures and best practices, things like setting the app to minimize leveling announcements and the best way to switch between individual, team, and squad channels. She finished with a few worst-case-scenario instructions, so everybody would be on the same page.

"Lastly and most importantly, do not under any

circumstances stand inside the boss." Lynn swallowed. She wanted to tell the truth—or at least what she suspected. But that would make her sound like a crazy person. So, she took another approach instead. "I know some of you have heard about what I did at the qualifiers, but that was a one-time thing. The competition judges told me directly that the tactic is now listed as illegal. And besides, it messes with the app and glitches have been known to happen. The last thing we want is a massive glitch just when we're about to hit the motherland of experience and loot. So, I repeat, *everyone stay away from the boss.* They don't usually move much, but if it advances towards us, back up and stay out of its way. Got it?"

As the acknowledgments rolled in, Lynn glanced at the time on her overhead display and noted that her two missing teams still hadn't shown up. Shoving that worry away, she spoke again.

"If there are any more questions, ask your team captains. Captains will address it to their squad leader, and if the squad leaders don't know, they can ask me.

"Now, squad leaders, assemble and decide on team order within your squads. Make sure everybody knows where they're supposed to be and what we're doing. Go!"

Lynn crossed her arms and waited, hoping against hope that she'd made wise selections in appointing her squad leaders. It was the hardest part of being in charge: Depending on your subordinates to do their job and do it well. It was so tempting to step in and micromanage, but she knew from painful experience that doing so would be disastrous.

To distract herself, she turned back to her own guys, subvocalizing to Hugo to switch to her team channel.

"Any questions?" she asked, looking at each of her team members in turn.

"Nope," Dan said, bouncing on his toes. He already had his batons out, and he spontaneously flicked them back and forth, miming various martial arts moves from one or another of his favorite action vids.

Mack was a little pale, but his face was set in determination. Lynn was weirdly struck by how...mature he looked. He'd bulked out over the past nine months and had managed to *almost* grow an entire goatee—even more impressive, he'd convinced his mom to let him keep it. If Riko had been a real person, Lynn wouldn't have faulted her pick in a man to admire.

Ronnie, of course, looked as composed and serious as ever. His eyes were unfocused, and she assumed he was reviewing their assigned formation. Though, being at the tip of the spear with Edgar, all he had to worry about would be killing TDMs as efficiently as possible and staying alive.

It was up to Lynn to keep an eye on the whole formation and direct the squad leaders as needed to keep them together in a cohesive fighting force. Dan would be doubling as sniper and tactical, while Mack juggled fighting tactical as well as keeping them all supplied. In the prior weeks, Lynn had instructed each captain to designate a team member as their supply personnel. Being a Hunter Strike Team had its perks—any hunting group created by Skadi's Wolves had special abilities, like being able to share supplies across the whole group. Their biggest challenges would be collecting loot dropped without slowing down and keeping good com discipline. The whole group had practiced operating together several times in virtual, but there was always that one idiot who kept forgetting to mute themselves or switch to the appropriate channel.

"You ready to rumble?" Lynn asked Edgar.

He grinned down at her.

"Like a boss, boss."

Lynn rolled her eyes but couldn't help smiling.

"Remember, team, we're using game handles, not names."

"Yeah, yeah, we know," Ronnie grumbled. "Now, can we get this show on the road?"

Lynn redirected her attention outward and was relieved to see that the crowd had shifted into four loose groups. Most everyone was quiet, listening to their squad leader's instructions over their individual channels.

"Hugo, you ready for this?"

"I was created ready, Miss Lynn."

"Har-de-har-har. Just a regular comedian there, aren't you."

"I have my moments, and they are entirely your fault."

"What? How so?"

"My primary function is to assist my users, and nothing engenders a better working relationship than adopting the personality traits uniquely attractive to each Hunter."

"So, you're saying you're snarky and difficult because I *like it* when you're snarky and difficult?"

"Just so, Miss Lynn."

Lynn was speechless for a moment, then remembered she had more important things to do than fuss at her AI.

"We'll come back to this, Hugo, I promise."

"I do not doubt it in the slightest."

Lynn's eyes narrowed, but instead of retorting, she told Hugo to switch to her squad leaders' channel.

"RavenStriker to squad leaders, sound off. Are your squads ready to go?"

"DeathShot13, Gold Spear ready to go."

"IAmAgentFranks, Green Spear ready to go."

"FoxyMulder, Gold Wing ready to go."

"Kharneth666, Green Wing ready to go."

"Okay, everyone form up their squads and get ready to move out. Skadi's Wolves will be leading down this access road about a quarter mile before we spread out into our formation and go into combat mode."

A chorus of acknowledgments responded, and as each spoke the squad leaders' names popped up on her display. It was a nice function that meant she always knew who was talking whether they identified themselves or not. She preferred players stick to standard radio etiquette, but in a fast-paced battle situation, she knew a lot of those rules would fall by the wayside.

Lynn mentally shrugged. They were gamers, not soldiers.

With Skadi's Wolves in the lead, the whole crowd of TD Hunter players headed down the access road toward their biggest battle yet.

"Incoming chat request from DeathShot13," said Hugo. "Would you like to accept?"

"Accept."

"I'm impressed, RavenStriker. You've organized something truly remarkable today."

Lynn smiled to herself, glad her friend Yoda was behind her and couldn't see her face.

"I have a championship to win. We do what we have to do, yeah? Don't be too impressed yet, though. We still have a boss to kill. For all I know this little op will fall down around my ears the moment we go hot."

"I don't think it will. My squad won't, in any case. You can rely on us."

"That's why you get the best seat in the house, DeathShot. I figure you all can take the heat."

"Thanks for that," he replied, amused sarcasm in his tone. "My kill-to-damage ratio won't thank me, but my wife certainly will. She loves getting it stuck in."

Lynn coughed. "Uh, right. Well, if it's any consolation, I'll be right here beside you when shit hits the fan. We can enjoy our dipping scores together."

"Oh, I'm counting on it, my friend."

Lynn gulped. Was that stereotypical Canadian politeness? Or had he guessed who she was?

No time to worry about it. She had an op to lead, a boss to kill, and over a hundred people depending on her to do a good job.

She only hoped she was leading them all to victory, not possible injury—or worse.

Chapter 15

THE WALK DOWN THE ACCESS ROAD WENT QUICKLY, and it didn't take long for everyone to get into position. Gamers they might be, but anyone who assumed that meant they didn't take their games seriously was in for a rude awakening.

Lynn's mind worked methodically, checking and double-checking her strategy, considering worst-case scenarios, reviewing contingency plans. Every time a worry popped up or her insecurity tried to dig in its evil tentacles and derail her thought process, she buried herself deeper in the mission. Larry or Lynn, both or neither, it didn't matter who she was.

She had a job to do and nothing else mattered.

"Okay, Hugo," she subvocalized on her team channel. "Time to take us live."

As much as it pained her to do so, they'd told Mrs. Pearson all about Operation Boss Bash, and the PR manager had helped them come up with a workable plan for capitalizing on its potential without sacrificing operational security. GIC had been hyping a big announcement from Skadi's Wolves for several weeks, implying it would happen at GIC headquarters with all sorts of fanfare and corporate shine. The misdirection helped discourage any enterprising paparazzi from shadowing the team members—though Lynn and the guys had still sneaked out of their respective houses before light that morning and met at a random restaurant for breakfast and to change into their gear.

Now, with people worldwide glued to their streams waiting for the "big announcement," Lynn and the guys switched on their live views. Helen had already set up their stream to play various prerecorded clips to keep people occupied until the live feed started, and Lynn knew their standard five-minute delay would be in effect as well.

Time to rock and roll.

"RavenStriker to Skadi's Horde, heads up everybody," she said, noting all the gold and green dots on her overhead were lined up in the proper formation. "This is it. Once we go into combat mode, we're not coming out until we've utterly obliterated this boss, or we're dead. You all are the best of the best, the top-scoring, most professional teams on the North American continent. I expect to see great things from you, and I'm proud to be the one leading you. Remember to listen to your captains, support your squad, and of course, have a freaking shit ton of fun."

A few hoots of approval sounded around her, and one side of Lynn's mouth twitched upward. She was being more verbose than she liked to be during an op—in combat you used the fewest words possible, or your enemy would frag you while you were still jabbering to your men. But she had a live audience to please and a small army of gamers to inspire, so she tried to keep that in mind while her Larry brain just growled at her to shut up, hurry up, and start killing things.

"Today, you are Skadi's Horde," she said, pitching her voice to battlefield volume. "Today, we fight for the Horde!"

"For the Horde!" many voices yelled, drowning out Mack's muttered protestations about "the Alliance" and "far superior."

"Blood for the Blood God!"

"Te morituri salute!"

"IT'S BEER AND CIRCUSES! *BEER*!"

Other war cries rang out up and down the line spread out across the road and into the woods.

"On my mark!" Lynn yelled over the clamor. "Enter combat mode and begin a measured advance in three, two, one, *go*!"

Hugo flipped the switch, and her overhead map turned blood red.

"Whoa!"

"Shit!"

"There's too many of them!"

Yells of alarm sounded over the channel and through the air, and Lynn gritted her teeth. Her team was already attacking, Edgar and Ronnie in the lead with Dan and Mack on either flank and her in the middle, dodging back and forth in support and killing anything and everything within reach.

"Everybody but team captains, get off the open channel!" she yelled. "Captains, clear your immediate area, then advance. These are low-level mobs. Sweep the floor with 'em."

It took them a few minutes, but soon the swarms of imps, grinder worms, Grumblins, demons, and other low-level TDMs had been pulverized and nothing else was close enough to detect them, thanks to the area cloaking of Skadi's Bastion that Lynn had equipped. She'd been ecstatic when she'd learned from Hugo that Bastion's defense and stealth bonuses applied to *any* "team" she formed, including a hunting group, as long as she was the one who created it. If they were her people, then Bastion would protect them. In her other hand, she held Abomination, ready to rain sweet destruction down on the TDMs.

It was not her preferred role. But such was the sacrifice of leadership. Besides, once they hit the lines of Alpha Class monsters around the boss, they would need all hands on deck and she would see enough action to keep even the most bloodthirsty gamer happy.

Lynn switched to the squad leaders' channel and had everyone check in. Then, they advanced.

Edgar and Ronnie set the pace at a measured walk, killing as they went. Lynn kept a careful eye on the formation and relayed to her spearpoint when to slow or speed up. They couldn't advance too quickly or they'd leave behind their wings spread out in the woods. Neither could they form a simple patrol line and double-time it down the access road to their objective. That would leave too many enemies behind them and waste opportunities to pump up their group experience bonus. This slow sweep leading up to the rings guarding the boss was less exciting, but entirely necessary.

It also gave the squads a chance to iron out any wrinkles in their movements.

"Green Wing Leader, tell your squad to quit stopping for loot. This isn't a daisy-picking party. Grab and *go!*"

"Sorry, RavenStriker. On it."

"Gold Spear Leader, your squad's pulling ahead. Put a damper on it until we hit the rings. If your

boys and girls have extra energy, start grabbing loot
and transfer the excess to the group."

"Roger that," DeathShot said, amusement in his
tone. "We'll try to keep busy while you lot catch up."

"Don't worry," Lynn told him, having Hugo switch
her to a private channel with Yoda. "I'll send the Nundu
your way when they show up. That'll keep you busy."

Nundu, the upgrade from Yaguar, was as fast as a
striking Creeper and as relentless as the night-loving
Varg. The four-legged, low-slung creatures looked like
scaled panthers with spikes down their spine and a
whiplike tail they used for balance and to strike you
as they sped past. They were *not fun* to fight and
played hell on Lynn's kill-to-damage ratio.

"Sonia will take care of them," DeathShot promised. "She's got a sniper augment that would make
you weep with envy."

"Oh, I know," Lynn said. "I saw it when I was
making the team assignments. When I told my sniper,
DanTheMan48, his head almost exploded. I'm not
convinced she can make the shot, though. Those
things move too fast."

"Bet you one of those famous taco pizzas I keep
hearing so much about that she can take one down
with her first shot."

Lynn grinned. "You're on."

They made good progress for the first quarter
mile. The Delta, Charlie, and even Bravo class TDMs
that started crowding in were easily dealt with by
such experienced teams. Many of them had augments
with area bonuses, so each team's damage and armor
capabilities increased exponentially for being in a
squad formation. Though the TDM were thick on

the ground, they fell like wheat to the scythe of Skadi's Horde.

After some initial disorganization, the formation's lines straightened up and in the open air Lynn could hear good-natured banter going on between teams on their individual channels. After she'd chewed out the first few people who mistakenly broadcast on the group channel, nobody else had made that mistake.

By the time they reached the last quarter mile, things started to get intense. Lynn could see where the access road opened out into the mesh node clearing up ahead. But between them and the node were ranks upon ranks of monsters. Not just four or five like they'd faced before, but over a *dozen*. Lynn felt a chill run down her spine.

There were *a lot* of monsters in front of her. But that didn't mean the game was out to get her or that some antagonistic force beyond the game's algorithm was messing with the TDM levels.

Besides, in the end it didn't matter. A dozen lines or one, Skadi's Horde would crush them all.

"Heads up, Skadi's Horde. Shit's about to get real. Tighten up, pay attention, and bring your A game. We've got to pick up speed, hit them hard, and *keep moving*. Assault *through* the enemy, don't stop. Spearpoint teams, open a gap, spearhead, widen it, and wings, blast it to smithereens. I'll signal the wing squad leaders when they should fold in. Now, let's utterly obliterate these bastards and send them crying like babies to their digital god!"

There were some hoots of approval, while Lynn rotated through her other channels.

"RavenStriker to squad leaders, double-time and

hit these bogies hard. Don't forget, head on a swivel and keep your formation tight.

"RavenStriker to team captains, keep an eye on your team's levels and keep the supplies flowing. We're only as strong as our weakest link, so don't let anyone run out of juice."

Acknowledgments flowed over the channel as Lynn's focus turned to the TDMs in front of her team.

"Skadi's Wolves, let's wipe the floor with these bastards. You set the pace, so I want maximum output. Mack will push you ichor if you need it. Listen to Hugo and re-up your levels as needed. If anything big comes, I've got your back. Go!"

Edgar and Ronnie broke into a trot and Edgar's eerie *choo-hoo-HOO* war cry rang out through the woods. Lynn could just imagine the grin on his face as he prepared to hit the first line of TDMs like a herd of rampaging elephants. The pounding of footsteps on gravel and the crash of underbrush changed to the swish of grass as their hundred-plus-man formation swept into the clearing around the mesh node.

The first line of Orculls, Penagals, and Spithra vanished into explosions of sparks before the hunters got within a dozen yards. The next line was swept away in similarly effortless fashion. By the third, Namahags and Managals were showing up, soaking up fire and lasting a few seconds longer than their weaker counterparts. By the fourth and fifth lines, Rakshar were dominating the lines while lone Manticar and Yaguar attacked from the sides. Lynn remembered last September—it seemed so long ago, almost another lifetime—when she'd been terrified of Manticars. Now their lionlike roar and the subtle vibrations of their approach just made her smile with predatory anticipation. Yaguar were more of a problem simply because they were so small and fast, but their team had spent weeks perfecting just the right tactics and response for each of the different TDMs.

They knew what to do.

Edgar blasted away, switching ammo smoothly from armor piercing to poison to incendiary as needed. Ronnie was in the thick of it all, his Splinter Sword flashing, finding every weak point between armor plates and spikes as he sliced the monsters to bits. Mack was methodical but effective, his movements tight and economical as he destroyed TDMs while scooping up supplies to transfer to his team. Dan cackled with bloodthirsty glee and shouted smackdowns at the TDMs as he put bright blue bolts through their brains and "showed them who was boss."

Over the roaring cacophony of TDM cries and the very real shouts of the Hunters around her locked in augmented-reality battles, Lynn heard the occasional wailing shriek of Tengu and the deeper, but much more terrifying, screech of Kongamatos. Those monstrosities were the Alpha Class upgrade of Tengu: giant, armored pterodactyl-like beasts with mouthfuls of teeth that could rip away half your health in a single attack if you didn't dodge fast enough.

Wisely, Lynn had put the teams with the best snipers in their formation's wings, and they'd already been briefed on their job of keeping the skies clear. If Lynn had looked up, she would have seen the air filled with blue energy bolts from Spitfire sniper rifles and the exploding sparks of Rocs, Tengu, and Kongamatos.

Ronnie and Edgar's momentum didn't slow until they were halfway through, around the sixth line of TDMs.

That's when they were ambushed on both sides by a group of Strikers patrolling between the lines. Lynn hated them even worse than Creepers. Because they roamed instead of lying in wait, their heavy camouflage and soft, sibilant hisses made them difficult to notice in a press of bigger, louder monsters. They were much sneakier—and harder to kill—than the ghosts, Ghasts, and Phasmas of Delta and Charlie Classes.

By the time she, Mack, and Dan had helped destroy the Strikers, the bigger monsters were crowding in and their momentum was largely lost.

"Horde, tighten up!" Lynn bellowed, seeing on her overhead that the clusters of green and gold dots had started to spread out, caught in the heat of battle as they pursued the TDMs.

"Squad leaders, spearpoint is stuck in. Don't let your teams chase every monster, let them come to us. Switch to ranged if needed, and use the breather room to distribute supplies.

"Green Spear, Gold Spear, we're bogging down. Focus your fire forward and *push!*"

Lynn accompanied her words with action, renewing her flurry of fire from Abomination, taking out Rakshar one at a time with clean headshots right through their ugly, fanged faces.

Controlled chaos raged around them as their spearhead slowly pushed forward through the sixth, seventh, and eighth lines. They got dangerously close to losing Hunters as their "supply officers" raced to keep up with shrinking health levels for those in the thickest fights. It would have been worse but for the defense bonus of Skadi's Bastion. Lynn kept moving, trying to draw the fire of any ranged TDMs and using Bastion to protect her and those nearby as the ranged monsters were taken out by snipers.

"Holy crap, what is *that!*"

Someone's horrified yell rang out over the group channel, and Lynn's eyes snapped up, searching for the source of the alarm. When she saw it, her lips thinned.

Lovely.

Half a dozen Spithragani, a good six feet taller than the lesser Spithra, stepped over the lines of TDMs, headed toward the Hunters. Unlike *some* Hunters, Lynn and her team did their homework and had already studied the Spithragani and fought against them in the TD Hunter app's simulations, so they weren't daunted by the monstrous spider-crab-like beasts with armored shells and pincer mouths. They were terrifying to see coming toward you on their spiked stilt legs. They were also devilishly hard to kill in melee combat as their armored bodies were a good seven feet in the air.

"DanTheMan, Sonia, I want those Spithragani *gone.*"

"On it," Sonia said as Dan echoed her. Blue bolts started hitting the Spithragani, mostly splashing over their tough armor but some finding their mark in the monster's vulnerable mouth and eyes.

Skadi's Wolves led the formation through the ninth rank of TDMs, fighting tooth and nail for every foot of ground. The wings had gotten bogged down and were starting to come apart, so Lynn gave the command for them to fold inward and tighten up, creating one large spearhead. The teams were close enough together that the ones in the rear could support the ones further up with ranged fire while the tip of the spear raged in melee battle with the biggest and toughest monsters.

The snipers kept the Spithragani from stomping

all over the teams, but with their attention tied up it was up to the melee and tactical fighters to keep the mobs of other TDMs from washing like a wave over their lonely spearhead. Lynn found herself charging out again and again, using Bastion to block, bash, and push back particularly aggressive monsters to give her fighters breathing space.

If only we had a shield wall, Lynn lamented to herself as she charged a Rakshar and blasted away at a Spithragani close enough to step on them. There were a handful of other Hunters in their group with shields, but not nearly enough. She body-checked the Rakshar away from Ronnie, who was busy slicing up a clutch of Strikers trying to ambush them from the side. The Rakshar came back for more, so Lynn ducked under its lumbering swipe and stepped into its reach to shoot rapidly up through a vulnerable spot under its chin. It exploded just in time for her to raise Bastion and block a shower of poison spray from the Spithragani's pincered mouth. Seconds later the spider-crab monster exploded from blue bolts to the brain and her attention flicked to her map, checking on her Hunter group's formation.

It was holding.

We can do this.

Lynn grinned and spun, bashing away the clawed strike of another Rakshar before jamming Abomination up under its chin and firing away. Through the resultant sparks she spotted DeathShot, ducking, dodging, and dancing between targets as his twin pistols spat fire in tandem faster than Lynn could fathom. How in the world he was able to aim at all—much less accurately—in two different directions at the same time was beyond her. His pistols were a named set and Lynn made a mental note to ask him some time how he'd earned them.

Regardless, he was a machine, and Lynn suspected he kept his supply guy busy with a mind-boggling level of power consumption.

Skadi's Wolves broke through the tenth line, Team Light Brigade on their right and The Lone Gunmen on their left. Lynn was breathing hard, but deeply. She felt the fatigue of battle in her aching muscles and burning lungs, but knew she had plenty of fight left in her. The thick of a fight was all about mind over matter, and her mind could push her body much further than it wanted to go.

Spin. Strike. Dodge. Roll. Shoot. Again and again and again.

She fought almost on autopilot, the movements imprinted in her muscles through hundreds of hours of hunting and simulation practice, while her eyes slid smoothly from overhead to display to the battle before her. There was no panic, no tense worry about what was happening or what would happen. Just smooth input of sights, sounds, and data, and cold, calculating output of decisions.

A growling scream heralded the arrival of the Nundu Lynn had predicted. It shot past, leaping over their heads in a streak of gray, and Mack's body flashed red with damage.

"You're up, Sonia!" Lynn yelled, trying to keep the thing in view while still fighting two other TDMs simultaneously. If she could keep herself between it and her team, Bastion could stop the damage from its whiplike spiked tail and razor-sharp claws that moved too fast to dodge.

Out of the corner of her eye, Lynn saw Sonia back up from the line of battle as the Hunter switched weapons, going from the higher-powered and longer-ranged Spitfire to something more suited to close quarters. Sonia gave herself space as her rifle muzzle tracked the Nundu's movements. Lynn lost track of what the woman was doing when she had to block a Striker that had slithered at her from between the feet of the next line of TDMs. But she was close enough to hear the shot Sonia took and see the small shower of sparks in the air close above them.

"Guess—I owe you—a taco pizza," Lynn panted after shifting channels.

"Darn straight—you do," DeathShot replied, sounding just as out of breath.

"I think you mean you owe *me* a taco pizza," came Sonia's amused voice. She did *not* sound out of breath. "DeathShot can have a taco pizza when he shoots his own Nundu."

"Don't be greedy, Sonia. You can't possibly eat an entire pizza by yourself."

"Sounds like a challenge," Lynn said, grinning and ducking under a Rakshar's swipe.

Their banter fell silent as more and more monsters crowded in and Lynn had no more thought for anything but moving and killing.

"Miss Lynn, be aware, you are within five percent of advancing to Level 37," Hugo informed her.

Crap.

Leveling was good, but not in the middle of a pitched battle. It couldn't be helped, though, and she knew from reviewing the stats of all the teams she'd invited that others would be facing imminent leveling as well. It would make them stronger, but it would also invite the attention of the toughest monsters out there.

After what felt like an eternity, though her display told her it had only been a few minutes, Lynn forced herself to re-evaluate their position. Their forward momentum was gone. They were holding their ground, but for every TDM they killed, two more filled its place.

It was impossible to advance. There were simply too many enemies.

She made a decision she'd hoped to avoid, but there was no help for it.

"Green Wing, Gold Wing, execute Contingency Scenario B. Squad leaders, direct rearmost two teams to focus out and behind, forward three, fire out and forward. Let's get this boss. Move!"

With surprising swiftness, the squads shifted, the wings sliding inside the spear to make a double line powerful enough to break through the mobs of TDMs. The sounds of pistol and rifle bolts, and the shouts and calls of group members increased. Lynn didn't take her eyes off her enemies before her, just used her overhead map to ensure the formation shift was finished before she called for another advance.

A firestorm of bolts hit the lines of TDMs in a tsunami of damage, and several ranks of monsters simply vanished in a whirlwind of sparks.

"Advance! Go! Go! Go!" Lynn shouted, egging her Hunters on. She could see the massive cloud of glittering mist between the spiked legs of Spithragani and lumbering shapes of Rakshar.

And that was when she leveled.

As if summoned by the tantalizing scent of her

newly promoted self, a line of Jotnar appeared between the last line of TDMs and the boss's sparkling mist.

Lynn swore the most colorful, dirty, Larry swear she could think of, and heard a flurry of snorts and guffaws over the group channel that she had forgotten to exit.

Oops.

Hopefully nobody in the group had heard that particular Larry expletive before and wouldn't wonder where she'd gotten it from. She already knew Helen would edit it out of the livestream, so at least she didn't have to worry about that.

"Jotnar incoming," she told the group in a more normal voice. If she had leveled, that meant everybody else had or would be leveling soon, since her invites had only gone out to teams as high level as Skadi's Wolves. Jotnar were Orculls on steroids, with legs and arms like tree trunks and hide just as thick. Their crushing attacks did massive damage, and their only weakness was how slowly they moved. They would take forever to kill, giving all the other TDMs around the boss time to crowd in, trapping Skadi's Horde and diverting their damage and attention away from the boss that was their primary objective.

So, as usual, Lynn acted.

It wasn't that she acted without thought, more that she didn't let thought hold her back from acting. Her plan was untried, but if it worked, it would be the difference between success and failure.

"DeathShot," she said on the squad leader channel. "You have command of Skadi's Horde. I have to go do something only I can do. Squad leaders, push forward and prepare to form a firing line, Spear squads firing on the boss, Wings covering our rear. Get your TD

Hunter app analyzing the boss. We need it identified, stat."

To her relief, none of the squad leaders questioned her decision. They simply acknowledged and got to work.

Well, all except one.

"RavenStriker, what are you up to?"

"Focus on your command, DeathShot. I know what I'm doing."

"Do you? I heard the rumors. Last time you 'knew what you were doing' you got a concussion."

Lynn's mouth thinned and she didn't reply while she fended off an attack to her head and blasted the offending TDM with Abomination.

"Follow the plan, DeathShot. I'll be back," she finally said, voice tight. She turned her head enough to suck a quick gulp of water from her built-in hydration pack on her compact backpack. If she collapsed this time, she wanted to be darn sure it wasn't from dehydration.

But she didn't intend to collapse, nor jump inside of a boss. Her plan was much less suicidal, but still risky enough that she couldn't let anyone else do it.

Not after she'd seen what this boss had done to Mack and *failed* to do to her.

With a last storm of fire, the tip of their spear broke through the final line before the towering Jotnar, and Lynn sprinted forward, passing between Edgar and Ronnie as she headed straight toward the nearest Jotnar. Both her friends shouted in surprise as she passed, and she could hear Edgar calling for her to come back.

She would have, but she was the one with Skadi's Bastion.

Shield held at chest level, tight to her right shoulder,

Lynn charged the Jotnar in front of her and rammed it right in the stomach.

Instead of going through it like she should have, she met a strange, marshmallow-like resistance. Contact with it sent uncomfortable tingles up through her hands and arms. But then the resistance vanished as the Jotnar *bounced backward*. It was only a few feet, but that was further than it should have moved at all, based on everything Lynn had seen in TD Hunter so far.

Lynn didn't waste energy wondering why, she simply drew back and charged again, knocking the Jotnar back further toward the ominously twinkling boss.

By that time her Horde had caught up and started pelting the line of Jotnar with fire, distracting them from all stomping on Lynn at once. Still, she had to dodge huge, trunk-like feet and duck under ponderous swings as she kept charging the monsters, pushing them further and further back toward the boss.

She was gulping in lungfuls of cool spring air by the time she'd gotten the first one at the very edge of the sparkling mist. It kept trying to step forward, but she drove it back, half herding, half pushing it into the mist. She had no idea what would happen once it was inside. But even if nothing happened, she'd used her unique item and high tolerance for damage to distract deadly enemies that would have rampaged through their firing line before the Hunters had a chance to kill them.

With one last ramming charge, Lynn bounced the Jotnar back into the mist. She jerked away, retreating as a tendril of mist seemed to reach out for her. By the time she'd jumped out of the way, the Jotnar was completely surrounded by the sparkling stuff.

The TDM stopped moving. Lynn couldn't be sure,

but she thought its image in her AR sight flickered. Or perhaps that was just an effect of the mist.

Triumph surged through her, though she couldn't take time to enjoy it. The other Jotnar nearby attacked, and she got to work herding another into the mist as *finally* the one closest to the firing line of Hunters exploded into sparks.

By the time the rest of the Jotnar were neutralized, she'd taken more damage than she would ever have voluntarily exposed herself to. But there were four Jotnar immobilized inside the boss while the three others had been wiped out by the Hunters.

As she dashed back to the line and rejoined her team, she spoke on the squad leader channel: "RavenStriker to DeathShot, I have command. Green and Gold Spear, focus all fire on that boss. Let's kill it and boogie."

"You are the craziest gamer I've ever met, Raven," DeathShot said over their private channel. "If we survive this, I should be the one buying *you* pizza."

"Make it a rare steak and I'll accept," Lynn said, too tired to laugh, though her lips twitched in amusement.

A quick survey of her overhead map and the data on her display told Lynn her crazy stunt might not be enough. She shook her head in disbelief that she'd thought they could wipe out *all* the TDMs around this boss. They'd been fighting like mad for over thirty minutes. They were exhausted and would soon be facing limited supplies, yet they'd barely destroyed a third of the TDMs surrounding the boss. They had already lost a few members who hadn't been able to keep up with the onslaught of damage, and they would likely lose more before they were done. Worse, they'd barely begun to chip away at the unidentified boss.

Speaking of.

"Hugo, you've got a hundred sensors analyzing this thing. Give me something!"

"Patience, Miss Lynn. It's not simply a matter of the volume of data collected. I need time to analyze the TDM's attacks and responses to its environment."

Lynn kept Abomination spewing fire at the boss as she eyed the edge of the sparkling mist. It was definitely closer, but by how much? The Jotnar were no longer visible within it, either because of a game glitch or simple visibility issues.

"Hurry up. That thing is coming. For *us*."

"I assure you, your entire group will be informed immediately as soon as I finish my analysis."

"Skadi's Horde, warning, boss is mobile. I repeat, boss is *mobile*. Keep an eye on it, prepare to retreat as needed. Green and Gold Wings, *you* have to make a path. Try not to have too much fun while you're doing it."

Lynn kept her tone light and amused, but the reality of the situation was much more grim. If the TDMs behind them grew too thick, they wouldn't be able to retreat from the slowly advancing boss. They might be forced to retreat *through* the TDMs, taking on massive damage. Not all of them would make it out, and they definitely wouldn't have enough members left to destroy the boss.

The alternative—trying to fight the boss from the inside like she'd done at the qualifiers—was out of the question. Somehow, deep in her bones, she knew it wasn't safe. Why she couldn't say, and that freaked her out even more. But she wasn't about to ignore her instincts with the safety of her fellow Hunters on the line.

Thousands of hours of gaming had conditioned and strengthened Lynn's trigger finger. Even so, it was threatening to cramp from the stream of no-holds-barred fire they were pouring into the slowly advancing boss. Her omnipolymer pistol grip was hot and sweaty from her exertions and she imagined she could smell the ozone that would be filling the air from their whirlwind of plasma bolts if they'd been fighting for real.

"Entity analysis partially complete." Hugo's voice broke through her concentration, and she felt a surge of adrenaline as the mist suddenly flickered to horrifying life.

This time it wasn't just her swearing over the group channel.

"Holy cow that thing is *ugly*," Dan shouted.

Lynn couldn't agree more. The monstrosity looked like something from a Cthulian horror novel, unspeakable and all. It wasn't as towering as Mishipeshu had been, but it was far more vast, like a giant, oozing blob of flesh. What made it truly horrible, though, were the hundreds of arms, legs, and heads sticking out of it—not human parts, but parts from every TDM the Hunters had ever fought. It was as if the designers had taken dozens of each monster in the game and smashed and melted them all together into a giant mass. The thing was inching toward them, dragged along by hundreds of mismatched limbs grabbing, lifting, and pushing its disgusting bulk.

"Unknown entity has been designated Gyges, Alpha Class boss," Hugo said. "It has a single attack, Devour, which is fatal. It is only effective within close proximity, however, and it has no ranged attacks. Defenses include blubber-like hide that affords it an armor bonus. Detection, Level 30. It has no stealth, and its only special ability currently detected is Crawl, giving it limited mobility. I will spare you the lengthy list of discovery credits. A full analysis and additional bonuses will follow once the boss is defeated."

The end of Hugo's spiel went in one ear and out the other as Lynn focused on the tactical information. There wasn't much, except the chilling confirmation that none of them wanted to get *anywhere* near it.

Devour. Was that what it had done to the Jotnar she'd pushed into it? Had it eaten them? Had that tendril of mist reaching out for her been the ghostly zombie arm of some TDM this boss had previously devoured and assimilated into its bulk?

Regardless, Lynn tucked away the mental note of her successful, if unorthodox, tactic with dispensing of the Jotnar.

"RavenStriker to Green and Gold Wing. How's our back trail? This boss is slower than a launch-day patch, but once it gets here, we're screwed."

"It's pretty dicey back here," FoxyMulder said, and Lynn made a quick subvocalized request to Hugo to turn up her left earbud volume so she could still hear the squad leader over the uproar of TDM noises, bolt blasts, and shouts of Hunters around her. "I'm thinking once we kill the boss, we skedaddle and leave these fellas in the dust. Otherwise, we're liable to end up cold and dead."

"Noted," Lynn said, still out of breath. Her trigger finger was killing her.

The next minute was excruciating, from the tension of a slowly approaching monstrosity that made her sick to look at, to her burning lungs and cramping finger, to the rising fear that their firepower wouldn't be enough—and she was going to get them all killed.

With less than a dozen yards left between their double line and the boss, Lynn shouted, "Green Spear, Gold Spear, back up! Boss is too close."

"Would love to, but then we'd get our heads ripped off by Spithragani," IAmAgentFranks grunted.

Lynn looked for a weak point in the wave of crimson dots surrounding their position, but there wasn't one. Nowhere to break through, nowhere to retreat. Certain death in front of them.

With nothing else to do, Lynn gave an order she'd *really* been hoping not to give.

"Skadi's Horde, we're breaking regular formation. All snipers, on the boss. Use everything you got. Assault and tanks, get in close and dirty with your highest-damage weapons. *Be careful.* One strike from this boss and you're dead. Everyone else, fire to the rear and keep us alive. We've got one shot at this. *Move!*"

Hunters dashed forward, monsters roared, and chaos reigned. Putting the hardest-hitting two-thirds of their force at the front was her last desperate attempt to kill the boss—if they weren't destroyed from behind first. But better to die trying than to have never tried at all. Though if a hundred Hunters weren't enough to kill an Alpha Class boss, she didn't know what was.

First one, then another Hunter's blue dot winked out, and Lynn swore. They'd run out of Oneg and weren't killing enough TDMs to keep up with demand. She just hoped the Hunters that died followed her orders and got the heck off the battlefield and away from the boss. In her prebattle brief she'd instructed Hunters to re-enter combat mode far enough away to avoid the high-class TDMs, but close enough to still get the group experience and item bonuses. That way they wouldn't miss out on the rewards despite the cold chill of death penalties that kept them from rejoining the main battle.

More Hunters died, and Gyges inched ever closer. If it came much further, the assault fighters, Ronnie included, wouldn't have room to maneuver and still avoid all those grotesque arms reaching and flailing.

Just then a flash washed over them, so bright Lynn reflexively lifted an arm to shield her eyes. In the same moment the handles of her weapons blazed with heat and her hands spasmed open, dropping them to the ground. She dove for them, still blinking and trying to clear the spots from her vision, only to realize they were surrounded by an eerie stillness.

"Hugo, what the heck?" Lynn subvocalized, frozen in a kneeling position on the grass as confused shouts rose around her.

"Congratulations, Miss Lynn, you have destroyed an Alpha Class boss. I am completing my unknown-entity analysis. Your achievement notifications and reward selections have been minimized, as requested, and await your perusal."

"Not the boss, dummy! Why are all the TDMs frozen?"

For some reason, the AI didn't reply. Lynn was distracted from asking again by her squad leaders' insistent voices. She scooped up her weapons—still warm, but touchable—and started barking orders.

"Green Wing, Gold Wing, double-time it to the other side of the ring where those monsters are thinnest and start shanking the bastards. Open us a hole. I don't know what's going on, but let's not waste the opportunity. Gold

Spear, comb the area, grab any items you can find. No point wasting good loot. Green Spear, spread out. Thin the ranks of TDMs closest to us. Go for highest class and rack up the experience."

Her Hunters moved with renewed energy as half of them sprinted across the wide-open space of grass left by Gyges' much-deserved demise. The rest hurried this way and that, mercilessly tearing into the mysteriously immobile monsters.

Then, as suddenly as the silence had descended, it lifted. A clamoring roar washed over them and the ranks of TDMs surged forward. Hunters backpedaled and shifted stances, retreating from their previously helpless prey, though they kept at their assigned tasks.

Lynn stood at the base of the node tower in the middle of the open grass and spun in a quick circle, taking a few precious seconds to survey the swiftly contracting ring of monsters around them. The ranks of TDMs were not as thick to the south where her wings were trying to break through, but they wouldn't be able to make a hole before the avalanche of TDMs on every other side buried them.

Time to make the call.

"Good work, Skadi's Horde! We killed the boss and got the loot. What do you say we make ourselves scarce? Or does anyone have a death wish?"

"Aw, spoil sport!" came Edgar's voice over the channel. "I was gonna go out in a blaze of glory!"

Lynn rolled her eyes. "That was a rhetorical question. If there's no one else who'd prefer to stay and die a glorious death, then everyone exit combat mode. Go!"

Hugo obliged and the clamor of sounds and the flashing movement of hundreds of monsters abruptly vanished. For a moment Lynn could only stand there, ears ringing, catching her breath.

Then the cheering started.

A smile spread across Lynn's face at the sounds of celebration, animated chatter, and backslapping filling the grassy clearing.

They'd done it.

She had done it. Not a virtual alias hiding in the shadows, but her. In the real. Leading people who liked and respected her.

A strange buoyancy filled her chest. Was it . . . hope? She'd defied her fears and spat in the face of her doubts. She'd fought for victory and had won.

For the first time since she'd joined Skadi's Wolves, she genuinely believed they might win the championship.

All she had to do was keep fighting.

Chapter 16

ALPHA BOSSES, AS IT TURNED OUT, WERE WORTH an insane amount of experience.

That was fortunate because the total experience needed to achieve each level increased exponentially. Together with the group and achievement bonuses, Operation Boss Bash collectively bumped Lynn and her team up an entire level, from 37 to 38. That benefit alone lowered Lynn's stress level considerably, though with barely three months left until the June fifteenth championship—and school finals coming up to boot—she knew they would be hard-pressed to achieve Level 40 in time.

The op's rewards went beyond experience, though. Everyone who participated got a random rare augment on top of a choice between five unique weapons with significantly better stats than the standard. None of them were as good as Wrath or Abomination, since those items leveled with her and benefited from the Skadi's set bonus. But Lynn picked what she thought was the most competitive weapon anyway to sell at auction later.

For the rest of her team, it was like Christmas come early. Edgar picked up Snazzgun of Da Boyz, a two-handed monstrosity that looked as if someone had bolted together a grenade launcher, a flamethrower, and a cannon all in one. From the way Edgar giggled in glee at reading the stats, Lynn assumed there would be many spectacular explosions in their future. Dan went all starry-eyed over the Ambanese Sniper Rifle outfitted with a Splinter Blade bayonet—"I can shoot and stab at the same time!"—while Mack hooted at a pair of deceptively plain-looking pistols called the Croft Desert Eagles. Their high-damage, low-energy ammunition would make Mack a terror on the battlefield.

Ronnie's new sword was probably the most impressive, though its name made him grumble. Lynn thought he should have been grateful for the jaw-dropping stats and left it at that. Instead, he argued with Mack about whether "Zelda's Sword of Mastery" was a terrible insult to a historic game or a hilarious inside joke.

An even greater reward than the experience and items, though, were the friendships that were forged. After the battle, most of Skadi's Horde descended on the nearest Happy Joe's pizza and emptied their entire kitchen of food. DeathShot—or Derek as Lynn found out once they got around to real introductions—and his team joined Skadi's Wolves and several other teams for taco pizza. There was great celebration and many exaggerated retellings of their most impressive kills before players finally started trickling away. Many of them had airbuses to catch and long flights before they reached home. Lynn wished them safe travels and tried not to worry. During lunch she'd gotten a brief message from the captain of one of the two teams who hadn't shown up, letting her know their airbus had malfunctioned on the way to Cedar Rapids and had been forced to make an emergency landing. The message stirred up paranoid thoughts and conspiracy theories that she tried to ignore. Thoughts like why airbuses seemed so unreliable recently, and what Connor's next backstabbing attempt at sabotage was going to be. He and CRC had been suspiciously quiet the past month and Lynn had no illusions that it was because they'd decided to play fair and leave Skadi's Wolves alone.

But Lynn had a victory to celebrate and deserved a break from her overactive brain, so she did her best to focus on her teammates and friends.

Focus was especially necessary to play it cool and not give herself away to Derek. She avoided the topic of WarMonger entirely. But there were still a few times when Derek's knowing look made her wonder. If he suspected anything, though, he didn't mention it—for which she was desperately grateful. Ronnie would murder her if he ever found out about Larry Coughlin, and she shuddered at the thought of the story getting out on the streams.

Speaking of streams, in the immediate aftermath of the battle, their team channel's viewing numbers jumped by thirty percent and their subscriptions passed one hundred million. Kayla pinged her while they were at Happy Joe's and full-on flipped out over text. Lynn mentally resigned herself to listening to endless new vid ideas from her friend come Monday.

"You too are mortal," Lynn muttered to herself as she eyed the last slice of taco pizza on the table. Just as she was going to grab it, Dan leaned toward it, still chatting with Sonia about his favorite sniper-rifle settings. Lynn made a split-second decision and dove across the table, scooping up the pizza right out from under Dan's fingers.

"Hey!"

"I'm the team captain! It's my right!"

"But I'm hungrier than you."

"How do you know?"

"I'm a guy, guys are always hungrier."

"Says you. Have you seen how many ounces of steak I can eat in one sitting?"

Dan tried to argue further, but Lynn was already stuffing the pizza into her mouth while their teammates laughed and Sonia gave Dan a sympathetic slap on the back.

"Better luck next time, eh?"

Later, when people were trickling away and the food was all gone, Lynn was absently scanning some of the more esoteric numbers from their battle, things like time spent in combat mode, distance traveled, and monsters killed by class and type.

"Hugo, can you run some numbers for me?"

"Certainly, Miss Lynn."

"Don't tell me now, just put them together so I can think about them later. If you have access to the data, I want to know the Hunter-to-TDM ratio of that boss battle."

"What are my criteria? Only monsters engaged with and destroyed by Skadi's Horde?"

"No, count all the monsters we engaged plus all others within, say, three hundred yards of Gyges."

"Very good."

"Oh, also, I can't see the more detailed data of the fight from each of the individual Hunters, just the total ranked scores in the main categories like Kill-to-Damage

Ratio, Kill Count, stuff like that. I don't suppose there's any way you could, um, poke around and get that individual data for me? I've got this idea and, well, I'm looking for patterns and it would be really useful..."

"While that is a nonstandard request, since you were the group leader for Skadi's Horde, I could see what data may be acquired."

"Thanks, Hugo."

"Your wish is my command."

"Don't even start. I ask you to do things all the time that you won't do."

"Such as, Miss Lynn?"

"Like that time I wanted you to prank Ronnie and make him think he'd accidentally gone into combat mode in the bathroom."

"I beg your pardon, but that was *not* a legitimate command."

"It would have been hilarious, though, you gotta admit."

"That is beside the point..."

Mr. Krator's private conference room was a sweet deal. Not only were all the chairs a top-of-the-line body-mold brand, but there was one of those new SNAC machines—Simple Nutrition Automative Construct. It was straight out of science fiction, and would "build" whatever snack you wanted using basic food molecules. Or something. Steve didn't need to know how it worked to enjoy its "snacs."

He was munching on a double-fried, bacon-wrapped corn dog when the conference room door beeped and admitted a familiar face.

Steve rose.

"Derek! Long time no see, brother. How you Canucks doing these days?"

"Better than you cowboys down here, but only because we have less infrastructure to go haywire."

The two men clasped forearms. Though Derek was smaller than Steve in stature, there was no less power or confidence in his grip. Steve got his friend settled— Derek opted for an entirely healthy and boring peanut-butter-covered banana bar—and they chatted while they waited for the rest of the meeting's attendees to arrive.

"So . . . that boss battle," Steve said.

Derek shook his head.

"I can't believe she actually did it. I have to admit I was skeptical at first."

"Nah, I knew she would pull it off."

"I can hardly believe it and I was *there*."

"At least this time she didn't try any suicidal stunts," Steve growled.

"It was a close thing, my friend. Did you see what she did with the Jotnar? I didn't even know that was possible. Who thinks of crazy things like that?"

"Gamer teens, man, I'm telling you. They're cheeky as hell and think they're immortal."

"I've been gaming my whole life, Steve, and I didn't even consider it."

Steve leaned forward, propping his elbows on the conference table.

"Yeah, but you and I grew up when things were first starting to take off. They didn't even have legit VR back then. The first VR headset I got as a kid was complete crap compared to what we have now. Lynn though? She's been steeped in this tech since she could walk."

Derek made a "hmm" noise, his expression contemplative.

"Besides, we've spent our entire adult lives training to follow the rules. I mean, there's a *ton* of enthusiastic gamers in the military, but as a type, we aren't the most 'think-outside-the-box' bunch when it comes to gaming."

Derek tilted his head.

"I would disagree with you there, but our 'think-outside-the-box' skills are entirely focused on human-oriented situations. Not gaming and technology."

Steve waved a hand and was about to continue when the door beeped again, and Mr. Krator himself strode in.

"Hello, Derek. Thanks for coming all the way out to my humble headquarters for this debrief. You could have remoted in, you know."

"I prefer to keep things old school when I can, sir," Derek said as he shook Mr. Krator's hand.

"Well, thank you. Now please, let's all sit and get things started. The others should be arriving soon."

Mr. Krator fiddled with the control panel at the head of the table and the lights of the room dimmed. Steve's LINC synced automatically with the Tsunami display system, since he was an employee, and he assumed Mr. Krator had already sent an invite to Derek's LINC. The shared display appeared on all their various AR mediums. Steve wasn't surprised to see Mr. Krator using stylish AR glasses rather than implants as most would expect of the most high-profile game designer in the world. As a rule, those deep in the tech industry trusted their own tech much less than the end user did.

Before long, two holograms joined them at the table:

Colonel Bryce, head of Force Training for Taskforce Sanctus, the US branch of CIDER's unified mobile units; and General Kozelek, who had the unenviable task of herding the mob of cats that was CIDER's unified military command. This debriefing was, honestly, not something the general needed to attend. But Steve wasn't surprised the man wanted to hear an update straight from the horse's mouth, so to speak.

"I want good news, Mr. Krator," the general began without preamble. "I've just come from a meeting with the Joint Foreign Secretaries of CIDER and the only news I have patience left for is good news."

Mr. Krator shrugged.

"It's a mixed bag, I'll admit, General. But I'll start with the good news: a group of gamers successfully—and without injury, I might add—attacked and destroyed a major nodality that was causing problems in the electrical grid of northeast Cedar Rapids."

"That was Lynn Raven's operation, correct?"

"Yes, sir. We had one of our Alpha Tester teams join for observation and intervention—if needed. It was led by Mr. Peterson, here, and he'll be giving us a full rundown of the details."

"That's definitely good news, but if you would, remind me of the significance?" General Kozelek said.

"Well, one of the biggest limiting factors we face in this war is the need for secrecy. While we *can* field some undercover rapid-response teams to deal with immediate infrastructure threats, and of course we have our research and development teams testing weapons and searching for the incursion point, we are extremely limited in how else we can physically respond to these entities. Drones help, but again, too much sustained and regular activity will be noticed. It's why we can't just mobilize thousands of military teams worldwide for a mass extermination push. If we failed to eliminate enough of the nodalities—or they kept multiplying anyway, which seems probable until we can pinpoint the source of the incursion—we would then face global societal upheaval. That would likely cause far more damage than the entities are capable of themselves—at least at this stage of their evolution.

"Our solution of mass extermination under the guise of something else—a game—buys us time to develop our disruptor technology, and is relatively risk-free. The exception, of course, is the physical danger posed by direct contact with the major nodalities. Some of them are more mobile than others, and we've seen an extremely aggressive defensive response whenever we've attacked one. In the early days, before we truly understood what was going on, we had widespread neurological injury and even death from the varied and unpredictable way the nodalities responded. It's one reason the TD Hunter interface is so important. We designed the algorithm specifically to analyze and assign a predictive form and behavior pattern to the entities so that our poor human brains can comprehend them enough to destroy them. TD Hunter isn't just a game, it's the actual technology by which we track, analyze, and disrupt this alien invasion.

"All that to say, sir, because we have a decentralized system of recruitment and training through the TD Hunter app, there's only so much we can do to progress the 'Hunters' toward our ultimate goal without blowing our cover. We can equip and prepare them as best we can through the tactical forums, but it's up to them to take the initiative. And, up to this point, none have had all the factors of initiative, sheer skill, *and* social clout, to take out a major nodality in a way that is survivable and replicable for other Hunters. Lynn Raven is the first."

General Kozelek looked thoughtful.

"You mention social clout. What does that have to do with a global battle against aliens?"

"A global battle against aliens *in the form of a popular game*. That's the key, sir. CIDER's scientists still haven't managed to create any disruptor bigger than the equivalent of a hand grenade. The military's usual advantage in war—big guns—is moot here. Therefore, the only way to eliminate them at this point is sheer numbers."

"The military has numbers, Mr. Krator. So why is Lynn Raven's successful operation so significant?"

"Secrecy, remember, sir? We have to balance maintaining the cover of TD Hunter with the rate of the entity incursion. If we move too aggressively, too soon, our cover will be blown and we'll have that whole global-panic problem to deal with. If we move too slowly, we'll be overrun before we can find the incursion point. It's a terrible, terrible balance, and for all we know, we're already doomed and we just haven't realized it yet."

General Kozelek sighed.

"I said good news, Mr. Krator. Good news."

The CEO chuckled and spread his hands.

"Lynn Raven is your good news, sir. She has the popularity to recruit all the manpower she needs to take on these nodalities while perfectly maintaining TD Hunter's cover. Early on, there were hundreds of promising players across the world that might have pulled ahead of the pack to do what Lynn Raven is doing. We even had teams of Alpha Testers competing under cover, like Mr. Peterson here, to be that catalyst if necessary. But so far, Lynn is the one whose unique combination of skill and celebrity status has gotten the job done.

"Obviously, the hope is that we'll have a weapons-development breakthrough soon, create some disruptor nukes, and be rid of these entities in one fell sweep. But until that happens, Lynn Raven leading by popular example for our 'attack force' of millions of gamers worldwide, well . . . she's our best hope."

The general shook his head.

"The fate of humanity, resting in the hands of a teenager. Based on the behavior of my own teens, I can't say I'm thrilled about that."

"She's good people, if I may say so, sir," Steve interjected. "Hardworking, responsible, honorable, and one of the best gamers I've ever encountered."

"She's a good leader, too, sir," Derek added. "We could certainly do worse."

"And she'll be eighteen soon, if it makes you feel any better," Mr. Krator said with a shrug.

General Kozelek waved a dismissive hand.

"Putting aside the Lynn Raven fan club, gentlemen, let's get into the meat of things. I know Colonel Bryce has hundreds of units ready to implement whatever new tactics you come up with, so let's not waste any more of his time. Mr. Peterson, if you would."

Derek sat up straighter and fiddled with his LINC, populating their shared display with aerial images of the Boss Bash battlefield and various bits of relevant data.

As the Alpha Tester started summarizing the op, Steve leaned back and took a sip of coffee from his Everheat mug. Since he was a civilian now, he wasn't privy to the team movements and tactical details of Taskforce Sanctus, nor its sister units in the allied CIDER countries. But being on the leadership team of TD Hunter's tactical department, he *did* see the increasing TDM numbers on a daily basis. He wasn't sure General Kozelek or any of the civilian higher-ups truly appreciated how fast these bastards were multiplying. He understood that Lynn—heck, an entire world of gamers—needed time to learn and adapt. But if CIDER didn't enact Phase II of their plan soon, it might be too late.

The National Championships couldn't come soon enough.